NO ONE'S GONNA TAKE HER SOUL AWAY

AMANDA B. WEAVER

No One's Gonna Take Her Soul Away by Amanda B. Weaver

Published by Amanda B. Weaver

WWW.ABWWRITES.COM

Copyright © 2024 by Amanda B. Weaver

For permissions contact: AMANDABOLDENWEAVER@GMAIL.COM

Cover by RaeKwon Groover

Edited by La Purvis

Interior design by C. M. Lockhart of Written in Melanin LLC

Disco Ball: Image by pngtree.com

ISBN: 978-1-7349854-8-1

Printed in the United States of America

First Edition

AUTHOR'S NOTE

Dear reader,

This book contains some scenes and instances that some readers may find disturbing. They are: drug and alcohol use, violence, anxiety, depression, torture, gore, cannibalism, emotional and mental abuse, and murder. If these things are triggering, please be mindful when reading.

Amanda B. Weaver

OTHER BOOKS BY

AMANDA B. WEAVER

(formerly Amanda Ross)

NOVELS

To Astera, With Love

To Ilaris, In Desperation

In the House of Transcendence

ANTHOLOGIES

Girls of Might and Magic

Kindred Kingdoms

THE SEVEN MISDEEDS

ENVY

sad or resentful covetousness towards the traits or possessions of someone else.

CONNIVANCE

willingness to secretly allow or be involved in wrongdoing.

VAINGLORIOUSNESS

inordinate pride in oneself or one's achievements; excessive vanity.

TREACHERY

those who deceive with the intent to harm.

RAPACIOUSNESS

aggressively greedy/grasping.

DESECRATION

treat sacred place or thing with disrespect, to violate someone.

MALEFICENCE

cause harm or destruction, do evil.

For anyone brave enough to be their own savior. This one's for you.

PART 1: HEART OF GLASS

CHAPTER 1

SAPPHIRA

EVERY SATURDAY NIGHT, Sapphira Gail performed the same ritual.

She showered and dressed in her most extravagant attire; this time a gold jumpsuit that glistened against her golden-brown skin, and a caramel-colored fur coat to stave off the December chill. She'd do her makeup — gold eyeshadow, red lipstick, a set of false lashes. She'd style her dark hair to resemble Donna Summer's and spritz on Opium, her favorite perfume. Lastly, with the most reverence, she'd strap on her gold, platform heels.

She'd cross the hall and push open the door to her twin sister's bedroom, and chuckle as she saw Persephone sitting at her vanity, picking her hair out and reading *Something Wicked This Way Comes*. She knew her sister like the back of her hand, so when she said she only needed five more minutes, Sapphira knew she really needed twenty. At the same time, their friend Frankie would enter their apartment unannounced, humming "I Want Your Love" by Chic or "Disco Inferno" by The Trammps, a joint in hand and ready to share.

She would meet him in the living room. They'd spark up, smoking at least half the joint by the time Persephone emerged from her room, their black cat, Dorothy, in hand. Before they left, they'd go to their alter in the far corner of the living room, across from a poster of Sapphira's favorite movie, *Mahogany*, and light nine candles. They'd whisper prayers to their gods as their fingers brushed over bracelets made of nine gemstones, one for each god, repeated three times.

Then they'd leave their apartment, hail a taxi, and thirty minutes later they'd arrive at their favorite club, Kaleidoscope. Sapphira had performed this ritual without fail for the past year. She knew it by heart. But what she didn't know was that this time, in less than three hours, she would be dead.

It was snowing and the headlights of cars reflected off the snowbanks on the sides of the road. They walked to the back of the line, hustling past the other clubgoers, each of them hugging or shaking hands with some of the regulars they knew. They could hear the music pumping from where they stood, "Knock on Wood" from the sounds of it, and Sapphira tapped her foot in time as they waited for the bouncer to let them through. The sound of the music and the cars and the numerous conversations around her made Sapphira buzz with energy. Ever since she was a child, she longed for the nightlife, and she was thankful that her sister and their friends were also night owls.

"Claudia meeting us?" Persephone asked, inquiring about the last member of their crew.

"Yeah," Frankie said, plunging his hands into his olive-green leather jacket. "In about an hour or so."

Sapphira nodded.

"Dante's going to meet us, too," she said. She looked at her sister and their best friend, and out of the corner of her eyes she saw Persephone grimace. Sapphira turned to Frankie, who kept his face blank, but she knew by the way he sniffed that he was also disapproving of her boyfriend.

"I know he's not your favorite person, but just give him a chance! They might play the song he wrote and he wanted to hear it."

"That's great, Sapph," Persephone replied, her smile not quite reaching her eyes.

"Yeah, the more the merrier," Frankie added. Sapphira frowned, hating the way her stomach clenched and her heartbeat quickened when she brought up Dante around them. Sapphira sighed and pushed away the anxiety that gnawed at her, threatening to ruin the night, and plastered a smile on her face as she listened to Persephone and Frankie gossip about their hot neighbor down the hall.

Minutes later they crossed the threshold into Kaleidoscope. They checked their coats and Sapphira took in the scene before her. A chrome bar took up the back half of the club. Above the shelves of liquor bottles was a mirror outlined by a rainbow-colored neon sign, the club's name written in barely legible script. To the left and right of the bar were chaise lounges, tables, and four small pillars. A dancer gyrated atop each pillar, decked out in red and gold club wear. And in the center of it all was the dance floor. Unlike the rest of the club which had dark wooden floors that were perpetually sticky from alcohol, the dancefloor was pristine, smooth as marble, with lights inlaid into the tiles that shone all the colors of the rainbow intermittently.

There were people she recognized standing by the bar, a few camped out at a table taking shots. Sapphira waved at them all but didn't bother to chit-chat. She strutted toward the dance floor, her gold heels clicking as she stepped down the three short steps to her destination.

Sylvester was playing. As Sapphira lost herself in his voice; in the synths, the chugging beat, the heat of the bodies pressing in around her, she felt exactly as he said: mighty real. Persephone and Frankie joined her and the three of them danced until sweat beaded on her forehead and streamed down her chest and back. She lifted her hair to try to get some air on her neck.

Three songs later, Claudia arrived, dressed in a white maxi dress and pink boots, her dark hair piled up in a bun atop her head, and her brown skin was dusted with glitter. When she approached them and gave each of them a hug, Sapphira could smell cigarettes and sweat and the perfume she was using to cover it all up.

They collectively groaned as the beat dropped for "Stayin' Alive" And surged to the bar.

Most people were on the dance floor, so they perched at their usual spot at the corner.

"How was work, Claudia?" Sapphira asked. Claudia shrugged.

"Good night, but the men were extra handsy."

"The worst," Persephone said. She was a waitress at an upscale restaurant on the Upper West Side. Sapphira knew she'd gotten the job because it was close to Columbia, but she'd come home telling Sapphira stories of being groped, or having lewd comments said to her by men dressed in Ralph Lauren as she poured them coffee. One night, after a patron slapped her ass, Sapphira, Claudia, and Persephone went down to the hardware store, each of them buying a small weapon. They each carried it when they went out by themselves.

Claudia snorted. "Yeah, but I got Peggy Sue with me at all times, so nothing ever gets truly out of hand."

They all laughed at Claudia's mention of the switchblade that she carried with her.

"What're we drinkin' tonight?" Frankie asked.

"How 'bout shots?"

Sapphira turned to see Dante standing behind her. Instantly her cheeks warmed and her heart beat wildly out of her chest. He wore all black— leather pants, a sheer black shirt, black platform boots. A gold chain with a medallion hung around his neck bearing the symbol of Xira, the goddess of love, passion, and creativity.

His eyes glittered in the golden light of the club, pupils already dilated as though this wasn't the first party he attended that night. Sapphira smiled at him, scanning him once again trying to gauge his mood. She hated the range of emotions that coursed through her whenever she saw him. There was lust, always washing over her like a tidal wave, making her body ache for his touch, only it to be tempered by uncertainty and curiosity at what mood he was in. Dante's presence was so all-consuming that his emotions quickly bled into her. On more than one occasion she'd left the disco in the grips of anxiety, a lump in her throat, moths batting around in her stomach, and the inability to look anywhere but the ground. But when he was in a good mood? When Dante smiled and laughed and danced? Sapphira felt higher than she ever could from alcohol or weed.

Dante's eyes met hers and a smile spread across his face.

Does it reach his eyes? She thought. When it did she exhaled and let her shoulders relax. She raised her arms toward him. He sat on a barstool and pulled Sapphira off her own and into his lap, gripping her butt and pulling her into a kiss so rough and passionate it left her breathless. She could hear Persephone groan, and Frankie and Claudia chuckle, but she didn't care. He was there, and he was in a good mood, and it was Saturday night, the best night of the week.

He pulled away, lust written all over his face, before nuzzling into her neck. "Dammit, girl, you feel what you do to me?"

Sapphira giggled, her cheeks warm and the seat of her jumpsuit wet. "You wanna feel what you do to me?"

"Why don't you two just get a room?" Persephone asked, breaking through their lust-fueled conversation. Dante sighed and pursed his lips before casting a sidelong glance at Persephone.

He set Sapphira down and turned toward the bar to hide his erection. "Nice to see you too, Persephone."

Sapphira's twin rolled her eyes.

"I wish I could say the same, *Dante*," Persephone replied. Sapphira noted how she said his name like it was poisonous, and her eyes darted back to him. She noted the clenched jaw, felt his energy change, and all the anxiety she'd felt when he first walked in returned. Her stomach churned.

"Oh, c'mon you two, all this fighting over me is unbecoming," Sapphira said, leaning back over the bar and throwing a hand across her forehead in a mock faint. She could fix this evening, she had to.

Persephone snorted. "Why the hell are you always so dramatic?"

"Tell me about it," Dante said. "Went to see The Exorcist at a midnight show the other night and this one couldn't stop shouting at the screen."

Persephone laughed. Dante did, too. Sapphira sighed, hoping this tenuous connection would last throughout the night, even if it had to be at her expense.

"Yeah, she did the same thing when we were kids. I used to get so annoyed watching movies with her," Persephone replied.

"Well, at least you know you'll never be bored when I'm around," Sapphira said in a sing-song voice. She draped an arm around Dante's shoulder, and he wrapped one around her waist. "Anyway, what are we drinking?"

"How about some champagne?" Dante said.

"We celebrating something?" Frankie asked, lifting a brow.

"Yeah, the DJ's got my record. He's about to play my song," Dante said. He turned back to the bar and ordered a bottle of champagne. Persephone and Claudia exchanged looks.

Sapphira could tell they were unimpressed, and she was glad Dante didn't see this. It pained her to think that her friends and her sister didn't think much of him. It hadn't always been that way. When they first met at an open mic night hosted by their local cafe, each of them had been taken by him. Dante struck up a conversation with her after he played, and the five of them went to Gertie's, a '50s-style diner next door. They all laughed and talked until the sun rose and Sapphira felt more hopeful than she ever had. She'd met someone who piqued her interest more than any other man or woman she'd dated before. Her sister and best friends seemed to like him and had even said they thought he was a great catch.

But somehow, throughout their relationship, they'd all changed their minds about him. When she asked why, they gave vague answers like "he just gives me bad vibes," "I don't think he's the right one for you," or "he's got a very particular personality."

Sapphira cornered Persephone once and the two argued until Persephone finally shouted: "Because he changes you! I don't like him because he changes you, and not for the better."

Sapphira's stomach dropped. "What the hell does that mean?"

Persephone crossed her arms. "You know exactly what I mean."

"No, I don't, Per," Sapphira spat. "Why don't you, the English major, tell me in a way I can understand."

Persephone groaned. "You get skittish whenever he's around. You stop being you and having fun and it becomes all about him, how he's feeling, what he wants, and what mood he's in. If he's not in a good mood, he drags you down, too."

Sapphira had sat at the table then, dumbfounded, her cigarette burned down to the filter. She hadn't known that the things she was experiencing were so on the surface they were obvious to her sister and friends. At that moment she knew Persephone wanted to say more but Sapphira got up and left the apartment before she had the chance.

Here she was now, back in the present, doing the same thing her sister told her she was doing. *No,* Sapphira thought, shaking her head. *There's nothing wrong with making sure my man has a good time and is in a good mood. I'm not skittish. Just intuitive.*

"We'll take a bottle of Moët & Chandon," Dante said.

"That'll be $30," said the bartender as he slid the bottle and five glasses across the bar. Sapphira blinked hard, surfacing from her thoughts just as Dante locked eyes with her, an expectant look on his face.

"Oh, right," she said.

"Seriously?" Claudia whispered. "We could each get four drinks for that much."

Sapphira didn't look up at them, instead focusing on her purse. She rummaged through it, hoping she had enough for the bottle. She made ok money working at Macy's, enough to pay for her half of the rent and bills and groceries, and the scholarship she'd gotten paid for school. She had enough spending money to get by, but she'd never ordered something so expensive in one night. Her ears pounded and her cheeks were warm as she shakily pulled thirty bucks out of her purse and slid it across the bar, her heart a lump in her throat.

The bartender wordlessly accepted the money and turned away from them but not before looking between the two and shaking his head. Dante stood and made a big show of opening the bottle. Sapphira plastered a smile on her face and watched as he poured champagne into the five flutes and set the bottle back on the bar. She handed a glass to Persephone, Frankie, and Claudia, each of them looking at her with reproachful gazes and she braced herself for their comments which would come later.

As Evelyn "Champagne" King sang about wanting to be back in the arms of her lover, Sapphira lifted a glass, determined once again to lighten the mood, hoping if she lightened the one around her, then the tumultuous emotions raging within her would calm.

"Your song's about to play and you're gonna be a star! Congratulations, I'm so proud of you, baby," she said.

"Congrats," Frankie said. Persephone and Claudia followed suit, and they all clinked their glasses together. She looked at Dante and felt a pang in her stomach as she noted the frown on his face when he drank. Sapphira downed her champagne, the heady feeling the bubbles gave her giving her momentum to keep trying to lighten the mood.

"Who's ready to get back on the dance floor?" she asked.

"Let's go!" Claudia said, grabbing Frankie's hand. Persephone followed and as Sapphira turned to go, Dante caught her hand. She closed her eyes tightly.

Maybe he just wants a kiss.

But when she turned toward him, she knew there was something wrong.

She took a deep breath, replaying the events of the night in her head and trying to figure out what she'd done wrong so she could get ahead of it. When she couldn't identify it, she dug her nails into her palm to steady herself. "What's up, honey?"

"You haven't said you love me yet," Dante stated, his voice reproachful. He looked down his nose at her as though she were a child who'd gotten in trouble for the millionth time. There was a pang in her belly, her mouth dried up and all the good feeling she'd gotten from her champagne evaporated.

This wasn't the first time he'd pointed out that she'd failed to love on him; once when she'd arrived at his apartment she'd gone straight to the bathroom, having ridden the subway from school to his place with a full bladder. When she came out of the bathroom, he was moody, frequently sighing and barely responding to her.

"Are you alright?" she asked.

"Fine," he replied, but she knew better. When he was in this place, she had to be delicate with prying the truth out of him, like pulling a knot out of hair. At first, she asked how his day was. Then she asked again if he was okay and if he was tired or hungry. Finally, exasperated, she questioned him.

"Are you mad at me? Have I done something wrong?"

"Yes," he replied. That caught her off guard. He'd never been explicit like that before.

"What did I—"

"You didn't kiss me when you came in."

She knitted her brows. *Is that all?*

"Honey, I'm sorry, I had to pee bad. I'll kiss you now," she said, planting a kiss across his pouty lips.

"That's not the point. You just walked past me when you came in. It makes me feel like you don't love me. Like I'm not a priority to you."

"But babe you are! I had to pee is all."

"I'm important to you?" he questioned. She grabbed his hands.

"Yes, the *most* important."

"Then I need you to care about what's important to me. And that's you coming in, kissing me, and telling me you love me first thing when we come together."

Sapphira swallowed, not wanting to continue the argument. She simply nodded. They spent the rest of the day in uneasy silence, one in which she kept wondering why he never asked what was important to her.

"I love you, Dante," she said in the present. She cupped his chin in her hands and stared into the deep wells of his eyes. "I've loved you since the moment I met you."

He nodded. "It's just really important to me that I know how you feel."

"I know."

"So why didn't you tell me?"

"Because we're... because I..." Sapphira sighed. She didn't have an answer, only looked down at her shoes, hating the bile settling in her throat, the way the champagne now made her stomach upset. "I'm sorry."

"It's just important to me, and I want to feel like these things matter to you."

"They do."

"Then why'd you forget?"

"Dante, please, I said I'm sorry," she said, tears welling in her eyes.

"I'm not looking for an apology," he said as he looked at her, wounded. He opened his mouth to speak just as the music changed and his eyes lit up.

"Ephemera." She'd recognize the track anywhere. Kaleidoscope was playing his song, and the pure joy on his face, the tears that now welled in his eyes, made Sapphira altogether happy and exhausted. Tension from the night settled in her shoulders and clavicles, making them ache.

"That's my song!" Dante shouted, turning to the bartender, and to the other patrons at the bar. "That's my muthafuckin' song!"

He grabbed Sapphira's hand and pulled her onto the dance floor where they joined the rest of the group. They wore matching looks of concern on their face as they took her in, and she wondered if her makeup was smudged. She knew she'd have to wait until the song was over to go to the restroom.

"It's his song!" Sapphira shouted, getting back to playing the dutiful girlfriend. Frankie dapped Dante, and both Claudia and Persephone clapped.

"This is huge! You're gonna be famous, Dante!" Claudia gushed.

"Yeah, you're gonna be big. Next thing you know, they'll be playing this at 54!" Persephone added.

"You know it!" Dante said. "I'm already talking with the DJ at 54 to get this on rotation."

As she danced, Sapphira looked around the dance floor for the reactions of the other people in the disco. Many of them seemed to look at each other, spending more time talking about the song than dancing to it. *No, no, no, please just dance.*

She shimmied through the crowd, connecting with the other regulars she knew and telling them that the song was by her boyfriend, that it was already on rotation at 54, and that they should tell their friends about it.

"He plays Thursday nights at The Mean Bean by himself, and on Monday nights with his band at Garden Grove," Sapphira said. One of the regulars, a white couple with matching long, blond hair and sunglasses, scoffed.

"Must not be very good if he's playing for the Monday crowd."

"No, it's not like that. He's just getting started is all," Sapphira said.

"Well, if he's as big and good as you say, he wouldn't be playing for such small crowds. But this song's ok," the woman said.

"Needs some more funk to it," the man said.

"What do you know about funk?" Sapphira spat before turning and dancing back through the crowd. The song ended. And though there had been a modest amount of people on the dance floor when the song played, the second the beat dropped for "Get Off," the floor became even more crowded. Dante stopped dancing. His shoulders slumped as he walked off the dance floor.

"Shit," Sapphira said.

"What's going on, Sapph? Why's he acting like this?" Persephone asked.

"He's upset, Per, anyone would be. That was the first time his song played in a club and not that many people seemed to like it."

"I liked it," Claudia said. Persephone cast a pointed look at their friend. She shrugged. "What? I did."

"I'm sorry about the song but that's not what I'm talking about. I saw you two talking at the bar, you looked like you were about to cry," Persephone said.

Anger sparked in her belly. "We were just talking, Per. You don't have to be so nosey."

"Nosey? Sapph, you—"

"*Sapphira.*"

She grit her teeth at the sound of her name, the pitch of his voice making her stomach drop.

"I've got to go."

"Go? But we're still dancing," Persephone said.

Dante walked back to the stage, placing a hand on Sapphira's lower back. "You ready?"

Sapphira looked at her sister, at her friends, then at Dante. It felt like she was in the middle, a position she had been thrust into so many times over the past few months, and one she was tired of tap dancing on the line of.

"I'm gonna call it a night," Sapphira said. "You all keep dancing.

I'll see you later."

"Can't you stay for one more song?"

"She said she wants to go, Persephone," Dante said. "Why you always so controlling?"

"*I'm controlling?*" Persephone yelled, her voice carrying over the music, making people turn toward them. Frankie placed an arm on her shoulder and stepped in front of her.

"Let's all just keep it cool. If Sapph wants to go, let her go. We'll see you back home later."

"I... I think I'll be at Dante's tonight."

Frankie's face fell, but he recovered quickly. "No biggie. Tomorrow. Breakfast at Gertie's?"

Sapphira nodded, a thin smile on her face.

Frankie reached out to dap Dante, who returned the gesture. Sapphira hugged Frankie as Dante stood back, not bothering to say anything to Claudia or Persephone.

"Take care," Frankie said.

"You too, get home safe," Sapphira said.

She walked toward Persephone and Claudia. Her twin stood with her arms crossed, lips pursed. Sapphira wrapped Claudia in a hug.

"Be safe," she whispered.

"Always," Sapphira replied.

"I mean it," Claudia said, pulling back slightly. "Take care of yourself."

Sapphira turned toward her sister. "Have a good night."

Persephone sighed and pulled her sister into a hug. "I wish you wouldn't go."

"Per, I'll be fine. I'm staying over at Dante's. I'll be back in the morning. We'll get breakfast so you three can get rid of your hangovers and then we'll go shopping or something. Don't worry."

"Sapphira, let's go," Dante warned.

She pulled away from her sister quickly. "I love you."

Persephone's brows knitted and Sapphira was overwhelmed by the concern written across her face.

"I love you, too. See you tomorrow."

She turned and walked away, letting Dante grab her hand and squeeze it. She cast one look over her shoulder, watching as her sister stood at the edge of the dance floor, her face etched with worry.

CHAPTER 2

SAPPHIRA

S HE TURNED LEFT as they exited the club, but he jerked her arm toward the right, heading not toward the subway station but toward Central Park.

"C'mon, let's take the scenic route," he said as he slid his hand into hers. She furrowed her brows; thankful his mood had changed but wondering why they were going through the park in the early morning. Sapphira let herself be led. He wrapped an arm around her shoulders and planted a kiss on her temple.

They'd walked through the park so slowly, and the smile he'd worn in the club was replaced by a contemplative frown. The timbre of his voice changed as he waxed poetic about their relationship and the future of his budding music career. People didn't know who he was yet, but everyone would one day. He was convinced of that. He brushed snow off a park bench and sat, pulling her into his lap just as he'd done at the disco.

"You're so wonderful," he whispered. "I don't deserve you."

"Dante—" Her heartbeat had quickened. Dante kissed her again, trailing kisses down her neck and chest. She leaned back, giving him access to her. She closed her eyes in ecstasy, her temperature rising.

"I don't. But I have you, every part of you, including your love. Don't I?"

"Of course, baby," Sapphira said eyes closed as he brought one hand down and cupped her pussy. He wrapped his other arm around her, keeping her steady as his thumb rubbed circles over her clit.

"You'd do anything for me, wouldn't you?"

"Yes. Anything," she breathed.

"I knew you would. That makes this so much harder."

He moved his hand away. The heat she'd felt between them dissipated, bringing her body back to reality. She felt the winter chill again, the breeze kicking up and licking its way up the sleeves of her jacket. She leaned against him, her emotions surging through her.

"You mean keeping me out in the cold and making me wait for you?" She chided.

"Uh-uh," he said, his breath hot against her neck. "This."

A sharp pain shot through her torso. Her eyes snapped open, and she yelped, looking down and bringing her hands to her stomach to touch the source of the pain. It wasn't until the pain went away and then returned that she realized what it was. A knife. Planted in her stomach. She screamed as Dante stabbed her again and fell onto her side in the snow. She scrambled on her hands and knees, trying to get away from him, but he lifted her onto the bench, laying her on her back. She winced at the feeling of the hardwood; the cold snow pressed up against her back.

"No! Stop, please!" Sapphira screamed. He lifted the knife up over his head, his eyes still locked on hers. A chill ran down her spine as she saw how unfazed he was at the sound of her screams. She screeched as the knife sliced into her gut, making a squishing sound as he pulled it out. He ran a finger across the blade, coating it in blood, and began to draw on her chest.

"I'm gonna be famous, Sapphira. People everywhere gonna know my name, singing my songs. But I had to make sure it would happen," he said.

"Why?" she asked. Blood spurted from her lips, flowing down her cheeks and onto the snowy park bench. When he was done writing, Dante brought the knife down again, puncturing her through her belly button before pulling it out.

Dante, the man who she'd loved and who she thought loved her, the man who brought her flowers and wrote songs about her and made her question everything about herself, looked Sapphira in the eye, his dark eyes misty yet resolute, and buried the knife once more in her stomach. The blade had hit her just below her ribs with such force that Sapphira could feel it run through her body and touch the bench.

She tried to take a deep breath, but the blood made it hard to do anything other than pant. She could feel it coating the back of her throat, seeping out of her nose and onto the bench beneath her. She was going to die. She would drown in her own blood, covered in snow on a park bench in Central Park.

No, she thought. *He doesn't get to win. He doesn't get to be big.* She reached out and tried desperately to hit him, but he kept dodging her, that unbothered expression still on his face.

She grabbed the hilt of the knife and tried to pull it out, all the while her heart galloping in her chest. The sound reverberating in her ears and morphing into what sounded like hooves on pavement. Her vision went cloudy for a moment, her mind's eye coalescing into the shape of a carriage emerging from a thick blanket of fog. She blinked rapidly and then she was back, staring up at Dante as he hovered over her, her vision restored.

"I don't think you'll be able to get that out, or if you'll want to. Probably the only reason you're still alive," he said.

"Fuck you," she spat, spraying blood on his clothes. He groaned and stepped back, brushing her blood off his jacket.

"Help!" She groaned, but she could hear how slurred the words were. It was three in the morning in New York City. Anyone who heard her probably thought she was drunk rather than dying, but she didn't care. She had to try.

"Help!"

"You know that's not going to help," Dante chastised.

"Why you still here?" Sapphira slurred. Her fingers and toes felt tingly and cold, as though she'd stuck them in a bucket of ice. She struggled to keep her eyes open, a bone-deep exhaustion settling in.

I'm dying.

As if to punctuate that thought, a horse whinnied in the distance. In the back of her mind, she knew what that was. And as she thought about the image of the carriage, she'd seen moments ago, she shuddered.

"I have to make sure you die," Dante said. Though her vision had started to twist, she could tell he was frowning at her. He pulled the knife out of her stomach and she gagged. Then he dragged the blade across her throat. Her blood spurted out of the wound and sprayed his clothes, coated her jacket.

Where before her body had been in pain and aching, there was a languidness to it; the bleeding out, the slow drowning from her blood. But this wound sent pinpricks up her arms, widened her eyes, and made everything feel more urgent. Sapphira's body was in overdrive. Every nerve fired, every muscle ached. She pressed her hands against her throat trying to stop the bleeding. She heard a tree ruffling in the distance, followed by footsteps tracking through the snow.

"Hey, man, what the fuck?" she heard someone say. And Dante was gone, sprinting through the opposite side of the park, taking the bloody knife with him.

Then there was a hand pressing against her stomach, another joining hers against her throat, tilting her head up and angling it toward them, the new angle making her dizzy. A Black woman with a red afro held her up and made shushing noises trying to calm her.

"Baby, you gotta get to a payphone. Call 911!" She urged. She heard running again, and the sound made her heart skip a beat.

"He—" Sapphira choked.

"No, he's gone. Chased him off. Who was he?"

"Dante," Sapphira tried, but her voice came out in little more than a whisper.

"I hear you. We'll report him and get you to a hospital. You gone be just fine, honey," the woman said. Tears streamed down Sapphira's cheeks. "Just hold on."

Sapphira grit her teeth, the pressure keeping her lucid as the woman held her head up and stroked her hair.

"Cold," Sapphira groaned. She was used to the snow, having been born and raised in Harlem. But this was a different kind of chilly. This was the kind of cold she felt in her marrow, so cold it stung like the heat from a candle. Her teeth chattered.

The man who'd accompanied the woman returned. She could hear them speaking in hushed whispers before he took his jacket off and placed it upon her. That helped stave off the cold just barely, but at least it was something.

"You hear it?" Sapphira asked.

"Hear what, honey?" the woman said.

"The horses," Sapphira replied, the sound of hooves against the pavement, wheels spinning endlessly, and the tinny neighs of a quartet of horses taking over in her mind, drowning out all the other sounds. But then the sound crystallized, and she could see the whirring lights of red and blue lighting up the distance.

"You're gonna make it," the man said. "You're safe."

"Safe," Sapphira mouthed, hearing the clip-clopping of hooves.

The first time Sapphira thought about death was when her Granny Olivine died. She'd raised Sapphira and Persephone until she died from tuberculosis after interacting with a sick patient. Sapphira still remembered the day she died, how dark and stormy it had been, how she and Persephone had sat by her hospital bed, teary-eyed and mortified by the constant cough that wracked her body and turned her tissues into blood-smeared messes.

She'd been the one who taught her and Persephone what happened when a being died — their souls were taken to Purgatore and judged by Simyasha, goddess of fate and arbiter of death — where they'd either be sent up to Caelum or cast down to Pandemonia.

It was Granny who gave Persephone and Sapphira their first prayer bracelets, and Sapphira felt the weight of it on her wrist now as she tried to pray. She tried to repeat the names of the gods and their corresponding gemstones, but all she could remember was opal for Enefri, moonstone for Simyasha, and ruby for Xira.

As Sapphira's lungs filled with blood, she marveled at how strange and yet fitting it was that she would die in the same way her granny did — drowning in her blood. Dying at 22 was not how she thought her life would go. She thought she'd be much older, dying in her lavish apartment in Paris, surrounded by friends and family. *I haven't even finished college. There's so much more I need to do.* she thought. *It's not my time.* But then, as her grandmother said before she died, "Death arrives exactly when he's meant to."

Only, she hadn't said death, had she? She said a name, something with a G—

The sound of a horse grunting in the night made Sapphira snap to attention.

That's just the ambulance.

Sapphira wasn't alone, thank the gods, but the person holding her was a stranger. How she wished it was Persephone or one of her friends there to hold her hand and tell her she'd be ok as she drifted in and out of consciousness. Her entire being ached. The pitter-patter of her blood against the snow made her nauseous. When she closed her eyes, she saw a black carriage emerge from the darkness, the rider draped in black smoke, eyes embers, bony hands gripping the reins.

A shiver slithered down her spine. She could hear the horses, the wheels of the carriage grinding closer and closer, and it was as though something primordial within her was more afraid than she'd ever been.

Then the sound stopped. And her head rolled to the side again. A group of EMTs rushed toward her, their faces stoic and their voices level. Two officers followed suit, one of them striding toward the man and the other grabbing the woman's attention. She reluctantly stood but not before looking down at Sapphira.

"You're gonna be okay," she said.

"Thank you," Sapphira replied. The EMTs were upon her, pressing gauze to her throat and stomach to staunch the bleeding.

"We've got you, Ma'am," one of the EMTs said to her. Then he turned to the other three EMTs he arrived with and began to bark orders, but Sapphira was barely able to comprehend what he was saying to them. A strange red glow in the distance caught her eye. She looked beyond the EMTs, and her stomach dropped. The carriage stood beneath the lone streetlamp, the green-blue light of it casting the carriage and its rider in an eerie glow.

Sapphira sat up, marveling at how she was able to do so despite bleeding out not a minute before, and the mess of people that had swarmed around her. There was something that pulled her to the carriage, and she stood and took a step toward it.

The rider was still as Sapphira stared at his profile. A bony and gaunt face, a black, wide-brimmed hat, and a black overcoat. Something needled at the back of her mind and Sapphira stopped. *I know what this is,* she thought. *I've heard of this before.* Granny spoke about the rider clothed in black smoke, his eyes aglow, shining the same crimson as his horses. He'd sit atop a bench seat, manning a —

Carriage. Sapphira gasped as the realization hit her. This was no mere carriage before her, no random rider. This was Gwydion, the one who drove the carriage of the dead.

As though reading her thoughts, Gwydion's head snapped toward her just as she realized who he was and what he was doing. He was here to take her to Purgatore.

"No, I'm not ready," she said. She turned to walk away but there was a cracking sound and suddenly she was no longer standing in the cold of Central Park, snow up to her ankles. She now sat in the carriage, her hands brushing over the red velvet seats. Her face pressed against the glass window as the carriage took off. She turned to the side, looking back to where she'd just been. There was no one there by the bench, no EMTs or police officers, no couple anxious after having just found a girl stabbed in the middle of a park. She screamed and banged on the window, desperate to free herself as the carriage sped through the park, the snowy trees blurring as they rode.

"Help! Help!" she screamed, noting how strong she sounded now when her voice had been slurred and weak moments before.

"Only the dead can hear you," Gwydion said, his voice deep and devoid of emotion. "And they won't be much help, I'm afraid. Purgatore awaits, Sapphira Gail."

Tears streaked down her eyes as she shouted again and again until she was hoarse. They were almost out of the park when she heard shouting in the distance. She jerked her head toward the sound. But there was still nothing.

"There's no use fighting. Everyone tries, but no one succeeds," the rider said.

"Yeah, well, I'm not just anyone, asshole," Sapphira replied, and punched the window.

"Sapphira."

She snapped to attention, a breeze caressing her cheek. She was surrounded by EMTs, watching as they lifted her off the bench and onto a stretcher. They wheeled her out of the park and toward the ambulance which was double parked next to a red Mustang. They guided her up into the back of the ambulance, and she watched as they closed the doors, removing the park, and everything in it from her view, including the carriage, and its rider. They put an oxygen mask on her and another EMT began the process of hooking her up with an IV, and the beep, beep, beeping sound of the vital signs monitor filled the back of the ambulance and mixed with the sound of the siren as the driver sped down the streets. They cut open her jumpsuit, exposing her breasts and belly and suddenly she felt self-conscious at the thought of these men seeing her naked.

As they worked to patch her up, talking to her the whole way, Sapphira's gaze was drawn to the large window at the rear of the ambulance. The carriage had caught up with her, it seemed, for the rider peered into the window, its glowing and stoic gaze trained on her.

"No," she gagged.

"Don't worry, Ms. Gail, we're working to keep you with us," one of the EMTs said. But Sapphira wasn't talking to him. She was talking to Gwydion, who stood on the other side of the door, lifting a leather whip over his head. Sapphira's eyes widened.

"Ok, pulse is slowing, we need to get the paddles," said one of the EMTs. Sapphira wanted to rip the oxygen mask off and free herself from their grips. She wanted to yell at them, ask them couldn't they see the man who'd broken into the ambulance? Didn't they know he was coming for her? But when she looked at the doors there was nothing. They were closed. "Just hold tight, we're almost there."

Almost there, she thought. *Almost, almost, al–*

Snow surged into the carriage. She watched as a single snowflake drifted in and landed on one of the EMT's glasses, but he didn't seem to notice. The carriage now galloped behind the ambulance. Sapphira could see into the eyes of the horses, see their smoky black nostrils flaring. They neighed as they pushed forward, their black manes whipping in the air. The rider lifted his whip again, cracking it against the ambulance door, the sound making her tense up in the same way as nails on a chalkboard.

"No, you cannot take me yet," Sapphira said, surprised once again by the strength of her words when seconds ago she could barely swallow.

"It is not up to you to decide when it's your time to be plucked from this mortal coil. Simyasha calls all souls back from whence they came," Gwydion said. The whip cracked for the third time, wrapping around her waist as it had earlier in the park. "And it is I who must deliver them."

Sapphira screamed as she was ripped from the stretcher. She tried to grab the EMTs' arms, the bench seat, the ambulance door, anything heavy enough to give her leverage, but nothing she did helped. Her head cracked as it connected with the pavement of Columbus Street. She was being dragged, and she could hear the machine that had been tracking her heartbeat slowing, the sound fading in the distance. Sapphira screamed, hoping that she'd catch someone's attention on the street and get their help. But aside from an uptick in dogs barking, no one seemed to hear her.

"I thought you weren't evil," Sapphira spat as the rider slowed the carriage, moving the horses from a gallop to a trot. "They always say that you're not evil."

"I am not."

"Then why are you doing this to me?" The carriage ground to a halt and Sapphira slid into a snowbank on the side of the road, screeching from the cold.

Gwydion slowly dismounted and walked toward her. "Because you ran."

She grunted as he pulled her out of the snow. By the time they reached the carriage, all the fight drained out of her. She was silent as Gwydion untethered the whip and placed her in the carriage.

The carriage pulled away, the horses trotting slowly at first before picking up speed. She'd tried so hard to stay alive. She'd spent the last hour of her life fighting, making it through the most excruciating pain she'd ever felt, only for it all to be for naught. She died anyway. As she realized there was nothing she could have done to save herself, Sapphira let out an anguished scream.

CHAPTER 3

SAPPHIRA

THE MARK DANTE drew on her chest in blood had seared itself into her skin like a brand. She rubbed at it, tracing the upside-down triangle, the crescent shapes within it, and the ones pressed against the outside of it, a small circle tucked beside each crescent. With her other hand, Sapphira played absentmindedly with the gold earrings she'd borrowed from Persephone.

Thinking of her sister brought fresh tears to her eyes and she forced herself to take a deep breath. Sapphira clenched her fists and stared at the sky as the carriage carted her from one realm to another. The skyscrapers passed like a blur as they moved through the city, only to be replaced by an amorphous fog. She knew that meant she was headed into Purgatore — "piercing the veil" as her Granny and all the elders of their communion said. The dense fog was the color of an early morning sky. To Sapphira, it looked like cotton candy, and her stomach lurched, and she wondered how that was possible. She was dead, after all, that fact was enough to make a fresh set of tears flow down her cheeks. But how was it that her chest still moved up and down? Her heart still beat and she shivered from the cold. When she looked down at her jumpsuit, she saw there was no wound there. Her fur coat looked like new. Even her shoes, which had been soaked with snow, were pristine.

"Hey!" she called. "How am I still breathing? I thought I was dead."

"You are dead. Very much so. You know it. Your sister is soon to discover it."

"How do you—"

"I'm the herald of death, Sapphira. I know all things as they relate to the dead."

"Then you know that I didn't deserve this, right?"

"This?" Gwydion asked, and that one word sparked a rage within Sapphira. No, she didn't deserve *this*. She didn't deserve to be dead, or to be stabbed by her boyfriend, or to never have left New York. She wanted to see the world. She wanted to design clothes and become a household name like Halston or Gucci. But now she'll never do any of those things. She'll never see the pyramids or the Champs-Élysées or Hollywood. The more Sapphira thought about the things she'd never get to do, the more she understood those horror movies full of angry ghosts. Life wasn't fair, and neither, it seemed, was the afterlife.

"This. Being dead. Being stabbed to death and getting dragged down the street by some skeleton in a stereotypical black robe. Are you trying to take over the Grim Reaper's gig?" Sapphira questioned. She braced herself for Gwydion's reaction, wondered if he'd stop the carriage and harangue her or if he'd just ignore it. Surprisingly, he did neither. Gwydion chuckled, a deep, grating sound that set her teeth on edge.

"You are funny, Sapphira. Pity that humor will be wasted on the dead," he replied. "And to answer your previous question, you breathe and your heart beats because in Purgatore you are remade. Once a soul pierces the veil, they become all they were before, flesh and blood and sinew and soul, restored to who and what they were just before their death."

"Why?"

"Some say it's so those that go to Pandemonia can be sufficiently tortured; what good is torturing a soul who has no lungs with breath to steal or heart to rip from the chest?"

Sapphira shivered at the imagery. *Thank the gods I won't be anywhere near Pandemonia*, she thought. That was the one thing she held on to. She knew Simyasha would weigh her good deeds and misdeeds against each other and find the decision to send her to Caelum an easy one. She took hope in the fact that she'd not be like all those souls whose misdeeds outweighed the good and were cast down to Pandemonia, or those whose deeds equaled out, giving Simyasha the ultimate say in their fate. Or so Sapphira had been told.

Whether it was true or not, Sapphira knew where she belonged — in Caelum, with Granny Olivine, with her ancestors, and someday, with Persephone. *At least I'll get to hug Granny again*, she thought and crossed her arms over herself against the cold of the fog around her.

"What do others say?"

Gwydion scoffed. "Others say that it's because you are reborn into your next life once you pierce the veil, whether that be one of peace or one of perdition."

Sapphira knitted her brows, unsure of what to believe. They rode in silence again, Sapphira watching the fog hug the carriage and listening to the galloping of the horses as they moved through its density. She let her mind drift to what Gwydion had said about Persephone and how she'd soon find her body and the thought made a scream bubble up in her throat. She couldn't bear seeing her sister in pain, never could, but at least then Sapphira had been there to comfort her. Now, she'd have their friends, but it wouldn't be the same. She wondered how she'd look to them — her cold, stiff body covered in blood and snow. Would they know who had done this? Would they ever know what she went through to try to get back to them?

She tried to take a deep breath and struggled. It felt as though someone gripped her lungs and squeezed, robbing her of oxygen. Her heartbeat pounded against her ribcage, threatening to bust through. She gripped the door handle with one hand and dug her nails into the seat with the other, stretching her legs out as tears stung her eyes. She closed her eyes to try to center herself but all she could see was the knife jutting out of her belly as she lay on that snow-covered bench.

I'm dying again. I'm dying, I'm dying, I–

Then, as quickly as that imaginary hand gripped her lungs, it let them go. Sapphira gulped for breath, her temples and the back of her head tingling. The vision of her death drifted away from her mind's eye, replaced by one of her, her sister, and their friends sitting on the floor by the fire. She felt the warmth of the fire caress her skin, the sweet smell of cinnamon and bourbon filling her nostrils.

Her heartbeat returned to normal. She slowly opened her eyes and relaxed her hands. When she gazed out the window her eyes settled on a wholly different landscape. The fog was gone, revealing a canyon, and above it the tiniest sliver of sky, all purple and pink and orange like at sunset. Gone was the shivering cold she'd felt when she first crossed the veil; now there was a dry warmth that carried a sweet scent in the air.

She pressed her nose against the window, looking at the striations of the rock formations. They were a smooth burnt orange, with lit torches hung in a neat row on either side of the canyon. The road they were on was narrow and twisty, taking them around sharp bends and up and down hills with such quickness that Sapphira's stomach lurched. She swallowed the bile that formed in her throat.

"Are we almost there? I feel like I'm going to be sick," she said.

But Gwydion didn't respond. He simply sped up, taking a left turn so sharply the wheels lifted off the ground and pushed Sapphira up against the carriage door. The side of the carriage made a high-pitched metallic sound as it scraped against the side of the rock. Another turn, this time to the right, then to the left, and the narrow road began to widen. They passed through a clearing, and then the horses trotted to a stop.

Sapphira's heart leaped as she watched Gwydion dismount and walk to the side of the carriage. She stared at him as he unlocked the door, pulling it open with a creaking sound and letting in a rush of fresh, warm air. Sapphira breathed deeply, sucking in the cinnamon-sweet air. Gwydion held a bony hand out and Sapphira reluctantly took it. She leaped out of the carriage, her feet sinking into the sand. They stood in a clearing surrounded by rocks jutting up toward the sky. There were no clouds, only the lavender and pink hues of twilight and a magenta moon looming above them.

But it wasn't just the sky that left her in awe. Before her, carved into the rock was a temple. In the center was a large archway framed by pillars made of bone. She shuddered as she recognized the femur and tibia bones that were the same copper color as the canyon. A slab of gold-painted rock sat atop the pillars which served as the foundation for three smaller archways framed in skulls. There were two more rows of bone-framed archways that sat beneath spires, also made of bone, that stretched toward the sky.

Sapphira gulped and looked back at Gwydion.

"Do I have to go in there?" she asked. His ruby eyes seemed to stare right through her. She closed her eyes and sighed. "Of course I do."

"Best get going," Gwydion said. "Patience is not a trait Simyasha is remembered for."

"Yeah, yeah, yeah," she replied.

She turned back toward the temple and slid her hands into her pockets. She heard Gwydion's boots kicking up sand as he turned to leave, and without looking back heard him as the carriage drove away.

Now alone, Sapphira whimpered as she slowly trudged through the sand toward the temple. The closer she got the larger it looked, and the more details she saw. The skulls that lined the top of the pillars all had jewels placed into their eye sockets. Some of the skulls had long fangs, others had longer snouts with longer teeth like that of a wolf. Sapphira knitted her brows, confused as to why some of the skulls looked so inhuman. She placed a hand against the temple's surface as she stood before the dark entrance. The surface was cool and smooth, and she forced herself to take a deep breath as she chest as stared into the entrance. She could hear the rhythmic sound of drumming and the spicy-sweet smell of cinnamon intensified. Smoke wafted out from the entrance toward her, as though beckoning her in.

She walked into a darkened antechamber, the only source of light coming from the room ahead of her. She moved quickly toward the light, entering a narrow, torch-lit hallway. The firelight danced against the stone, illuminating paintings that stretched to all corners. Sapphira stopped before the one on the right. In it, Simyasha sat atop her throne, piles of bones at her feet. One hand held a fanged skull while the other clutched a scroll, pressing it against their chest. The goddess smiled wickedly, and when Sapphira turned to look away, she could swear the eyes followed her.

The painting on the opposite wall also featured the goddess. This time looking down at a scroll while a person knelt on the ground before her, hands up in supplication.

Sapphira fluffed her hair. She adjusted her breasts in her bra, then licked her lips. She didn't know what she looked like, but she was sure as hell not planning to stand before the goddess who'd decide her fate looking a fool.

"C'mon, girl. You've got your boogie shoes on," she said to herself. She stood up straight and walked down the rest of the long hallway. Seconds later she stepped into the throne room of the goddess.

It was a large semi-circle, the back wall gone and looking out onto clouds as far as the eye could see. The walls were covered in moonstone. The torches around the room illuminated the jewels, casting a kaleidoscope of color around the room. Sapphira marveled at the number of people who took up space in Simyasha's throne room, some playing music with ancient-looking instruments, others kneeling before the goddess just as that person in the painting. Though she'd been told that some souls ended up staying in Purgatore, a fact some would say was a blessing and others a curse, she thought she'd appear before the goddess alone. Somehow, having other beings there as she met her fate made Sapphira feel even more anxious.

"Sapphira Gail, it is nice to meet you, my child."

She trembled at the sound of the goddess's voice. It was silky smooth, deep, and terrifying. Sapphira fell to her knees, leaning down so far her forehead pressed into the stone floor, the coolness of it easing the anxiety raging through her body.

"Such pretty manners," the goddess chuckled. "You may stand."

Her knees wobbled as she stood. Sapphira's eyes widened as she gazed upon Simyasha. Her wide-set eyes were white from corner to corner, shimmering like an opal in the light. Her cheekbones were pronounced as was the point of her chin. Her full lips were set in a smirk, and Sapphira's gaze drifted down toward her simple, white, chiffon dress, a stark contrast to her dark brown skin. The sides of her raven-black hair were shaved, leaving only the top, which she wore in three small buns stacked on top of each other and tied off with gold thread.

She was exquisite, and Sapphira realized now why all these people would want to kneel before her and worship. One of the people kneeling before the goddess sat up, and Sapphira took a step back when she saw how strange they looked — its body was covered in fur. Its ears were pointed, and its nose and mouth were elongated like that of a wolf. In the corner behind the goddess, Sapphira saw a being with wings and spindly limbs, and she shook her head and blinked wondering if what she was seeing was correct. As though reading her mind, Simyasha spoke.

"You humans amuse me."

"How so?"

"You write about vampires, werewolves, fey, and all manner of supernatural creatures," Simyasha said pointing at the beings as she called them out. "And yet when you see tangible proof of them, you balk at their existence."

Sapphira sucked in a breath and buried her hands in her jacket pocket. "Well, a lot of things happened tonight that I wasn't prepared for, so please forgive me if finding out that vampires and werewolves and shit exist freaks me out."

She eyed the goddess, bracing herself for an explosive reaction. All she did was laugh.

The sound filled Sapphira with dread, but she wasn't going to let her know how terrified she was. She would be poised and stand perfectly straight as Simyasha told her she was to go to Caelum, as she showed her the path that led toward the sky. Toward her Granny.

"Well, I suppose we ought to get to the business of where you belong," Simyasha said, her eyes scanning Sapphira's body and landing on the symbol at her chest. Sapphira nodded. She kept her outward appearance blank, all the while her heart pounded in her chest. *This is it*, Sapphira thought. *The moment all of this will be worth it.*

The goddess's clapped her hands and a scroll appeared in her hands. She unfurled it and stared at the parchment. Sapphira thought back to the painting on the wall at the entrance, where Simyasha held a scroll in her hand while telling a soul about their fate. She knew from the stories she'd been told at communion that every being had a life scroll, with all their events etched upon it. Simyasha would read the scroll and determine their fate.

"Sapphira Gail, born May 14, 1956, died December 13, 1978, 22 years old. You are a beautiful woman with good manners and a meek spirit."

Sapphira bristled at the insult but remained silent.

"The symbol on your chest is confirmation of that."

She looked down at the symbol etched angrily into her skin.

"What does it mean, goddess?" she asked. Simyasha quirked a brow.

"My girl, do you not know the marks of a demon?"

Sapphira's stomach dropped. She stared, wide-eyed, at the goddess before her. The other beings in the chamber murmured.

"I—"

Simyasha waved a hand at Sapphira. "No matter. Your fate is sealed."

"But what—"

"Quiet," the goddess hissed. She rolled the scroll up and in an instant it disappeared from her hands. The room grew silent, the only sound the whistling of the wind beyond the cave. Sapphira bit her lip to keep from crying.

"Sapphira, you will spend eternity in Pandemonia."

Sapphira's jaw dropped and tears sprang into her eyes. *Pandemonia?* She thought. *I don't belong there. There must be a mistake.* She opened her mouth to speak just as Simyasha continued.

"You will be cast down to the seventh island, Maleficence. May you spend eternity in atonement."

The other humans and creatures in the room whispered amongst themselves. But to Sapphira, it sounded like white noise. Her vision twisted and she took a shaky step toward the goddess. "This isn't... this can't be..." she whispered.

Simyasha scoffed. "Take your time absorbing this news. It's not like you don't have all of eternity."

The beings in the room laughed. Sapphira closed the distance between herself and Simyasha and sank to her knees at her feet.

"No, but I — I never killed anyone. I never harmed anyone. Ok, maybe I did break Jennifer Lance's arm in tenth grade but she broke my nose! And I shoved Adam Gilray into the street once, but he shoved his hand up my skirt. I was defending myself."

"I know all of this, Sapphira," Simyasha soothed. "It does not change your placement in Pandemonia."

"But I'm not like the people who belong in Pandemonia. I've done good things, many good things! I — I took care of my Granny before she died! I made sure Persephone stayed out of harm, I went to school, I had friends. I... loved," she cried. Sapphira hated how strangled her voice sounded but she couldn't help the sorrow that crept into her voice, nor the tears that fell from her eyes.

The goddess stood and heaved a sigh, sounding irritated. Though every impulse in Sapphira's body told her to stop, she shot up and followed the goddess as she strode toward the back of the throne room.

"Please! I don't deserve this. I'll do anything! I'll give you my jacket!" Sapphira shrugged out of her jacket and held it out to the goddess, whose lips curled in disgust at the sight of it. "Or... this bracelet! You like jewels and gems, right? It's got one for all of you. All the gods I mean, see? Moonstone here for you."

Sapphira cupped the bracelet in her hand and thrust it toward Simyasha who took a step back. The goddess shook her head.

"Please," Sapphira sobbed. "I don't deserve this. I was murdered."

She fell to the ground, stretching her hands out toward Simyasha's feet. Sobs wracked her body, and she could hear the whispers, and chuckles, even from the denizens of Simyasha's court.

The goddess pulled Sapphira up to her feet. She grabbed Sapphira's jacket from the ground and shook it before sauntering behind Sapphira.

"Let me help you, child," she said. Sapphira sniffled as she let the goddess slide her jacket onto her arms. Simyasha adjusted the collar of the jacket. Sapphira marveled at the rings carved out of bones and set with gemstones that studded each of Simyasha's fingers. Her touch was cool against Sapphira's skin. She smelled like fire and honey, and yet beneath all the sweetness, there was also the stench of decay.

"You're so... delicate. I can feel your bones if I press hard enough here," Simyasha pressed her fingers into Sapphira's chest, and Sapphira grimaced at the pressure. "They'll crack. It wouldn't take much, not from a god. I've always found that to be interesting, how much you all try to fight when really, you're just a sharply applied force away from disintegration."

The goddess pressed into Sapphira's chest, the pressure making her cry out. Simyasha seemed to perk up at the pain and smiled, showing a row of perfect teeth. Despite her beauty, Simyasha's smile made Sapphira shiver. It was too wide and exposed more teeth than Sapphira thought a being should have. Her eyes remained open wide even when she smiled.

She stood in place, knowing now why the god kept so many beings in their court, why they all seemed to be equal parts attracted to and terrified of her.

Sapphira swallowed. "Can I stay here with you, goddess?"

Simyasha cackled.

"Where was this fight when your lover stole your eternity?"

"I did fight him! Even as he stabbed me I—"

"Your fate has already been decided. Besides, if you stayed here, it'd only be a matter of time before you ended up like them." She pointed toward the pile of bones in the corner. "Unless you'd be willing to be a sacrifice? Go on, answer honestly. I won't hold it against you."

Sapphira looked at the bones in the corner and realized now why every being in Simyasha's court was afraid of her. It wasn't just that she could send them to Pandemonia. It was that she could kill them, too. From what little Sapphira had learned about the goddess in the short time she stood before her, it seemed like the goddess would enjoy murdering them, too. She shook her head.

"I thought not."

"But I don't belong in Maleficence."

"That symbol on your chest guarantees that you do, my child."

"I didn't draw this on me. The one who killed me did, with my own blood," Sapphira said. "I don't even know what it means."

Simyasha canted her head to the side, her gaze softening. She looked at Sapphira as though she were a child. "Whether you drew it or not, that symbol guarantees you an eternity in Pandemonia. I'm afraid you chose the wrong lover, Sapphira Gail."

"But goddess, you've made a mistake, I—"

Simyasha's hand snaked to Sapphira's throat and squeezed. Her milky eyes pulsated as she glared at Sapphira and sneered.

"You insolent, petulant child. You pathetic peon. Do you really think saying that I, the goddess of fate, the arbiter of death, am wrong, will help you?"

Sapphira gagged as Simyasha's grip tightened.

"I have existed for eons," Simyasha began, her voice growing louder. "Before the Christian God, before Buddha, before Kali, before them all. I have seen everything, judged every type of soul there is, and you think you're special? You think you, a little orphan from New York with nothing but a cat and a sewing machine to your name, will be the one to change the hands of fate?"

Sapphira's lungs burned. Her neck ached from the pressure on her throat and black spots danced across her vision. She drew her hands up toward her neck, but the goddess swiped at them with her free hand, knocking them down.

She didn't respond as the goddess lifted her off her feet and walked, turning toward the rear of the temple. It was only when she felt the shock of icy air at her back that she began to struggle. Simyasha dangled her over the edge, and Sapphira's eyes welled with tears. She kicked out her legs and hands, scrambling for solid ground.

"Please," she coughed.

The goddess smiled ruefully. "Your pleas have no place here, Sapphira. I cast you down to the seventh island, where you will be met with horrors beyond your most terrifying nightmares."

Simyasha pulled Sapphira in close and whispered in her ear, the goddess's breath hot on her cheek. "I wish I could be there to see them rip you apart."

Then the goddess let go and Sapphira sucked in a breath, arms flailing, as she was tossed backward into the clouds.

CHAPTER 4

SAPPHIRA

THE WIND WHIPPED through her hair as she plummeted toward Pandemonia. She was falling backward, her hands and legs still kicking out, desperate to find purchase. She tried to scream but the swiftness of the wind stole her voice. Her eyes and mouth went dry. Her cheeks and ears burned. With great effort, she flipped over so she was no longer falling backward but face-first into the realm.

She shivered as she passed through a layer of dark red clouds, the cold sensation of it brushing against her body chilling her. When she passed out of the clouds, she saw the place she'd been dreading her entire life. An ocean stretched as far as her eye could see, the water black despite the sun sitting high above the horizon. A string of seven islands sat below her, each connected by a narrow bridge. Some of them were barren and desert-like while others were densely populated by forest.

Her stomach roiled and her heartbeat so fast in her chest that she felt as though it would burst. As she got closer, she saw that she was falling toward the seventh island in the chain, a hilly terrain full of barren trees, the branches spiking up toward the sky.

She was getting closer, closer to the trees, closer to the sandy beach, and the torture that awaited her on the seventh island. The air had gotten warmer as she descended, and where she'd been freezing when Simyasha first let her go, now she was burning up. She was so close she could make out the people below, some of them running, others impaled on trees. Shouts and screams reverberated in her ears and replaced the ringing.

And then she was mere feet away. Sapphira hugged her legs and pressed her head down between her knees. She held her breath as she hit the ground and then skidded across the gravel-covered beach on her left side, pain shooting from her leg to her neck.

Once she finally came to a stop, Sapphira groaned. She rolled onto her back and opened her eyes to a dark sky scattered with the red clouds she'd passed through looking heavy with rain. As she lay listening to the sounds of twigs snapping, feet crushing in gravel, and guttural screams of rage and terror, it began to rain. The droplets beat against her face and body, stinging her eyes. She blinked several times and wiped her eyes with her hands. When she pulled them away, she was startled to see her hands covered in red. She looked down at her shoes and noticed the little red splotches collecting on them. She held a hand out. A small pool of rain collected in her palm and she brought it to her nose and sniffed, lips pulling back in a grimace as she smelled the metallic scent of blood. She dropped the liquid and gagged.

Sapphira dug her hands into the gravel to try to push herself up and instantly regretted the movement. Her ears rang and throbbed, feeling clogged and reminding her of the time she had an ear infection. The entire left side of her body ached.

She tried again, this time wincing as something sharp pressed against her palm. She looked at her hand and saw a piece of gravel jutting out. Sapphira plucked it out and examined it. Her eyes widened as she registered not a pebble but a small incisor, coated in her blood. She shrieked and tossed the tooth to the ground. Looking at it now, she realized that what she had initially thought to be gravel was something so much worse — teeth. The beach was covered in them. She stifled a scream as she crab-walked backward, incisors and bicuspids and molars pressing into her hands as she did so.

She stood and brushed off the back of her jacket and jumpsuit. The air was thick with humidity, but Sapphira shuddered despite the intense heat. She looked out at the ocean and was unnerved by how perfectly still the black water was. A head popped out of the water a few yards out. It was almost as dark as the water, its skin smooth and its oil-slick colored eyes large, almost bigger than its face. It stared at her, motionless. And Sapphira remained rooted in place.

She had never known what Pandemonia would look like. No one at communion ever spoke in detail about it, just that it was the place where bad people went, those who committed the seven misdeeds—envy, vaingloriousness, connivance, treachery, rapaciousness, desecration, and maleficence. They said souls would be tortured but never mentioned what exactly happened to them, so she'd always associated it with what she'd read about in the Christian bible. She began to think of Pandemonia as a barren wasteland full of fire and brimstone, where souls were burned forever, and where a cloven-hooved devil delighted in their torture.

Of course, she knew that Pandemonia wasn't without its overseer. The god Tartagnon presided over this realm, and he was as beautiful as he was fearsome, according to the paintings she'd seen of him. She knew some people even worshipped him, hoping that would keep them out of his domain, but now that she was here, she wondered just how much of what she'd learned had been inaccurate.

She continued to stare at the creature in the water for several minutes, feeling instinctively that this was a predator and if she moved or took her gaze off it then it would charge at her. Finally, it sniffed, displacing the water around it before disappearing beneath the depths of the ocean. She let out a breath, and bent over, resting her hands on her knees. She felt sticky, sweat pooling in her panties and at her armpits. She slunk her jacket off her arms, letting it rest just above her elbows. The bloody rain had not stopped and now coated her caramel-colored jacket. She sighed and turned toward the interior of the island, noting how the barren trees were dark and dripping in sap.

A twig snapped behind her, the sound making Sapphira squeak. She closed her eyes and gulped down the lump in her throat and slowly turned around. There was a trio of creatures standing before her, two of them holding knives and the other one holding a crude saw made from what looked like bones. They stared at her with the same hungry expression; eyes narrowed and a wide smile splitting their faces in two. The one holding the saw seemed to be the leader, as he stood in front of them a few paces, towering over them. He was bulky, his bare chest and arms all corded muscle and smooth, jet-black skin. A network of glowing orange lines snaked up his arms, face, and body, and Sapphira realized they were the creature's veins. She took in its bald head and orange eyes. Despite its bulky frame, its face was gaunt, the skin pulling back from its face as it smiled looking like it could rip at any moment.

She stood still in the same way she had with the creature in the water. Her heart hammered in her chest, her limbs tensing and poised for flight. Sapphira did her best to keep her breath steady and not make any sudden movements. The demon took a step forward, and the two creatures behind it — both gray with mottled skin, egg-white eyes, and a single slit in the center of their face for a nose — followed suit.

"Don't mind me," Sapphira said, holding her hands up and out, letting them know she wasn't a threat. "I just—"

"Pretty thing must've just landed," the demon said. The timbre of its deep voice made her skin crawl. The two gray creatures chuckled maniacally. *Goons*, she thought. *This demon has goons.*

She stepped backward, careful not to step into the water.

"Go get her for me," the demon said. "I can think of a few ways we can welcome her to the seventh island."

Sapphira didn't waste any time waiting to see if the goons would comply. She turned and ran in the opposite direction, pumping her arms and controlling her breath, thinking about all the times she'd had to focus on her breath control while dancing. She could hear the goons running behind her, their heavy feet crunching in the teeth on the shore. She knew there was no way she'd be able to outrun them on flat, relatively steady ground. She took a sharp right turn and ran into the wood, passing by a tree just as one of the goons launched its knife at her, the blade lodging in a tree trunk. She yelped but kept running.

The ground here was no longer covered in teeth. Instead, it was muddy, her shoes sticking in a foul-smelling, crimson-colored muck. Bits of bone were scattered about on the ground. Hair dangled from a few trees like Spanish moss. She passed a tree on her left, this one taller than the rest, a small, round fruit hanging from its limbs. The closer she got, though, the more she realized that it wasn't fruit hanging from the tree but eyes. There were hundreds of eyeballs, the nerves tied together and hanging from the branches. She whimpered as she ran around it, and she could swear that the eyes shifted their gaze to follow her as she passed. The air was heavier in the wood, making it harder for her to breathe.

Save for the body parts strung around them, the trees seemed barren. Only a handful of them were fruiting, and the ones that bore smooth, bulbous black fruit the size of an apple. She stepped on a fallen fruit and it squished beneath her foot, red liquid leeching out of it and staining her shoe red. The metallic, rotted smell of it drifted up toward her and made her gag. She hopped over a large branch before tripping on a lifted tree root and nearly falling face-first into a pile of intestines and feces.

She stifled a scream and looked around, then stepped behind a tree and pressed herself against it, wincing at the way her hand stuck to the bark. She caught her breath, her mind catching up to the situation. She was being hunted. She could hear the pounding sound of feet running through the mud. Of twigs snapping. Of screams.

She trembled and leaned further against the tree. She tried to steady herself, but she couldn't help the way her hands shook or the heat crawling up her chest, neck, and cheeks. *I'm going to die here all over again*, she thought, as she looked around and put the pieces together. All the bones and body parts, strewn about or fashioned into ornaments, the bone saw the demon had been carrying. This island was a hunting ground, the place where the murderers were sent to be murdered, their bodies defiled, for all eternity.

"Fuck," she whimpered. She had to get her mind right. She had to figure out how to survive. Then maybe she could find someplace safe to hide.

She turned to the right, preparing to dash toward another tree just a few yards ahead of her, and ran right into one of the goons. She gasped as her body connected with it. Up close she could see just how ugly this creature was. Its skin looked like it was peeling, as though it was shedding like a snake. Its teeth were sharp and stained pink as it smiled at her. It fixed its milky gaze on her, still wearing that hungry stare, and it gripped her right arm in one hand and ran the blade of its knife down her neck and sternum, pressing in as it passed over her sternum and drawing blood. She winced but didn't want to give this goon the satisfaction of her cries.

"Pretty little thing, indeed," it said, its voice a little deeper than a toddler's. It reached out and brushed its fingers across the brand on Sapphira's chest. "And look! She's branded."

"Is she now?" the demon said. "Looks like a bargain, the pitiful lamb. Wonder what she got in return. Must've been something tremendous for her soul to have been called back across the veil at such a tender age."

"I'll bet she asked for fame and fortune," said the goon.

"No, I'll bet it was a man she bartered her eternity for, the meek ones are always so desperate and lustful," said the other goon, eliciting a cackle from the demon. Sapphira punched the goon in the nose, surprising herself with how hard she hit him. His head whipped back, and it dropped its knife. She watched it land a few feet away in a puddle of piss.

She thought the goon would be angered by her actions, but instead, it turned back to her with a gleeful expression on its face.

"Oh, pretty thing wants to play!" the goon said. "I love to play."

The goon returned the gesture, its punch connecting with Sapphira's chin. The force sent her reeling back, and she landed on her butt in the muck. She stood and was met with a punch to the gut. She doubled over as her stomach twisted in on itself. She grumbled as she stood, flailing a handout and trying to reach out for the tree she'd been standing by, hoping to catch her breath.

She felt a large hand grip her arm and twist. Sapphira screamed at the searing pain shooting through her arm and shoulder. The pain went away just as quickly as it came, replaced by a numbness in her extremity.

Her head was jerked back toward the sky, and she saw the demon staring down at her. She hated the triumphant grin that spread across his obsidian face, hated the orange eyes that regarded her with equal parts rage and lust, the body that stood over her which was all compact muscle.

"What's your name, pretty thing?" he questioned.

"Why do you care? You're just going to kill me," she replied.

The demon chuckled. "True, but I collect the names of everyone I kill."

"Jane," Sapphira said, giving the demon her middle name. "I'm Jane."

"Don't look like a Jane," said another voice, Sapphira guessed the other goon.

"How the fuck would you know what a Jane looks like?" She spat, her eyes still trained on the demon.

Another punch to her gut. This time Sapphira couldn't double over to alleviate the pain.

"Fiery one, this Jane. My favorite. I love breaking them down."

"Yes, yes. What fun is there in eviscerating the damned if they have no fight in them?" replied the other goon.

Sapphira kicked her foot out in response, but she connected only with air. The goons howled with laughter. Sapphira's cheeks grew warm with shame. The demon seemed to grow bored with the banter and tossed her against the tree. She hissed as her back connected with it, pain radiating in waves along her back. She pushed herself to stand but still leaned against the tree. The goons stared at the demon in anticipation. Behind them ran a stream of people all being chased by another demon the same size and makeup as the one before her only its skin was slick and iridescent as though it had just stepped out of an oil spill. Their screams rang through Sapphira's ears, replacing the sound of her heart jackhammering in her chest.

"The first death is always the most fun," he said. One of the goons handed him his bone saw. "I hope you don't mind that I take my time."

The demon advanced on her and Sapphira realized there was nowhere for her to go. She was trapped. A single tear fell down her cheek and she blinked rapidly, fists and jaw clenched, refusing to face this death with her eyes closed. She'd already been unsuspecting when Dante killed her and sent her to Pandemonia. She'd not make the same mistake twice.

Just as he lifted his blade, another creature leaped from the wood and tackled him to the ground. Two other beings joined the fray — a human in a zoot suit and a fairy with broken blue wings. They launched themselves at the goons. The creature who tackled him grunted as it clawed at the demon with its bare hands before sinking its teeth into the demon's neck. He struggled against the creature, but its grip was strong.

She didn't know if these beings were there to kill them all or just the demons, but Sapphira knew she couldn't wait around to find out. She searched the ground for a weapon she could use. She made it to the knife that the first goon dropped, grimacing as she dug through piss to retrieve it.

She heard slow footsteps behind her and Sapphira whipped around, holding the knife out before her. The creature looked from the knife to Sapphira, an amused expression on its face. Despite the blood coating the bottom half of its face and its neck, she could see its fangs. A vampire. His pupils were so dilated that Sapphira could barely see the whites of its almond-shaped eyes.

"You shouldn't play with things you don't know how to use," the vampire drawled.

"Don't talk to me," Sapphira said, holding the knife out toward the vampire. She brought her second hand around the hilt, hoping that would give her more leverage.

The vampire chuckled as he pulled a dirty handkerchief from the pocket of an equally dirty, emerald-colored pea coat.

"Very well," he said as he wiped the blood off his hands and patted it off his face, licking away the excess before sliding the handkerchief back into his pocket. "I'll leave you to your business then."

He turned to leave but, against Sapphira's better judgment, she called out to him.

"Wait!"

The vampire kept walking.

"Wait!"

He ignored her still.

"Wait, please!"

That made him stop. He turned toward her and in a matter of seconds stood before her again, so close she could smell the blood radiating off him. Sapphira took in the vampire's appearance — he was tall, and though most of his body was covered she could see the impression of lean muscle beneath his clothes. Black coils framed his face and complimented his manicured beard. His pupils had returned to a normal size, revealing mahogany irises rimmed with a blue ring. His fangs rested on his lower lip. His dark pants and boots were covered in dried blood and mud. His dress shirt and green vest were unbuttoned halfway, showing off his brown skin. Despite seeing what this vampire was capable of up close, she couldn't deny how handsome he was. He wore a similarly hungry expression as the demon, but Sapphira couldn't turn away.

"Well? Get on with it," he said.

"Why did you save me?"

He rolled his eyes. "I didn't."

"But—"

He held his hand up. "Let me disabuse you of this notion of being 'saved' right now. I've been looking for Florizeel for weeks."

"Why?" Sapphira asked as she took a step back. The vampire stepped forward.

"To invite him to tea. Why do you think? What else could I possibly want to do with the demon in charge of this Enefri-forsaken island?"

Sapphira was starting to regret calling back to him.

"I—"

The vampire stepped forward again, Sapphira backward, the movement pressing her straight up against a tree. The vampire smiled again and stood in front of her, not touching her but not allowing her the space to move. She held the knife out, the tip pressed against his sternum.

"Well, even though you didn't intend to save me, thank you anyway."

"You're polite."

"Thank—"

"That trait won't get you far at all here."

"And what will?"

"Cunning. Quick reflexes," he said as he knocked the knife from her hand and flipped the blade back onto her. She pressed against the tree as the tip of the knife touched her throat. "And an understanding that in Maleficence, the only thing that matters is kill or be killed."

He dropped the knife onto the ground and disappeared into the woods.

Sapphira trudged through the forest well into the night. She didn't know where she was going. All she could think of doing was keep moving. It would be harder for someone or something to kill her if she never sat still. Her clothes were covered in muck, hair matted with blood. She was thankful for the moonlight to light her way, even if the light was an eerie, blood red.

"Get back here, you motherfucker!" someone shouted. Sapphira's heartbeat spiked, and she dove to the ground, pressing herself against an overturned log. She struggled to steady her breathing, terrified of moving a muscle lest she be heard. Footsteps pounded close by. There was another set, this one kicking into the log Sapphira hid behind.

She gripped her knife and braced herself for a blow. But it never came. The fight remained on the other side of the log, and though she couldn't see it she could hear the violence all the same.

Sapphira lay there for what felt like hours as the shouting and cursing turned into grunts and whimpering, of bone-crushing and blood squelching. It stopped and for a moment, there was silence. Her breath hitched as all she could hear was the sound of her heartbeat.

She tentatively stood and walked slowly toward the body lying mere feet from the log. The face was caved in. Its ribs poked through its torso, the skin hanging in jagged strips. What was worse was that its hands were still moving, roaming on the ground as though searching for something.

The demon — Florizeel, the vampire had called it —had mentioned a "first death." This being had been tortured in ways no being should have been able to recover from. Was it possible to die in Pandemonia and then be reborn? The thought of being tortured, dying, and then having to relive it all again knocked the wind out of her.

Just keep going, she thought. She turned away from the body. It started to rain again as she did so, and Sapphira whimpered as the sticky, metallic-smelling rain beat down on her. Clouds now filled the night sky, obscuring her vision.

It was then that Sapphira began to cry. What started as a silent sob turned into a wail, and then she was bent over, hands on her knees, trying to breathe around the snot that clogged her nose. The blood rain streamed down her face from her hair, mixing with her tears and stinging her eyes. She crouched down, pressing her face into her hands to try to quiet herself. The rain fell in a torrent, the sound of it smacking against the ground would've been comforting for Sapphira were it not for the screams. The sounds of violence had picked up again, and this time in the dim light she couldn't see where it was coming from.

She stood, exhaled, and held her knife in one hand and kept the other aloft, trying her best to feel her way through the darkness. Still, she cried. She wept for everything she'd lost, for every ounce of pain she knew she'd likely gain. She had no idea where she was, no idea where she might go for safety. She was more scared than she'd ever been in her entire life. She walked back toward the tooth-covered beach but narrowly missed another trio of souls fighting on the beach.

The rain stopped. The clouds shifted and the moon came out again. There was a sliver of light off in the distance, at a slightly higher elevation. *Could that be some kind of fire?* She wondered. She sniffled and started toward it, stumbling over tree limbs as she did so. Her left foot sank into a pile of what felt like entrails. She grimaced at the slimy texture of it against her toes. She pressed on, the light getting closer and closer. She could see a little of the terrain around her. She was zig-zagging her way up a hill. At the top loomed a large cave, and before it sat a bonfire. Two people stood across from each other about the fire, holding their hands out toward it for warmth; one wore a zoot suit, the other a frilly dress with a pair of broken blue wings at her back. The same two who'd been with the vampire who'd inadvertently saved her. Now she stood at the tree line mere feet away from the firelight and wondered where the vampire could be.

She felt the air around her shift before she was tackled to the ground. Her teeth clicked as her chin connected with the rotten soil. She struggled against the weight of the creature that lay on top of her, shuddering in its grip as it wound one hand around her chin and the other gripped her hip.

"What did I tell you about the rules here, human?" The vampire questioned. Sapphira closed her eyes at the smoothness of his voice. His touch was cold but firm.

"I... I just wanted to get somewhere safe."

The vampire grunted and shifted his position before flipping her onto her back. He pinned her down, gripping her neck and tilting her head to the side to expose her throat to him.

"You naive little child. You're in Pandemonia. Safety is a rarity."

She trembled as she met his gaze, feeling even more fearful of him as she noted how his pupils reflected the light, reminding her of a cat.

"I'm so tired of running," she whimpered.

"My word, it hasn't even been twelve hours yet here you are, blubbering like a baby."

"I—"

"I've been tracking you since you started your ascent up the hill. It's a wonder you managed to get this far unscathed."

"If you're going to kill me or rape me, you may as well do it now."

The vampire leaned in toward her, so his eyes were inches above hers. She could see the disdain in them, noted his sneer and the way his nostrils flared.

"What kind of monster do you take me for?" he asked.

The expression on his face, the way he sounded so affronted; both things filled Sapphira with anger and for the second time that day she found herself pressing a knife into this vampire's body.

"The kind that did enough damage when he was alive that he landed here in Pandemonia, on the worst island of them all."

He huffed; his breath warm against her skin. "I'm a lot of things. A vampire. A killer. But a rapist I am not. I've never had to stoop so low to get the pleasure I wanted from anyone I desired."

"Then why the fuck are you still on top of me?" Sapphira spat. She applied force to the vampire's chest with the knife, this time drawing blood.

"Is it making you amorous?"

"Hardly," she spat. The vampire chuckled. He leaned in and sniffed at her neck. She winced. "But you sure seem to be getting off on this."

"Don't flatter yourself. I was going to feed on you, probably drain you dry," the vampire scoffed. "But now you've bored me."

He sprang to his feet and held out a hand to help her up, but she ignored it, instead standing on her own.

"Sorry, I'm still trying to get used to this whole, 'I'm dead and in a place I don't belong,' thing," Sapphira said. The vampire rolled his eyes dramatically.

"Everyone says that. It's rarely true."

"It is in my case," Sapphira shot back.

"That brand across your bosom would beg to differ."

Sapphira scowled. "What do you know about this brand?"

The vampire shrugged. "Enough to know that you most definitely belong here."

The comment set her teeth on edge, and she thought to strike out at him with the knife.

"What does this *mean*?" She questioned.

"Do I look like your professor, here to teach you the ways and rules of Pandemonia? Fuck off and take your questions elsewhere, human," he said as he turned to leave.

"But—" she stepped toward him, and he rounded on her, fangs bared. She gulped and held the knife out before her, but even in the dim light she could see how much her hand shook. He sighed and leaned against a tree, crossing his arms.

"Fine. Ask your silly little questions before I change my mind."

"You said that you knew enough about this brand to know that I belong here," Sapphira said. The vampire nodded. "When I got to Purgatore, Simyasha said my lover had stolen my eternity. And that demon, Florizeel, said something about me bartering my soul."

He shrugged. "Yes, that's what happens when one makes a pact with a demon."

Her throat went dry. "A demon pact?"

"Seems like a powerful one, too. I hope whatever you received in return was worth it, seeing as how you must've not had it for long, that is unless you made the pact as a young girl."

"Is it... is it possible for someone to..." she said, struggling to catch her breath. The vampire titled his head to the side. "Trade someone else's soul?"

The vampire uncrossed his arms and stroked his beard.

"I suppose so," he replied. "From what I gather, a demonic pact needs three things — communion with the demon, a verbal agreement on terms, and the demon's symbol drawn onto the recipient, usually in blood."

"You'd do anything for me, wouldn't you?" Dante had asked.

"Yes. Anything," she'd said. A verbal agreement.

Dante's fingers, slick with her blood, flashed in her mind. She'd watched him trace the symbol on her chest and wondered what it was. The demon's symbol drawn in blood.

"Holy shit," Sapphira breathed.

"I don't know why this is surprising, you had to have done all of this already unless—"

She looked at him. Seconds later his eyes widened.

"Oh. *Oh.* What an unfortunate hand you've been dealt."

"*Unfortunate?* I've been damned to Pandemonia because my boyfriend—"

Her breath came out in ragged spurts, stealing her words. Her body shook and her ears grew warm.

"I can't. I can't—" she said, dropping the knife in her hand and clenching and unclenching her fists as her breath escaped her in ragged bursts. She backed up slowly and pressed against a tree. The vampire walked toward her. Tears stung her eyes as she trembled, drawing her shoulders up to try to protect her neck. But instead of biting her, he picked the knife up and held it out to her. She took it with a trembling hand.

"Take a deep breath," he said. "Now."

Sapphira struggled to calm herself, even as the vampire loomed before her. As though sensing her fear, he stepped away from her, keeping his hands at his sides. She held her knife aloft as she worked to soothe her breathing. Minutes later, her lungs no longer felt like they were seizing, and her heartbeat returned to normal.

"Feel better?" he asked. She nodded.

"Now, you were headed toward the camp I share with my companions."

She looked from the vampire toward the bonfire. The flame was doused and both people who'd been there were now gone. She sighed and leaned back against a tree.

"I saw the fire and I thought maybe... maybe they'd let me sit by it for a while."

"Oh, gods no. Those two would've ripped you apart before you got the chance to even ask."

"Great," she replied.

She shifted her weight from side to side, flexing her toes. When she'd chosen her platforms for the evening, she'd done so because they were the most comfortable heels she owned. They were reliable and didn't pinch her toes or nip at her heels. She could wear them all night to dance and then saunter home, drunk, high, or both, without issue. But she'd never thought she'd be spending eternity in them. She hated the way her feet ached, and she wished she could take off her shoes and lay down. But there was nowhere clean or safe to do so.

"However," the vampire began. She could feel the vampire's eyes on her. "I suppose I could convince them to pause their murderous endeavors for the rest of the evening if you still need a safe haven."

"Why?"

"Pardon?"

"Why are you offering me this? Why are you being nice?"

"I wouldn't go that far," he said. Though his expression wasn't quite as disdainful as it had been moments ago, she could feel his annoyance for her radiating off him. *Why is he still here?* She thought. "It's just... well, you look pitiful. About as terrifying as a... kitten. And knowing now what happened to you..."

She wiped away her tears with the back of her hand. "I don't need your pity, bloodsucker. I can figure this place out on my own."

He laughed, and the sound made her cheeks warm in anger.

"Pitiful and foolish. What a wonderful combination. I bet you left all the boys and girls in a tizzy where you're from."

"I hope you choke," she said.

Sapphira slashed at him with the knife, swiping the blade across his cheek. His eyes widened in surprise before giving her a wicked grin.

"Well, perhaps you've got some fight in you after all, human," he ran a finger across the cut then slipped the finger into his mouth. Sapphira shuddered yet found herself unable to look away from those lips. "Come. Take some time to rest, get your bearings."

"No thanks, I don't want to spend my night being insulted by a smug-ass leech."

The vampire held his hands up as if in surrender. "I won't say one disparaging word."

She shook her head, but her resolve was waning. He was right. She needed rest. The chance to let her brain slow down and process what she was going through, come to terms with what Dante had done to her. But how could she trust him? How could she trust anyone again after what Dante had done to her? No, better to be on her own. At least then she won't have to worry about being betrayed.

"For Enefri's sake," he said, throwing his hands up. "If you want to take your chances out here in the wood at night, that's your choice. Don't say I didn't warn you."

He turned to leave, but the sound of footsteps close by and a scream off in the distance made her reach out and grab his arm. "Wait, ok. I'll go with you, but only until it gets light out."

"Very well."

"And please just, don't kill me. I'm not ready to die again."

"It's not so bad once you get used to it. After a while, it feels about as normal as taking a nap."

He led her up the rest of the hill, and she walked slowly behind him, gripping her knife in her hand. They got to the mouth of the cave and her heart skipped a beat. The vampire gestured toward the cave, where firelight danced somewhere far down a long corridor.

"Here we are. Gird your loins, kitten," he said before walking into the cave.

CHAPTER 5

SAPPHIRA

APPHIRA OPENED HER mouth to reply but no words came out as she took in the cave before her.

Two torches illuminated a space no larger than a bedroom. Stalactites hung from the ceiling in jagged spikes. There were a handful of rocks scattered about the cave, a pile of leaves in one corner and a pile of bones in the other. It smelled like piss and blood. The smell tickled her nose, and she found herself scrunching and un-scrunching her nose involuntarily.

Perched on top of a large rock sat the creature with the broken blue wings. She looked more monstrous up close; her eyes glowed in the torchlight. Her face was long and boxy, with eyes too large and too small a nose and mouth, which she wore in a severe frown as she locked eyes with Sapphira. Seated on the floor with his back pressed against the rock was the man in a zoot suit. His hat sat low on his brow but Sapphira could still see his pale skin and the frown that spread across the lower part of his face.

"Maxwell, you've brought home a pet," drolled the winged creature, sounding as though she was bored of the conversation already.

So that's his name. Maxwell, Sapphira thought as she looked at the vampire. He with his hands in his pockets, his posture perfect and his blue-brown eyes reflecting the torchlight.

"Shut up, Kiava. She's not a pet, she's... a guest," he replied.

"A guest? Why in all the years we've lived in this cave I've never once seen you invite someone in, have you, Harry?" Kiava wondered.

"Never," the man in the suit replied. He crossed one leg over the other and slid his hat back on his head. Sapphira took in his sunken eyes, his crooked nose, and the small slit of a mouth. Though his frown dissipated he still regarded her with malice, the same as Kiava.

"And I can assure you, you likely never will again. But right now, she..." he paused and leaned toward her.

"What's your name?" he whispered.

"Sapphira," she replied.

"Sapphira," he said as though testing out how the name would sound aloud. "Sapphira is our guest. That means no maiming, murdering, raping, or generally hellish behavior, are we clear?"

Sapphira could tell by his tone that he wasn't giving them the option to say no. She tried to grip the hilt of her knife tighter, but it kept slipping out of her sweaty palm. Her eyes darted around the room, and she startled at the sound of Kiava sliding off the rock. Sapphira stepped backward and pressed herself against the wall of the cave. Maxwell shifted to lean against the wall opposite her and pressed his boot against it.

"Oh, she's scared of us," Kiava said. "Isn't that adorable?"

"Maxwell, just how fresh is your little... guest?" the man asked. He stood and sauntered over toward her.

"I can speak for myself" Sapphira said. She hated how meek she sounded, but at least she was saying something. "You all saved me from Florizeel right after I landed."

"Saved you?"

"Yes, I said saved. I know that wasn't your intention, but you did save me. And of course, I'm scared of you. You look mean, you sound meaner, and I don't belong here."

Kiava rolled her eyes and hissed. "That's what everyone says. No one wants to cop to what they did to get here, 'cept me and Harry over there. Not even Maxwell wants to talk about it."

Sapphira glanced at the vampire and saw the way his brows knitted, and his lips pulled at the corners in a frown.

"Ever consider that whatever it was is some messed up shit he doesn't feel like reliving?" Sapphira said. Quicker than she thought possible, Kiava was on her feet, and in front of her, pressing Sapphira into the wall of the cave, she winced as the sharp edge of a rock pressed into her back. The fairy scowled, her thick brows knitting and her small mouth frowning.

"You've got some nerve, crabapple. We're being nice to you, helped keep you alive and now offering shelter and yet you want to threaten us? You want to talk about messed up shit? You've never seen messed up shit, not yet," Kiava said. She punched the cave wall next to Sapphira's head, making the entire cave shake. "But don't worry, I'll show you. I'll—"

Maxwell caught her arm just as she went for another blow, this one, Sapphira was certain, meant for her head. The vampire flung her across the cave, the fairy's body connecting with a stalactite. The contact made the cave shudder, and Sapphira's eyes snapped up toward the jagged spikes, and she wondered whether that had been enough to make them fall.

"Do that again and I'll rip your throat out," Maxwell growled.

Kiava sneered as she stood and straightened herself. "Don't know why you're so on fire to save her. She's just a human."

"I have my reasons. Now get the fuck out of my sight."

Kiava glowered at them but disappeared into the rear of the cave, blowing out one of the torches and casting herself in darkness. Only the reflective dots of her eyes were still visible, her malicious gaze still following Sapphira's movements.

"You saved me again," Sapphira said. "Why? Are you expecting something in return?"

Maxwell smirked. "And what sort of thing would you be willing to offer?"

Sapphira pressed her lips together and narrowed her eyes at him. "Not a damn thing."

A smile split Maxwell's face in two. "You're catching on quick, aren't you, kitten?"

"Why did you stop her from hitting me?"

"You ask a lot of questions."

"I need a lot of answers."

"It's vexing," he retorted.

"Then here's one more — why am I the first person you've brought back here?"

Maxwell huffed and turned away from her. He walked toward the other side of the cave and gently sat on a short, squat rock. He leaned forward, pressing his elbows to his knees and steepling his hands. He looked up at her through thick, dark lashes. "I highly doubt you'd be able to survive on this island without a companion. Believe me when I say I died over a hundred times before I was able to even survive for longer than a few days, and I'm a vampire, preternaturally stronger and faster. I have better senses than you ever will. Most of the time I don't blink at the sight of weaker beings on the chopping block. But you looked..."

The confident smirk he'd had on his face was momentarily replaced by something almost worried. "You looked so scared...yet defiant, even after what you've been through. I think you deserve a chance."

Sapphira didn't know how to respond, so she said nothing. After a few minutes, she slid down to the ground and leaned back against the cave wall.

"How long have you been here?" she asked. Then she clapped a hand over her mouth realizing that she'd asked another question.

He shot her a knowing look before replying: "1897."

Sapphira's heart leaped. Eighty years in Pandemonia. She wondered what she would be like after even a year in this place.

"What year is it for you?" he asked.

"1978, almost 1979," she replied. She crossed her arms and squeezed her toes together, trying to bring some sensation back to them. Maxwell sighed.

"Does it feel like you've been here for almost a century?" Sapphira asked.

"Yes, and no," Maxwell said. "I've died over a thousand deaths and yet it feels like just yesterday I was tossed down from Purgatore."

"Why are you here?" Sapphira asked. His eyes darted toward hers, the irritated expression on his face making Sapphira's cheeks grow warm. She ducked her head down to avoid his gaze.

"Why are you so nosy?" he questioned, glowering at her with those reflective eyes.

"I don't know what else to say."

"Why do you have to say anything?"

"I just..."

"Look," he said, quickly moving from sitting across from her to kneeling before her. She clutched the knife in her hand like a talisman, and Maxwell frowned but he did not move closer. "You are in Pandemonia. There's no making friends here. There are just people you kill, people you avoid, and the reluctant allies you make to survive."

"Wha—"

"And before you ask which one am I in that bravado of yours, right now I'm the third one, but if you keep pressing me, I'll very quickly turn into number two. You don't want that, right?"

Sapphira shook her head.

"I didn't think so," he stood. "Now, why don't you just sit a spell, *in silence*, and rest. You'll be fresh and capable of leaving in a few hours."

She didn't respond as he walked out of the cave. Harry raised a brow at her before shaking his head and following Maxwell into the night. Sapphira drew her knees up to her chest and rested her head on them. She turned her head to the side, toward the dark depths of the cave. Kiava's eyes still glowed in the darkness, staring at Sapphira, unblinking.

Somehow Sapphira fell asleep and when she awoke it was to the sound of grunts and moans. She heard skin slapping against skin and when she snapped open her eyes she saw, in the far corner, Maxwell and his companions having sex.

The torches had gone out but in the dim light of the morning, she could see Kiava on her hands and knees. Behind her, hunched over her back was Harry, his hands gripping her wings as he thrust into her. Maxwell knelt behind him, and Sapphira watched as he dug his hand into Harry's hair and pulled the man back, exposing his neck.

Maxwell sunk his fangs into the man's neck as he moaned. Then he dislodged himself from Harry's neck and pulled him away from Kiava. The fairy hissed but turned to watch as the vampire pushed Harry onto his stomach and thrust into him. Both men grunted and as Maxwell increased his rhythm, Sapphira's cheeks grew warm and she was suddenly aware of the slight throbbing between her thighs, a fact that made her cheeks warm even more. She sighed. Maxwell and Kiava's heads whipped toward her at the sound. Though Maxwell made eye contact with her, he didn't stop his thrusting.

"We got a peeper," Kiava crowed. "Does our little guest want to join? I promise not to hurt you too bad, unless you like that sort of thing."

She could see Maxwell smirk, his gaze never leaving Sapphira as he continued to fuck Harry. She scrambled to her feet and ran out of the cave, leaving her knife and jacket. Her stomach clenched and she doubled over, pressing her hands against her knees.

"What the fuck?" She whispered. Tears sprang into her eyes and she knelt and covered her face in her hands. She was horrified at her circumstance — cast down to the worst part of the realm, taking shelter with a trio of creatures who were just as likely to kill her as they were to fuck each other right in front of her. What's more, she was in Pandemonia because Dante bartered her soul. She stared out at the wood before her. The early morning light barely crested the treetops, and already she heard the screams of the damned. Or had they always been there? Had she already started tuning them out?

I don't belong here. The thought reverberated in her mind and she fought the urge to scream it aloud.

She hadn't known why she was in Pandemonia. She'd assumed it was the mistake of the goddess, though in all her years she'd never heard that Simyasha could be wrong. But finding out that she was cast down to the seventh island because Dante bartered her soul? It was too much to bear. Because it meant that not only had he never truly loved her, not only did he put her through such turmoil when she was living, but he was literally responsible for her going through it now that she was dead. It meant that he *had* won. That he was enjoying whatever it was he'd traded her soul for. She pictured him standing on a stage, singing his songs for thousands of people, while her sister and friends mourned her death. Her stomach rolled at the thought, and she bent over and retched, bile steaming as it hit the ground.

She straightened and looked back at the cave, where she could still hear the trio grunting and moaning. She couldn't face them after they'd seen her watching them, after she'd felt her body ache at the sight of them together. She marveled at that, wondering how she could even feel anything close to horny with all that had happened to her, with where she was. Her best bet was to leave and take her chances on her own.

But then she'd left her jacket and more importantly, her knife, in the cave. She'd be foolish to think she could try to survive in Maleficence without a weapon. She clenched her fists and resolved to grab her things and leave. This was never supposed to be a long-term arrangement anyway. Maxwell offered her rest, a chance to get her bearings and though she'd gotten the first and not the latter, she had to keep moving. Maybe she'd find her own hideout, a place to spend the rest of eternity away from the torture if such a thing was possible.

Eternity. The thought was dizzying. But she took another deep breath and stepped toward the cave. In the space between her steps something lodged in her back. She squawked, arms bowing backward before she fell onto her knees. She reached back to try to pull whatever it was out, her hand becoming slick with blood as she did so. There was a giggle behind her, high-pitched and cloying like nails on a chalkboard. The sound grew closer. She tried to get to her feet but was kicked in the butt, the blow hard enough to send her down onto her face, the cartilage in her nose crunching and sending a searing pain up between her eyes.

A foot pressed against the back of her neck, driving her face deeper into the muck. She could feel a bare foot with long sharp toenails scrapping against her skin.

The blade dislodged from her back and the pain of the wound only increased as her blood seeped out more freely. She couldn't speak. She could feel the mud and muck infiltrating her nose and mouth and thought idly about whether parasites were a thing in Pandemonia.

Whatever stood above her removed its foot from her neck and slid it to the small of her back before pressing down, shoving her body further into the dirt. The being chuckled as it ran the knife up the center of her back, the tip of it barely touching her skin but still sending a tingling feeling up her spine.

She lifted her head and spat out the muck in her mouth, that had gotten stuck in her throat, a rancid taste still on her tongue after her mouth was unobstructed. As the tip of the knife slid through her skin, Sapphira flailed her arms and legs in pain.

"You've got such a beautiful scream," the being croaked. "I'm gonna have fun making you squeal."

"No!" she cried. Tears welled in her eyes, blurring her vision. She clawed at the dirt and tried to wriggle out from beneath her captor's foot, but no matter how hard she tried she barely moved an inch. "Please, stop."

She hated the tremulousness of her voice as she said it, hated the way it made the being chuckle even louder as he dragged the blade further across her spine. It shifted position again, this time slamming its knee into her back and pressing a clammy hand against her cheek, forcing her gaze to her left, toward the forest.

She heard fast footsteps behind her, and she pressed her eyes tight, bracing herself for the end. Instead, she heard the being pressing down on her squawk. Instead, she felt the knee in her back lift, the hand against her cheek slid off, and then the sound of cracking bones. A warm liquid sprayed across her body, and she heard a plunking sound right in front of her. She slowly opened her eyes and didn't bother fighting the scream when she saw the severed head of an ancient-looking vampire before her. Its milky-white eyes rolled up toward the sky, its mouth slack-jawed and the skin at its neck looked like tattered bits of fabric.

Sapphira willed her body to move but she remained pressed into the dirt. Though she was thankful for the rescue, how could she be sure that whatever it was that saved her was any better than what she'd been saved from?

She blinked away the tears and the sticky blood and waited for her fate.

"Well, you can officially count that as the first time I saved your life."

Maxwell knelt before her, bloody hand outstretched. He stared at her with an amused expression on his face, and Sapphira's stomach roiled. She recognized the patronizing look on his face; it was the same one Dante and so many other men had given her over the years, as though they regarded her as little more than a child. She dug her hands into the earth and pressed herself up to stand, ignoring the vampire's show of support and the gaping wound in her back.

Maxwell stood with her, one dark eyebrow raised as he regarded her, wearing only his pants held up by suspenders and his mud-covered boots.

"You didn't need to do that," Sapphira said.

Maxwell chortled.

"*Please.* You were seconds away from being carved up like a turkey."

"I would've figured it out myself."

"Yes, I'm sure you would've."

Sapphira growled and balled her fists. "Stop talking to me like I'm fucking stupid!"

"Then stop acting like it, kitten," Maxwell said.

"Don't call me that!"

Sapphira shoved him, but it did little to move Maxwell off his position.

"What would you like me to do, then, huh? Should I have watched as that vampire, who's been here longer than any other creature I know, split you open and dig around in your insides? You would've died, but then you would've come back to life to find your guts rearranged or your lungs pulled out of your back like a pair of fucked up wings."

Sapphira's heart skipped at the last part.

"I..." her breath hitched. Maxwell sighed.

"Do whatever you feel you need to do, it's your eternity," Maxwell said. "I'll not worry about you anymore."

"You were worried?"

The vampire knitted his brows, seemingly annoyed with his own use of the word.

"I'll not *bother with you* anymore," he corrected. But Sapphira felt her shoulders relax just a little, and she took a deep breath. Already she could feel the blood stop oozing out of her wound. The pain was slowly going away, too.

"Are wounds always this quick to heal here?" She asked.

Maxwell hooked his thumbs into his suspenders. A bright, clementine-colored sun had risen in the sky. The light caught his eyes, illuminating their warmth. Sapphira scanned his face, finding its beauty, until she got to his blood-soaked beard. She blinked and turned her attention away from him. *Trust no one, not even the beautiful vampire cast into damnation.*

"Still full of queries, I see." but there was no edge to his voice as there had been the night before.

"If I'm to spend eternity here, I need to know what I'm dealing with."

"Well," Maxwell sighed. "I suppose I can be of assistance, help you put your best foot forward, keep you from dying unnecessarily and all that. At least, if you want my help."

She looked toward the forest, where the cries of the damned reverberated through the barren trees and wondered if she could afford to go on without Maxwell's knowledge. But then, could she afford to stay with him? Would it mean having to deal with his companions who, as he said, would merrily tear her limb from limb if they got the chance? How could she trust anyone after what Dante had done? How could she even trust herself?

She could feel Maxwell's eyes on her. She looked at him and was surprised to find not pity in his gaze but something that looked like concern. Sapphira took another deep breath and tried to steady her racing heart.

"Ok. You can help me."

CHAPTER 6

SAPPHIRA

AFTER PUTTING ON the rest of his clothes and grabbing her jacket and knife from the cave, Maxwell led Sapphira to the highest peak on the island. He didn't protest as she pressed the knife against his back during the trek. Even now as she stood beside him wheezing, legs sore and lungs burning, she gripped the hilt of the knife in her hands.

"Do all humans lack stamina or is it just you?" he asked.

She glared at him, and he chuckled as he ran a hand over his dark coils. The sun was starting to wane in the sky as she stared out at the terrain before her. From where she stood the screams, the sound of violence, had faded and were replaced by the whistling of the wind. It was almost peaceful, if she didn't think about what had caused her to be there in the first place. A single tear slid down her cheek but she didn't bother to wipe it away.

"You're crying."

"Betrayal will do that to you," she said. "So will having to come to terms with spending eternity in the worst place in this realm and the next."

"May I ask, since you seem to have a lot of questions for me..." he trailed. She looked at him and nodded. "What happened, with your lover?"

The question hit Sapphira right in the chest, spiking her heart rate and making her sweat.

"He, Dante," she said. Even just saying his name aloud made her stomach clench. She took a deep breath and started over. "His name was Dante. And he was beautiful. Is beautiful, I guess. And so, so talented, a singer. He writes his own songs, wrote a few about me. He made me feel like princess... most of the time."

"And the other times?"

"Other times... he made me feel like I was losing my mind," she replied. She blinked up at the vampire, whose expression grew solemn. She stepped back, needing to put more space between them before she spoke again. "So, uh... where are we?"

"It's ok to keep talking about him if you need to. Enefri knows you probably need it."

"Why would you say that?" she questioned.

He surprised her by holding his hands up in surrender, brows raising. "I just meant… if my lover was directly responsible for damning me to the bowels of Pandemonia, I'd need to pour my heart out, too, cold as it may be."

"I don't think your heart's cold," she said without thinking. The vampire smiled but there was no joy in it.

"Sweet of you, but unnecessary, kitten. I know what I am, what I've done to get here. I don't need your flattery."

"Then what do you need?"

"I don't know. I think I'd just settle for knowing more about the jackass who sent you here," he said. He took a seat and crossed his legs. She followed suit but kept her distance. They sat in silence for a long while before she spoke.

"We got into a fight, that night."

"What about?"

"I didn't tell him I loved him. I was so focused on stopping him and my sister from arguing that I didn't remember to tell him I loved him."

Maxwell's brows knitted as he grimaced. "Sounds quite pathetic if I am being honest."

"No, no, it's not like that," she said. "He just… I should've remembered to say it when I first saw him that night. I didn't want to upset him, I always tried so hard not to."

"Why?"

"Because…" she trailed. *Because I worried about how he'd react. Because it never felt safe.*

"What a silly question," she said, leaning back and bracing for Maxwell's reaction. But all he did was shake his head. "I mean, no one wants to upset their lover."

"No, of course not. You cherish their feelings as if they are your own," he replied.

"Yes, so—"

"But, that doesn't mean you must betray yourself and your own feelings in the name of his comfort, which I sense you had to do quite often."

"What do you know?" she breathed. She got to her feet.

"I mean no harm with my statement, kitten," Maxwell replied. He did not move, but she held her blade out before her as though it could block the judgement radiating off him.

"It doesn't matter. I don't even know why I'm telling you this. You're just as likely to kill me as you are to snark and sneer at me."

He stood then, and she took another step back, glancing behind her only to make sure she wasn't close to the edge.

"Sapphira."

She stopped at the sound of her name on his lips.

"I mean you no harm, nor judgement. Please, just tell me what he did to you."

"Why?"

"Because holding it in will only poison you, trust me, I know. It's been eighty years and I've told not a soul about my past. And I can feel it festering within me like a wound, taking over nearly every thought of mine."

"He did it because... I think he bartered my soul to become famous. He said the whole world would know his name, and that he had to make sure it happened."

The vampire was on his feet and closing the distance between them before she could register what was happening. She leapt backward, knife out, gripping the handle so tightly her knuckles turned white. He grabbed her jacket, pulling her toward him.

This is it, my second death, she thought, and wondered if it would hurt more than the first. To her surprise, all he did was set her down beside him.

"You were about to fall," he said, gesturing to where she'd just stood, right on the edge, on ground that seemed ready to give way if she prodded it.

"You could've just let me," she said.

"Then consider this the second time I've saved you," he said, and flashed a wide, indulgent smile at her.

She didn't return the gesture, unsure of how to handle his sweetness. So instead, she walked back to where they'd stood and looked out at the opposite direction, past the barren trees and toward a yellow fog that shrouded the area it surrounded in mystery.

"What's that?" she asked.

"That, some say, is where Tartagnon's palace is. No one who has ever left this island has come back to report it as such, though, so perhaps it's just another island worse even than this one."

"People can leave?" she asked. Maxwell nodded.

"How... how do people leave?"

"The path of the damned."

"The path of the damned?" she questioned.

"You know, if I had a nickel for every question you asked, I'd be rich."

"Hardly," Sapphira replied. "I've barely asked ten and in 1978, fifty cents won't get you more than a cup of coffee and a croissant."

Maxwell looked affronted by the revelation. "Sacrilege."

"The path?"

Maxwell turned on his heel and walked toward the edge, boots sending debris down the side of the mountain.

"The path of the damned stretches between every island from here to the first, and beyond to a beach, where a small, hidden path leads to Purgatore," Maxwell cast a sidelong glance at Sapphira. "Or so I've heard."

Sapphira narrowed her eyes at him. "And you've never tried to escape before? You been here almost a hundred years and you've never once tried to leave?"

"Presumptuous, aren't we?"

"Maxwell," Sapphira warned.

The vampire heaved an exaggerated sigh and pursed his lips before speaking. "That path is dangerous. Not only does one have to make it out of these woods alive, but they must cross the path without being killed both by the demons of the island, like Florizeel, or the creatures in the abyss."

"The abyss?"

"Do they no longer teach about the abyss in communion?"

Sapphira shook her head. Maxwell clucked his tongue.

"The preachers of your age have gone soft. That is the abyss," he said, pointing out toward the ocean. "All the demons and even the great beast Tartagnon himself, is afraid of it."

"How could the evilest being in existence be afraid of water?"

Tartagnon was one of the first gods, created by Enefri along with Simyasha and Damsuul. He was the creator of Pandemonia, father of demons, originator of every torture method known to man. It blew Sapphira's mind to think that he could be afraid of anything, let alone an ocean.

"Not just any water," Maxwell said. "The abyss is older than all the gods, and every being who ends up in it dies. Only they don't reanimate. The abyss takes them forever, to their final death. I don't know if it's the same for demons and gods. I just know that it's the one thing every being is afraid of."

The terror in Maxwell's voice was palpable, and Sapphira shuddered at the thought of a final death. Then again, she wondered what could be on the other side that would be worse than this?

"How hard is it to cross? It didn't look that narrow."

The vampire shook his head. "The path gets flooded over often throughout the day. Even if you made it through the wood, if the path was flooded, you'd have to wait until exactly the right time to get across, and risk being killed or dragged back. Plus, if one does get to the sixth island, who knows what mayhem lay in store there, or how hard it will be to progress."

"But I thought the seventh island was the worst?"

"It is, but that doesn't mean the rest aren't terrible in their own right."

Sapphira sighed and let Maxwell's words—his fear—sink in. There was a way out, that was good. But according to him it was treacherous, and if she didn't get it right, she could be killed. But what was the alternative? Hiding in caves, running around the island like some even more horrific version of *Lord of the Flies*? No, this would not be her fate. Not when her sister and her friends needed her, not when she had a life she deserved to live. Especially not when she thought about Dante and how he traded her soul for his success. She wanted to flee this hellscape and do to Dante what he'd done to her — take away not only his life but his future.

In that moment, Sapphira decided she would do it. Even if it meant she had to fight her way out, die trying, then try again once she reanimated. She looked at the vampire then. He stood unnervingly still as he looked out at the rest of the island toward the abyss. There was a part of her that wanted to run through the forest and across the path right then and there, try to see if she could make it on her own. But there was still so much she didn't know, and though she wasn't sure she fully trusted him, the reality was that she needed Maxwell, and not just for his help. There was also a small part of her that was starting to like his company. She stepped up next to him, letting her hand relax around the hilt of her blade.

"Dante didn't just trade my eternity; he took my life. Stabbed me on a park bench in the middle of the night. I didn't even get a chance to say goodbye to my sister, my friends. They were all I had and then he…" Sapphira's breath hitched. "He took so much from me, and when Simyasha cast me down here, she said she wished she could watch them all rip me apart."

Maxwell looked at her, surprised. "What did you say to make her respond thusly?"

"That I didn't belong here and that she made a mistake," Sapphira began. She was afraid and anxious, but there was something else stirring within her, a fire that sparked and grew the more she spoke. "But I'm going to escape this madness. I'm going to cross the path to the sixth island, the fifth, the fourth, and every one after that until I get to Purgatore. Then I'm going to look the goddess in the eyes… and demand she send me back."

Maxwell chortled and crossed his arms.

"An ambitious, albeit foolhardy, plan if I've ever heard one," the vampire replied.

"You should come with me," she replied, saying the words before she fully thought about it. But it felt right, somehow. She didn't want to be alone, and so she hoped that this vampire would be her companion rather than her undoing.

"I beg your pardon?" he questioned.

"Come with me, Maxwell. You've been here too long and from what I've seen, you don't belong here."

"Who are you to decide who belongs where?" he questioned.

"I'm only saying... It's a chance to change things for yourself."

"And what if I deserve to be here?" he asked softly. "What if what I did was so heinous I don't deserve a second chance?"

Sapphira took a step toward him and placed a hand on his shoulder. He flinched but then looked at her, and there was such vulnerability in his expression.

"Everyone deserves a second chance."

"Even vampires who killed their family and friends? Who watched their lover executed?"

Despite Maxwell's revelation and the way it made her anxiety flood, Sapphira didn't move her hand from his shoulder.

"Even them."

Maxwell's brows knitted. He looked like he might cry but instead clenched his teeth and stared at her.

"This is a fool's errand."

"What've either of us got to lose?" Sapphira said.

"Our lives."

"Oh, you mean your weird little fuck fests you have in between running away from bloodthirsty killers?"

Maxwell smiled wryly. "I'm hungry in more ways than one, kitten, what can I say?"

"Say you'll come with me."

"Let's say we make it to Purgatore and Simyasha sends us back. What then?"

"At least we tried. And if we feel up to it, we try again as many times as it takes."

"You're a lunatic, Sapphira," Maxwell said. Sapphira bristled at the use of her name instead of kitten. "But... ok. I'll accompany you on this reckless, perilous, bound-to-fail mission to escape Pandemonia. But when our asses get caught, you're on your own."

Sapphira smiled as hope swelled within her. Without thinking she took his hand and shook it, ignoring how frozen it was. He grimaced at her but didn't move his hand away.

She had always been ambitious. At ten she decided she was going to be a fashion designer, at fourteen, she was going to go to the Pratt Institute, and at nineteen she was going to design a dress for the world's most famous women. And now, at twenty-two, she was setting her most ambitious goal yet — breaking out of Pandemonia, heading to Purgatore, and demanding the goddess of death make her alive again.

"When's the best time to leave?" she asked.

"The tide is low at first and last light," Maxwell said.

"Then we'll try tonight."

CHAPTER 7

SAPPHIRA

THE MOON WAS a crescent in the cloudless, starless sky as Sapphira stood on the beach. She waited for Maxwell, who'd spent the rest of his day with his companions. He'd insisted it was necessary, saying he didn't want them to catch on to their plan. She'd wanted to ask why, but by now she knew better than to ask too many questions. As though reading her thoughts, he answered anyway:

"I don't trust them any more than I must. We hunt together, we fuck, and we survive. That's it. Letting them in on our little scheme will result in us getting caught."

"Wouldn't it be better to have them join us? More people to fight off the creatures we'd come up against."

"Or more people to kill us to get ahead or abandon us when we need them most. Best to keep them out of it."

"How do you know that I won't abandon you or kill you to get ahead?"

The vampire laughed, a deep, beautiful sound that made Sapphira smile despite herself.

"Kitten, if you manage to kill an overturned log in this place I will rejoice. No, I don't think you'll be killing me."

"I could leave you," she replied, but the words rang hollow even as she said them.

He shrugged. "You're more than welcome to try. I've survived this place for decades; I think I could manage many more if I had to. I'll meet you back here in the dead of night."

He left her then, and once he disappeared into the trees Sapphira went about finding a hiding place. She was almost caught by a strange-looking creature that was half human half goat, but she managed to knock it unconscious before crawling into a large, hollowed-out log at the edge of the beach before the tree line. She spent the rest of the day there, dozing in and out of sleep, moving from one nightmare to another. In one she was being chased, another she was burned, but in every single one it was Dante doing the torture. In the nightmares he was as tall and bulky as Florizeel, and his dark eyes bore into her, filling her with equal parts terror and pleasure.

When darkness fell over the wood, Sapphira inched her way out of the log. There was a fire glowing from the other side of a tree line and she knew if she stood, she'd be seen. She grit her teeth as she crawled on her hands and knees across the tooth-covered beach. Her fingers plunged into a pair of eyeballs, and she pressed her lips together so hard it hurt to stave off a scream. She kept going, stopping behind a felled tree when she heard moans.

Sapphira peeked her head up just far enough to see a man on his knees before a woman, his face pressed in between her thighs. She kept moving, stopping at the sound of each scream or moan. She was sweating by the time she reached the path. She sat on her haunches and stared into the tree line as she waited for the vampire.

What seemed like an hour passed before she saw a pair of eyes reflecting in the darkness. She fought to keep her heart and her hand steady as she held her blade up, bracing for a fight. But then the shape closed the distance between them within seconds, and she recognized Maxwell.

"Thought you'd changed your mind," Sapphira said.

"As if you could do any of this without me," he replied huffily. She sniffed and rolled her eyes, watching as he sauntered past her.

The pathway was clear. The water all but still. It looked to her close to a mile walk, and even in the dim light of the moon she could make out the island across the pathway.

"Well, what're you waiting for?" the vampire asked, gesturing to the path before them. Sapphira smiled quickly and stepped toward it, a lump forming in the back of her throat.

The teeth crunched beneath her heels. The air was crisp, just cold enough to set her teeth on edge. *I can do this*, she thought as she stood before the path.

"Looks like we've got a pair of escape artists," came a gruff voice from behind them. Sapphira whipped around to see Florizeel flanked by three other demons quickly closing the distance between them. Harry and Kiava trailed behind them. Maxwell stepped in front of her.

"And? Two less souls for you to have to mind, Florizeel."

"You think that shit will work on me, blood sucker?"

"Well, you know," Maxwell said. "I had to try."

He launched himself at Florizeel, who gripped the vampire's neck in one hand tossed him to the side, where the two goons quickly set upon him. Seeing that Maxwell was preoccupied, Florizeel closed the distance between himself and Sapphira and grabbed her blade from her hand and tossed it away before pushing Sapphira to the ground.

One of the goons stood holding a torch behind him, while the other was sparring with Maxwell.

"Did you think it would be that simple, Jane?" Florizeel questioned.

"Jane? That ain't her name," said Harry.

"Uh-uh. That bitch is named Sapphira, and she's just some demon's whore," Kiava spat. The fairy kicked Sapphira in her back, and she yelped at the pain that radiated up her spine. Florizeel brought his bare food down onto her wrist, the bone crunching beneath his weight. Pain seared in her already swelling limb, turning her vision black momentarily. Sweat beaded on her upper lip and forehead as she clutched her arm to her chest.

Florizeel chuckled and turned from Sapphira to Maxwell, pulling him away from one of the demons he'd been sparring with.

"I hear you've been searching for me," the demon said. "So, what do you intend to do to me now that I'm here?"

Maxwell lashed out at the demon with his hands, but Florizeel dodged it and landed a blow against Maxwell's jaw, hitting him so hard Sapphira heard a popping sound, saw how his jaw hung unnaturally to the side. The vampire groaned in pain as Florizeel dropped him to the ground in a heap.

"No!" Sapphira yelled.

She threw herself forward and tried to crawl toward him. Florizeel stepped in front of her and knelt. His thick finger pressed her chin up to look at him.

"I've got so many wonderful things I could do to you. So many ways I could torture that unsullied body of yours," he said. Sapphira squeaked, more afraid than she'd ever been before.

Florizeel pulled her up by her broken wrist and she screeched at the pain. He stepped toward her, pressing his body against her and sniffing her neck.

"Please stop," she whispered. The demon chuckled.

"It's time I officially welcome you to Maleficence," he said.

She closed her eyes and clenched her fist, praying to a goddess she knew had no power in the domain of the great beast. There was a tug at her coat and then the sound of wind whipping through the air, coupled with screams and a loud thud.

"Fresh souls, ripe for the taking," crowed one of the goons.

"You go get 'em," Florizeel said. "I've got business to attend to."

He turned his attention back to Sapphira, but the new souls landing was just enough of a distraction to allow her to punch the demon in the throat. He dropped her and wheezed, and she scrambled toward her knife, gripping it in her hand just as the demon pulled her ankle toward him. She whirled around and buried the blade into his stomach. He sneered at her as his large hand closed around her wrist and pulled the blade out of his stomach.

"Glad you've got some fight in you still. It's so boring when souls are docile," he said. He stepped on her ankle, pinning her in place. He knelt over her and held her blade up above his head, and Sapphira braced for the blow.

Maxwell snaked forward and gripped the demon's head in his hands, breaking his neck. Florizeel fell to the ground and Maxwell looked at her.

"You ok, kit—"

Harry tackled Maxwell to the ground. Sapphira got to her feet. Her ankle wasn't broken, probably just sprained, but it hurt nonetheless. She knelt to grab her knife when a blow from the back sent her down to her knees.

"Looks like I'll have to deal with you myself," Kiava said. She pushed Sapphira to the ground and flipped her on her back. Kiava straddled her.

"Why are you doing this?" Sapphira asked. She swiped at the fairy, her nails digging into her skin.

"You chickenshit," she snarled. Kiava screamed and punched Sapphira in response. Kiava grabbed Sapphira's blade from her hand and pressed it against her throat.

Sapphira headbutted the fairy, making the fairy fall to the side. Black dots danced across her vision, and she willed herself to focus, knowing that Kiava would only be off her game for so long. She stood and tried to run, but the fairy was faster. She tackled Sapphira to the ground and pounded her head into the beach and Sapphira yelped at the pain, at the teeth that dug into her cheeks and pushed into her nostrils and mouth with each blow. Sapphira's wounded arms were outstretched before her, and she felt the water from the abyss lick the tips of her fingers.

"You don't belong anywhere but here," Kiava said as she grabbed Sapphira's hair and pressed the knife once again to her throat. "This is to remind you of that fact."

"No!" Sapphira bellowed as she rolled over, trapping Kiava beneath her. She brought her elbow to the fairy's side and pulled the blade from her hands, before rolling to her side and burying the blade into Kiava's eye. The fairy's body twitched before it went limp. Sapphira screamed and scrambled backward, crashing into Florizeel's body just at the demon was starting to stir.

"C'mon kitten, we've got to go," Maxwell said, pulling her up.

She fought to catch her breath. "Wha—"

"We've got to hide or else we'll fall into Florizeel's grip." He grabbed her hand and ran, forcing Sapphira to outright sprint as they sped down the right side of the beach. They reached a rock formation and Maxwell began to climb. She groaned and heaved herself up. Sweat beaded on her brow and her chest as she struggled up the rocks. Though her arms were starting to heal, it took her longer to reach the top and by the time she got there, her arms ached. He pulled her up to stand and grabbed her hand again, running along a river filled with bones. They took a right into the woods, bypassing a group clustered around a fire, fighting and yanking bone from flesh. Down a hill they went, until they hit a large tree. He let go of her hand and pulled up a log wedged in front of the tree. Then he pushed Sapphira toward the entrance. She ran in and he followed, pressing the log against the tree to bar the entrance.

"Shh," he whispered. He sat on the ground and pressed against the wall, and Sapphira did the same. They waited, and a minute later she heard the demon and its goons roaming around.

"Be on the lookout for that vampire and that human with the fur coat. They're mine, especially the girl," Florizeel said.

They stayed wedged against the wall for what felt like hours, listening to the sound of screams and torture. Then it went quiet, and

Sapphira's head swam.

Maxwell moved away from her. She gripped her not-quite-healed arm in her other and took slow, light breaths.

Maxwell quickly started a fire and minutes later she stared into his eyes over the small flame.

"What the fuck just happened?" she asked.

"An ambush, that's what," he said bitterly. "They must've learned about our plans."

"How could they? Did you tell them?"

"Absolutely not. They must've attuned."

"Or followed you. That fairy was one shifty little bitch," Sapphira said. Maxwell scowled but didn't say anything.

"Well, what do we do now?"

"We must wait," he said.

"How long?"

"I don't know."

"What do we do 'til then?"

"I. Don't. Know," he replied.

She huffed and pressed against the wall, looking away from him. Her arm still ached, and her broken wrist hadn't quite healed. Her feet were numb, hair wet, and though she was trying to keep on a brave face all she wanted to do was cry.

"Let me help you," he crawled over toward her.

"No, I'm fine."

"You're mad at me?"

"Yes. No. I don't know. Your friends are the ones who gave us up."

"They were hardly my friends."

"Fine, your fuck partners sold us out and now we'll never get to leave."

"We certainly won't if you don't set your wrist."

"It's already healing."

"Bones may heal but if they aren't set, they'll still heal poorly. You need to be able to actually use your wrist if you want to leave."

"What's the point I'm just gonna fail."

He chortled. "One setback and you're ready to give up? You really don't have a chance here."

She whipped her head around and glared at him. He returned the gesture, and the two stared.

"You're an insufferable asshole," Sapphira spat. "I bet you told them our plans because you didn't think I could actually escape this place."

"And you're a foolish, fragile little woman. What do I care if you leave? One less human threatening my existence," the vampire replied.

"I thought you said I couldn't kill you?"

"At the rate you're going you couldn't even kill a flea."

"Fuck you, I'm the one who killed Kiava."

Maxwell bristled. "Beginner's luck. Now let me set your arm or you'll be at a disadvantage when we try to escape again."

She opened her mouth to speak but stopped. His brows shot up. He looked at her and sighed, gently holding her wrist in his hand. He grabbed a piece of wood with the other and began the process of setting her arm

"Yes, I said *we*. I still want to try this, even though it is a very foolhardy plan."

"Do you always have to say something shitty?" she asked as she watched him wind his handkerchief around her wrist and the plank of wood.

"Do you always have to ask so many damn questions?"

Again, they stared at each other, his hands still holding hers.

He moved away first, clearing his throat and scooting to the other side of the fire. She looked down at the pretty bow that tied off the splint.

"Thank you," she said softly.

"You're welcome."

"Why do you want to go with me?"

"Because... you've given me hope, as much as that may make me sound naive. I never thought I deserved to leave, given what I've done," he replied.

Silence stretched between them. "What did you do?"

"I killed my family... well, most of them, anyway."

Sapphira was silent but drew her knees up, creating a barrier of sorts between them. Maxwell seemed to notice and looked at her with a pained expression on his face.

"You don't understand."

"No, I don't. What could compel someone to murder their family? I couldn't..." Sapphira's voice broke. "I couldn't even think about hurting mine."

Maxwell chortled. The sound was bitter, resentful. He fixed his eyes on her and spoke:

"That's what I thought, too, back then. When I was still human. I didn't think I could bring harm to them despite the harm they wrought onto me."

The vampire grabbed a handful of dried leaves and tossed them into the fire, stoking the flames. The hole they sat in was so small that she was already starting to sweat from the heat.

"What did they do?" she asked.

Maxwell picked at a spot of dried blood on his coat as he spoke:

"I was born and raised in Chicago. My father was a preacher and he, along with his immediate family had the ability to pass—which they did often. My mother was the daughter of our family's maid and she, like the rest of her family, could not pass. Still, they lay together. A bit of 'youthful frivolity,' my father called it. Affronted, my grandmother beat her son mercilessly and fired my grandmother. For her sins, my mother was sent away to a place upstate until she gave birth. As my father put it, the only reason he stayed in contact with my mother after that was to see how I would come out. Whether I'd inherit his 'blessing' or her 'curse' as he called it.

When she gave birth to me and he realized I didn't have the ability to move through white society as his family did, he shunned me. My father married a woman of the same status and color as he. But, when my grandmother died and my father's parents slipped into old age, he hired my mother and I on as staff. I was ten at the time, and I watched as my siblings reaped benefits of his wealth while my mother and I spent our lives serving them. When my father took his father's place as leader of his communion, his distaste for me turned into cruelty. It didn't help that I had a wondering eye during his sermons and paid attention to the both the women and men in his congregation."

Maxwell drew his knees up to his chest and stared at the fire. "I knew the pain of broken bones, bruised ribs, swollen eyes before I even finished school. His wife ignored me. Most of my siblings ridiculed me, cursed the gods for the way I looked, except for one, my sister Julietta. She stole extra food for my mother and I, brought me books to read and paper to write on."

"Do you come from a family of vampires?" Sapphira asked.

"Vampires aren't born, they're made," Maxwell added. "I was made into a vampire when I was twenty-three. A stranger came to my father's communion, and he had the most beautiful face I'd ever seen. He said he had traveled from Boston, and that he wanted to find a church family. Despite his color, my father could see that he was dressed in such a way that hinted at wealth, and so he let this man into the church and sit not in the back with my mother and I, with the rest of those my father's family felt were too dark for their taste, but near the front. I remember watching him, Evander. I remember the way his dark brown skin seemed to glow from the kiss of the sunlight, how he always seemed to wear a perpetual smirk. He passed me one morning on the way to communion and I remember thinking how like Umiyo he looked."

Sapphira nodded and thought about the goddess of the sea, whose devotees wore jewelry inlaid with blue topaz to model the color of her eyes and who held their weekly communion in the water. She watched Maxwell with rapt attention as he told his story.

"Just as I looked at Evander as though he were cast in a god's image, I soon learned he looked at me in much the same way. We came together quickly and in secret and it wasn't long before I was opening my veins to him."

"He turned me one fall night, the harvest moon high in the sky. Only my mother and Julietta noticed the difference in me, how I skulked around the house during the day, lethargic, but came alive at night. I was a young, hungry vampire in love and together we drank our way through town. We rarely killed on the first night, and Evander always hypnotized our victims to forget our presence."

Maxwell looked wistful then, as though recalling a memory he wished he could live in forever. Then he ran a hand over his coils and sighed.

"I'd only been a vampire for six months when they came for us. They thought if they killed Evander then I would revert to being human, because the old wife's tale of killing the maker to rehumanize the nascent vampire was a commonly held belief back then. But it didn't work, obviously. And when they realized that my father attacked me. So, in return for his years of cruelty, for my family's indifference to my pain, I made my way through the house ripping their throats open and draining them all except my mother and Julietta. When it was all done, I made them take whatever money and valuables they could and flee, somewhere I could never find them."

"What happened to Evander?"

A single, bloody tear spilled from Maxwell's eye as he turned his gaze back toward Sapphira.

"Before I killed my family, my father and my brothers beat me harder than ever before. Being a vampire, the wounds began to heal almost as soon as they issued them, but I was still broken. They said if I told them where Evander was then we would start fresh. They'd welcome me into the fold with open arms, and my mother and I would no longer need to serve them. So, I gave him up."

Sapphira's heart dropped at Maxwell's words. She saw how revealing his truth pained him, the way the bloody tears flowed freely down his face, matting his beard.

"They killed him and I... I didn't stop it. I just watched as they staked the man I loved, as they cut his head from his body. I thought he'd been a vampire for so long, surely, he could defend himself, but there was no way I could have known he couldn't. Yet still, I should have done something."

Sapphira moved to sit beside him. She placed a hand on his, and he looked up at her, his dark eyes red from corner to corner.

"You were trying to protect yourself," she said. Maxwell smiled ruefully.

"I should have protected him, too. He would have done everything in his power to save me, he never would've betrayed me. Yet, I was only too happy to surrender him to my family."

"Is that why you saved me?" Sapphira asked. Maxwell was silent, contemplative, before he replied.

"I told myself I'd never falter when I had the chance to save someone again."

"Surely you've had plenty of chances in the time you've been here," Sapphira said.

"You severely overestimate the goodness in others, kitten," he said as he wiped the tears from his cheeks.

"I always have," Sapphira replied. "I suppose it's part of what landed me here. But that's a story for another day."

Maxwell nodded, and Sapphira let out a breath, thankful that he didn't try to press her. Instead, he tossed more leaves into the fire, leaned back against the dirt and closed his eyes. And Sapphira, feeling relaxed for the first time in days, did the same.

CHAPTER 8

SAPPHIRA

MAXWELL SLOWLY PUSHED the log back from the hole in the tree and Sapphira stood behind him, heart hammering in her chest. Once the coast was clear, Maxwell slithered out then bent back to help Sapphira. The sky was the color of a bruise. The air was fetid and dry, and though it was early morning already it was too warm. The clearing was empty, but Sapphira could still hear movement not too far away. Wordlessly, Maxwell grabbed her hand and she nodded, though she kept her blade ready in case she had to use it, even on him. They made their way down to the beach on what felt like an endless set of switchbacks, Sapphira almost tripping and toppling them both over the edge of the cliff before the sun fully rose. They passed another stream, and she looked at a knot of intestines that floated by dispassionately, barely flinching when she saw a big toe bobbing in the water and wondered what type of hell she'd see on the sixth island.

"I don't remember this from yesterday," Sapphira said quietly, examining the hilly, sparsely populated terrain they now walked around.

"There's more than one way to get to the beach," Maxwell said. "This way takes us away from where we last saw the fiend."

"Florizeel," Sapphira said, the sound of his name sending shivers up her spine.

"This way takes us the long way, but we're less likely to run into him."

"Yeah, but it looks like we're not out of the woods yet," she said, pointing toward the tree line ahead, where a group of gray demons clustered around a trio of humans.

"Can we get past them?" Sapphira whispered. Maxwell pursed his lips.

"Those demons are what stand between us and the path. We have no choice but to go through them."

Sapphira took a step back, suddenly gripped by fear. How could she fight them off? The last demons she'd encountered were formidable. Even Kiava was ferocious; Maxwell had been right that Sapphira killing her had been a fluke.

I must do this. Persephone needs me, Sapphira thought. But not even the thought of her twin compelled her to move. She willed her feet to take a step as she fought to calm her ragged breath. Bile rose in her throat. Memories of her sister and her flashed before her eyes. But then she saw Dante and her stomach cramped. She saw him holding that knife and plunging it into her belly, heard him talk about how he needed her gone so he could achieve his dreams. As his face flashed before her eyes, the fear that was buzzing about her body was replaced by an anger so acute she had to stifle a scream.

I deserve the life that was stolen from me.

Sapphira knew she had to get back to the land of the living, even if she died trying. She gripped her knife tightly, her hand throbbing around the hilt. She ignored the pain and turned toward the vampire.

"I'm ready."

Maxwell let go of her hand and walked ahead of her, his feet barely making a noise as he trekked lightly through the muddy forest. Once they got closer, she could see how ghastly the demons ahead of her looked; up close she saw that their skin was mottled and sloughing off, teeth blackened and eyes as milky-white as Simyasha's.

One of them held a small carving knife in its bony hand. It pressed the knife against the leg of one of the humans it had captured, an elderly woman, and ran the knife across the midsection of the thigh. The woman screamed as blood flowed down her thigh from the wound. The demon squealed in delight and dug one of its long nails into the wound, and Sapphira watched in horror as it removed a long strip of skin from the woman's thigh and ate it.

"What the fuck?" she whispered. Maxwell looked back at her; judgment written all over his face.

"You've seen people be gutted, viscera hanging from trees, and you draw the line at cannibalism?" he said.

"Fuck off," Sapphira shot back. They were so close it was only a matter of time before one of the demons looked up and noticed their presence. She stepped into a puddle, the splash sound reverberating through the wood. She clapped a hand over her mouth, staving off a scream at the feeling of the sticky liquid between her toes. Ahead, the demons stared at them, slow smiles spreading across all of their faces.

"Get ready," Maxwell whispered.

Without warning one of the demons lunged at them. Maxwell dispatched it easily, gripping its head in his hands and snapping its neck. He bent forward and picked up the demon's weapon, a bat studded with nails, and sprinted toward the third demon just as its companion closed the gap between itself and Sapphira. She drew the knife across its throat, but the wound was superficial and closed within seconds. It cackled and Sapphira shuffled backward.

It closed the gap between them and she lashed out with her knife again, this time grunting as she sliced its throat properly, this time leaving a wide, yawning gash across its trachea. She shot to the side as the demon fell. She huffed as she looked around the wood, now touched by the early morning sun.

Their fighting had attracted the attention of another group, who looked hungry for a brawl. Even two of the humans on the ground who were being actively tortured by the demons stood and looked as though they were ready to cause pain.

An arrow whizzed past Sapphira, grazing her cheek before it landed in the tree in front of her. She whipped around in time to see a young woman about her age clad in a linen dress and sporting a bowl cut. Sapphira looked for cover, but the woman was already loading her bow with another arrow and pointing it straight at Sapphira. She ran toward Maxwell, who was beating a stocky, naked man back toward a tree.

Another arrow sailed by her, landing in the tree inches from where Sapphira stood. She turned toward the woman, who was running at her with an arrow in hand. Instead of loading it up in her bow, she held it like a knife and plunged it into the meat of Sapphira's thigh.

"Bitch!" Sapphira screamed. She pulled at the arrow with one hand but the woman swatted Sapphira's hand away before punching her in the jaw. The blow jerked Sapphira's head to the side and warm, stinging pain shot up the back of her head. Stars danced before her vision when she righted herself. The woman bent down and grabbed Sapphira's knife before sliding it into her quiver. She looked at Sapphira solemnly, her flat blue eyes devoid of emotion.

"Tell me how you wish to die," the woman said in clipped English.

Sapphira grimaced against the pain in her thigh, against the chain of body parts the woman wore around her neck, the centerpiece an ear with a pearl earring.

"Of old age." Sapphira spat in the woman's face, but it barely phased her.

"Slowly, then," the woman said. She gripped the arrow lodged in Sapphira's thigh and twisted. Sapphira screamed but managed to drive the palm of her hand up into the woman's nose until she heard a crunch. Then the woman slackened and fell to the ground. She pulled her knife from the woman's quiver and limped toward her companion, knowing that the woman wouldn't be dead for long. More souls had gathered here, hemming Sapphira and Maxwell in. Though he still fought, Sapphira could see his movements dulling. He was getting tired. They had to try to make a run for it, otherwise they'd never make it.

Just as he dispatched an elderly man in a priest's habit, a werewolf launched itself at Maxwell.

"A little help here!" he yelled, as the werewolf rolled on top of him and swung his hands in wide arcs, his long nails slicing into Maxwell's body. Sapphira dug the knife into the creature's back and yanked the blade down, splitting the skin like a zipper. The werewolf rounded on her and growled, but Maxwell was just as fast. He grabbed the wolf and buried his teeth in its neck, violently slurping the blood that gurgled up from the wound until the wolf stopped moving. He dropped him to the ground and grabbed Sapphira's hand, tugging her out of the way of a demon as it thrust a pitchfork toward her side.

Dozens of bodies filled the clearing, engaged in an all-out brawl. Just entering the clearing was Florizeel, flanked by even more grey demons. The sight of them sent a pang through Sapphira's body. Her wrist twinged at the memory of his rough foot breaking her bones. Her head swam as she watched the look of glee on the demon's face as he cut through the creatures between them, his gaze never leaving Sapphira. Maxwell shook her out of her reverie, tugging her toward the tree line.

"We've got to make haste!"

She turned on her heel and followed him, pressing through the thickening crowd. She dodged a blow to her neck but took one in the breast, and yelped as she felt a blade slice across her Achilles. She stumbled, and without a word, Maxwell tossed her over his shoulder and kept running.

"Put me down, I can—"

"No, you can't. Let me carry you."

"But..."

"Sapphira, let me help you, please," he breathed.

They broke through the clearing. The path lay straight ahead, a lone strip of muddy land sticking out from the abyss, the water tossed by small waves that licked at the pathway. Thick, ruby-colored clouds had moved in and kicked up wind. Maxwell sprinted, his boots crunching in the toothy gravel. He pressed a hand against her butt to keep her secure and gripped the nail bat in the other.

She watched as Florizeel and his retinue spilled out from the forest, closing the gap between them. *Will we make it off this Enefri-forsaken island?* She wondered, just as an axe buried itself in Maxwell's free shoulder. He fell to the ground, knocking the air out of Sapphira.

"C'mon, we've got to go," she said. She pushed him to the side and leaped to her feet, instantly regretting it. She looked down at ankle, the hem of her gold jumpsuit soaked through with her blood. She knelt behind Maxwell, wincing at her pain. But she couldn't think about that now, nor any of the other wounds she sustained in the brawl. The vampire lay on the ground, gasping for air, dark blood oozing from his back.

"Take out the axe," he breathed. "It's...silver."

"Silver really harms vampires?"

"Not really the time to discuss the physics of vampiredom," he replied. She rolled him on to his side and yanked at the axe. It was lodged deep into his skin. She looked back toward the demons, who were feet away. She didn't have time. They had to go.

"It's stuck, we've got to get across the path."

"Can't carry you with this in me."

"You don't need to. I can take you," she said. She groaned as she hoisted him to his feet. She tossed one of his arms around her shoulder and started toward the path.

"C'mon, you can do this, we're gonna make it," she soothed. He pressed his fangs into his bottom lip, drawing blood that seeped into his beard.

"I'm coming to get you, Sapphira," Florizel yelled. His demonic goons giggled. But she didn't quit. She shuffled down the path, half-dragging the vampire at her side. They were halfway down when she felt the first drops of rain.

"Oh fuck," she said, pushing herself faster.

"Let me go, I don't want to stop you," Maxwell groaned.

"Shut up, we're almost there."

Within seconds the rain became a deluge. Thunder rolled in, the sound so loud it hurt her ears. Lightning crashed before them, landing mere feet away.

She groaned from the exertion as she pushed herself faster. Her ears pounded, and her ankle felt completely numb. *Almost there*, she thought. *Almost there.* They were close to the sixth island now, and it reminded Sapphira of the images she'd seen of tropical islands in Vanity Fair and Vogue, all palm trees and a white-sand beach.

"We've got to jump," Maxwell said. "The water's too close, we won't make it."

"Are you fucking kidding me?" she breathed. But she knew he was right. She was already moving as fast as she could.

"Let me go, I've enough strength to close the distance," he said. He slipped from her grasp and launched himself at the beach, landing just at the edge of the water. He turned on wobbly legs and held his hands out toward her.

Sapphira sucked in a breath and launched herself at him, her body connecting with his and knocking him off balance. He grunted as he fought to stay on his feet. She righted herself and blinked against the bloody rain, watching in terror as the demons picked up their pace.

A tentacle snaked out of the abyss and wrapped itself around the ankle of one of the demonic goons. It pulled him up into the air, making the other demons and even Florizeel stop to try to grab him. But it was too late. Whatever creature that had grabbed him pulled him down into the water, and he disappeared beneath the surface with barely a splash.

"My lord, it's too dangerous to cross," shouted one of the other demons.

As if in response thunder cracked again, and a bolt of lightning struck the water near the path. Florizeel yelled before turning toward Sapphira and pointing his knife at her before turning and sprinting back to the seventh island.

Maxwell collapsed beside her. Sapphira startled and ran to his side, sinking to her knees. She pulled at the hilt of the axe, but it was slippery from the rain and the blood stung her eyes.

"Leave, it's ok, I just need a rest. I'm suddenly very weary," Maxwell said. She squeaked as he closed his eyes and his mouth hung open. She pressed a foot into his back to give herself leverage and grabbed the hilt. She dug in and growled as she pulled, finally getting it free. Blood poured from his wound and her eyes widened. It wasn't closing, not like all the other wounds she'd seen him have.

"Maxwell? Maxwell!" She called. She shook him but he didn't move. "Fuck."

She wiped at the sweat and blood on her forehead. *Blood. Maybe he needs blood,* she thought. She pushed up her sleeve, then paused. *What if he drains me dry and leaves me?*

And then, as her gaze rose to look at the picturesque but no less foreboding island before her, she wondered, *can I make it from here on my own?*

She rolled him onto his back and pressed her wrist against his mouth.

"I give you permission to feed on me, provided you're not dead. But please don't kill me," she said. There was the slightest movement before she felt his teeth press against her skin. When they pierced her skin it felt like a needle puncture, and she sucked in a breath as she watched him drink. After a minute his eyes sprang open. They were black from corner to corner, and they stared at her with such hunger that she started wriggling her wrist out of his mouth.

He didn't protest, nor did he fight her. He let her wrist go and once he licked her blood off his mouth he sat up, snaked an arm around her head, and kissed her. Her eyes widened and she gasped against his lips. Despite her surprise, she found herself leaning into him for the briefest second, feeling the way his lips didn't press against her lips but fused with them, sending fire up and down her body. He moaned and she pulled away, pushing him to the ground.

"What the fuck was that?"

He gazed up at her with his blue-brown eyes, now back to normal, and winced.

"I'm sorry. The effects of blood drinking can be... unpredictable. Sometimes it merely energizes me, other times it makes me... amorous."

His words sent a throbbing sensation between her legs, but she crossed her arms against herself.

"Well, take those feelings and fuck off, I can't... we can't..."

He stood and nodded, his unbothered expression returning.

"As you wish, kitten. Best we get going, that rain won't fall forever."

She walked past him toward the interior of the island, butterflies raging in her stomach.

Maxwell fell in step beside her as they walked toward the interior of the island. Though it had been cloudy and raining over the seventh island, here the sun sat high in the sky. The wind carried a pungent, acidic smell that made Sapphira's nose scrunch instinctively.

The smell worsened once they passed the tree line. Here palm fronds and other flora blanketed the ground. Sapphira listened, waiting to hear screams or shouts, anything that would indicate the danger of this island. But there was no such noise. Only a low, persistent moaning sound nagged at her incessantly.

Something crawled across her toes and she squeaked. She kept walking but the sensation never went away. Soon she began to feel like things were squirming between her toes and inching over her shoes. She shook one leg than the other, but the feeling persisted.

"Are you alright?" Maxwell implored, his voice low.

"I think there are bugs—" Her shoe caught on a rock and she fell forward, catching herself against a tree.

Sapphira righted herself but her hands came away sticky. She examined her palms, her nose scrunching from the stench of the greenish-yellow fluid on her hands. She gagged and wiped her hands on her jumpsuit.

"What is this?" she said. Maxwell shrugged.

"I don't know, and I don't know that I want to find out."

The vegetation of the forest grew denser and wilder, with kudzu snaking up the palm trees and wildflower bushes dotted in between the fronds. She stretched a hand out to caress a petal, only for it to snap closed on her finger. She hissed at the sharp pain and pulled her hand back, wincing at the small cut across her cuticle.

"Me neither," she said, shaking her hand and trying to dull the pain in her finger. "But what's that sound?"

"I cannot place it."

"C'mon, don't vampires have superhuman hearing or something? Least that's what the books all say," Sapphira replied. Maxwell snorted.

"Yes, we do, but I'm sure the books are little more than hogwash," Maxwell replied. "But pray tell, what do these tomes have to say about my kind?"

"That you're all evil. You can't be in the sun, hate garlic, crosses, silver. Have no reflection. And that you're all pasty white men with a widow's peak."

"As I stated — hogwash. These stories sound like the brain trust of white men seeking to demonize that which they do not know."

"So, you're not evil? You're cool with crosses? Garlic? Did you sleep in a coffin?"

The vampire sighed and turned back toward Sapphira, boredom traced all over his fine features. "I could care less about the Christian symbols, nor that pungent vegetable. And why sleep in a coffin when a bed and crisp linen sheets exist? As for being evil," Maxwell said, lifting a brow and smiling wryly. "I suppose that's a matter of perspective."

"How could that be?" she questioned. "Things are either evil or they are good. There's no in between."

But even as she said it, Sapphira doubted her words. Hadn't she been with someone who fit that exact description? Hadn't Dante been equal parts good and evil? Angel and demon? She swiped the errant tears that welled in her eyes as she thought of him and looked up at the vampire, who watched her with curiosity. Sapphira's cheeks burned from his scrutiny.

"I'm fine," Sapphira said, brushing away his concern. "C'mon, let's keep going. I can keep telling you about all the things our world has gotten wrong about vampires. Or I can tell you about all the historical things that've happened since you died. Or I can—"

Maxwell placed a cool hand against Sapphira's shoulder. She stopped and looked up, her dark brown eyes meeting his blue-brown ones.

"You do not have to pretend, not with me, kitten," Maxwell said.

She scowled at him, uncertain still of his motivations. Against her will tears spilled down her cheeks, and she collapsed against him in a fit of sobs. She allowed herself to weep in the arms of this vampire. But the tears couldn't be stopped and so she didn't try. She thought of her sister, her friends, her Granny. Of the internship she'd applied for and the life she'd always imagined for herself. The memory of Dante's half-hearted smile, the way he'd tear her down and follow it all with such lovely words, like "I love you more than life," and "You're the only person who makes me happy." His words swirled in her mind and tugged at her stomach, pulling her further down to the ground. All the while Maxwell silently moved with her, his hands cupping her shoulders and pressing her to him. When she pulled away, they locked eyes again.

"Thank you," she said and sniffled.

"You're welcome, kitten," he replied, and tenderly wiped a lock of hair from her face.

"We should probably keep going if we—" she began, but the feeling of something gripping tightly around her ankle made her pause. She looked up at Maxwell in confusion before falling backward onto her ass so hard she bit her tongue.

"How did I not realize how clumsy you are?" Maxwell chided, but the statement sounded more amused than his normal level of annoyance.

"There's something wrapped around my ankle," she said. She cut down the vegetation at her feet with her knife, revealing a hand tapping against the ground, reminding Sapphira of The Thing from the Addams Family show she used to watch as a kid. The moaning sound grew so loud Sapphira scrambled to her feet and plugged her ears.

Maxwell pressed a finger to his mouth and turned back to the vegetation. He peeled it back with his hands, revealing the ground below. She realized the hand wasn't some amorphous, unattached thing. It belonged to an arm, which connected to a body covered in kudzu. The vampire grimaced as the arm flailed out toward them, trying desperately to grab one of them.

"What's wrong with them? Why can't they move?" she asked. But the vampire didn't respond. His lips set in a grim line as he got to his knees and pulled away the plants that covered the body. Once the body was uncovered, Sapphira's stomach lurched. "What the fuck?"

"Gods," Maxwell whispered.

The body lay on the ground, its mouth forced wide open by the trunk of a tree that burst forth from the opening. Another tree, its trunk roughly the width of a tire, protruded from the body's stomach. Bits of bone and intestine clung to the root, and Sapphira realized now that the sticky greenish-yellow substance on the tree had been stomach bile, which had coated the tree as it burst forth from someone's stomach.

And now she understood what that persistent sound was they've been hearing ever since they arrived—it was the sound of thousands, maybe hundreds of thousands, of people groaning from pain and the weight of the trees that sprung from their bodies. Sapphira's stomach churned as she clawed the vegetation off another tree and saw another body with a tree jutting out of its chest. This had once been a woman, a vampire by the looks of her teeth. Tiny saplings protruded from its eyes and mouth. Despite this, her hand reached for Sapphira, trying to pull her down and either doom her to their fate or beg her for help.

Sapphira looked at Maxwell and for the first time since she'd met him, she could sense his terror. They turned around, searching for a way beyond the grasping, needing hands. Above them, the trees rustled, and then, she heard whistling.

Without warning Maxwell grabbed Sapphira's hand and started to run. They pushed their way through the oppressive flora, the palm fronds leaving stinging scratches on their skin where they made contact, the petals of the wildflowers stretching out to them, sniffing for them in the air and longing for a taste.

The rustling and whistling followed them as they ran.

"Don't look back," Maxwell urged. "We have to make it out of the forest."

"There's no way I'd want to stay here," Sapphira said. Her limbs ached. She was already so tired of running for her life and she was only on the sixth island. She still had so many more to go, and she dreaded what horrors each of them had in store.

The trees parted several feet ahead of them, and it was all Sapphira could do not to collapse. The whistling and rustling sound followed them as they fled, filling Sapphira with dread so acute she nearly collapsed.

They made it to the clearing and onto the beach just as a hand grasped the ends of Sapphira's hair. She screeched and shot forward, losing a clump of her hair in the process. She sank to her knees and whipped her head around in time to see a pair of large, reflective green eyes staring at them unblinking before retreating into the forest, a whistle still on the creature's lips. Sapphira sank onto the beach, her lungs burning.

CHAPTER 9

SAPPHIRA

"WHAT DO WE do now?" she asked, looking out at the flooded path before them.

"We've got no choice but to wait," he replied. Maxwell sat with his back to hers, his eyes trained on the forest and Sapphira's on the path of the damned. After a while, her breath got back to a normal timber, her shoulders relaxed, and she leaned her head back against the vampire. She rubbed at her temples, hoping to massage out the pain that had settled there, which felt like someone taking a chisel and carving out either side of her head. Her nostrils stung from the smell of blood and bile on their skin and clothes.

"Never could I imagine such brutal torture," Maxwell said. Sapphira stopped massaging her temples and turned toward him.

"I can't believe I thought Maleficence would be the worst," she replied.

"Yes, we're both about to be enlightened as we move through the rest of Pandemonia, I suspect."

There was dread in his voice and Sapphira couldn't help the guilt it sparked within her. *He probably hates me now*, she thought. *Gods, why did I do this? How could I have put him in danger just so I could leave?*

Sapphira bit her lip.

"There's still time to go back... if you change your mind."

"Sick of my company already, kitten?" he questioned.

"You did kiss me without my consent," she said. His face grew solemn.

"That was a weak moment on my part, it shan't happen again. Given what you're going through, it was irresponsible."

"My boyfriend killed me in the middle of Central Park, bartered my soul and sent me down to Pandemonia. Now I'm trying to escape with a literal vampire who's a stone-cold killer but still polite enough to apologize for kissing me without my permission. I can't believe this is my life."

"You mean your afterlife," he quipped.

"Maxwell," Sapphira groaned. He chuckled and shifted to lie down on the sand. She followed suit, lying with her head next to his and her feet pointing in the opposite direction. She rested her blade on her stomach but kept one hand on top of the hilt. They lay in silence for a long while, the sound of the wind and the distant moaning keeping

Sapphira's focus away from Dante.

Maxwell broke the silence first.

"I know that we just met, and you're uncertain if I am trustworthy, but despite the horror we saw on this island and the horrors that no doubt lay ahead of us, I want you to know that I do not regret joining you on your quest."

"I thought you said it was foolish?" she said.

"It is, but that doesn't mean it's not brave, and that I wish to be anywhere else," he replied.

"So, you're saying I've got you on my side?"

He turned toward her and smiled.

"Yes, I suppose you do."

The path cleared at twilight, just as the sun fell below the horizon. Somehow, she'd fallen asleep on the sand. She woke up with a start, sitting up straight and taking in her surroundings. Maxwell sat beside her, braiding the top of his hair back from his face. He smiled at her as he bound the braid with a ribbon.

"Hello," he said.

"Hi," she replied.

"I think the coast is clear," he said. He stood and held out a hand to help her up. This time she took it, wincing as she realized her legs were asleep. They were all pins and needles as they began to walk, but she was thankful for their luck. After the battle they'd faced on the seventh island, they'd passed through the sixth relatively unscathed. She hoped that this was a marker of what was to come, rather than a fluke.

Maxwell's bat rested against his shoulder, and she held her knife aloft, both of their heads on swivels as they braced for a fight. But they were alone, and once they got several feet away from the island the moaning sound stopped and then there was silence save for their feet on the road and the sound of her heartbeat in her ears. The closer they got to the fifth, the more she marveled at the different terrain. She'd heard the Christian tales of Pandemonia, or what they called Hell. It was all fire and brimstone, layers and layers of torture leading down to a pit where the devil himself lurked.

Though she'd never been taught to think much about or even speak about Pandemonia, she'd thought about it in her deepest, darkest thoughts and nightmares. For her, it had always been a place of complete darkness, riddled with fire and the screams of the damned. Sometimes she thought of Tartagnon sitting there watching the torture with glee. Other times she thought of just a black, fire-filled void.

But as they finished crossing the path and made it to the fifth island, a place yet again populated by lush, tall trees that stretched high into the orange and purple evening sky, she realized that this was worse. That she probably could have handled darkness and flames. But the picture-worthy sunsets, the palm trees, the jungle-like terrain, filled her with more dread than fire and brimstone ever could.

Sometimes the horror comes not from ugliness but from beauty, she thought. And her mind drifted toward Dante. How beautiful he'd been. She'd been stunned by his presence ever since she met him and yet it was not a stranger that attacked her. Sapphira carried a knife. Claudia, a switchblade. Persephone, a hammer. All in the name of fighting off strange, leering men at work or while walking down the street. Yet it was not a stranger that attacked her. It was the man she'd let into her bed and into her heart that was the one she should have worried about most.

She swallowed the lump that had formed in her throat and focused on the present. She stepped off the path onto another pristine beach. Feet ahead were large trees covered in Spanish moss and wisteria, large ferns and other flora packed so densely she wondered how they'd make it through. Though the sun was down, she could still feel the humidity. It licked at her skin and hair, and it made Sapphira think of summers in the city, where it got so hot she and her sister would try to boil eggs on the sidewalk just to see if they could. She rolled the sleeves of her jacket up and pulled her hair to one side to cool herself off. But she knew that nothing could stop the humidity, just like she knew that her hair would suffer for it.

Sapphira stepped forward this time, determined to lead the way through what was closer to a jungle than a forest. She used her blade to swat away the ferns and smaller trees. Everything was so green. She marveled at how lush it all looked but remained leery after encountering the palm fronds with razor-sharp edges and the bloodthirsty wildflowers on the last island.

Insects buzzed all around her and she swatted at them. In the distance, she heard a scream.

Her heart raced as she looked at Maxwell and noticed the apprehension on his face.

"Careful, kitten," he said. "I don't have a good feeling about this place."

They pressed further into the island, her feet sinking into the marshy land. "How are we able to walk here? Doesn't this water come from the abyss?"

Maxwell didn't respond. He wore a scowl on his face as he lifted one foot and then the other, examining his boots.

"You'd think after all that blood and guts I've stepped in on that accursed island that I'd be fine with a little mud but, gods, I'd murder to be clean right now," he said, and Sapphira groaned. She hadn't thought about a shower but now all she could think about was how good it would feel to scrub her skin clean, removing what felt like ten layers of dirt off her body.

"Please don't remind me," she said. He chuckled and then stopped as they reached a clearing marked by a vast lake, the edge of it dotted in bonfires. As far as her eye could see, there were logs and small boats that jostled and bumped into each other in the lake. The persistent sound of buzzing and the screams they'd heard when they arrived were louder here, all rising from the boats in a cacophony. There was a sweet smell on the air that the smoke from the fires carried toward them.

Sapphira and Maxwell hastily dashed behind a tree just as a demon dragged a man who looked to be the same age as Sapphira behind him. The man's screams took over the cacophony, and they watched as the demon bound the man to an overturned log next to a small fire, a pot sitting atop of it.

The demon's face pulled into a manic grin as he grabbed the pot off the fire and poured it over the man. Sapphira cupped a hand over her mouth as the man cried out in pain, the burning, sweet-smelling liquid hissed as it met the man's skin. The demon poured some of it into the man's mouth as if to stifle his screams. A mixture of honey and saliva and vomit cascaded down the man's chin and chest. The demon cooed in satisfaction, dipping a finger into the mixture and sucking it into its mouth. Sapphira gagged, pressing her hand against her mouth even tighter.

The demon paused and looked in their direction. Sapphira and Maxwell ducked down further until they were practically laying on the ground. They kept their gazes down, staring at the ground and listening for any movement. After a minute Maxwell peered up over the tall grass.

"Coast's clear," he whispered. Sapphira slowly peered over the bushes, watching as the demon pushed the log and the man he'd tortured into the pond. Seconds later a swarm of bugs covered the man like a shroud. She shuddered as she thought about what it would feel like to have her entire body covered in swarming, stinging bugs.

The demon moved away, toward another cluster on the other side of the lake. Sapphira and Maxwell looked at each other and he nodded before slinking away, crouched low in the brush. Her thighs ached from the position but she knew if they stood, they would be discovered. Ahead of her Maxwell tripped, grunting as he did so. Sapphira rushed toward him, righting him, and seeing what he tripped on. It was another fairy. She was covered in bug bites and open sores, her mouth smeared with brown liquid.

"Help me," the fairy whimpered. Sapphira turned toward Maxwell, who looked from the fairy to the demons off in the distance.

"We've got to keep moving," he whispered. But as they turned to continue crouching and walking through the brush, the fairy grabbed Maxwell's ankle and pulled, dragging him to his butt.

"Unhand me, you wretch," he spat. When the fairy didn't let go Maxwell bent and dug his teeth into its throat. The creature screamed before Maxwell pressed a hand to her mouth. He drank hungrily, moaning and gripping the fairy's shoulders. He pulled himself away with a gasp and licked at his lips, his face bloody and his eyes once again reminding Sapphira of a shark.

"Let's keep going," he said, slightly out of breath. But as they both went to move, Sapphira felt a pair of hands grab the back of her jacket and lift her out of the brush.

"Well, well, well, what've we got here?"

Sapphira was face to face with a demon, this one looking much different from the ones on the seventh island. Its skin looked like that of a snake, complete with red stripes that made their way down its arms and bare chest. The other demon had smooth, almost oily-looking orange skin and glowing yellow eyes. It smiled menacingly at Sapphira with a mouth devoid of teeth.

"Looks like a few more morsels for our pets, my sweet," the demon said, its voice high. Before Sapphira could respond the sound of rushing water made her head snap toward the pond, where a creature that resembled an alligator but twice the size and twice the teeth shot out from the water, its mouth gaping, and bit the head off a young man. Blood erupted from the body and squirted into the air. Then the beast dragged the rest of the man's body below the brackish water.

Pets, Sapphira thought. *Demons have pets now.*

The orange-colored demon grabbed Maxwell. Though he tried to fight, the demon thrust a hand up against his chin hard, knocking the vampire out. It hoisted him over its shoulder, before smiling yet again at Sapphira, its eyes unblinking, and turning to walk away. The other demon fell in step behind its companion, dragging Sapphira along the ground in her jacket.

The demons dragged them toward the pond, where the alligator waited. Its bulging yellow eyes eyed her hungrily, sending a shiver down her spine. Maxwell was still unconscious but that didn't stop the orange-skinned demon from tying his arms and ankles and tossing him into a hollowed-out log before slathering him with honey. It was only then that Maxwell awoke. She could hear him pushing against the log and shouting curses at the demons.

"Untie me, you foul-faced harpy!"

"Your feistiness won't save you, blood sucker," the demon replied. It giggled and Sapphira hated how that sound made the hair on the back of her neck stand up. Maxwell continued his threats, and the demons ignored them. The snake-skinned creature grabbed Sapphira by the nape of her neck and pulled her jacket off.

"Hey," she shouted. The demon kicked her legs out from under her in response. She fell to her side, tearing her jumpsuit as she landed on the ground. She rolled to her back just as the demon grabbed her arms and legs and bound them quickly. Then it doused her with honey. Sapphira scrambled as the molten liquid made her skin bubble and boil. She writhed and clawed at the sticky liquid as blisters broke out all over her body. In the areas where blisters hadn't formed her skin felt tight and raw, as though it would split if she moved. What's more there was this deep ache all over her body that remained even as the honey began to cool. Her lips were stuck together. Honey clung to her eyelashes practically gluing them shut. She whimpered as she tried to unstick them. Her eyelids stung at the pain, and she felt a few lashes fall onto her cheek in the process, until finally she was able to see. Honey seeped down her cheeks and into her ears, plugging her ears as it cooled.

She felt herself being hoisted up and into a log like Maxwell's, the middle hollowed out but the sides shallow. Then she heard a chuckle and suddenly the log was moving.

"No, no, no!" She tried to say, but it came out as one muffled protestation. The log sank a little as it floated into the lake.

What the fuck am I going to do? Sapphira thought. How could she make it out of the log with her wrists and legs tied? If she did fall into the water, what would stop that alligator from eating her whole? She wondered what happened to the souls the alligator ate. Would they reanimate or were they doomed to spend eternity in the bowels of this creature?

A tiny prick on her breast pulled her attention back to the present. She looked down and saw a small insect in the shape of a hornet. But this bug was translucent, its eyes the milky color of decay. It pierced her again on one of her blisters, the stinger lodging deep into her skin. Sapphira jerked from the stinging and shimmied her upper body trying to shake the insect off. But her efforts were in vain; two other insects joined the first, one landing on her cheek and the other on her arm. She kept jerking around in the log, feeling water splash over her. She stopped herself just as she felt the log about to tip over completely.

"Careful, cheri."

Sapphira stopped at the sound of the voice. It wasn't Maxwell. This voice was deep, French, and when she lifted her head up to see over the side of the log. Her eyes widened at what she saw. Someone — or rather some creature — had pulled its broken and hole-filled log right next to hers. It looked like a wolf, its fur oil-spill black and its eyes the color of sunflowers, glowing in the night. It had a wolf's snout and pointed ears, but it had the hands of a man, albeit covered in fur. Its clothes were tattered and old, reminding Sapphira of all the paintings of men from the Renaissance age.

"The more you thrash, the quicker you'll get attacked by the kaimong," the wolf man said again.

Sapphira pressed and rubbed her lips together trying to heat the honey so it would loosen. Finally, she was able to part her lips but not without feeling as though she'd completely removed the top layer of her skin. But she didn't have time to think about the pain. She had to figure out how to get out of the log off the island and away from the bugs. They were swarming her now. The same translucent bugs were now joined by other, larger black bugs with long, spider-like limbs and fat bodies. They flew like gnats but once they landed on Sapphira, they bit her, their bodies swelling with her blood. Her eyes watered from the pain of the bites and stings and boils that riddled her body.

"What do I do? How do I get out of this?" she asked. The wolfman looked around, his glowing gold eyes flitting from the shoreline to the center of the lake as though searching for the demons to see if they were watching. He seemed to realize their attention was elsewhere and surfaced a long strip of wood which he slid into the water and used as a paddle to close the distance between them. Once he was closer, he grabbed the edge of her log and steadied himself.

"Try to turn away from me," he said. Sapphira began to twist but the wolfman tsked. "Slowly, slowly. Yes, that's it."

Once she had her back to him, she could feel his furry hands working quickly through the ropes. *Hurry*, she thought, as more insects stung and bit her arms and back, suckling on her blood. One landed on her cheek and stung her, the feeling sending an instant shock through her body.

"Hold still," the wolfman warned. She could feel the ropes loosening. Her heartbeat hammered in her chest and her breath heaved. "There, all done."

The ropes fell away from her hands and Sapphira slowly flipped onto her back and stretched her hands out. They were purple from lack of circulation, the skin around her cuticles especially dark. She flexed and shook them to try to get the feeling back.

"Thank you," she said, swatting at the bugs swarming her and squishing the ones that had landed on her body. Even in the firelight, she could see the welts, the boils that had risen even more because of the venom from the stingers. Her whole body felt like one big itch. She moved to scratch her arm but the wolfman grabbed her hand. She looked up at him and he shook his head.

"That's a quick way to peel all your skin off. You've got to ignore it," he said. Her eyes narrowed.

Why was he being so helpful? She sat up and looked out at the water, searching for Maxwell.

"Why are you helping me?" she asked.

There was something hungry about the way he spoke to her, the way his eyes followed her as she bent forward to untie the ropes around her ankles.

"Well, I need to get off this lake, of course," he said. She could feel his eyes on her as she finished untying her ankles. "But to do that, I'll need a distraction... and a new log."

Before she could respond, the wolfman tipped her boat to the side, thrusting her into the water. She barely had time to suck in a breath. Her eyes snapped open, taking in the dark swampiness of the water. She struggled to surface, but when she did, she spat out water, glowering at the wolf who had somehow slid into her log.

"What the fuck?" she shouted. She grabbed the edge of the log just as she felt something brush past her legs, its skin scaly. She tried to pull herself up and out of the water but the wolfman swatted her hands.

"I'm so sorry, mademoiselle. I need this to get to shore since mine, as you can see, is worse for wear."

From her peripheral she could see it tilting, half of it already underwater.

"So why untie me? Why not just push me out and make it easier for that thing to eat me?"

The wolfman scoffed, pressing a hand to its chest, seemingly affronted. "I'm not a monster. Now you have at least a fighting chance."

He paddled away without another word. Sapphira trod water, her fear making her thoughts swarm her mind all at once. Again, she felt scales brush against her thigh, and she whimpered.

"Maxwell!" she shouted again. "Help!"

"Where are you, kitten?"

Her heart leapt when she heard his voice, though she couldn't make him out amid the dim light. She raised her hand, the gesture making her sink in the water slightly.

"Here! I'm here! Can't you see me?" she cried. Her vision blurred as tears welled in her eyes. "Please help me. I don't how much longer I can do this, there's this alligator and it's—"

Teeth clasped around her ankle. She could feel her bone shatter in the kaimong's mouth as she was pulled beneath the water. It let go just as suddenly as it grabbed her. When she surfaced, she grit her teeth against the pain and heaved a breath.

"Maxwell, please!"

She turned in a circle, her eyes scanning for any sign of movement.

Suddenly she saw his reflective eyes, his arms gesturing wildly.

"I'm here, swim toward me and I'll paddle," the vampire said. The kaimong's tail swatted at the leg it just bit, sending a shockwave of pain through her.

"I can't—"

"Yes, you can. You can do this, kitten," Maxwell shouted.

She sniffled and pressed her eyes tightly together and took a deep breath trying desperately to center herself. She opened her eyes and got into position, lifting one arm then the next out of the water, kicking as best she could with one leg. She was slowly closing the gap between them. Ahead she could see Maxwell pushing himself toward her using his arms as paddles. She felt the kaimong press its warm, scaly body against her side below the water. It was toying with her. She pushed herself harder, harder, despite the blood loss and the way her whole body ached.

All around her the cries of the damned reverberated. To her left she saw another soul being dragged beneath the surface by another kaimong, a spurt of blood arcing into the sky as the beast bit down on its prey, crushing its torso in its teeth.

Please, Enefri give me strength, she prayed to the creator, though she didn't know if her prayers could reach the goddess's ears. Surely, she wasn't the only soul who cried out for her mercy only to receive none.

Then the kaimong dug its teeth into her stomach. She screamed louder than she ever had before she was drug beneath the surface.

Water invaded her mouth, sliding down her throat and filling her lungs. She looked down at the beast, saw its radiant yellow eyes even in the darkness. She pressed down against its snout, then balled her fists and punched it. But that only made it clamp down harder. Sapphira felt like she was being crushed, her ribs breaking and pressing into her organs.

Her blood mixed with the water, turning it red. She was losing blood. She was losing oxygen. Her head swam and her vision blurred. She wondered what it would be like to die again in Pandemonia. Would it be like dreaming or would there be a vast nothingness? How long would it take to reanimate and if she did while under the water, would she be doomed to repeat this moment over and over? Forever trying to claw her way out of the jaws of this beast?

Her blows glided off the kaimong's snout now, limbs growing heavy. *Maybe it's best this ends here*, she thought. *Maybe Dante wins, after all.* The memory of how he looked at her when he stabbed her surfaced in her mind. No hesitation, only clarity in his eyes.

Eyes.

She imagined she was staring into Dante's eyes and with her last bit of strength she made her hands into claws and dug them into one of the kaimong's eyes. It released its grip and flitted away. But now she couldn't feel her legs.

The black dots that had been creeping up at the edge of her vision coalesced into one large dot at the center. Then all she saw was nothingness. Her arms slackened.

I never could have made it anyway, Sapphira thought, before her mind, and every thought within ceased to be.

PART 2: LE FREAK

CHAPTER 10

TARTAGNON

O F ALL THE gods in the cosmos, Tartagnon was one of the few who loved everything about his existence. He was a primordial being, having been created before the continents formed, before life was little more than protozoa flitting around the ocean. He'd existed for eons, and that meant he'd seen it all. He'd watched as those same protozoa turned into other life forms, evolving and changing until they grew two legs and clawed their way onto the earth.

He had watched the comets fall on the dinosaurs. Watched as the first primates discovered fire. Delighted in seeing them evolve their higher consciousnesses because that meant that his time would soon come. He waited and waited for these beings — humans, vampires, werewolves, and every other supernatural creature in existence — to become what they would be for millennia. He waited for them to live and to die, for them to be collected by Gwydion and sent to Simyasha, where she would cast down the souls of the damned. Where his demons and his islands would be waiting, welcoming in their own way, ready to give them what they deserved.

He was punishing them for their misdeeds, making sure they knew without a shadow of a doubt they belonged with him, with his retinue, in Pandemonia. Not every god was so transparent. Not every god thought creatively about how they would treat those who crossed their path, either by entering their domain or by calling them down through worship. But he was different. He was magnanimous. Exacting. And when it came to torture, no one could think of better ways to punish the damned. There were many who felt that he was a villain, that he was terrifying, the root of their deepest, darkest nightmares.

And while Tartagnon delighted in their terror, he knew that without him, without the fear that his very name caused, whether whispered in an ear or shouted from a rooftop, the beings across the veil would never do right by each other. For most of them, the thought of eternal torture was the only thing that kept them kind.

So, he was happy to be the keeper of Pandemonia, the guardian of the damned. Other gods, like Umiyo trapped in the ocean or Xira, the beauty, there to ensure the continued existence of all living things through procreation, may have been bored with the monotony of it all. But Tartagnon delighted in it. He'd seen it all, tortured them all, and maintained the status quo.

That is, until this very evening.

He was sitting on his throne, as he often was, posed with one leg draped over the arm of the throne and his head resting on his slender, obsidian-colored hand. His long, ember locks spilled down his right shoulder, brushing against his cheeks. He stared straight ahead, his lips parted and his gaze resolute. He was being sculpted by one of his favorite artists, a Renaissance-aged sculptor whose torture it was to spend his afterlife carving statue after statue of the god of Pandemonia, when a demon entered his throne room looking completely vexed.

Tartagnon huffed but didn't shift his position. "What's plaguing you, Garwill?"

Garwill, a demon whose grey skin was covered in buboes, paused before responding.

"My dark lord," he started, his gravelly voice already grating on Tartagnon's nerves. "There's been an escape."

Tartagnon rolled his eyes. "Of course, souls are trying to escape. This is Pandemonia. No one wants to be tortured for eternity."

Garwill stepped closer. Tartagnon cut a glare at him, and the demon stepped backward to his original spot.

"This time there are two souls, one vampire, and one human woman."

"Splendid."

"My dark lord, they came from Maleficence and are on now on

Rapaciousness."

Tarragon pursed his lips but kept his posture the same. *So what?* He thought. *They've only made it to the fifth island. There's no way they'll make it much further.*

He made a mental note to torture this demon later for interrupting his sculpture time. The demon cleared its throat and Tartagnon slid his burning gaze toward him. The demon took a step back and raised his hands as if in apology.

"Apparently they mean to reach Purgatore—"

Tartagnon laughed. "I'm excited to see them try."

"But there's more to it than that," Garwill said.

"Then you'd best get to the point," Tartagnon growled.

"My ddark lord, the woman has been branded, her soul traded to a demon. She appears to be headed to Simyasha ... perhaps to try to renegotiate her fate?"

That got Tartagnon's attention. His left leg fell from its perch across his throne.

"Sire," the sculptor objected. Tartagnon twisted his fingers, not bothering to look at the man as his neck snapped. He fell to the ground, his body thudding on the marble concrete.

He stood, rising to his full height, and descended the steps of the dais his throne sat on. Garwill stepped backward, his face riddled with uncertainty as Tartagnon strode toward him, his black robes puddling on the ground around him.

"So, they're headed to Simyasha with a plan," Tartagnon said, throwing his arm casually around the demon. "This could be interesting. Most beings who try to escape don't know what to do with themselves when they do. They try to go to another island, thinking it'll be less torturous because the misdeed is lesser."

The god chuckled, thinking about past escapees who fled from the sixth or the fourth island to the second or even the first, thinking they'd be better able to tolerate the different types of torture. How wrong they were. How they still screamed in agony, even more so after realizing their mistake.

But it seemed this woman had a score to settle, especially if she truly was not the one to barter her soul. Even if the goddess shunned them, getting to Purgatore was so close to the veil that all they had to do was make it out and go through the gorge. And if they didn't get lost in the fog or fall off the path, they'd return to the land of the living. Of course, they'd be revenants, but if they were planning an audience with the goddess herself, they might be able to get what they want.

"So... what do we do, my dark lord?" Garwill said. Tartagnon groaned, pushing away from the sycophant. What to do, indeed.

He began to pace, his feet fitting into the groove of black marble he'd worn down after spending so many millennia pacing in this exact spot. After several moments he stopped and thought of the place he wanted to be in his mind's eye. Then he was no longer in his throne room, a circular dome with the ceiling open and exposed to the red sun, the floors and walls black marble. Now he stood in a dimly lit cave, the bones of the dead in one corner and the fawning denizens of this realm in the other. He stared out the cave's opening and marveled at the clouds that obscured the view of Pandemonia. The goddess of death stood in the center of the cave, her back toward him.

"Well, if it isn't the lord of the damned," she said, her voice devoid of mirth. Tartagnon's lips pulled back from his mouth in a grimace, and he strode toward Simyasha and came to a stop by her side.

"Greetings, lover," he said.

"What pulls you away from your domain? Are there no more artists to paint you or carve your visage out of marble?"

Tartagnon chuckled. He always enjoyed Simyasha's banter. It was one of the things that drew him to her so many centuries ago. "There are two souls who've escaped from the seventh island."

"Oh?" Simyasha said as she looked at him. But she seemed unmoved by this information. Her nonchalance irritated Tartagnon. It was a trait she employed not because she was unbothered, he knew, but because she knew that, especially in the face of possible peril, was irksome even to the most serene.

"Yes. Apparently, it is a vampire and a human woman, one you cast down to Pandemonia not too long ago."

There was the slightest shift in the goddess' energy. *So, she does know the woman.*

"Darling, you'll have to be more specific. I send thousands of souls a day down that dreary place you call home."

"I think you know who I'm talking about, Simyasha," Tartagnon stated. "And I think you know why she'd be on her way to you."

Simyasha rolled her milky-white eyes and turned away from him. "Tartagnon, we have been in existence for eons. This isn't the first time the damned have tried to escape."

"No, it's not. But this soul has been branded, soul bartered against her will."

"That's not my problem," Simyasha huffed, waving a hand at him. "Last I checked, that's permitted. Enefri's golden feathers won't be ruffled by it."

Tartagnon narrowed his eyes at the mention of the divine goddess. "Oh, my demons can make any type of deal they please. But this is the first time a branded one has hatched a plan to come to you. And given that her circumstance was one outside of her control, one could argue you judged her harshly. I'm told this soul has recruited a vampire to her cause, one whose been in my realm for decades. What if she recruits even more souls? What if they band together with a clear plan not to escape for lesser punishment, but to escape from our realms altogether?"

Simyasha smiled but the gesture didn't reach her eyes.

"You sound worried. I should think that the god of Pandemonia, the overseer of the damned and originator of every delicious method of torture, wouldn't be so rattled about a pair of souls."

Tartagnon shifted and instantly stood by the goddess's side, gripping her thin but muscular arms in his hands, pressing his fingers into them. He looked down at her, knowing her affinity for pain. She peered up at him hungrily. He sighed and let her go, striding back toward the opening. She sucked her teeth at his refusal to meet her pleasures.

"Who said I was worried?"

"Then why have you come?"

"To warn you. If these souls successfully cross the path of the damned without getting captured or sucked into the abyss, they could make it here," he said.

"No matter, I'll just send them back."

"And if they return? If they keep returning? What will you do then?" Tartagnon questioned. "You are not just the goddess of death but of fate and order. Need I remind you that souls escaping their fate and potentially piercing the veil again isn't very *orderly*."

Simyasha hissed and closed the gap between them, slicing at his bare chest with her long nails, leaving five long, jagged gashes in their wake. Tartagnon looked down at the already-healing wounds and smiled. *She's rattled.*

"Who are you to question me on this? Were it not for your inattentive demons, this would not be an issue."

"And that is why I mean to take care of it. But I thought I'd give you the courtesy of a warning, lover."

He stood before the cave's opening, reveling in the breeze that whipped at his beard and tossed his robes about him.

"And how will you take care of it?"

"Simple. I'll send our children, of course."

Minutes later Tartagnon stood in the middle of the dead forest of Maleficence. He closed his eyes and pictured his son, drawing the demon to him in an instant. Florizeel stood before him, shoulders pin straight and his retinue of demons kneeling before their god.

Tartagnon smiled and clapped his son on the back.

"How goes the torture?"

"Rapturous, father, as always."

"Always? Does that include those little souls you lost track of?"

Florizeel's eyes widened before he returned his composure.

"We... we lost them. But the girl, she's been torn apart by a kaimong. No doubt it's there she'll stay."

Tartagnon stepped toward his son. He grabbed his shoulder, squeezing so hard he saw the slightest wince pass over Florizeel's face. "Best to be sure, huh? Get back to the fifth island find them. Make sure she really has met her true death, or at the very least, make sure she doesn't get to Purgatore. I trust that won't be too hard for you this time, right, son?"

"No."

"Good."

Without another word, he disappeared. He returned to his palace and traveled down to the depths of it until he no longer treaded on marble but on wet, foul-smelling earth. He walked until he approached a ring of fire outlining a containment circle. At each of the seven points within the circle stood a guard, just outside of the flame. Kneeling within was a demon he hadn't seen in two centuries. Her arms were stretched above her head, palms flat on the ground and wrists shackled, the chain so small it forced her face almost to the ground in supplication.

Her black tunic was tattered and dusty, the back of it ripped away, revealing the gaping wound on her back. Her skin had been peeled away from her bones and her ribs cracked open and bent back so they faced the ceiling. Her lungs were skewered with knives no larger than his hand, but he knew their presence made it hard to breathe. Even now he could hear how she wheezed, a wet purring sound that filled the chamber.

Though she knelt, the demon was tall, almost six feet. Her skin jet black, lips and nose full, her cheekbones and chin as sharp as her mother's. Ginger braids stretched down to her waist. The spidery network of her veins was traced in a fiery glow that pulsated the same amber as her eyes. She was gorgeous, a work of art, crafted to look just like her parents — Simyasha and Tartagnon himself.

"My...lord." she rasped.

"Astraphelle, my dear," Tartagnon began. Her eyes met his and he smirked at her. "Have you been faring well all these dark centuries?"

She sucked in a breath.

"Has it been," she paused. "That long?"

She let out a long, hacking cough and spit up blood onto the stone floor. Tartagnon chuckled. He clasped his hands behind him and stalked around the circle, ignoring the guards who shuddered and stepped back from him as he passed.

"It has. I must confess, I have missed you, young one."

"And I you...father."

Tartagnon bristled at the biting way she said father but didn't bring it up.

"Is that so?" He waved a hand and the flames before him parted. He stepped into the circle and knelt before his daughter. Unlike Florizeel, Astraphelle didn't flinch at his presence. She always was the stronger of the two.

"Yes. I've been... regretful."

"You mean when you tried to kill me after I stole the soul of your human lover? The one whose soul you were supposed to tempt into damnation?"

Astraphelle looked down and remained silent. Tartagnon could see the grim set of her lips and her clenched fists, and he delighted in her discomfort.

"Yes."

"Do you wish to make it up to me?"

Astraphelle looked up at him through her long lashes, and he recognized that calculating look well; it was one he often wore himself. She nodded in response and Tartagnon snapped his fingers. Instantly her shackles and the knives in her back melted away. Astraphelle slowly sat up on her haunches. Her shoulders were dislocated, so her arms hung loose in her lap. She looked pitiful, and Tartagnon sighed, feeling a pang of sadness for his daughter. But it went away as fast as it came.

"Come, let me care for you as I once did."

He walked over to the edge of the containment ring and wiped at it with his hand, breaking the spell that kept her in a suspended state of torment. Then he picked Astraphelle up to her feet and shoved her arms back into their sockets. He bent down and picked her up in his arms and pressed her close to his chest like one would a baby, careful not to touch her broken back.

"Guardians, thank you for your service all these years. I bid you farewell."

He turned on his heels, his ears filling with the sound of the guards' necks breaking one by one.

Astraphelle clung to him as they ascended the stairs and when they reached the main palace she hissed as the light of the sun shone upon her. He took her to her quarters and sat her down. Her knees wobbled and he held an arm out to steady her. Already her ribs were stitching back together with her spine and some color was returning to her sickly face.

With the snap of his fingers, a tub appeared, filled with steaming water and fresh jasmine. Another snap of his fingers and clothing appeared on the bed.

"Meet me in the throne room after you've refreshed yourself."

Tartagnon lounged on his throne, face titled toward the sun when his daughter approached. Gone was the tattered tunic she'd worn while captured. Now she stood in her rightful garb as the daughter to the god of Pandemonia. She wore a black breastplate. Her skirt was layered with lace and leather, and around her ankles and upper arms were golden bands inlaid with carnelian. The front part of her braids was twisted into ram's horns, the edges dipped in black dye. Black kohl was painted in a thick black bar across her eyes and swiped across her lips. And between her knuckles, a set of golden knives that curved like claws.

"You always did look better in these clothes than anything you'd don across the veil," he said. "I never did understand your love of corsets."

"They make the most beautiful silhouette," Astraphelle said, her voice still raspy.

"Well, once you do what I need you can go back to wearing them, though I do think you'll find they're considered archaic."

She pursed her lips.

"Two souls have escaped from Maleficence. They are on Rapaciousness, and I need you to find them."

"Would you like me to bring them to you?"

"I would like you to join them."

Astraphelle huffed. He narrowed his eyes at her, and she stood back at attention. Good. He never wanted her to forget that though she was the daughter of two of the most powerful beings in the universe, he was still a god, and she was merely a demon who was not above being tortured. It was a lesson he'd just finished dispensing but had no qualms about dispensing again.

"I want you to get close to them. Find out their plans and do everything you can to stop them. Do not let them cross out of Pandemonia."

"I mean no disrespect, my lord," Astraphelle started. "But why join them? Why not send them back to the seventh or even bring them here to be tortured?"

"Because this will be infinitely more fun," he said. He leaped to his feet. "Think about it, getting close to them, stoking hope within them, all the while sowing chaos. If they're close, get between them. If not, widen the gap between them until it's a chasm. If they don't die before they hit the bridge between Pandemonia and Purgatore, then that is where you will end them. And I'll be there, watching them realize they never had a chance."

"What's in this drawn-out game for you?"

"Why, entertainment of course," he said. "Careful, Astraphelle, you're starting to sound sympathetic. We don't want you returning to the pit, do we?"

She flinched at that and he smiled.

"No. That won't happen, I will do this, in your honor, Father," she said.

"Good."

She turned to leave.

"Astraphelle?"

She stopped.

"Errant souls can be tricky to deal with. But don't worry. I'll always have an eye on you, watching out for you, making sure you complete your task... *safely.*"

She clenched her fists and walked out of the throne room and out the long hallway toward the palace doors.

He sighed and lay back down, his long hair spilling over the edges of his throne.

CHAPTER 11

ASTRAPHELLE

STRAPHELLE SLUNK OUT of the throne room, her fists clenched and her head held high. It'd been centuries since she last walked these halls, hell since she last walked at all. She could hear the murmurs of the guards as she passed them.

"Can't believe he let the blasphemer out of her cage."

"Wonder what favors she committed to finally get let free."

"I give it a week before she's back to her old ways."

Their comments made Astraphelle's skin crawl and it was all she could do to keep her composure and not drive her blades straight into their throat. But she knew that reaction would only validate their gossip and word would get back to her father that she hadn't changed. That even though she was a demon, no, *the* demon, one of the very first created by her mother Simyasha and her father Tartagnon, she was still utterly, bitterly weak. Still so susceptible to human emotion that she was willing to fight the god himself on behalf of a single human soul. She could tell her father believed the same of her. Why else would he decide to let her out? Why else would he tell her he had eyes on her at all times? He was testing her. And though it made her blood boil, it was a test she would make sure she passed. She was never going back into the pit, forced to kneel until her legs atrophied and her eyes couldn't handle any light stronger than that of a flame.

Though surrounded by guards she'd been so completely alone. At first, she screamed, and once she broke her vocal cords she sobbed. The containment spell meant she would barely heal, and so once her eyes swelled and dried out from the tears all she had were her thoughts. For decades her torture flashed before her mind so viscerally it was like she was living it over and over again. There was no way she was going back there, even if the price she had to pay was toying with a few errant souls who fancied themselves as escape artists. Once she delivered the souls to her father, she'd be free.

Two guards opened the palace doors for her, malice shaping their small, pinched faces. She glowered at them as she passed. They were sycophants, fawning obnoxiously at her father as he passed or asked them for the simplest things:

"Clean this blood off my boots."

"Pick this bit of viscera out of my hair."

"Create another sculpture of me, the god of the damned."

Even before her detainment, she hated every one of them. Hated every island, with their toothy beaches or bile-covered trees, and loathed its blood-red snow. But she was a demon, after all. Hatred was probably her default setting. Astraphelle stepped out of the palace and onto a black sand beach. She saw the seventh island across the abyss, the shoreline partially obscured by a fog that prevented most from seeing the seat of Tartagnon's power. Only those who knew where to look ever made it to the palace. The sun cast everything in a bloody glow, and she squinted, eyes still adjusting to the light. Unlike the pit, which was dank and damp and cool, there was a heat so dry it took her breath away.

Let's get this over with, she thought.

Astraphelle strode onto the causeway, her bare feet pressing into the slightly damp soil. The further away she got from the palace the less she smelled the cardamom and burning wood that filled the halls of Tartagnon's domain. Now the smell of blood and shit stung her nostrils. She walked into the wood, avoiding the puddles of intestines and piles of skin. The screams of the damned were a familiar refrain. Once, centuries ago, she'd found them comforting, back when she still believed in what Pandemonia stood for. Now, it was a sound that set her teeth on edge. She passed a tree adorned with eyeballs, all of which turned to watch her as she went.

"Well, well, well, I guess the bitch is back."

Astraphelle stiffened. She closed her eyes and rallied her strength before turning toward that voice. Her brother stood a yard away, both feet resting on the head of a roughed-up fairy. He wore a smug expression and Astraphelle remembered now why she always wanted to break his face.

"Florizeel."

"Princess," Florizeel spat. Astraphelle ignored the poisonous way he said it and squared her shoulders. "Father finally saw fit to let you out. Pity. I would've kept you down there 'til your lungs disintegrated."

"The spell would've prevented that from happening, as I'm sure you know," she replied, unable to hide the edge in her voice.

"Good to know," he sneered. "Now how 'bout you fuck off? I'm a bit busy doing my job, the one I've never hesitated to carry out, as I'm sure you know."

She crossed her arms. "Is that so? I heard you had a run-in with a young woman recently."

"Been many young women recently, you'll have to be more specific."

She stared at him blankly, her orange eyes boring holes into him. She knew he knew who she was talking about. He just wanted her to explain it, to exasperate her and make her squirm. And she wouldn't give him the satisfaction. Astraphelle turned on her heel and began to walk away.

"Okay then," she replied.

When he realized she wasn't taking his bait, he balked. Typical.

"Wait. If you're talking about that sweet thing with the fur coat who was rescued by a vampire and his cronies, then yeah, I know who you're talking about."

Astraphelle turned back toward him as if to say, "I'm listening."

"So you're aware they escaped this island?" She said.

"Yes," he replied

"And the sixth? And the fifth?"

Florizeel's nostrils flared and he grit his teeth as he looked down at her. He stepped off the soul he'd been torturing and moved to her side quickly and she scrunched her nose at the funk of decay he brought with him. They fell into an easy step together as they proceeded to walk through the wood.

"I've heard that. I sent word ahead of time, but it seems that those other demons aren't so good at their jobs."

Astraphelle lifted a brow at him. "It would seem to me that, had you and your retinue stopped the girl and her vampire, none of the rest of this would have happened," she said.

Florizeel growled and Astraphelle turned her incredulous expression into a grin. Of course, the truth would set him off. They escaped the seventh island, the one he oversaw, the place where those who'd spent their lives butchering others were butchered. That feat alone could be enough to galvanize any other soul who was foolish enough to try to take their chances at running.

The demon didn't respond as they walked through the island and Astraphelle admired all the different ways these demons and souls thought of killing each other. She was partial to disembowelment herself, had even once worn the entrails of an Italian explorer known for his atrocities as a necklace for a while. But here was a human who tied up a vampire to a tree, a manic smile on her face as she carved into the back of the vampire and snipped away at its ribs. The sound of the bones splitting made her grit her teeth.

"Having flashbacks?" Florizeel said, catching Astraphelle's gaze. She rolled her eyes and pushed forward, ignoring the cries of the damned. "Is that why you're here then? Trying to get back into the beast's good graces? I'm already on it. But go ahead, I don't mind you cleaning up our messes like a good little maid."

Astraphelle gripped the metal bar on her palm that kept her daggers in place. Without a word she turned and buried the daggers into the demon's neck, slicing across his jugular before pulling the blades out. His purple blood sprayed across a large oak tree as Florizeel dropped to his knees, bringing both hands up to his neck.

"I've... always... hated you..." he choked out before falling face-first onto the ground. She stepped back, not wanting blood on her feet. She bent down and grabbed his head, knowing he still had a few more seconds before he died. Of course, he'd be coming after her when he reanimated, but she'd deal with that later.

"The feeling's mutual, brother."

She slammed his head into the dirt before walking away. She wiped her blades on her skirt, not caring that the blood left aubergine smears on the lacy fabric. She'd find these escaped souls and make sure they didn't leave her father's domain, even if it meant tossing them into the abyss before they reached Simyasha's shores. And then, if her brother had his way, she'd probably be captured by him and tortured for days before he killed her. But at least she wouldn't be in the pit. At least then she'd be free from her father's torture. At least she'd feel something, even if it was a blade slicing through her gut.

The trees of the sixth island swayed in a warm evening breeze and Astraphelle walked across the beach and into the forest with brows knitted and her teeth ground together. The incessant moaning sound of the damned on this island always made her ears ring, and the atonal whistling of the tree-dwelling demons always stuck with her long after she left.

She ignored the grasping of the damned who lay on the ground, trees bursting forth from their bodies. What could she even do for them? What could anyone do for them but chop their heads off and end their suffering, at least until they reanimated?

One soul became particularly grabby, managing to tear off a chunk of her skirt. She growled and fixed her ember gaze on the creature, a satyr from the looks of it, and dug her knives into the creature's face.

"There, now we both get what we want. You get to die again and stop your suffering, and I get to be left alone."

But the whistling sound above her reminded Astraphelle that she wouldn't ever truly be left alone on this island. She looked up as a demon with spindly limbs and slits for eyes leaped out of the tree above her and tackled her, whistling all the while.

"Are you fucking serious?" she said. It extended its long, bifurcated tongue and drew it across Astraphelle's cheek, her skin sizzling from the poison it left in its wake. She lifted the demon up just enough to gain purchase and sliced across its belly. It shrieked and she growled as the demon's brackish blood spurted from the wound. She tossed it to the side just as another demon leaped from the trees and scurried across the ground toward her.

Astraphelle rolled her eyes but secured her knives on her hands and stood at the ready.

"It's the princess, finally free after two hundred years of torture," came a maniacal voice from behind her. And just like the damnable whistling, she felt it nagging all along her spine.

Astraphelle sighed and stood her ground, not wanting to turn her back on the acid-tongued demon before her.

"Care to come out and face me? Or are you just going to let me slaughter your puppies?" She spat.

The demon chuckled and Astraphelle shuddered. She could hear it rustling in the trees, moving about the canopy quickly.

She strode toward the eyeless demon and drew her knives across its back. It fell to the ground with a shriek, and then Astraphelle turned her attention toward the trees. She closed her eyes and listened for the demon's movements. It was right above her. She knelt then jumped, knives at the ready, and sliced the demon's foot off.

It screeched and fell out of the tree, its green eyes radiating in the darkness. Astraphelle grimaced as she wiped her blades across the shirt of the body the tree grew out of. It turned its head toward her and moaned.

"Yeah, yeah, you need help, you're damned, you've been tortured too long," she mocked. She turned her attention back to the demon at her feet. Its spindly hands clutched the stump of its leg, its head tilted away from Astraphelle. She huffed and hunched over the demon and pressed her knives against its cheek to turn its focus toward her.

"A pair of souls are on the run. Have you seen them?" she asked sweetly.

The demon's eyes widened briefly, which told Astraphelle all she needed to know. But she kept silent. She knew that sometimes the way to get what she wanted was to stay silent and let people tell on themselves. It was a trait she'd inherited from her mother.

"I watched them cross the path."

"And you didn't think to stop them?" she questioned.

"Not my job," the demon replied, the same mania in its voice as when she first arrived. Astraphelle pressed her knives into its mottled green cheek, drawing blood.

"Did you plan to tell that to Tartagnon when he discovered that a pair of souls were fleeing the realm of the damned?"

The demon shook its head so intensely it grounded its own cheek on her blades.

"Well then, I suggest you don't keep talking about what isn't your job and tell me what you saw and heard."

"A vampire. A woman. She's shiny and new here, and her scream sounds like breaking glass, so beautiful. She cries, and the vampire soothes her."

Astraphelle rolled her eyes. "Two souls of the damned bonding over torture. How cute."

"I heard them on the beach, talking about their lives and death and survival and reaching Simyasha to—"

Astraphelle sighed. This is useless.

She pulled her arm back and positioned her blades above the demon's eyes, ready to drive them straight into its brain stem.

"Wait! Wait! You seek errant souls out but know not what they look like," the demon hissed. "I can show you!"

Astraphelle paused, her blades mere inches from the demon's eyes.

"You make a good point," she said. "I think you can show me."

She plunged her knives into the demon's eyes and plucked them out, reveling in the snapping sound of his optic nerve severing from the brain. It screamed and flailed beside her, but Astraphelle stopped paying attention. She stood and licked her lips before peeling first the left then the right eye off her blades with her teeth.

Eyeballs weren't her favorite part of a creature. They were chewy and unctuous, but they held a lot of power for those who could wield it. Without another word she turned and walked out of the forest and onto the beach, ignoring the moans of the damned, their hands reaching for aid. The demon whose eyes she now swallowed had disappeared up into the tree to nurse its wounds.

The moon loomed large in the sky, casting the beach in a crimson glow. She stared across at the flooded causeway, knowing she'd have to wait for the water to dissipate. It wasn't that she couldn't get around it; she was more powerful than most demons in Pandemonia, after all. She had strength beyond measure, could glamour her appearance, and she could teleport herself just by thinking of a person, place, or thing she wanted to reach. But without knowing more about these errant souls, she'd never find their precise location. She sat on the beach and crossed her legs. She closed her eyes and cleared her mind and let the demon's vision take over.

Images appeared in her mind's eye of a woman dressed in fur, her dark coils spilling over her shoulders and her face a mask of trepidation. The demon was right, she was a beauty. And beyond her fear Astraphelle could see something else — determination. Her companion, a tall and lithe vampire with clothes stained in blood, had the look of a soul who'd been damned for decades. She also saw them speak, watched them say each other's names. She made out the words "Maxwell," and "Sapphira."

Sapphira. A beautiful name for a beautiful woman, Astraphelle thought.

The last image she saw was them disappearing into the tangle of flora on the fifth island. It was midday when they arrived on the island. If their luck faired the way it had so far, they were already well on their way to the fourth island.

"Or perhaps their luck has run out," she said aloud. Astraphelle stood and adjusted her skirt. Then she closed her eyes and pictured Sapphira in her mind's eye and seconds later she was on the fifth island, watching as the woman was dragged under the water by a kaimong.

CHAPTER 12

SAPPHIRA

SAPPHIRA CAME BACK to life with a gasp.

She was no longer in the water but on solid ground. Her fingers dug into the grass beneath her, the leathery coldness of it making her eyes water. She felt the warmth of the sun and the humidity of the fifth island. She lifted one leg then the next, feeling the joints crack and tendons pull.

"I'm alive," she whispered, and this time she didn't try to stop the tears as they cascaded down her cheeks.

"You're reanimated, thank Enefri," Maxwell said. He sat beside her, a hand on her shoulder. He looked worried, an expression she wasn't used to seeing on his face. When she'd succumbed to the water and died, she'd been terrified. She hadn't known what was on the other side. But she didn't remember anything about it. One moment she'd been dead and the next she was alive.

"What happened?" she asked.

"I dove in after you, but you were already dead — that kaimong bit a chunk out of your stomach and your legs were barely connected to the rest of your body. I got you into the log and paddled to shore. Would've gotten caught if it wasn't for our new friend over there."

Maxwell's tone grew edgy when he said the word 'friend'. Sapphira followed his gaze toward the other side of the small clearing where the wolfman sat against a tree, fiddling with the lacy sleeves of his shirt.

"You!" Sapphira shouted. "What the fuck are you doing here?"

"Why, helping to keep you alive. You're welcome," Luquin scoffed.

"I only died because of you."

"We don't know that. That kaimong could've had your scent from the second you entered the water. That's how they hunt, you know, scent." He sniffed at the air. "Besides... I knew your blood-sucking companion would help you sooner or later."

Maxwell growled. The werewolf cleared its throat. "Sorry. Not bloodsucker. I forgot you all prefer the term 'leech.'"

Maxwell lunged at Luquin, picking him up by the collar and lifting him off his feet. The werewolf looked unimpressed.

"Do let me know when you're done with your tantrum, vampire. I believe we have more pressing things to discuss, like your escape plan."

Sapphira sat up and instantly regretted it as pain shot up through the back of her neck and to her temples. She pressed her hands to her temples and hissed.

"You ok, kitten?" Maxwell dropped the werewolf and knelt before her. Sapphira nodded.

"Kitten? Oh, so you're a couple after all," Luquin teased.

"Not at all," Maxwell spat. "We're just... friends."

Sapphira looked up to see the werewolf shake his head. "Yes, and I'm Louis the fourteenth."

"Do you have a point?" Maxwell asked.

"Or a purpose for being here?" Sapphira questioned.

Luquin lifted his hands in surrender. "Ok. To the point I go. I know you're trying to escape. To what end I don't know, but I do know you need me."

"How do you know that? Did you say something to him?" Sapphira asked.

"I barely even talk to you, why would I tell our plans to this buffoon?" Maxwell replied.

The werewolf clapped a hand to his chest, affronted. "I beg your pardon?"

"Because it was your friends who told Florizeel and his goons about our plans!" She shot to her feet, and Maxwell rose to his. They stood toe to toe now, and she glared up into his eyes. "We never would've gotten hemmed up back there if you hadn't—"

"How many times must I tell you I had nothing to do with that?

I don't know how they found out, maybe they were spying on us!" Maxwell shouted.

"You would say that, that way you don't have to take responsibility for—"

The werewolf placed a hand between them.

"Now, now. You can save the angry fighting and subsequent fucking for later. Right now... let me answer your question, despite you calling me a buffoon, which is quite offensive, I must say."

"Offensive? You called me a leech!" Maxwell yelled. The werewolf hushed him.

"You're so loud. If you're not careful we'll get caught."

"I—"

"Anyway, I pegged you as escaped souls the second I saw you. I've been on this island since 1705. Believe me when I say I've seen it all. I know every soul here. And though you look new to Pandemonia, mademoiselle, I'm quite certain I'd remember you if I'd seen you before," the werewolf said.

"Why? Because of some weird vampire, werewolf beef?" Sapphira asked.

Luquin chuckled.

"Not at all! I find vampires fascinating. All that blood and self-loathing that's so characteristic of their kind. No. It's because he's *beautiful*. And I make it a point to remember all the beautiful creatures, like yourself," Luquin grabbed Sapphira's hand and slowly planted a kiss on the back og her hand, his golden eyes never leaving hers. Sapphira bit back a smile. Despite him having a hand in her death, she had to admit he was quite charming.

"Ok, that tells us how you knew we're not from this island, but what makes you think we have a grander plan?" Maxwell huffed. His arms were crossed and he scowled at the werewolf.

"Oh, because you just confirmed it with that little argument of yours," he replied.

Sapphira and Maxwell looked at each other, mouths agape.

"Anyway, shall we skip to the part where you tell me where you're going?" Luquin asked.

"Why should we?" Maxwell questioned.

"Like I said, you need me."

"Bullshit," Maxwell snarled. "We're doing fine, just us two. We don't need some... peacocking lycan giving us away."

"Oh, such *rage*. I bet you came from the seventh, eh?"

Maxwell clenched his fists and growled, and Sapphira stepped between them.

"Look, you seem to be very observant and your being here for centuries gives you an advantage but why should we include you?" Sapphira asked.

"Because not only do I know how to get off of this island, but I know how to get you to Simyasha's shores," Luquin stared down at his nails. "If that sort of thing would be helpful to you."

Sapphira opened her mouth and closed it, nonplussed. She looked at Maxwell, who was still seething at the werewolf's presence.

"Can you give us a moment?" she said to Luquin.

"Of course, bijou, take your time." He turned and walked over to the tree and crossed his arms and closed his eyes.

"What do you think?" she whispered.

"It doesn't matter how low you talk, he can probably hear us," Maxwell grumbled.

"Yes, I can!" Luquin shouted. Maxwell shook his head and grabbed Sapphira's hand, pulling her toward the edge of the clearing.

"Do you think he's telling the truth?"

"Not at all. I think he's a grifter who'll give us up any chance he gets," Maxwell said.

"I think it's risky to take him too, but... what if he's right? What if he really does know how to get to Simyasha?"

"Then he should've escaped centuries ago. It's not our fault that he didn't have the wherewithal to do so. I don't trust him."

"Neither do I," Sapphira said. "But then again, I wasn't sure I could trust you and... I was wrong."

His brows lifted. "You... trust me?"

Sapphira shrugged and looked at the ground. "I suppose I do. But we're both out of our depth here. If he does know how to get us off this island, maybe we can make it off before Florizeel finds us. And if he's lying, you can just... kill him."

She surprised herself with how nonchalant she sounded when she said those last few words. Maxwell seemed to share her surprise, as his brow shot up before a wicked smile spread across his face.

"I'd do it with pleasure," he said.

"I know you would," she said. "It also may be nice to have someone else who's strong around. I'm sure you're getting sick of me tripping and struggling to—"

Maxwell cupped her cheek. "You're stronger than you realize, kitten. And you're getting stronger every day."

She looked into his eyes and the softness within them made her breath hitch. Part of her wanted to lean into his touch but the other part was filled with guilt and dread. The guilt uncoiled in her belly as she chided herself for even finding another person attractive so soon after her relationship ended, even if it ended because he killed her. Dread coursed through her nervous system, and she found herself leaning away from his touch because how could she be certain that he wouldn't hurt her, too?

He moved his hand away and nodded. "Whatever you say, kitten. I'm with you 'til the end... or as long as you'll have me."

Her cheeks warmed at his comment. She wanted to reach out to him then, grab his cool hand and entwine her fingers. Instead, she simply nodded, let out a shaky breath, and turned back toward the werewolf. She strode across the clearing, Maxwell close behind.

Luquin was perched on a tree limb. His eyes were closed, and his hands were folded over themselves, legs crossed at the ankles. He looked at peace, except for the sorrowful tune he hummed.

"We've decided to let you come with us," Sapphira said.

He jumped down instantly and stood before her.

"Excellent, let us make haste then," he turned but Sapphira caught him by the arm.

"Wait..."

"I won't lie to you and pretend I'm not pissed at you for getting me killed."

"Why don't you kill him back?" Maxwell whispered in her ear.

"What?" she balked.

"He'll reanimate and then you two will be square." She looked from Maxwell to Luquin, her heart pounding in her chest.

"Is this all part of some plan of yours to stop him from joining us?"

"No. But I can't say I won't beat his ugly ass all the way back to the seventh should he continue to irritate me," Maxwell said, glaring at the werewolf.

Sapphira sighed, suddenly weary. All she wanted to do was rest, but she knew that was a luxury she couldn't yet afford.

"Why don't you two take whatever weird male aggression you have with each other and save it for when there's an actual threat. Unless part of all this aggression is you wanting to fuck him?" Sapphira asked.

"*Please*. He's hardly my type." Maxwell rolled his eyes.

"You should be so lucky, Maxwell," Luquin said as he jumped out of the tree.

"This is about you getting the vengeance you deserve," Maxwell said, ignoring the werewolf.

Vengeance, she thought, the word turning over in her head as she watched the vampire shrug and slide his unbothered mask back on.

Sapphira caught the werewolf's eyes and held his gaze as she spoke:

"You may know how to get to the goddess, but you're conniving. And you got me killed, and I think if Maxwell hadn't roughed you up, you probably wouldn't be here now."

"Bijou, I—"

She held a hand up to silence him. "But I've got no idea what I'm really doing or where I'm going, so if I'm going to get out of this place, I need someone like you."

There was a rustle in the bushes behind them and all three of them jerked their heads to the source of the sound. Sapphira's unease deepened as she wondered what manner of demon could be on the other side.

"So..." she paused, swallowing the bile that rose in her throat. "I'm going to kill you now. And when you reanimate, we'll leave."

She braced herself for his reaction, leaning away from him, but all he did was nod. "Very well. It's only fair that you avenge yourself."

Sapphira stared at the werewolf. He said he'd been on the island for over three centuries. Longer than Maxwell, and so much longer than she'd been. As she took him in, she wondered what it would be like to spend three hundred years in Pandemonia. Three hundred years of torture, pain, and dying over and over again. She had no idea what she'd turn in to if she stayed here, and as she thought about what all this werewolf could have seen, she wondered if this was the right thing to do. Afterall, he was offering aid. Maybe he hadn't done it on purpose, as he said. Then she thought back to the way her legs had instantly gone numb when the kaimong bit into her stomach and she shuddered. She deserved her retribution.

Maxwell stepped up next to Sapphira and held out her knife to her.

She wrapped a hand around the knife's hilt, her heart pumping wildly in her chest. Could she really do this? Could she willingly end Luquin's life, not for self-defense but retribution? She squeezed the blade so hard her hand hurt. She swallowed the lump in her throat and locked eyes with the werewolf. He nodded at her and smiled reassuringly.

She stepped toward him. Her hand shook as she brought the blade up to his throat. She locked eyes with him as tears blurred her vision. She blinked them away and pressed a hand to his shoulder to steady himself.

"It's ok," he whispered. He placed his large hand over hers and steadied the blade, pressing it against his throat. Blood bubbled to the surface and Sapphira stifled a scream. She dropped her knife and backed away from Luquin, who looked at her so reassuringly that a lump formed in her throat as she fought back tears. Her back connected with Maxwell's chest, and she jumped.

"It's ok, kitten, I've got you," he said, wrapping his arms around her. This time she let him touch her and hold her as she processed what had just happened. She had the chance to get retribution and instead, she let her fear get the better of her. She didn't know why — it wasn't like she hadn't killed before since she'd been in Pandemonia. Perhaps it was the way he looked at her, the way he accepted his fate, even tried to help her cut his own throat. Sapphira tried to tell herself that was the reason, but then she thought about crossing the veil and shuddered. How could she get the revenge she deserved when it came to Dante if she couldn't get it here, in a place where creatures reanimate?

"Do you feel better, kitten?"

"No," she replied quickly. "And I don't know if I ever will."

There was rustling in the bushes again, which spurred Sapphira out of her bitter thoughts. "We should probably start moving. We've been here too long."

"Only if you feel you're ready," Maxwell said.

Sapphira snorted. "I don't think I'll ever be ready for anything here. Let's just keep moving."

"This way," Luquin said, gesturing to them to follow. Maxwell pressed a hand to her back as they walked out of the clearing.

They emerged near another, smaller lake, which was overflowing with the hollowed-out logs of the damned. They rounded the right side, sticking to the marshy ground next to the lake, where their location was hidden by the large bushes surrounding the shore. Something splashed in the water, and she yelped before clapping a hand over her mouth. They stopped and waited for the sound of someone having found their location, but when nothing happened, they kept moving.

"It's ok," Maxwell whispered. Sapphira inhaled deeply, trying to center herself. But the closer they moved to the water the more memories of her death the night before flashed in her mind's eye. She saw herself back in the water, the jaws of the kaimong wrapped around her stomach, cutting her in half. She'd lost feeling in her legs, had felt her lungs burn as she drowned. She vowed to do whatever it took to avoid that same fate.

They passed by the lake and strode along more marshy land. The further they got from the water the more humid it was, and Sapphira fanned herself with one hand while gripping her blade with the other. Large Cyprus trees dotted the landscape, a soul tied to the trunk of every one of them. They seemed to have gotten the same treatment as those on the lake — bodies covered in honey and insects biting and burrowing into their skin. They passed a man with hollowed-out eyes, bugs pouring from the socket, moving in and out of his nostrils and open mouth. A large hole in his stomach exposed his intestines. Sapphira gagged at the sight and the smell. Somehow the scent of blood and honey and feces was stronger here.

"You get used to it," Luquin said, as though reading her mind.

"It's quiet... pungent," Maxwell replied. His nose was scrunched, and his eyes were watery with blood. Sapphira wondered if the smells were even more intense for him given his heightened senses. They trudged through the dense swamp, Sapphira fighting the urge to gag every time she saw a soul throwing up the honey mixture and having it fed back to them. It was deep into the night when they reached the path of the damned. Sapphira looked back at the island and shuddered, but when she looked toward the path she was filled with dread, wondering what fresh hell awaited them on the fourth island.

"What did you do to get you trapped here for all eternity?" Sapphira asked as they stepped onto the path.

"Isn't it obvious? This is Rapaciousness; he probably stole some old dowager's fortune or conned a family out of their home."

"Must you always think the worst of every creature you meet?" Luquin asked.

Maxwell glowered. Luquin clucked his tongue.

"I bet you were a delight at parties," the werewolf said.

Sapphira sighed.

"Yes, because at least my friends and family didn't have to worry about getting conned by some overgrown pet," Maxwell retorted.

"Nor did mine," Luquin replied lightly.

"Oh, cut the bullshit, you were on an island where people who spend their lives being greedy and gluttonous are sent. You cannot tell me that whatever it was you did was a small, inconsequential little con."

"I wouldn't be so quick to judge, bloodsucker," Luquin cautioned. "After all, you either came from Maleficence, where the murders are sent, or Desecration, an island filled with rapists and defilers. I bet if we compared stories, the brutality of yours would beat mine out any day."

Luquin spun on his heel, but Maxwell yanked the fur at the back of his neck, tugging the werewolf's head backward and exposing his neck. Luquin's eyes widened as Maxwell's jaw opened and his fangs brushed against his neck.

"Stop, please!" Sapphira said.

"You're tap dancing on my last nerve, Lycan," Maxwell said. "I wonder now if it's a good idea that you join us after all. I'm having a hard time not tearing your larynx out and shoving it up your—"

Luquin swiped his claws across Maxwell's face. The vampire hissed and let him go, both his hands springing to his face as blood seeped through his fingers.

Maxwell growled. Luquin returned the stare, his ears flattening against his head and his lips pulling back from his teeth. He looked more inhuman than he had in the time since she'd met him. Sapphira's old anxiety kicked into overdrive as the two creatures circled each other. *I've got to do something*, she thought. She stepped between the werewolf and the vampire. Both looked at her in surprise.

"Please stop this, Luquin's just trying to show us how to get out of here."

"You're taking his side now, kitten?"

Sapphira's heartbeat quickened at the growl in his voice, now directed at her. Her eyes darted from Maxwell, who'd been there with her from the beginning, to Luquin, her new companion who was the key to getting toward Purgatore.

"I'm not taking sides. It's just everything's ok. We don't have to fight, we just need to get to Purgatore, and then—"

"You're cute, bijou, but neither I, nor that bloodsucker, need you to fight our battles." Luquin gripped Sapphira's arm gently and pulled her out from between them, then closed the space between himself and Maxwell. He was taller than the vampire by at least half a foot, but Maxwell's presence still loomed large.

"I'm not, I just..." her voice broke. "Please don't fight."

Luquin was the first to break his gaze and turn toward her. She looked at him with glassy eyes, a lump lodged in her throat and her chest tight. She bit the inside of her cheek and tilted her head back to try to blink the tears out of her eyes.

"Oh, Bijou! There's no need to cry."

Maxwell blinked, his eyes returning to normal. He looked at her and the menacing expression on his face softened. He stepped in front of her and gently pressed his hands to either side of her neck, cupping her chin with his thumbs.

"Shhh, it's ok," Maxwell said. Luquin scratched at the fur on his chin, an embarrassed look on his face.

"I don't know why I'm doing this," she said. But that was a lie. She'd always been sensitive, attuned to the moods of those around her. It had gotten worse when her Granny died and they entered foster care, and even worse than that when she got with Dante. It felt as though she was supposed to be responsible for the moods of everyone around her, always making sure they were in good spirits, having a good time, that they weren't mad. Because if they could be mad at each other, they could be mad at her. And that meant yelling. Silence stretching on for days. Being called "a nag," or "a bitch," or worse, "a cunt." And sometimes, it meant a thinly veiled threat that maybe, just maybe, words weren't the only thing he could throw in her face.

"You don't have to apologize, kitten. Sometimes I forget how unused to the brutality of Pandemonia you are. I've spent decades fighting every day that I sometimes don't know how to do anything else," he leaned in close to her and she stared into the deep pools of his eyes. Her cheeks warmed. "I'm sorry for being so callous. You are safe with me, okay?"

She nodded cautiously. This wasn't the first time she'd been told that. Granny had told her and Persephone one stormy afternoon the same thing, and months later she was gone. And so had Dante, after they made love for the first time. He'd held her in his arms, and he'd felt so solid and warm that she'd started to panic when he shifted on the bed.

"You're a precious thing, Sapphira. And precious things need careful handling. I will be careful with you, I promise."

He smiled then, but now she was examining the memory, she realized it hadn't reached his eyes.

When she looked at the vampire before her now, whose cold hands felt like salves against her flushed skin, she saw his lips slowly spread into a smile, one that made his left cheek dimple and the edges of his eyes crease.

"Okay," Sapphira said. "Please just stop fighting, for me?"

"You have my word," he said. He stepped back and grabbed her hand and planted a kiss across her knuckles. Then he slid his hands into his pockets and sighed.

"I am sorry for making you uncomfortable," Luquin said. "I'll do my best to get along with your companion during our journey. Shall we press on?"

"After you," Maxwell said. Luquin gave him a tight smile and proceeded toward the fourth island.

CHAPTER 13

ASTRAPHELLE

THESE SOULS AND *their fucking sentimentality*, Astraphelle thought as she watched the two creatures pull the woman out of the river. They bickered the whole time but wore twin expressions of concern as they tried to rescue her. The vampire held her torso and the werewolf held her legs, barely connected to her body by a few strips of skin and tendon.

They carried her, struggling past demons and other souls towards a clearing where they could let her heal and reanimate safely. This action sent a pang in her belly, but she took a deep breath to suppress it, knowing that this same sentimentality is what got her cast into the pit in the first place. She focused instead on the tension between the two creatures as they waited for the woman to arise.

When she did, she and the vampire spoke about whether to cut the werewolf into their escape plan, ultimately deciding to bring him along, something Astraphelle never would have done herself, but not before the vampire convinced Sapphira to seek her vengeance and kill the werewolf.

To Astraphelle's surprise, Sapphira almost did it, and she felt a glimmer of respect for the woman. It wasn't easy, she knew, getting vengeance against the people who hurt you, especially when their power greatly exceeded your own. But that respect diminished when she saw the woman break down as her companions began to fight.

She begged them not to fight and even though Astraphelle felt her weak, she could tell that there was a story there. It wasn't just the desperate way that she pleaded with them to stop fighting. It was the way that she moved after the creatures stopped fighting— taut, like the bowstring of an arrow that would snap with too much pull. It was the way she tried to keep the conversation going between them all, even when her companions gave one or two-word answers. It was all of that, and the brand etched into her breasts that piqued Astraphelle's curiosity.

Remember your plan, she reminded herself, shoving down her lingering feelings, and continuing to follow the trio, invisible. They made their way through the rest of the fifth island, through the forest, to the pathway to the fourth.

Night had fallen. The moon was a bloody orb in the starless sky, hanging so low it kissed the still waters of the abyss. The bonfires of the fourth aisle burned in the distance as though beckoning the trio toward its shores.

The trio walked along the narrow path toward the island and Astaphelle silently trailed behind them. The vampire and werewolf kept their heads on a swivel, and the woman held her knife at the ready.

At least they're being vigilant, Astraphelle thought.

Unlike the fifth, sixth, and seventh island which were densely populated with trees and rolling hills, the fourth was flat and arid, marked by bonfires that burned day and night, a large mesa in the center of the island that stretched as far as even her demon eyes could see to the left and right, and overgrown cacti the color of puke with spines that were so poisonous that Astraphelle had been killed by them once, long ago.

The demons on this island were particularly excited about the brand of torture they got to dispense, and at one point, Astraphelle moved among them. She should have been on this very island, instead of in New York, when she met the soul that would spark the light of humanity inside of her. A soul that was responsible for her landing in the pit.

She heard the woman up ahead talking wondering aloud about whether they'd be able to make it through the fourth island unscathed. Astraphelle chuckled at this, her mind drawn back to the present.

Every island had its own unique torture, and though the

misdeed of the fourth aisle, Treacherousness, was lesser than that of Rapaciousness, Desecration, and Maleficence, the torture there was no less abhorrent. A fact that these souls would find out soon enough.

The second their feet touched the shore, a horde of demons set upon them. Sapphira screamed as a demon gripped her shoulders and hoisted her over its shoulder, before her companions even had the opportunity to defend her. One demon thrust a knife deep into the vampire's neck and pulled it out just as quickly, making his blood spurt and coat the werewolf's fur. Another broke the werewolf's neck, sending him down to the ground instantly.

They cackled as they dragged these souls across the desert, and Sapphira screamed all the way. Astraphelle continued to follow them across the long plain of the island and towards thousands of cages where the damned were held, awaiting their punishment. These cages were small, and she watched as the woman was tossed into one and tried to stand but could only hunch.

Her companions were slumped in their cages like ragdolls, and she cried as she waited for them to reanimate. The vampire was the first to wake up.

"Maxwell!" Sapphira shouted. She reached her hand through her cage, and he clutched her outstretched fingers to his chest.

Thousands and thousands of people batted against their locked cages, screaming for help, screaming to be let go, and screaming as they watched the horror of what happened before them.

One demon with large antler-like horns tied a soul to the back of its carriage with a long chain. Then he stepped in and snapped his whip, cracking the hide of a skinless horse with a mangy mane. It huffed black smoke that smelled like sulfur, and the demon rounded the bonfire not caring if the legs of the soul it dragged were kissed by the flames, burning its shins and feet.

She watched, unphased, as one leg, then the other, dislocated. It screamed as pieces of itself began to fly and fall away from his torso. The soul was long dead by the time the demon stopped riding its chariot. When he got off, he whooped and hollered, making the other demons in the area follow suit.

Astraphelle looked from this torture to the souls, seeing the horror written across their faces and knowing that they were wondering just exactly how fucked they were.

Time to make my move, she thought. Astraphelle glamoured herself, softening her features. No longer did her veins glow and pulsate beneath her skin. Her orange eyes dulled to a light brown, her braids uncoiled from their twists at the side of her head and hung loose down her back. Her clothes turned from a breastplate and a skirt to a tattered shift dress that came down to her ankles. She let her knives drop from her knuckles and pulled a bar loose from one of the empty cages. She covered her body and face in blood and dirt and ran towards Sapphira's cage, the bar high above her head. The werewolf stirred just as she reached Sapphira's cage.

"No, don't!" Sapphira called, covering her face with her hands.

Astraphelle brought the bar down against the lock on the cage, breaking it in four swings, though she only needed one. She pulled the door open and held a hand out to Sapphira.

"C'mon, we've gotta go, if they see that I've broken you out we'll both be dead."

"Wait, my friends... I can't leave without them," she replied.

"We don't have time," Astraphelle urged. Would this woman truly risk her life trying to save her companions as they had theirs?

"I'll make time, and if they kill me, I'll figure out how to save them again, but I'm not leaving them," she replied as she held her hand out toward Astraphelle. She frowned and pressed the bar into Sapphira's hand and watched as she broke the locks to Maxwell and Luquin's cages.

"Luquin, Maxwell, let's go!" Sapphira shouted.

Without a word she watched as the vampire took Sapphira's hand and began to run. The werewolf followed suit, and it was only once the woman turned back toward her and said, "Are you coming?" that Astraphelle joined the trio.

They ran past cage after cage, some empty, others filled with souls, so many that they became a blur. Had she been on her own, Astraphelle could have outrun the demons whose attention they now caught. But because she was hiding her full strength she ran as fast as a human could, and that meant when the demons descended upon them, she was caught along with them.

Of course, the demons could see through her glamour, but it didn't matter. Like the demons at the palace, these ones would be all too happy to torture the daughter of the great beast and the arbiter of death.

"Looks like a merry band of fuckfaces trying to escape their punishment," rasped a demon roughly the size of a bear. His name was Talthos, and he'd once been her friend. Now he wore a look of disdain that she knew was meant for her as well.

"Let us pass, we don't belong here, demon," the vampire spat.

He's got courage, Astraphelle thought. *But he's foolish as hell.*

Talthos chuckled and swung at Maxwell, his meaty fist connecting with the creature's jaw and sending him back on his haunches, ripping his hand from Sapphira's.

The werewolf emitted a low growl and launched himself at the demon, but Talthos grasped the wolf by the neck and tossed him to the ground beside the vampire.

He turned his attention to Sapphira, who trembled beneath his gaze.

"I think I'll start with you," he said. Astraphelle sighed. Was he really going to force her to kick his ass this early in the game?

She stepped in front of Sapphira just as he reached for her.

"You will do no such thing," Astraphelle said. Talthos narrowed his eyes and smirked at her.

"Is that so, human fucker?" he said.

Astraphelle bristled at the insult and narrowed her eyes at the demon.

"We will pass," she replied. "Even if we have to go through you."

"I'd love to see you try," Talthos drawled.

Astraphelle grabbed the metal bar from Sapphira's hand and swung at the demon, who caught it with one hand and smacked Astraphelle with the other. She stumbled but kept up her assault, not so much aiming to take the rotund demon down but trying to buy time. His focus was so trained on Astraphelle that he didn't notice the vampire approaching him from behind. The vampire gripped the demon's head in his hands and bit a chunk of flesh from his neck. The demon growled and reached for his neck with one hand and the vampire with the other, but the werewolf grabbed his arm and twisted it behind his back. The vampire locked his teeth around the demon's neck and sucked his blood, holding tight to him even as the demon fell to his knees.

Another demon ran over toward them, hearing the commotion, this one smaller than Talthos but no less ugly. She watched as he descended upon the werewolf, stabbing the creature in his shoulder then chest.

"Fuck you, demon!" Luquin shouted. He rounded on the demon and the two traded barbs, with the werewolf slicing the demon's thigh open, the skin bursting open like fruit. The demon stabbed Luquin in the hand, the blade tearing through tendon and flesh and coming out the other side.

While the two fought the vampire finished making a meal out of Talthos. He stood and licked his lips, looking euphoric.

"Are you ok, kitten?" he asked as he turned his attention toward Sapphira. She stepped out from behind Astraphelle toward her companion.

"I'm—"

Their reunion was short-lived as Sapphira was tackled to the ground by lanky demon with cracking white skin and blood-red eyes. Her head cracked hard against the dirt and the demon bit into the flesh of her left breast. Sapphira shrieked and punched the demon in the head, freeing its teeth but not its body. Maxwell was upon the demon in a flash and yanked the demon off.

Sapphira sat up, looking woozy, a pool of blood in her wake. Astraphelle knelt beside her and helped her up.

"This is the second time you're saving me, and I don't even know your name," the woman said, voice slurred.

"I'm Astra," she replied. "And you're losing a lot of blood. We've gotta get you out of here."

She grabbed Sapphira's arm and tossed it over her shoulder then hoisted the woman to her feet. Luquin and Maxwell had both been drawn into fights, this time the werewolf battling two demons at once, and the vampire, three. They were losing, and Astraphelle debated whether to save them. She had the soul her father ultimately wanted, the one who'd started this exodus, after all. All she had to do was take her to the path of the damned between the first island and Purgatore. But the woman was already shouting for her companions, and their skirmish had drawn the attention of a myriad of demons. Astraphelle was strong and powerful, but there was no way she'd be able to fight all of them off at once.

"We've got to help them," the woman said. Astraphelle sighed.

"Can you stand?" she asked.

Sapphira moved her arm from around her neck and stood on wobbly legs but nodded.

"I can help," Sapphira replied.

"You'll get yourself killed in the state you're in. Just stay here."

Astraphelle ran over and helped first the werewolf then the vampire. Once free, they looked at her with such appreciation it made her wince. *Disgusting*, she thought. *But was it, really?*

She pushed her thoughts away and strode back toward Sapphira.

"We've gotta go, those demons are on our ass now."

"How can we outrun them? There's nowhere to go," the werewolf said.

"I thought you said you knew how to get to Purgatore," the vampire added.

"I... only said that so you'd let me go with you," he wailed. The vampire rounded on him.

"You lying sack of—"

"We don't have time for this!" Sapphira shouted. She turned toward Astraphelle. "Do you know how to get to safety?"

Astraphelle nodded. "Follow me."

She ran without looking back to see if they followed and ended up caught in the pathway of the demons' chariots. She stuck to the right, avoiding a bonfire and jumped to her left just as a demon rounded another fire and nearly collided with her. She heard the trio of souls shouting in the background, heard demons shouting behind them, heard all their footfalls until the sound rose into a cacophony and her head pounded.

Ahead of her was a small opening in the mesa which she'd discovered nearly a thousand years ago. It led down into the depths of this island, to its foundation, the one her father created first before he made Pandemonia anew and created these islands as they were now. The creatures there were older than these demons and so primordial that, like with the abyss, even her father was leery of them. She knew if she led these souls into this darkness, she'd be risking all their lives. But if she didn't, she'd get stuck here and road hauled or worse, tell her father she failed. Better to take her chances with the darkness than to risk her father's wrath again.

"Up ahead, we're going through there!" she pointed.

They were yards away. She saw the entrance so clearly, and she pumped her arms, hating that she couldn't use her full strength.

And then, minutes later, she stepped into the darkness and turned. She held her arms out, grabbing hold first of the werewolf, who'd started running on all fours, then the vampire. Both creatures turned and held their arms out for the woman who ran toward them wide-eyed, mouth agape, hair flying behind her like a streamer.

Make it, Astraphelle willed. *You can make it.*

And before she had the chance to examine the spike of fear that shot through her at the thought of this woman getting captured, Sapphira ran straight into her arms.

CHAPTER 14

SAPPHIRA

SAPPHIRA TACKLED ASTRA to the ground as the shouts of the demons echoed through the cavern. She sat up and looked at her, taking her in for the first time and noting her smooth skin, soft against her hands. Her honey-brown eyes looked up at Sapphira in relief, and the smile that broke out on her lips made Sapphira's cheeks warm.

Just as Sapphira was assessing her, she could tell Astra was sizing her up as well. Oddly, she couldn't help the thought that she hoped the woman liked what she saw. It wasn't until Maxwell huffed that Sapphira broke out of her reverie.

"Oh, sorry," she said and scrambled to her feet. The woman sat up then stood with a fluidity that reminded Sapphira of Dorothy.

"That's ok," the woman replied. Her voice was deep and raspy like Tina Turner's. Sapphira took a deep breath to try to get her equilibrium back. This was not the first attractive woman she'd ever seen, she reminded herself. And if her plan to get back across the veil worked, it would not be the last. *Focus, just focus*, she thought.

"I— thank you for your help, you didn't have to do, well, any of that," Sapphira said.

The woman chuckled.

"I saw that you needed help and I helped," Astra replied.

"I'm Sapphira," she said, holding her hand out for a shake. The woman smiled and extended her hand, her long fingers brushing against the palm of her hand as they shook hands.

"Nice to meet you."

"And I'm touched by all of..." Maxwell's brows knitted and he moved his hand around in a circle. "This. But should we really be exchanging pleasantries so close to our former captors?"

"Maxwell—" Sapphira started.

"He's right, I hate to say. We're awfully grateful for your help, mademoiselle, but I feel like we should be moving elsewhere," Luquin added.

Astra nodded. "You don't need to worry about them. They won't come in here, they're too afraid."

"Afraid?" Maxwell scoffed.

Astra nodded toward the demons who loomed by the entrance to the cavern. "Look. if they wanted to come in and kill us, or snatch us up, they could've done it already. I learned long ago this was the place to hide from them because they'd never dare enter."

She looked around but all she saw were stalagmites that seemed to stretch on forever toward an endless ceiling. The air was stale, with an undercurrent of rot. The woman turned from her and began to move down a narrow corridor. Sapphira glanced at her companions, who both looked like the last thing they wanted to do was follow her. Sapphira was also hesitant; though Astra had saved them, she'd also brought them to a place that was arguably more dangerous than what they'd escaped. What if she was leading them toward some kind of trap?

"What is this place?" Sapphira asked, not moving from her position.

"I don't think it has a name," Astra said. She stopped and turned toward the trio. "But I've heard it said that this is the first place created by Tartagnon, and when he got tired of it, he simply got rid of everything but this one mesa, and the caverns beneath it. Those who stayed, demon and the damned alike, grew even more monstrous. They say these are the original demons and the oldest humans on this island. I don't know why they scare the others outside, but once I discovered that, I've been hiding out here ever since."

"If this is just a hiding place, why are you trying to take us further down?" Sapphira asked.

"This lets out on the other side of the mesa, just above the beach."

Sapphira and Maxwell exchanged glances.

"How convenient," the vampire whispered.

"I can lead you there, unless you want to take your chances with those demons?" Astra asked.

"Why are you helping us?" Luquin asked gently.

"Yes, why the thousands of other souls in peril," Maxwell added.

Astra stopped and turned to look at Sapphira. "You reminded me of the love of my life. You even resemble her. Same face shape, hair, and smile. Except when I last saw her, she was being pulled out of my arms and tossed into a burning pit. I don't know what happened to her after that, but when I saw you I just... I had to help you."

Sapphira's heart skipped a beat at this, not just because of the care in Astra's eyes when she looked at her but because, like the rest of them, she was also nursing a broken heart.

"C'mon, it's a long walk, but I promise I'll get you to the other side," Astra said. She pulled a torch from the wall and began walking down the corridor. Sapphira sighed and started to follow Astra, her stomach tying in knots with each step. Beside her, Maxwell scowled.

"What's wrong?" she asked.

"I don't like this," he replied. "There's something about her I don't trust."

Sapphira sighed. "You don't trust anybody."

"That's not true," he said. "I trust you."

She tilted her head and pursed her lips as she looked at him. He held his hands up.

"Look, I know you want to believe the best in everyone but..." he dropped his voice. "Look what happened with the werewolf. We believed him when he said he could get us to Purgatore and now we find out that he lied. What if this woman is lying, too?"

"I'm sorry for my chicanery," Luquin said as he sidled up to them. He stood, wringing his hands, looking contrite. "I just couldn't bare another moment on that island and when I heard your plan to escape, I seized my chance."

"I don't care why you lied. I should kill you for your deception." Maxwell spat. "Because of you, we're stuck deciding between letting this woman lead us through this cursed mountain or taking our chances in the open with those demons out there."

"I know. And I'm sorry. How can I make things right?" Luquin asked. Maxwell stepped toward him, his face mere inches away from the werewolf's.

"You can stay the fuck away from me for a while."

Luquin nodded, his head dipping low and his tail tucking between his legs. Maxwell turned back to Sapphira.

"And look, I know what you're going to say, kitten. That woman did save us but why? There were so many others she could have helped. And need I remind you of our plans and how a certain powerful, idiotic — but powerful nonetheless — demon is on our tail?"

"What does that have to do with..."

Maxwell gripped Sapphira's shoulders. "Think, kitten. Why would she save us? The ones on the run? Maybe she does see her lover in you, or maybe she's one of them, or working on their behalf to deliver us straight to the great beast himself."

Sapphira looked toward Astra, who was further down the corridor, seemingly unaware of their conversation. She looked back at Maxwell, her beautiful vampire, whose reflective eyes held such concern in them it took her breath away. He placed a hand against her cheek and ran his thumb over her lips. "I couldn't bear it if something happened to you."

She leaned into his touch and sighed and for the briefest moment, she envisioned what it would be like to fully give in to that touch, and her gaze fell to his lips. When he'd kissed her on the beach she'd been taken aback, not because he wasn't a good kisser — he was even better than Dante — but because it was all too much. She'd been murdered by someone she loved who she thought loved her. How could she give herself over to something like that again? Especially a murderous, sullen vampire whose touch was altogether soothing and electrifying? She shut her eyes tightly and thought of the moment in the park when the knife first stabbed into her. She focused on that pain, on the shock it caused, and pulled Maxwell's hand away.

He took a step back, melancholy written all over his face before he resumed his composure.

"Then come with me," she replied. Bile rose in her throat, and she took shallow breaths as she tried to tame her wild heart. "I don't want to do this without you. I'm scared to follow her too, but what choice do we have? What if this is our only way to freedom?"

Maxwell slid his hands into his pockets and fixed her with a nonchalant gaze. "Fine. I am once again at the whim of your decisions. We shall hope they do not come back to bite us in our asses."

He stalked ahead of her without another word, and Sapphira's shoulders sagged. She started after him, but Luquin placed a hand on her shoulder.

"Let him go, bijou. You'll come back to each other eventually. You always do."

She sighed and locked eyes with Luquin, who removed his hand and shied away from her.

"I'm sorry, again, for lying."

"I forgive you," Sapphira said. "Just don't do it again. I don't think Maxwell will let you live if you do."

"What will you do?"

She regarded him curiously. "Well, I suppose I'd let him do whatever he wants to you."

Luquin gulped. "Noted."

They fell in step behind Maxwell and Astra. Just as he had when he sat in the tree, the werewolf hummed some sorrowful tune. The melody made her heart ache as she thought of her fate. Her mind drifted to Dante, and she wondered not for the first time what he was doing on the other side. Did he mourn her, or was he rejoicing in her death? Her hand absentmindedly scratched at the mark across her breast, and she wondered whether he'd received the fame and fortune he sacrificed her for. Her eyes grew misty not just at the thought of the things he took from her, but at the thought of all he'd gain. He'll be the one that gets to go to Paris, draped in Yves Saint Laurent, strutting down the Champs-Élysées.

Luquin began to add words to his song and Sapphira slowed down to fall into step beside him.

"What was Paris like when you were alive?" she asked. Luquin smiled ruefully.

"It was beautiful and terrible all at once. A glittering city full of decadence, sex, and endless possibilities with the Sun King himself in the center, his court swirling around him. But if you were poor, it was hell."

"Were you…"

"I got lucky enough to have a generous benefactor sponsor me to go to the Académie Royale de Musique."

"You were a dancer?" Sapphira asked.

Luquin nodded. "I was a principal dancer from 1700 until my death. My occupation thrust me into the upper echelons of Parisian society; I performed for King Louis XIV himself. He was quite a patron of the ballet, having danced himself in his younger years."

"How did you go from a principal dancer in the Paris Ballet to spending eternity on Rapaciousness?"

Luquin laughed, but there was no mirth in the sound. He trailed his hand along the side of the cave and began to speak:

"When I took my spot as principal, I was on top of the world. And then I met her, my Ophelia. She was the most beautiful woman I'd ever seen. More than that she was... effervescent. And she was the only other werewolf that I'd met aside from my family."

"Wait, how long were you a werewolf before you met her?" Sapphira asked.

Luquin tilted his head. "Why, I was born one."

"Oh," Sapphira said, still blown away by the fact that vampires and werewolves existed. *I can't wait to tell Persephone—*

Her chest tightened as she remembered where she was. *I may never see Persephone again.* She shook her head and bit the inside of her cheek to bring herself back to the present. She could feel Luquin's golden eyes upon her, radiated in the darkness. She nodded at him, and he continued.

"We sought each other out, I think we could smell each other. We made love after our first rehearsal, then transitioned into wolf form and ran along the Seine. We danced number after number together, and oh, how they all talked about us! How they wrote about our love, evident on and off the stage."

Luquin's eyes darkened. "Ophelia was a brilliant dancer, but she was never happy. She always needed more. More sex, acclaim, money, drink. It started small for us. We'd dance, go out to celebrate, and drink ourselves silly. Stumble through the streets or change and run through the cemeteries. But it was never enough for her. And once she picked the pocket of an unsuspecting patron of the bar we frequented, she realized that was the kind of high she'd been seeking. She urged me to join her, and so I did.

"And we went from picking the money off a drunkard or two once a week to outright stealing from anyone we could as often as we could. After a while she began to hunger for it. We'd steal from street urchins or courtiers. It mattered not. All that mattered was the money, which she'd spend on anything she wanted. But it was only a matter of time before we got caught."

Luquin paused, and Sapphira noticed that even Maxwell had slowed his pace, seemingly to listen to the werewolf's tale.

"In my love-sick brain, I thought it made sense to say I was the one who'd thought of our subterfuge. Ophelia was only too happy to let me take the fall. I never saw her after I was arrested. Days later I was executed by the guillotine, just as I changed into the wolf before the whole crowd. The last word I heard before the carriage came for me was 'fiend.' I thought if only they knew I'd never been the one who wanted to do it. I spent centuries blaming her, wondering where she'd be, plotting my revenge for when she ended up in Pandemonia, likely on the same island as I. But I never saw her. And—" Luquin's voice broke. "And then I realized that whether or not she'd put the idea in my head, she did not direct my hands. I acted as her partner, not as her stooge. And I've felt like the biggest buffoon ever since."

He pulled a handkerchief from his pocket and dabbed his eyes. Sapphira placed a hand on his shoulder to soothe him.

"Luquin, I've known a lot of people, some of them buffoons," Sapphira said. "But you? You're not one of them."

"Yes, you may be conniving, silly, and dreadfully annoying, but a buffoon you are not," Maxwell added. Sapphira looked at the vampire in surprise. He'd stopped walking and looked over at them, his expression sullen.

"That means a lot, thank you, Maxwell," Luquin said. The vampire shrugged.

"No need to take it for anything more than what it is. You're not a buffoon, but you are a liar and a thief, and if you weren't handy in a fight, I'd have killed you and abandoned you for your lie. Just remember that."

He turned on his heel and walked swiftly toward Astra, who was now so far ahead Sapphira could barely see the light of the torch. She sighed, suddenly weary. Luquin squeezed her shoulder.

"Come, let's catch up to them. And while we do, you can tell me all about that little brand of yours... that is, if you want," Luquin said.

Sapphira smiled at him, and opened her mouth to speak when a scream up ahead made her startle. Without thinking she ran, and she felt Luquin by her side as she did so. The narrow corridor had widened into a dimly lit cavern marked by stalactites covered in a sap that smelled like rotten eggs.

In the far corner, Astra and Maxwell fought a dark creature that blocked their path forward. It swiped at Astra with its claws, tearing deep gashes into her stomach and spilling her intestines out from the wound. Astra groaned and doubled over, one hand on her belly, the other holding the torch in a shaky hand Luquin dashed over to help them. Though Sapphira knew they needed help, she stood rooted in place, her mouth dried up and her body trembling.

How can I help them when they're so much stronger than I am?

The thought reverberated in her mind as she saw that the creature moved in and out of form. One moment it was a nebulous fog and another it was a lanky, tall creature with claws the size of her face.

Astra cried out as the demon shoved her against the wall. She dropped the torch in her hand, the flames extinguishing as it fell to the ground. Sapphira moved on shaky legs as she stumbled to the wall. With trembling hands, she pulled one from its sconce and tip toed toward her companions, who were all bloody and beaten. Maxwell's left arm hung limp at his side as he fought with his right. Astra's stomach wound had started to heal but she moved stiffly, not getting out of the way of the creature's never-ending blows. Luquin managed to wound the creature but after seeing the wound stitch itself together almost as quickly as it received it, his eyes went wide.

"H-hey!" Sapphira called, drawing its attention toward her. She instantly regretted this after seeing the creature's eyes, dark and devoid of any color, almost as though absorbing what little light there was in the room. She swallowed the bile in her throat and steadied her breath as the creature stalked toward her. She slashed at it with her knife, but the demon moved too quickly. It rushed at her, knocking her into the wall. Her knife clattered to the ground. She moved to pick it up, but the demon raked its claws down her forearm. She screamed as blood bubbled to the surface. She held the torch aloft, almost like a shield. When she did, she noticed the creature shift backward.

Is it afraid of fire?

She shifted her grip on the torch so that the flames faced the creature. She pulled her arm back and grunted as she threw the torch at the creature with all her strength.

The torch connected with the creature's leg and the flames surged up its body. It howled, a hollow sound that sent a shiver up her spine, but that didn't stop it from stalking toward her, the flames engulfing it but not stopping it from claiming her as its victim. She darted to the right, and winced as her back connected with a stalagmite, just as the creature was mere inches away from her face. It screamed at her, its shadowy visage swirling and pulling all the sound of the cavern with it. Her breath came out in ragged gulps as tears cascaded down her cheeks. The creature lifted its hand, nails dripping with her blood.

I'm going to die again, she thought. *I'm barely closer than I was before.*

"You'll not touch her!" Luquin growled, jumping before her just as the creature's claws dug into the side of his neck, cutting so deeply his head lolled to the side.

"Luquin!" Sapphira screamed. The werewolf collapsed in a heap to the ground and Sapphira fell to her knees with him, her hands gripping his face. She sobbed and threw herself over his body as the creature screamed again. She prepared herself to feel those claws digging into the flesh of her back, but the stab never came.

There was the squishing sound of flesh being stabbed. She'd recognize it anywhere by now. And then there was silence. When she looked up, she saw that the creature had dissipated into nothingness, leaving behind only a puddle of dark pus that reeked of sulphur. Before her stood Astra and Maxwell, the former holding her knife, the blade covered in pus, the latter covered in blood.

"He's dead," Sapphira said. "Will he still come back even though he was killed by one of those things?"

Astra nodded. "C'mon. That thing won't stay dead forever and there'll be more where its coming from. We've got to out of here."

"Oh, now we've got to get out of here. Before this was the only place that was safe," Maxwell said.

"I never said it was safe, vampire. Just that it was safe from the demons on the top side. This is Pandemonia, no place here is safe. I thought you knew that," Astra replied.

"I know that," Maxwell seethed. "But you've led us into more danger and now my friend is dead. If he doesn't wake up, I'm holding you personally responsible and you won't make it to the other side of this mesa, certainly not in one piece."

For a moment Sapphira saw a dark, menacing look pass over the woman's face before she tore her gaze away from him.

"He'll reanimate. But we must go, now, or we'll all be torn to shreds."

Maxwell bent down and grunted as he hoisted Luquin up, one arm holding the werewolf's head in place and the other wrapped around his body. Sapphira got to the other side to stabilize him, and they began to walk with Astra leading the way. The cavern narrowed and widened at points, and all the while that same howling sound that the creature made reverberated through the caverns.

"How much further?" Sapphira asked.

"Almost there, look there's a light ahead."

Beside her Luquin groaned.

"Almost out," she soothed. They were so close. The light was growing closer. She could make out the sun in the distance, see the cloudless sky and the ocean beyond.

The howling grew closer. They picked up speed, leaving the cavern in the same anxious hurry as they arrived at it.

The smell of fire and burning wood assaulted her senses, and she welcomed it after the stale smell and sulphur in the caverns.

"This way!" Astra called over her shoulder, turning left toward a trail that led down into a canyon. Ahead of them the mesa dropped off steeply, and beyond that was the abyss, the water still oil-slick black and completely still despite the crimson clouds and gusts of wind that nearly knocked Sapphira off balance.

"Gods, we're out," Luquin whispered. Sapphira's heart leaped when she heard his voice, thankful her companion had reanimated.

"Thank Enefri," Maxwell said. "I really didn't want to have to carry your ass down this mountain."

Luquin scoffed and rolled his eyes. "You say that, but I know you're really glad to see me, my friend."

Maxwell glowered at the werewolf and Sapphira smiled. She slid her arm from Luquin's back and jogged to catch up to Astra. She had almost reached her, when an arrow pierced through her chest, stopping her in her tracks and stealing her breath. She rocked back on her heels before falling to her hands and knees, the skin on her palms splitting from the force of her fall.

"Sapphira!" Luquin and Maxwell both shouted. They ran to her side, but though she felt their presence all she could focus on was the tip of the arrow sticking out from her breast, covered in blood and gore. She didn't know whether it would be better to remove it or keep it in.

"What do I do?" she rasped. Each word felt like torture to get out. "It hurts."

Her companions grabbed her arms and pulled her to her feet, but her legs were full of pins and needles. Her knees buckled. Another arrow pierced her lower back, making her back bow. It hurt to stand.

It hurt to move. It hurt to breathe. She recognized the numbness, the cold that stung from the inside out, that slowly crept up her limbs. She was going to die again.

"Fuck!" Luquin growled. She tilted her head toward him just as the fletching of another arrow whipped through her hair.

"Who..."

"Hello, beautiful," Florizeel said.

She closed her eyes, her world spinning.

They've found us.

CHAPTER 15

ASTRAPHELLE

RAGE BUBBLED IN her as she turned to see Florizeel approaching the souls from behind. He held a bow in his hand, and Astraphelle was shocked to see that he'd hit Sapphira not once but twice. Rarely was he so accurate. She grit her teeth and strode toward them, fists clenched and aching for the feel of her knives.

"This will not end the way you want it to," she shouted. Her words made a smile break out across his face; his skin so taunt the movement looked like it could rip the skin like paper. Sapphira shuddered, tears flying down her cheeks. Her lower lip trembled and Astraphelle fought that pang in her chest and the desire to wipe her tears away. *Stop the sentimentality,* she chided herself. *You should be angry at Florizeel for trying to steal your gig, not sad about some human soul's torture.*

"How you figure, human?" he spat, and Astraphelle wished she could use her true strength and yank his tongue from his mouth, anything to shut his stupid voice up. She took another step and in one swift motion her brother dropped his bow, pulled the bone blade at his belt and dug it into the werewolf's side, quickly stabbing him three times. Astraphelle knew from experience that the blade had pierced Luquin's heart. She watched dispassionately as he crumbled to the ground on his side, spitting up blood and wheezing. There was a part of her that felt sorry for him after having been killed not an hour before.

The vampire dove down to try to secure his friend, but one of Florizeel's goons wrenched his arm behind his back. Florizeel stepped up behind Sapphira and grabbed her neck, holding her upright with one hand. He pulled the arrows from her wounds, her blood shower in the ground before her. Blood trickled from the woman's nose and mouth as she tried to steady her breathing.

"You're not going anywhere, vampire. Let the werewolf die. I've got a bone to pick with the rest of you," Florizeel said.

"You'll pay for this, demon," Maxwell growled. Florizeel laughed.

"No, I don't think I will, not this time. You're surrounded and you've got no one to save you," Florizeel replied, looking directly at Astraphelle.

Astraphelle assessed the situation. To her back was the trail that led to the beach. To her left, the cliffside, the beach and abyss below. The cavern loomed on the right side, the howling of the creatures within still echoing, as though calling for them. Florizeel and his trio of gray demons blocked the other side of the path, effectively boxing them in. The only weapon at her disposal was the blunted bone blade Sapphira had carried. She looked down at it, noting the blood and bits of intestine that clung to the end. It wasn't as good as her blades, but still, she'd killed her brother before with less.

"I think you're wrong about that, demon," Astraphelle shouted, packing as much venom into the word "demon" as he had when he called her a human.

"Oh? Are we really doing this?" He gave her a pitying expression, which only infuriated her more. But Florizeel was her brother, and she knew his tricks well; he was baiting her, trying to get a rise out of her so she'd foolishly rush toward him, knowing she was at a disadvantage. It had worked once, she had to admit, when they'd met across the veil in the late 1000's. She'd fallen into his trap, and he'd run her through with a spiked spear that only latched on to her insides the more she tried to pull it out. She'd died twice in the process of freeing herself. But then, she had gotten her revenge — and it took him decades to reanimate after she chopped him up and fed him to an anaconda piece by piece.

She kept her face blank as she took a step toward them.

"You won't make it to me in time to save them all. Why don't you go about your business and let me handle mine?"

"I wouldn't give you the satisfaction," she replied and strode toward him. One by one the gray demons came at her, freeing up the vampire to turn toward Florizeel, who sneered and dropped Sapphira. He was predictable in his lust for a fight that he willingly let go of the one soul he'd come to collect. Florizeel and Maxwell clashed, each of them throwing punches and slashing at each other with their nails. Sapphira languished on the ground, and from the sound of her breath Astraphelle could tell Sapphira was struggling to cling to life.

Astraphelle plunged her weapon into the demons before her, dropping them like flies. She finished just as Florizeel drove his knife into the vampire's left eye. Maxwell fell to the ground, the crunching sound of his skull against the ground enough to make even Astraphelle wince. Throughout it all, Sapphira panted. Florizeel pulled her to her feet and held her out in front of him like a shield.

"Am I supposed to be afraid?" she asked and cocked her head to the side.

"You know what I'm capable of. All I got to do is squeeze," Florizeel tightened his beefy fingers around Sapphira's neck. Her eyes widened and her hands sprang to her throat. "And I could pop her head off quite easily."

"I suppose you could, but not before I do this," Astraphelle replied. She sprinted toward them and brought the knife down on his arm, using her full strength to cast the blow, cutting off his arm. Sapphira fell to the ground, Florizeel's severed hand still around her neck. The woman clawed at the limb to try to get her neck free, and Astraphelle cast a sidelong glance at her before turning back to Florizeel and tackling him, sending them both over the cliff.

She heard her own bones breaking as she slammed onto the beach. She grunted as the dust settled and looked over at Florizeel, her piece of shit brother, and smiled with a mouth full of loose teeth. His face was caved in, legs bent haphazardly, bones jutting through the skin of his left leg and right forearm. He was still alive and glaring at her, but she chuckled nonetheless. She rolled to her side and spit in his face.

Her own wounds had already started to heal, which meant that her brother was not too far behind her. She approached him and stepped on his remaining hand, breaking the bones there. He barely reacted, his gaze following her as she walked around him and did the same thing to his feet. Astraphelle sat on Florizeel's chest, and his ribs gave a satisfying crunch beneath her weight.

"You know, it's a pity it's come to this," she said. "I hate to give you credit for... anything, brother, but you are a brilliant torturer. We could've had a most unholy alliance. Instead, you decided to hate me, and, well, here we are. Me about to toss you into the abyss and you about to go to your true death."

His eyes widened. The thought of him going under the water and never coming out filled her with such pleasure she allowed herself to smile. She sighed exaggeratedly and tore his shirt from his body and got to work plaiting it into a rope.

"What'll you do with the souls?" he choked out.

"Nothing you need to concern yourself with," she replied. She stood and grabbed his other bone blade from its hilt and slid it across his throat for good measure. Then she began to wind the rope around his ankles, tying it tight enough she could see it dig into his skin. It'd been so long since she'd truly tortured someone. The act restored her spirit, so much so that she began to hum.

"Stop that racket," her brother choked out. She arched a brow as she looked at him and pitched her voice louder.

"You know, I hear that there's a ship down there. Apparently, before our parents made either of us, some of their retinue tried to sail the waters of the abyss to get to Purgatore. I suppose you'll find out. Wish you could report and tell me, but..."

She pouted. Florizeel stared daggers into her. She tied his hand and his legs and hoisted him over her shoulder. She walked slowly, struggling a little to handle his weight, yet marveling at the fact that she was mere steps away from getting rid of her lifelong nemesis.

"I just have one question, brother. Don't you ever get tired of losing?"

She began to laugh, a deep cackle that she felt all the way through her entire body. The clouds had parted, and the sun glinted off water.

And in that moment things were almost perfect. She was almost happy. Almost—

Florizeel dug his teeth into her back. She fell to her knees, and he tumbled away from her, rolling onto his back to cut away his bindings. Already the hand he'd lost was starting to regenerate.

Fuck, I moved too slow.

They got to their feet at the same time and circled each other. He put his fist up, and Astraphelle sneered at him before hitting him in the jaw. He returned the blow in kind, the blow loosening her barely healed teeth. She spat blood onto the beach and continued her assault on him, landing a blow against his temple, clavicle, and sternum. Her blows knocked him back toward the abyss. For a moment he looked close to falling into the water where he'd meet his true death, but then regained his balance and launched himself at her with full force. He hit her hard in the gut and she folded in on herself. He grabbed her hair and wrenched her head back. She punched his chin, but he moved his head left and right, avoiding his blows.

"You're no closer to getting those souls," Astraphelle said.

"And neither are you," he replied. "Look at where you are right now... about to be tossed into the abyss. What was it you asked me, 'don't you ever get tired of losing?' Well, now you see, I never lose, not in the end."

He stroked her cheek. "Give my regards to those Enefri-forsaken sailors down there. May they be poor company for you as you ponder all the ways in which you've failed."

Without another word he stabbed her in the throat, pulling the blade out just as viciously as he slid it in before stabbing her three more times in her side. She looked down at her blood coating the gauzy fabric of her dress. Her vision twisted as her brother, hand still tangled in her hair, dragged her toward the abyss.

CHAPTER 16

SAPPHIRA

As soon as she healed, Sapphira ran. She gripped her knife in her hand so hard her knuckles throbbed. Up ahead, Florizeel had Astra by the hair and was preparing to toss her into the abyss. She pushed herself faster, faster, faster, knowing that if Astra went into the abyss there was hardly a chance she'd come out.

When she was close enough to touch him, she drove the knife square into the center of his back. His arms bowed and he wheeled on her, and Sapphira braced herself for his wrath. Then, just as before, an arrow whizzed past her face and implanted itself in Florizeel's shoulder.

He looked from Sapphira to the cliffside above, but Sapphira didn't follow his gaze. She stared at him as his eyes narrowed and his jaw clenched. But he let Astra go, and the woman dropped to the beach in a thud. Another arrow made contact, lodging into his side. His head whipped toward Sapphira, and she jumped away from him.

"We will meet again, Sapphira," he growled before disappearing.

She blinked at this, marveling at the demon's power. She turned toward the cliffs and saw Luquin on his feet, bow and arrow in hand. He nodded toward her and stepped out of eyesight, and she turned her attention to Astra.

The woman lay on her side, eyes cloudy. She rolled her on to her back and lifted her head, stroking her cheek just as the woman in Central Park had done for her.

"You saved me," Astra said.

"I had to return the favor; you've done so for me twice now," Sapphira replied softly. Astra lifted a hand and stroked Sapphira's cheek.

"Let's hope we don't have to keep doing that," Astra said. She coughed and a fresh trickle of blood ran down her chin. "I'm going to die now. I'll be back soon..."

Her hand slipped from Sapphira's cheek, and she went still. Even though she knew she'd reanimate, the more she got to know her companions the harder it was to see them die even if the death wasn't permanent. Minutes later, Maxwell and Luquin came to her side.

"We really shouldn't linger, kitten," Maxwell said. "Those demons are bound to come back for us."

"I'm not leaving without Astra. Help me carry her" Sapphira

requested.

Neither Luquin nor Maxwell moved.

"I won't leave her," Sapphira said. "She saved my life."

"So have I, so has the lycan," Maxwell retorted. "That doesn't mean you owe us anything in return. I'm still not sure we can trust her."

Sapphira glowered at him. "Trust her? Hasn't she more than earned at it, at least a little? She took Florizeel on all by herself. I'll carry her myself if I must, but we're taking her with us." She leaned down and slid an arm under Astra's shoulder.

The vampire grimaced and slid his hands into his pockets. He didn't meet her gaze. Luquin looked between the two and sighed. He gently plucked Astra from Sapphira's grip and cradled her corpse in his arms. Sapphira nodded at him and turned on her heel, not bothering to look at Maxwell as she started across the empty path. They crossed the path in silence, the wind raging around them but the water beside them remained still. Astra had reanimated halfway across the path. She and Sapphira walked together now, Maxwell trudging behind them and Luquin up front.

"Thank you for saving me," Astra said.

"It's only fair, you've done so much for me. Here, you should take this," Sapphira said, holding out her bone blade.

"No, please, you keep it."

"But you'll need something to protect yourself," Sapphira replied.

Astra shrugged. "Guess I'll just have to stay close to you from here on out."

The comment warmed Sapphira's cheeks and made her drop her gaze. "I'm not much of a fighter."

"Oh, I don't know about that," Astra said. "You saved my life before, and you've made it this far."

"I wouldn't be here without Maxwell or even Luquin."

"Perhaps. But I think you'd have made it this far with or without them," Astra said. Then she leaned into Sapphira and whispered: "Fighting is the easy part. You're the mastermind. Don't let them forget it."

Sapphira thought back to her conversations with Maxwell; he said he didn't think she was weak but what if he was lying? And what if Luquin felt the same? She thought back to how he'd deceived them and wondered whether she'd been a fool to bring him along with them.

She gripped the hilt of the bone blade. It was cool to touch and ground her amid the swirling thoughts in her mind. She remained silent as they trekked across the path. Luquin sang softly as they walked. Eventually Sapphira recognized the tune as "Ave Maria."

"You have a beautiful voice," she said.

"Thank you," he replied. "My mother always felt my true talents lay in the opera rather than the ballet."

"My mother wanted me to be a preacher," Maxwell said.

"Really? Even after everything your father did?" Sapphira asked.

"She was religious until the end," Maxwell said. "In fact, I think that the death of my father and his family made her even more drawn to the gods."

"What happened to her?" Sapphira asked.

Maxwell was quiet for a long while before he responded. "I told her to take Julietta and leave. Unfortunately, they didn't heed my advice. They were killed the same night I was, by the same men who came for me. But they never committed such egregious misdeeds that they should end up in this place. I very quickly adjusted myself to the fact that I would never see them again."

"I had a brother, and a child. Ophelia was pregnant when I was killed," Luquin said. "And I never got to see what they became."

Sapphira felt a pang in her chest as she thought about what her companions had lost.

"I'm sorry," Sapphira said, uncertain of what else to say or how to comfort them.

"Part of my penance here has been accepting the consequences my actions had for my family," Maxwell said.

"I must confess I still mourn the fact that I never got to know my child," Luquin said. "But I take comfort in the fact that his mother, conniving as she was, was hopefully good to them. And that they had a better life than I."

Luquin resumed his singing, and Maxwell joined in, humming the tune in a low tenor.

Sapphira's heart felt like it was breaking for her friends as they recounted all the people they left behind, people who they'd missed for centuries. Their grief only reinforced her need to get back across the veil. Persephone, Frankie, Claudia; they wouldn't become memories to her. Their faces and their laughter and their love wouldn't be just something to help her get her through the torture. Soon she would hold them. Soon they'd squeeze around her and Persephone's kitchen table and eat take out and talk about their futures. Soon they'd be on the dance floor again, feeling invincible.

"What about you, Sapphira, who are you longing to get back to?" Astra asked.

"I've got a twin, Persephone. And I miss my best friends, Frankie and Claudia. And I was in college, I had an internship I was waiting to see if I'd gotten accepted when..." her voice broke as she thought about that internship that she'd prayed to the gods for every night before bed. She'd envisioned herself opening her acceptance letter, boarding a plane for the first time, landing in Paris. She dreamed of meeting all the designers in the Yves Saint Laurent fashion house, of Paris fashion week. And now? There was someone else learning from the greats, while she struggled for her life, her Saturday night best ruined from all the blood and bile.

"You ok?" Astra asked.

"Yeah, fine," Sapphira replied. "I just can't believe I'm here; you know? Not just in Pandemonia but here as in all the bullshit that's happened so far."

Astra snorted. "Well, it is really bold of you to assume you could bust out of Pandemonia altogether."

Sapphira smiled ruefully. "That's me. Going into things guns a-blazing. My boyfriend used to say I didn't know how to read the room or know how to think about what I was doing before I did things. Said I was all action, no thought."

It had been a bright, spring afternoon when he said it. They'd had an argument when she told him she applied for that summer internship at Yves Saint Laurent, in Paris under the guidance of her professor who'd told her she'd be a shoo-in. Told her all she had to do was complete the application and she'd submit Sapphira's portfolio. How excited Sapphira had been that day. She'd gone to a payphone to call Persephone and tell her the good news. Then she'd gone to visit Dante, who'd greeted her with a big hug and soul-melting kiss. They'd fucked on his dining room table, her dress lifted, and panties shifted to the side. When they were done and sitting on the couch drinking coffee, she told him about the internship. Instantly his mood soured, and it was like all the color had drained out of him, the room, the atmosphere, and even her.

"What's wrong?" she asked, as he moved about his apartment, watering plants, cleaning, and huffing all the while.

"Nothing, it's fine," he said. But Sapphira could hear the tension in his voice. The way his stare was blank when he looked at her. The slammed cabinet doors, the heavy sighs. She spent the rest of the night with a tightness in her chest and every time she spoke, she found herself asking if he was ok. Finally, he broke down after she had sex with him again. But where their afternoon delight had been filled with pleasure for her, this time it was rougher, and he was so consumed by his own needs that he didn't even bother to try to bring her to climax once he'd gotten there first.

"You just don't think sometimes, you know?" he said, his pants and boxers still in a pool around his ankles. "You just do things without consulting me."

She chuckled at the sight of his dick still out and pointed towards her while he said such a serious thing. But when she caught his gaze, she realized that had been the absolute wrong reaction. He rubbed his face then stood and got dressed. He'd migrated to the kitchen, where he sat smoking a blunt, the sound of Marvin Gaye drifting through the apartment. She dressed and followed him, wanting to apologize, wanting to make a joke or ask him something personal, anything to get him to stop being mad at her.

"I'm sorry, I just thought... I mean, this is my biggest dream! This could be my big break."

"Yeah, and what about my big break? What am I supposed to do while you're out galivanting through Paris? I'm going on tour this summer, Sapph, or have you forgotten?"

Sapphira sat there, confused. She'd known about the tour and had even taken him to dinner to celebrate the news. But what she didn't know was what that had to do with her going to Paris. When he saw that she wasn't responding, Dante continued to speak.

"I'm gonna need you by my side. I'm gonna need costumes..."

"I can make those before I leave."

"Who's gonna help me if they rip?"

"Just don't do things to make them rip. They're just clothes, not fine china, Dante," she said. She could feel her anger surging inside of her, but there was also fear. She fought to keep her arms uncrossed, her palms unclenched. The last time they'd argued he'd gotten even more upset because her body language made him feel she had closed herself off to him. How could she tell him that she didn't take that posture because she was trying to close herself off, but because she was trying to feel safe. He sneered at her.

"Oh, stupid me. Here I thought I was trying to help you out, give you a chance to shine. Give you the credit when I get interviews, or, or when fans or other musicians ask where I get my sweet wardrobe. But I guess you don't want my help."

"No, Dante it's not like that, it's—"

"Nah, that's ok. I'm used to you just making decisions without even considering me. You know, you can be so selfish sometimes..."

Sapphira bit the inside of her cheek, desperately trying to claw her way out of that memory. When she looked up, she saw Astra looked at her with pity in her eyes. She turned away, unable to stand the expression, only to see that Maxwell and Luquin had stopped in

AMANDA B. WEAVER • • •

their tracks and were now looking at Sapphira with the same pitiable expressions. She shook her head and pushed forward.

"What did you see in him?" Luquin asked.

Sapphira stopped, her body suddenly weary. She sighed and closed her eyes, wishing she could run away. But there was nowhere to go in this place of the damned, nowhere that wouldn't be worse.

"He was the most beautiful, exciting person I'd ever met. Most of the time he was loving and romantic and funny. But his moods were all-consuming; like his moods, his happiness or anger would swallow me whole if I let them. And yes, we were still together when I died but... we aren't anymore."

"Because you're here?" Luquin asked.

"No, because he's the one who killed me."

She looked from Luquin, who looked sad at the revelation, to Maxwell whose face twisted in disgust. Then there was Astra, whose face was blank but whose eyes shone a hint of frustration. Sapphira sighed. She'd heard her companion's stories of how they got to Pandemonia, she supposed it was time for her to tell her own.

"We went dancing like I did every Saturday night with my sister and our friends and Dante joined us. He was a musician, trying to make it big. But it was always something holding him back — either he didn't have the right instruments or work got in the way or the clubs wouldn't play his songs. But then, he convinced my favorite club, Kaleidoscope, to play one of his songs. They did that night."

244 • • •

"Did that make him happy?" Astra asked.

Sapphira grimaced and looked down at her hands. That tightness in her chest again. Only this time it was coupled with a lump in her throat that made it hard to swallow. "Not really. There wasn't a good enough reception to the song, too many people went to the bar while it was playing and the people on the dance floor barely danced. We left right after. He said he wanted to take a shortcut through the park, but it was snowing and cold and I just wanted to go home. But I let him lead me and when we sat down to talk, he told me he had to make sacrifices for his dreams to come true. Then he started stabbing me. I didn't know what was happening at first, but the pain was..." Sapphira's voice broke. "Unbearable. Then he did this."

She turned toward the woman and opened her jacket, exposing the brand across her chest. Astra's eyes widened but she remained silent. "Thankfully a couple came and stopped him. But it was too late. I was already dying. I could already see Gwydion and the carriage even before the ambulance showed up."

Silence hung in the air and Sapphira buried her face in her hands. She couldn't look at them, couldn't see the way they watched her. Surely, they judged her for staying with someone who'd made her feel the way he did. Who put her through what he put her through. How could they not? It was all she'd been doing to herself since she was cast down to Pandemonia.

Then she felt arms wrapped around her and Sapphira looked

up to see Maxwell, her constant companion. He smiled down at her beautifully, the blue ring around his dark irises glowing in the light. He pressed his lips against her head and planted a kiss there before speaking: "Oh, kitten. You didn't deserve that."

"No, and you know what? He didn't deserve you," Luquin added.

Sapphira's cheeks grew warm at their words.

"He's right, you know," Maxwell said, his eyes boring hers. He ran a thumb over her lips, his arm still around her lower back and she realized that this time, she didn't want to shy away from his touch. "Anyone you choose should be so lucky to have someone like you as a lover."

Her heart skipped a beat at the sensuousness of his voice when he said the word "lover."

Sapphira stared into his eyes for a while longer before reality set in. She shook her head, returning to the conversation.

"Thank you. But it was my fault; I could've done more to prevent those arguments or been more mindful of his feelings. Maybe I could've dumped him sooner if I would've just listened to Persephone," Sapphira said.

"Blaming yourself isn't going to help you now," Astra said.

"Madame!" Luquin replied.

"I'm sorry for how rude that must sound, Sapphira, but it's true. Could you have broken off your courtship with him? Sure, but this man sounds like a real piece of work. I doubt he would have taken it on the chin. He sounds like the type to retaliate, and that would've happened whether you stayed or left. You don't need to feel guilty for his behavior."

"But I want to know why he did it. I want to see him and look him in the eyes and find out what made him... do all that he did," she said. She hadn't realized she'd wanted this kind of closure until she said it aloud. But it was true. She wanted to know why. Needed to know why. The question had been a quiet simmer in her mind, that now once spoken had turned up to a boil.

"I think if you do make it across the veil and speak to him, you'll be wholly unsatisfied with his answer," Astra said.

"What the fuck!" Maxwell shouted.

"I was only trying to be honest. I thought it could help her."

"Help her how?"

"It could give her the fight she needs to be able to keep going."

"It's not a fight she needs to be able to keep going, it's luck! With that demon on our tail, we'll be lucky if we make it to Purgatore," Maxwell said.

"You are insufferable!" Astra shouted. "You think you know what's best but you don't."

Maxwell stepped toward Astra, the pair so close that their torsos touched. Though she was just a few feet shorter, her presence seemed just as imposing as the vampire's. Sapphira could see the animosity in his eyes, the way Astra's fingers curled.

"At least I'm not trying to manipulate her. You're no better than that boyfriend of hers," Maxwell said.

"And with the way you talk to her and about her, as if you know everything, neither are you," Astra spat. Maxwell growled and bared his fangs.

"Ok, I cannot believe I'm doing this," Luquin said. He pressed his furry arm against Maxwell and pulled him away from Astra. "But you both need to shut the fuck up. Neither of you are helping, and if we're going to make it, we need to be working together not against each other."

"But she—"

"It doesn't matter," Luquin said.

"He—"

Luquin cut a glare at Astra. He bared his teeth at her and though Sapphira could tell she wanted to speak, she remained silent.

"Now, let's just—"

Without a word Sapphira began to walk ahead of her companions, letting the tears fall now that her back was to them. They were so close to the third isle. Even in the waning light she could make out the tall, craggy peaks of the mountains that seemed to consume the island.

"I'm sorry, kitten," Maxwell said as he caught up to her. When she didn't respond he grabbed her arm. She shrugged out of his grip and held the blade up to him. His eyes widened and his hands flew up in surrender.

"I don't want to hear your apology. Whatever your distaste for Astra is, she saved our lives back there, and she told me the truth. Whether you agree with that or not isn't my problem."

"I just don't think it was good for you," he murmured.

"And I don't care about that either. From now on, I determine what's good for me. Not you, not Luquin, not Astra, not Dante."

Maxwell frowned at the mention of her ex. Sapphira's heart skipped as she said it but she didn't try to backtrack.

"You got me?" she questioned.

"I just want what's best for you. I care about you, and I don't want you to get hurt," he said.

"I know you care. But what's done is done. I can push through. It wouldn't be the first time I've done it."

She turned back toward the path and kept moving, surging ahead of her companions. She needed space from them, and though she wished she could wallow in her misery, she kept putting one foot in front of the other. She thought back to all the times she'd had to stifle her emotions to survive, whether it was to avoid getting bullied by the other kids in the orphanage or to prevent Dante's mood from worsening. She hated it then, and she hated it now. But she could either let her emotions overtake her or she could use them as fuel to keep going, keep pushing. Sapphira put one foot in front of the other, determined to turn her pain and anguish into power.

CHAPTER 17

ASTRAPHELLE

THE THIRD ISLE greeted them with a blizzard. The wind whipped at them so strongly it nearly made Astraphelle tumble to her knees. The cold snatched her breath, and the snow made it nearly impossible to see, even for her, a fact that she was grateful for. It meant she could sneak away. Steal a few hours to find the demon responsible for the brand scorched into her chest.

"I can't see a damn thing," Maxwell grumbled. His beard had frozen into icicles that jutted out from his chin. Luquin's fur had become so frozen he looked more like a porcupine and less like a wolf. His teeth chattered. Astraphelle grit her teeth against the noise.

"It's as cold as a witch's teat," Luquin chattered. His arm was wrapped around Sapphira to help steady her as she trudged through the waist-high snow. Her skin was ashen, her nose the color of a bruise.

"I think it's only going to get colder and harder to see," Astraphelle said. She feigned a concerned look toward the interior of the island. Still the wind whipped and roared, and she looked back at the souls to see them shivering. It was still dark, and even though she couldn't see the moon, she knew it hung high in the sky, which meant that they still had several hours of darkness before the sun would show them the full extent of the third island, something she knew they'd never be prepared for. "Maybe we should stay here and wait the storm out."

Maxwell chortled.

"Why? We should just keep going while we have this momentum."

"Can you see far enough ahead of you to keep going?" She questioned.

"Yes, I can."

"But can Sapphira? I can barely see as it is," Astraphelle said. "If we're going to get through this island, we need to be able to see, and right now we can't."

"Luquin and I can see well enough for the both of you. We should just keep going. This blizzard will provide enough cover for us to make it through the island, hopefully unscathed."

"Yeah, but if we bust our asses doing so, or fall off a cliff, it'll take hours to reanimate."

"We'll deal," Maxwell said. "We have to keep going."

Luquin sighed.

"I hate to say it, Maxwell, but I think she's right."

Maxwell's head whipped toward the werewolf, his eyes narrowed.

"Why are you siding with her?"

"There's a blizzard," Luquin said flatly.

"Yes, I can see that. I'm fucking cold and my hair, your fur, all of it is freezing and turning into icicles. But we've got to go. We need cover, and this storm will provide it."

"And if something happens? What will we do when Florizeel, or some other fiend, catches but we're too focused on guiding Astra and Sapphira?" Luquin added. "We can't be their eyes and guard them at the same time."

The vampire was quiet for a long while, his eyes shifting from Luquin to Sapphira and finally to her. His upper lip pulled back momentarily in disgust as he looked at her. She kept her face blank, stuffing down her irritation.

"If you're itching for something to do, vampire, let's scout the area and make sure that we're safe here."

"Okay, fine, Luquin and I will go. I'll go to the left, and you'll go to the right."

"But—"

"No, you decided that we're going to camp here for the night, so I get to decide who goes to scout," Maxwell snapped.

Astraphelle clenched her fists and ached for the feel of her knives in her hands.

"Let her talk," Sapphira said through chattering teeth.

NO ONE'S GONNA TAKE HER SOUL AWAY

"I was just saying, if you two both go and something happens, it'll be harder for Sapphira and I, to defend ourselves. Maybe you should take one side, and I'll take the other. Luquin can stay here with Sapphira and make sure she's safe."

They all looked at each other for a long moment, assessing. It was clear Maxwell didn't trust her, and that was fine. She didn't trust the bastard either. It was clear that he was getting annoyed with Sapphira and Luquin siding with her. Good.

She was glad to be sowing the chaos her father so desired. But even though she delighted in it, there was still a part of her that felt a little guilty for doing so. She shook her head to push those thoughts away and turned her attention back to the present.

"I don't mind staying here with Sapphira," Luquin said.

"Yeah, I think it would be best for me to have somebody here that can help me fight," Sapphira replied.

"But Sapphira, don't sell yourself short," Maxwell said, taking a step towards her. "You can take care of yourself. You said as much last night."

"Yes, I can, but that doesn't mean that I always want to. I think Astra's got a good idea and you should go with her plan, even though it seems to pain you."

Maxwell sighed and threw his hands in the air.

"Fine, which direction do you want to go, Astra?" He spit her name out at the end.

■ ■ ■ 260

"I'll take the right. You go left," she said.

"Here," Sapphira said, handing her the bone blade. "You might need this."

Astra smiled tightly.

"Thanks," she said, even though she knew she wouldn't use a weapon at all. She'd have all the defense she'd need once she slipped off her glamour. She turned back toward the vampire, but he was already starting to walk away.

"Be back by sunrise," Luquin yelled. Maxwell waved with acknowledgment over his shoulder.

"If we're not here by sunrise, you two should keep going," she said. Sapphira opened her mouth to protest but Astraphelle held a hand up. "You keep going."

She turned and started to walk.

"Stay safe, please," Sapphira shouted.

"Good luck," Luquin added. Astraphelle laughed bitterly under her breath but didn't turn around.

She walked several feet toward the right, feet crunching in the snow. When she was certain she was out of sight she let her glamour dissipate like a mist. She was stronger, far aware, felt better without it. Now she walked atop the snow instead of trudging through it. Then she closed her eyes and disappeared completely.

Seconds later, she stood in the middle of a church across the veil. Dozens of people filled the large hall to worship Enefri. The building smelled of old wood and peppermint, the herb often used in offering to the goddess. Atop a large altar sat a statue of Enefri that, Astraphelle had to admit, looked close to the real thing. They captured her dark brown skin shimmering and bronzy in the light and her large doe-like mahogany eyes that seemed to look straight through the soul. The left side of her head was shaved, and dark braids spilled over her right shoulder. Her body was covered in a simple yellow, gauzy gown. These followers didn't seem to register Astraphelle's presence, and it was just as well. She wasn't there for them.

She looked toward the pews in the balcony where she made eye contact with the demon who had made the deal with Dante, which sealed Sapphira's fate. Aleteo sat with his legs wide, arms spread out over the back of the pew, casually glancing down at the worshippers. His long face was drawn into what looked like a peaceful expression, but what Astraphelle knew to be a hungry assessment. He looked like a human on the surface, but Astraphelle knew that it was just glamour, and a very good one. Underneath, his skin was a crumbling eggshell white that made his blue eyes look as dull as dishwater. His face was even longer, his bottom teeth jutting out in yellow spikes.

When he finally registered her presence, he nodded at her, and she moved quickly from where she stood near the door to sit beside him in an instant.

"Aleteo."

She folded her hands in her lap.

"Princess," he purred, not bothering to look at her. "Out of the pit, I see. What have you done to get your freedom?"

"None of your concern," she said, she said flatly.

"I suppose you're right," he replied. He made a show of looking down at his nails, but she knew him. He was a young demon compared to her, not as powerful and not as well connected. Even if her father hated her, he would still kill every other demon aside from Florizeel for her sake, of that she was certain. There was nothing to worry about from this sleazy, glorified salesman who spent his life corrupting humans and other creatures into severe misdeeds.

"What brings you across the veil? Back to your tempting ways?" he questioned.

"No," she replied. Astraphelle adjusted the metal bar across her palms ands he could see his eyes go to the blades, saw the look of fear in his eyes as he glanced at them.

"What are you here for?"

"I'm here for you."

"Why on earth would you be here for little old me?"

"Because of a deal you made."

"Oh, I make a lot of deals. You'll have to be more specific, darling."

"Because of a deal you made with a man named Dante."

His eyes widened for the briefest moment. Then he cleared his throat and sat up, adjusting his collar. "Lots of Dante's in the world."

She smiled. "Yeah... but not a lot with a girlfriend named Sapphira whose soul they bartered in place of their own."

When he didn't respond Astraphelle let her smile widen. "I know you've heard of what's happened. How this soul escaped and is on the run with two others."

"That's not my fault."

"If you think about it," she started. She lifted her left hand to let the sunlight catch the silver of the blades. "It sort of is. No matter. I'll fix things."

He made to disappear, but she grabbed his jacket, anchoring him to the present. She straddled him and pressed her knives against his chin. He shook beneath her, but despite his fear she could feel an erection pressing against her thigh.

"You're not going anywhere," she whispered into his ear. "I'm going to kill you, right here. And you know what that means, right?"

"I... won't reanimate."

"That's right. True death. More than what you deserve, but I'm willing to be generous."

Before he could respond she drove her knives into the soft skin beneath his chin and watched his eyes widen then dull. He made a grunting sound that Astraphelle knew most would read as an orgasm then his head flopped down to his chest. She stood, straightened her skirt, and disappeared back across the veil.

Her mother's domain was a fragrant tomb barely lit by a handful of torches. Her mother was seated on her throne and staring down at her worshippers as they writhed, naked, in a pile at her feet. Astraphelle grit her teeth and stood straighter, tilting her head higher. She couldn't show weakness to either of her parents, but especially not her mother.

"Hello, daughter mine," Simyasha said. Astraphelle fought the urge to roll her eyes as she approached the goddess cautiously. She held her long, slender hand out and Astraphelle took it. The goddesses' lithe frame was draped in silver, and Astraphelle saw in these moments why her father had fallen for Simyasha.

"Mother." Astraphelle bowed deeply before righting herself. The goddess smiled, her white eyes boring into Astraphelle's being.

"What troubles you?"

"Who said I was troubled?"

"A mother knows," she said, though her voice was more menacing than Astraphelle thought it ought to be.

"I'm not troubled, I come with a question."

"Then why stand so far from me?" Simyasha asked. She cocked her head to the side. "You're not still upset with me about the bite?"

Astraphelle pursed her lips.

"My word, Astraphelle, that was eight centuries ago, long before you landed yourself in that pit of your fathers. Certainly, that's more traumatic than what I've done."

Astraphelle clenched her fists, knowing any other outward sign of aggression would result in violence.

"It still feels fresh, Mother," Astraphelle replied.

Simyasha chuckled but kept her gaze on her daughter. Astraphelle chided herself to stay rooted in place even though every part of her body wanted to fight or flee. The goddess stopped laughing and a look of what Astraphelle could only read as jealousy passed over her face, gone just as soon as it appeared and replaced with pride.

"Your beauty is still lethal," she said. "Just like your mother."

Astraphelle was silent.

"Now, what is it you want to ask me?"

"There was a human who escaped—"

Simyasha scoffed. "The human, the human. Everyone is obsessed with her. Why?"

"She doesn't belong here."

Her mother slammed a hand on her throne, her white eyes darting to Astraphelle's face. "Do you think that I'm incompetent?"

"No."

"Do you think my judgment is unsound?"

Astraphelle grit her teeth.

"Of course not, goddess," she replied, emphasizing the word, knowing it would upset her mother.

"Then you must trust that I, Simyasha, goddess of fate, order, justice, arbiter of death, send souls to their correct place. That I do not make mistakes. That souls are sent to the exact place they are meant to go."

Astraphelle clasped her hands behind her back and paced before the goddess's throne. She could feel her eyes on her, milky white and unblinking. "You say that you're the goddess of order and justice. I've witnessed beings set up altars in your name and pray to you for justice for the wronged."

Simyasha shrugged and waved a hand at Astraphelle. "Yes, this is true. What's your point?"

"Wouldn't you say that a woman being sent to the very depths of Pandemonia for no reason is unjust?"

"What makes you think there was no reason?"

Astraphelle smiled. "I have learned of her story. I've seen the brand on her chest, the one drawn by her lover, who made a pact with Aleteo."

The goddess shrugged.

"I've killed Aleteo across the veil. He is truly dead and that means all his contracts are null and void."

Her mother simply blinked at her.

"She should be let go, as should all the souls—"

"No."

Anger radiated throughout Astraphelle's body, setting her stomach ablaze and making her temples ache.

"But—"

Her mother stood and closed the gap between them. Despite herself Astraphelle took a step back and winced. Her mother stopped and smiled wickedly at her.

"I've cast my judgement on every soul in this realm, your father's realm, and that of Enefri herself. My decisions are final. The girl stays in Pandemonia as do her companions and every other soul Aleteo damned. Good job, I suppose, of ridding the world of one your father's more pernicious demons."

Astraphelle grit her teeth and leveled a gaze at her mother. "She deserves better."

Her mother sucked her teeth and reached a hand out to stroke her face. "If it soothes you, Dante will end up in Pandemonia, and it'll happen sooner than you think. That girl will have the chance to exact her revenge on him for eternity, given how well-versed in torture she'll be by the time that man arrives. Just thinking of all the delicious ways she could annihilate him sends a delightful little chill up my spine."

The goddess giggled. Astraphelle grimaced and shrugged out of Simyasha's grip and stepped back.

"Well, I suppose that's settled then," Astraphelle said. "Justice will be served... eventually."

"Of course it will. What's more just in this case than retribution? Vengeance? Why deprive this woman of the chance to really settle the score between them by letting her return across the veil?"

Because such a delicate soul doesn't belong in Pandemonia, Astraphelle thought.

"If you're so concerned, why not ask your father for permission to torture him yourself once he pierces the veil?"

"I think that'd be quite boring."

The goddess chuckled and resumed her position on her throne.

"You've spent too much time with these creatures. You're getting soft on me, dear."

Astraphelle walked to the cave's entrance. The clouds looked like soft pillows, obscuring her view of Pandemonia. But the sun was rising. She had to return to the group. And though her mission had been to prevent them from reaching Purgatore, she wasn't so sure that she could.

"Don't worry, Mother," Astraphelle said. "I'm the daughter of death and damnation. I can assure you there is no softness in me."

Before the goddess could respond, Astraphelle leaped out of the cave and into the cold caress of the clouds.

CHAPTER 18

SAPPHIRA

THE BLIZZARD RAGED and Sapphira had never been so cold. She clung to Luquin for warmth, but his fur was so frozen and matted that it barely provided relief. She could feel him shivering against her as they sat on the beach waiting for their companions. Her toes were turning black. Her lips were numb, and Sapphira wondered what sort of monster or demon they'd find in this frigid temperature and what manner of torture they'd dispense. The thought sent a spike of fear through her chest. The wind stung her eyes and made them water, but the tears froze before they could even fall down her cheeks.

"I hate this," she said through gritted teeth.

"I must confess I never thought I'd long for the humidity of the fifth island," Luquin replied.

"This isn't fair. We shouldn't be here."

"Well, it was your plan to flee Pandemonia, so really this is all your fault."

She sighed and closed her eyes. "That's not what I meant."

"Oh."

"I mean, we shouldn't be in Pandemonia at all. I should be... in college. Getting accepted to my summer internship. You should've gotten to know your child, kept dancing, become some kind of Lord or something."

"I always fancied myself a Duke," he replied. "Luquin de Santigny, Duke of Normandy. Oh, the clothes I could have worn! How I would've spoiled my child!"

The werewolf chuckled and Sapphira smiled. Then he looked at her sheepishly.

"I like to think we would've had a girl."

"What would you have named her?"

Luquin smiled wistfully. "Désirée. I always loved that name. Though I don't know if Ophelia would've liked it."

"When you first arrived here, how did you handle the betrayal?"

The werewolf sucked in a breath and fixed Sapphira with a gaze. "I don't know that I ever fully have."

"But it's..." Sapphira's breath hitched. "It's not fair, you being here."

"Bijou, I was a willing participant in Ophelia's schemes."

"But she pinned it all on you. She got to keep living! She had your baby, ran away with another man, and didn't even have the decency to talk to you before you were executed."

His eyes were glassy as he adjusted the lacey sleeves of his shirt. "Yes. She lived. And at some point, she died. And I like to think she ended up in the worst of places, as terrible as that makes me sound."

"I don't think it makes you terrible. I think it means you've been hurt."

"I'd never felt such heartache as I did when the gendarme came for me, and she gave me up. She looked at me like she didn't care what happened to me. It tore me to pieces."

Sapphira's stomach clenched as she thought back to the way Dante had looked at her that night, not just when he was killing her but before when he'd cornered her about not saying she loved him, or that fight months before, when he picked a fight over his costumes.

"How can they do that?" she asked. "How can they go from treating you like you're their whole world to acting as if they never even cared?"

"It's maddening, I'll grant you that. I spent many a century picturing her face, wondering what I'd say to her if we ever met again. I scoured the island... that's how I knew how to leave it. I searched for her, and I didn't know whether I'd kill her or profess my love when I found her. But... being on this journey with you and Maxwell and, I guess even Astra, has made me feel something other the ennui for the first time since I landed. And all that pain, that aching for her, I feel it slipping away from me. And, oh, Enefri, do I feel lighter."

She turned away from him as a lump formed in her throat. She bit her lip against the tears that threatened to fall from her eyes.

"I wish I felt the same. But I can't let it go. He murdered me. Had the nerve to say it was so hard for him, that he had to sacrifice something to make his dreams come true. He even had the audacity to be annoyed with me for how long I was taking to die. And I'm here and he gets to keep living? He gets to thrive while I am..."

Her breath hitched and she stifled a sob. "He gets to thrive while I am damned? How is any of this fair?"

The werewolf pulled her closer to him. "A beautiful soul like you never deserved to be cast down here. None of this makes sense. But... it would be too easy to let those feelings consume you."

"What if I said my rage, the thought of crossing the veil and getting my revenge, is one of the only things keeping me going?"

He stroked her hair and sniffled. "I'd say it will only power you for so long. Because, in the end, escaping to get revenge is still centering him in your story. And I doubt that the revenge you seek will feel as sweet as how you're picturing it."

"He has to pay. He has to know how it feels to look your lover in the eye and know that everything they said about loving you was a lie."

She took a shuddering breath and then the dam broke. The tears she'd been fighting fell from her eyes in a deluge, freezing on her cheeks. But she didn't care. She let herself break down, the howling of the wind masking her sobs. All the while Luquin held her, rubbing a circle on her back and holding her tight against the cold.

Soon her nose became stuffed and all the devastation she felt was replaced by a numbness so acute it made her want to lay down in the snow and never move, never blink, or even breathe again for fear of the energy it would take. She pulled away from him and, wincing, wiped her nose on the sleeve of her jacket. The sight of her snot along with the blood and mud and bile that coated her once luxurious fur coat, the only truly expensive thing she owned, nearly made her break down again. She whimpered, sucked in a breath as she heard something howl.

Luquin's arms stiffened around her.

"What was that?"

"I don't know. But it's close."

"A werewolf?"

"Too big."

Her heartbeat quickened. Their visibility was low Maxwell and Astra hadn't returned and she was so distracted by her emotions that she hadn't been on her guard.

"Where are the others? They should be back by now. What if... what if whatever that is got to them?"

"Then let's pray to Enefri that they weren't mangled beyond repair," Luquin replied. She made to stand but he gripped her waist. "What're you doing?"

"We have to find them."

"No. It's not safe. They know we're here, if we leave now, we may never regroup."

"We can't just…"

"Yes, we can. They will return, bijou."

The howling again. She could see how on edge it put Luquin, and he stood, pulling her up with him.

"Better to stand if we should need to fight."

"Fuck," she said. She felt warm air against her knuckles as she did so and looked ahead of her. In the darkness she made out two glowing orbs, hovering before her. And then, teeth. Rows and rows of them, jutting out of a mouth as black as night.

"Luq—"

But she didn't have time to finish her sentence before those teeth clamped on to her hand. She screamed at the pain and tried to bring the blade down against the maw of whatever creature had bitten her. But she couldn't see it. Luquin grabbed her waist and pulled, but the creature's jaw was too strong.

"Your hand. We've got to sever it."

"What?"

" It'll grow back but it's the only way you'll get free."

"How do you suppose we do that? We don't have a weapon—"

Before she could finish her sentence, Luquin's jaws clamped around her forearm and tore at her flesh and bone. She wailed at the pain, and then suddenly her arm was gone, and blood spurted from the wound.

She stumbled backward and saw her arm disappear into the creature's maw.

"Run," Luquin whispered. He gave her a slight push with one hand and wiped her blood from his maw with the other. She stumbled in the snow, crying out as the mangled stub of her right arm connected with the cold snow, leaving a pool of blood in its wake.

She got to her feet as she heard another howl and took off running.

"I'm right behind you, bijou!" Luquin yelled.

She struggled through the waist-high snow as she ran. She could hear the footfalls of whatever chased her, and she could tell it was something large. It growled as it gained on them, and she could feel the heat of its breath behind her.

I'm so tired of running, she thought as her legs ached and her heart felt as though it would seize in her chest. Her lungs burned and the world before her began to tunnel at the edges. And still, the hand she'd lost throbbed, all her body heat rushing to the wound. She couldn't bear to see the sight of it, her missing hand, even if she knew it would grow back.

"We must head to the interior of the island," Luquin shouted. "Go left."

And she turned, sprinting and praying to the gods that they'd find a hiding spot, that they'd find their companions, that they'd get through this island unscathed.

Enefri give me strength, Damsuul fill my lungs with air even now as they seize, Itzeli grant me the fire to fight for my life.

Ahead of her, she thought she could see the craggy formation of a mountain. She ran toward it, not bothering to see if Luquin would keep pace with her. The creature behind her growled yet again and nipped at the edges of her jacket, ripping the bottom hem. She stumbled but kept running, pushing herself harder. She could now make out some of the rock formation, could make out a path stretching out before her.

Almost there.

"Bijou!" Luquin shouted, and at his encouragement she leapt up, hoping to clear a large bank of snow that sat before the rough edge of the mountain. She saw herself climbing the mountain in her mind's eye, going up, up, up all the way to safety. But when her feet connected with the other side of the snow bank the ground caved in beneath her.

"Luquin!" She screamed, throwing her hand into the air as she fell into the dark. Seconds later she gagged as she landed on wooden spikes. One pierced her throat, another her womb, and another, her gut. Sapphira choked spitting blood into the air before her. The air smelled dank, old, and unbreathed for centuries. Above her she could hear Luquin tussling with whatever creature had chased them and when she heard him scream in pain, a pang of regret shot through her. Her body relaxed and all the fight she'd had drained out of her, and she wondered whether she'd ever see Astra and Maxwell again.

Their faces were frozen in her mind's eye as her vision went black and death set in.

She came alive with a gasp, and then the pain set in. She moaned as she looked around, the memory of the spikes puncturing flesh and organ and bone surging back. She was thankful that she was no longer complete darkness; some light from above illuminated the small space around her. There was still time to escape. Above her she could hear fighting, shouts and bones breaking.

She couldn't scream with the spike buried in her throat and at that moment, Sapphira felt more alone than she had her entire time in Pandemonia.

She took a heaving breath and wiggled her fingers and noticed that her severed hand had regenerated. Her heart leapt at the sight of it.

How do I get out of here? She thought.

She tried to grip the spike in her hands to pull herself up. She cried out from the pain, her blood oozing down her chest. But she grit her teeth and lifted, and finally, just when she thought she would pass out, she felt the spike slide out of her throat. She gagged and began to pull herself off the other two spikes, eyes blurry with tears and snot and blood running into her mouth. By the time she'd freed herself, she was sweaty, and the light above her shifted.

She fell back against the cave wall, shaking and sobbing, pressing one hand to the gaping hole in her throat. Once the tears slowed, she tilted her head back to look up to the cave opening and dread settled in her belly. There were no grooves in the soil— how would she even be able to pull herself out?

Her brows knitted as she thought about her options. Then she turned to one of the spikes and pulled, gritting her teeth and leaning back to uproot it from the ground. Then she plunged it into the soil and pulled herself up. She continued like this, all the while hearing the fight occurring above her.

Sweat trickled down her back and beaded on her forehead. She slipped and nearly lost her grip on the spike until finally she righted herself. She planted the stick one last time and pulled and finally her hand touched the snow. She winced at the cold, at how numb and tired her arms were, and then pulled herself up again, this time coming completely out of the hole.

She stood just as a demon rounded on Astra, nearly severing her arm. Sapphira ran it through with the spike and turned toward the woman.

"Thanks," she said.

"Always," Sapphira replied.

Maxwell pressed a hand to Sapphira's shoulder.

"I'm glad you're alive," he said.

"Me too," Sapphira replied.

"What did I miss?" Sapphira asked.

"Hounds. And a minor demon horde," Maxwell said.

She looked at her companions, each of them looking worse for wear. But at least they were alive.

"We'd better go before more arrive," Luquin said as he wiped his forehead.

"How do we leave?"

"I've identified a path through the mountains," said Astra.

"Then let's make haste," Luquin said.

CHAPTER 19

ASTRAPHELLE

I T TOOK THEM three days to get off the island, all the while beating back the hounds who were responsible for Sapphira's death and dodging the souls whose eternal punishment it was to roll boulders up the side of the mountains and toss themselves off the cliffs, landing on spikes.

In Astraphelle's mind, it was one of her father's more poetic punishments — souls who tried to turn a blind eye and look the other way, were forced to watch their death rush toward them as they hurled themself off the cliffside.

The blizzard persisted, as did the intense cold. By the time they reached the beach, all her companions' limbs were numb and blackening, and even Astraphelle had started to feel the first dizzying effects of hypothermia.

I've gotten soft, she thought, as her teeth started to chatter.

She knitted her brows at this revelation and grit her teeth, trying to steal herself and remind herself of exactly who the fuck she was.

I'm the daughter of death and damnation. I'm a millennia-old demon, one of the first in creation. I do not get cold, I do not get weary, nor fall for humans.

At least not anymore, came another voice in her head and she swatted the space in front of her face as though the thought were a fly.

It was true that she had started to develop an affection for Sapphira. The woman was beautiful, had a heart bigger than any Astraphelle had ever seen, and what's more, she was brave. Not only had she saved Astraphelle multiple times, but she had managed to save herself. Astraphelle had tried to push her feelings away, reminding herself repeatedly of her mission—deliver the souls to her father on the bridge between realms.

That was all she had to do, and then she would be free.

But now, each time she saw the woman's warm brown eyes glinting in the sunlight, or the way that her nose scrunched slightly when she smiled, as she saw the way her hips swayed and the graceful way she walked, even through the snow. Astraphelle couldn't help the butterflies that flitted around her stomach. She couldn't help the fact that Sapphira's name had become a common refrain in her mind. She knew that this was bad news.

She knew that nothing could happen between them, not just because Sapphira was an errant soul, or because not delivering

Sapphira to her father meant Astraphelle's continued punishment. No, Astraphelle knew that they could never be together because of Astraphelle's lies.

She may have been a demon who delighted in violence and causing chaos, but even she knew that starting a relationship by lying about who you were was a recipe for disaster. Astraphelle's desire for Sapphira warred with her desire for freedom. She was so lost inside of her thoughts, she stumbled and nearly fell.

"Be careful," said Sapphira.

Astraphelle looked up to see Sapphira holding onto her arm, having just saved her from stepping into a cavern like the one Sapphira had pulled herself out of.

How caring, Astraphelle thought. *Damn it.*

"Thanks," she said quietly.

"Are you okay?"

Of course, she must have noticed Astraphelle's difference over the last couple of days. She was somebody who spent her whole life across the veil being hyper-aware of others as a result of her trauma.

The worried look on Sapphira's face sent a pang in her chest. Had anyone ever really worried about Astraphelle before?

Had her father?

Had her mother?

Her brother?

Of course not.

These were not creatures for whom worry was an actual emotion they could experience.

But it was clear that Sapphira cared for her, at least a little bit.

Shit.

"Yeah," Astraphelle swallowed. "I'm fine. I'm just ready to get to Purgatore."

"Tell me about it. I knew this journey would be a long one, but I'm so tired of dying and having to fight."

"You'd be having to fight regardless of if you were on this journey or stayed on the seventh island," said Maxwell, and Astraphelle felt irrationally angry at the thought of the vampire paying such close attention to their conversation.

"Yes," Sapphira said. "But that doesn't make it any less tiring."

Maxwell chuckled. "Oh, I forget how fragile you are sometimes, kitten. You're still so new to this."

Sapphira rolled her eyes, but Astraphelle could see the hint of the smile that played at the edges of her mouth.

She likes him too, Astraphelle reminded herself, envious that she had to share the woman's affection.

Soon they stood on the beach of the third island and stared across the brackish, eerily still waters.

"Gods," Luquin marveled. "We're almost there, just two more to go."

"Let us hope what awaits us is far less terrifying than what we've experienced so far," Maxwell said.

"Yes, I do too, but I find if I spend too much time thinking about it, I won't be able to put one foot in front of the other. So come on, vampire, we might as well just keep moving." Luquin said.

As if on cue, it began to rain. Astraphelle could feel all the hope her companions had slowly start to drain. It meant the path would be flooded for hours, keeping them on the third island for even longer. They turned to search for shelter and found a cave that appeared unoccupied. Maxwell and Luquin ventured in first, and once they made sure it was empty, gestured for Sapphira and Astraphelle to join them.

Maxwell sat just at the edge of the cave, staring out at the path. Luquin moved toward the rear of the cave, humming something melancholy. Sapphira slumped to the ground and removed her heels, wincing at her hypothermic feet.

Now it was Astraphelle's turn to check on Sapphira. "Are you okay?"

"I can't believe I made it this far. I didn't think I would, honestly. I wouldn't be here without you all."

Astraphelle swatted her arm. "Please, you would have made it by yourself just fine. You probably would have died several more times though, but you would have made it regardless."

"Nevertheless, I am thankful for you. I'm just glad we found you. Luquin and Maxwell are wonderful, but it is nice to not be the only woman on this journey."

Astraphelle laughed bitterly.

Woman, she thought. *Right.*

She could feel Sapphira's shoulder against hers and the contact sent a trill through her body.

"How long were you and Dante together?" Astraphelle asked.

Sapphira frowned. "Two years. We met at a cafe. I heard him sing and I loved that about him. I still do. You know, I always knew he'd be famous. I just wish he had more faith in himself to know that he could have gotten it on his own, but instead he—"

She sucked in a breath and looked down at the brand across her chest. Astraphelle followed her gaze there and clenched her fist, remembering the way it felt to dig her knives into Aleteo's gut.

"Do you plan to see him when you cross the veil?"

"I don't think I can cross the veil and not seek him out. I need to know why he did this."

"We talked about that already, right?" Astraphelle asked.

"Yes, but I have to know why he thought my life was worth so little that he could sacrifice it for himself."

"I don't think it's a matter of your life not being worth anything. I think it's a matter of him being an asshole."

"Yeah, you're probably right. But what he did to me, plus what Simyasha said to me when she cast me down... sometimes it feels like I don't... like my soul doesn't matter."

"The goddess can be harsh," Astraphelle said, speaking from

her own experience. "I remember when I met Simyasha. She was so beautiful. Radiant. All I wanted to do was serve her. I wanted her to love me. I know that's weird to say about a god, especially one such as her, but it's true. I wanted her love from the first moment I saw her, and I guess..."

She looked away.

"I guess that feeling's never gone away. And when I stood before her waiting for judgment, she bit me."

"She bit you?" Sapphira questioned.

"Yeah, the goddess likes her sacrifices, both across the veil and in her own realm. Did you notice, when you first landed, that pile of bones she collected in the corner?"

Sapphira nodded.

"Those are all the bones of the souls whose bodies she picks clean. They sacrifice themselves to her, and she tells them that if they do, they'll never be tormented, not like the other souls who go to Pandemonia. She doesn't tell them that she eats them alive, and they remain conscious the entire time."

Sapphira stared at her in wide-eyed fascination.

"Simyasha bit me in the shoulder, ripping tendons, cutting me to the bone. I was horrified, and sometimes that memory still plays in my brain, and I wondered why me? Why was I the soul she decided to bite? Why not—"

Astraphelle stopped herself before she could say, "Why not my brother?"

She couldn't invite any questions, though all the things she was telling Sapphira were true. She'd been so maddeningly desirous of her mother's love, wanting nothing more than to please her, that when she drew her close and said:

"I must talk to you, my daughter, I must tell you something," and then her teeth dug into Astraphelle's shoulder, the physical and emotional pain had been blinding.

"I'm so sorry."

Sapphira said, clutching Astraphelle's hand in hers. Her eyes looked impossibly brown, even in the dim light in the cave.

Gods, she's gorgeous, Astraphelle thought, and felt herself leaning in towards her, wanting to bask in her energy.

"It's okay. It happened so very long ago," she said.

"Yeah, but is it something you'll ever get over?"

Astraphelle pursed her lips. She didn't answer, but Sapphira knew the answer already, and so did she. You never get over the torment. You just learn to live with it.

"When we cross the veil, what will you do?"

Astraphelle chuckled. Of course, she hadn't thought about what she would do if she crossed the veil, because she wasn't planning to cross the veil, not in the same way that they were.

"I don't know," Astraphelle said. "It's been centuries since I was alive. Everyone I ever knew is dead. And this world, probably so different from how it was when I died, I wouldn't know where to start."

"Well, you can start with me. You can stay with me until you get on your feet. I bet Luquin and Maxwell will probably be there too."

"Thank you, Astraphelle said, leaning in even closer. "You care so deeply for people."

"I always wear my heart on my sleeve, everyone tells me that. It hasn't always served me well, but I don't know any different."

"You shouldn't change who you are to appease others. The right people are going to appreciate your gifts."

"Are you one of those right people?" Sapphira asked, smirking.

Against her better judgment, Astraphelle leaned in and pressed her lips against Sapphira's.

They were full, soft, and warm. Sapphira sighed and for the briefest second, Astraphelle felt the electricity between them, but then Sapphira pulled away.

"I'm sorry," Astraphelle said.

"It's okay, I've thought about doing that too, but the timing..." she trailed.

Astraphelle nodded. She looked out over the cave opening, and unsurprisingly, Maxwell's gaze had gone from staring out of the cave to looking directly at them, hurt etched across his face. When they made eye contact, she could see the envy within him before that nonchalant expression he so often wore slid back across his face.

Astraphelle stood, walking away from Sapphira towards the rear of the cave.

"What's wrong?" Sapphira asked.

"I just need to burn off some of this energy," Astraphelle lied.

In the rear, she saw Luquin dancing and noted how smooth and graceful his movements were despite his monstrous frame. He spun in a pirouette before landing and facing her. His eyes widened. Astraphelle held up her hands.

"Didn't mean to disturb. You danced beautifully, Astraphelle said.

"Thank you," Luquin replied.

"How long were you a dancer before you were killed?"

"Four years," he replied. "Well, four years in the ballet, a dancer for much longer than that. What did you do before you were cast down?" Luquin asked.

Astraphelle paused, scanning her brain for a plausible career that would make sense for her.

"I was a farmer, well... a farmer's daughter. I suppose I never thought about doing anything else, I never realized there could be anything else," she said, relaying the story of a soul she tempted back in the 1400s, but she was also surprised to know that the sentiment wasn't entirely foreign to her. She never had thought about being anything other than her father's daughter, her mother's daughter. A demon. A temptress. A princess.

"What do you think that you would have liked to do?" Luquin asked.

"I would have liked to have been a painter. It always fascinated me how somebody could take an image and render it so beautifully and so realistically that it looked as though you were looking at the real thing."

It was true, some of the best moments that she spent across the veil were visiting the museums and galleries.

"I'm sorry that you never got a chance to do that." Luquin looked at her with such care that Astraphelle had to look away. What is it about these souls and their insistence on being nice?

They stood together in companionable silence, Luquin still dancing and Astraphelle pacing back and forth, lost her thoughts.

"I saw you two kiss," Luquin said after several minutes. Astraphelle blinked up at him and grimaced. The werewolf chuckled.

"It's okay. It's obvious that she likes you."

"But Maxwell—"

"It's obvious that she likes him too, and he likes her. Of course, it's entirely possible to have affection for multiple people at once," he said as he smirked.

"Even while you were with Ophelia?"

She could see bringing up this woman had not been a good thing because Luquin stopped his dancing, Astraphelle didn't want to dampen his mood, so she stopped pacing and turned back toward the mouth of the cave.

"I'll let you continue your dance, I don't want to stop you," she said.

Luquin nodded. She walked past Sapphira, who had fallen asleep against the cave walls. She sat across from Maxwell who eyed her suspiciously. She lifted her hands in supplication.

"Don't worry, I'm not here to fight or argue," she said. "I just thought you could use a break from looking after everyone."

He sighed and rubbed his eyes with the palms of his hands.

"I take it you've always had to be the vigilant one," Astraphelle said.

Maxwell snorted. "Well, when you grow up in a house with a father and brothers who dispense beatings like candy, you always have to pay attention to your surroundings. But I suppose that's suited me well since I've been here, it's certainly not gotten me killed as much as others, I wish I could say that I've never died before, that shit hurts more than anything. Dying here hurts more than it did across the veil."

Astraphelle chuckled and nodded. "I think it's because up there it feels so final, but down here, you know that it can happen again, and you never know when."

Maxwell nodded. "I'm sorry I doubted you so."

She met his gaze and he looked at her with softened eyes. No longer did they regard her with suspicion, but a genuine apology. *Fuck, why are they making this so much harder?*

"You don't have to apologize, I was antagonizing you too."

"Yes, well, it will do us no good if we continue to do that for the rest of the journey, so... truce?" He held his hand out and she shook it. The coldness brought her back to reality.

Deliver the souls, get your freedom.

"So," she said, changing the subject. "I take it that what you did across the veil must have been horrific if it landed you on Maleficent."

He waved his hand. "Killed my father, brothers, and half his congregation in revenge for their treatment of me, and for them killing my lover."

"Before or after you were a vampire?"

"After. I don't think I would have had the strength to kill them all if I had been a human. Though I was always resourceful, maybe I could have managed it."

Astraphelle smiled. She had to admit he had a certain flair for violence that she had come to appreciate.

"Do you ever think about your family?" she asked.

"Sometimes. I often wonder if my father is down here, though with how religious he was, I wouldn't be surprised if Simyasha, in all her cruelty, sent him up to Caelum, where he absolutely does not belong."

Astraphelle snorted. She knew what it was like to be at the whim of her mother's decisions.

"Yes, the goddess does have a penchant for interpreting fate and justice in her own way."

"Truer words were never spoken."

They sat in silence, staring out at the bloody rain as it turned the snowy beach crimson.

She gave the vampire a sidelong glance. "Tell me, vampire, why is it you call Sapphira 'kitten'?"

Maxwell glanced at Sapphira, and adoration flashed in his eyes when he did so. "Because when she first landed here, I told her that she seemed as helpless as a kitten. Though I don't believe her to be so anymore... she is fierce, and I think if she didn't have us, she'd be able to make it to Purgatore even on her own."

"Hmm," Astraphelle replied. Maxwell crossed his arms and tilted his head.

"I know you share the same fondness I have for her," Maxwell stated.

Astraphelle didn't respond, only turned toward the beach and drew her knees to her chest.

"You know what she's been through," he began. "So, if I'm right, and you are fond of her, don't hurt her."

"I have no intention of—"

"I mean it," his voice hardened. "Do not hurt her. I can tell that she likes you."

"And she likes you, too," Astraphelle shot back.

"Yes. But whether she chooses me, or you, or only herself, it is her choice, and I will honor it. But if you hurt her..."

Maxwell leaned toward her, so his face was mere inches from hers. Astraphelle lifted a brow. "You know what I'm capable of."

This vampire was so bold, she had to respect it. "Yeah, I do. I may not be as capable as you, but I will issue you the same warning."

They looked at each other for a long while, assessing. Finally, Maxwell nodded and looked away from her and back towards the beach.

CHAPTER 20

SAPPHIRA

BURNING PYRES FILLED the second island as far as the eye could see, the flames filling the air with smoke and ash and the rancid smell of burning flesh. She covered her mouth and nose against the smell and kept her jacket on despite the heat.

The sun was rising, casting a sickly yellow glow about the air. As they weaved through the pyres the screams of the damned became like white noise to Sapphira, a fact that brought tears to her eyes. How she hated that this journey had desensitized her against the pain and agony of the souls she passed by, and she wondered if this aspect of her humanity was just suppressed or if she'd lost it completely. Yet another thing taken from her. Dread blossomed within her, tightening her chest and making her heartbeat so fast she thought it might burst. *What if we don't make it? What if he wins?*

Tears stung her eyes, and she wiped them away just as quickly. She didn't want her companions to see her crying, again, about Dante and the brand on her chest, about the horrors she'd never thought she'd be exposed to. *Stop, please stop.*

"Ophelia!"

The sound of Luquin's shouts pulled Sapphira out of her thoughts. She looked up just as the werewolf disappeared into the smoke ahead of them.

"Luquin, wait!" she yelled.

Maxwell groaned beside her. "What has that dumb wolf decided to do now?"

"Luquin!" Sapphira shouted. "We've got to find him!"

She chased after Luquin. The heat from the fires burning around her was so acute that it took her breath away and made running a near impossibility. Her eyes burned from the smoke, and she nearly gagged at the smell of burning flesh.

"Ophelia!"

Maxwell sped past her, leaving Sapphira and Astra to half-jog, half-walk through the maze to find their companion.

"He's over here!" he called, moments later. "Follow my voice!"

She and Astra looked at each other. Astra grabbed her hand, and they ran together toward the sound of Maxwell's shouts.

They emerged from a thick cloud of smoke to see Maxwell standing, arms crossed and scowling at the werewolf. Luquin stood before the pyre of another werewolf. Her russet fur was matted, and her snout was scared. Her green eyes glowed in the yellow light of the sunrise.

"Ophelia," he said. "After all of these centuries, I've found you!"

"Luquin, what are you doing here?"

"So, this is *the* Ophelia," Astra whispered to Sapphira, she glanced at the woman before turning back toward Luquin, her lips pursing.

"How long have you been here, when were you cast down?" Luquin asked.

"Not even a year after we parted."

"You mean after you left him?" Maxwell asked casually. Ophelia glanced at him but didn't respond.

"How?"

"Baring our child," she said. Sapphira could hear the sadness in her voice. "I didn't even get to hold her."

Luquin's head dipped. "I wish I could've been there to meet her, my little Désirée."

"So do I... but I didn't name her Désirée."

"What did you—"

"I named her Capucine. So much prettier, more unique than Désirée, Ophelia said.

Luquin's face fell.

"Prettier to whom?" Sapphira murmured. Astra chuckled.

"How is it possible that you're here? Have you been on this island all this time?"

"I was cast down to Rapaciousness."

She gasped.

"But I've escaped, with the help of my... friends," he pulled away from Ophelia and gestured toward them. She looked from Maxwell to Astra and finally to Sapphira. Her eyes narrowed.

"How? Why?"

"Why? Because I do not deserve such cruelty. None of us do. We mean to escape."

"Luquin," Maxwell warned.

"Escape? What madness are you speaking?"

"We're leaving, going back across the veil," Luquin looked around them at the pyres of burning souls. "Come with us!"

"Whoa... Luquin—" Sapphira began.

"Yeah, can we have a word over here, my *friend?*" Maxwell said.

"No," Luquin replied, his voice uncharacteristically firm. "She is coming with us."

He rounded the pyre Ophelia was tied to and leapt on the charred wood, his hands going to her bindings.

"I don't think that's a good idea," Sapphira said.

"So you're the only one who gets to invite people along?" he snapped.

"Well, it was her plan all along," Maxwell said, deadpan.

"I don't care! You protested when she insisted Astra join us—"

"So did you," Maxwell said.

"And then when she brought me into the fold and you threatened to murder me."

"I still might," Maxwell shrugged. "You lied to us, after all."

"No, you won't, vampire," Luquin growled. "You couldn't do it then and you won't be able to do it now. Besides, I've been nothing but a loyal companion to you all, and this is what I want and deserve, I will bring my lover with us."

"But she's not your lover. She left you to die, and—" Sapphira stopped as Astra squeezed her hand. She looked at the woman who glanced toward Luquin and his lover. When she followed her gaze, she saw the way Ophelia's eyes narrowed, teeth bared. Sapphira swallowed as fear rose within her.

"I know that you miss her, wolf. And I know that you love her, but instead of making this decision for her, why don't you ask her what she wants."

Sapphira looked at Maxwell, surprised by this moment of softness.

Luquin turned toward Ophelia. "If you come with us, we'll start fresh, we'll be alive again, we can—"

"No, I don't belong up there, and neither do you. Any of you. We made our mistakes, and we must deal with the results of our misdeeds."

"I committed no such misdeed," Sapphira said. "Nothing that made me deserve to be cast down to Maleficence and if Simyasha could make a mistake with me, imagine how many other people don't deserve to be where they're at."

Ophelia's head whipped toward her. "Well then, why have you not tried to free every single soul here? Or is it only a select few you've chosen that deserve to escape?"

"I, that's not..."

"It's awfully easy to assume that the goddess is incorrect, rather than accept our punishments."

Against her better judgment, Sapphira stepped towards her. Astra once again squeezed Sapphira's hand.

"We may not always understand why the goddess does what she does, but that doesn't mean we shouldn't respect her decisions, or abide by them."

"Ophelia, this is madness," Luquin said. "Nobody deserves this type of torture, no matter what they've done. Come with us, please. I want to live the life that was stolen from me."

"She's the reason it was stolen from you!" Sapphira shouted, breaking free of Astra's grip. "She's the one who started you stealing. She's the one who didn't say anything, letting you take the fall. And what's more, she hasn't even apologized. You deserve so much better."

Ophelia's harsh gaze bore into Sapphira's and even though she was terrified of what the werewolf could do to her, she took another step forward.

"You're wrong, Sapphira. Ophelia is the love of my life. And I've forgiven her." Luquin said. He freed Ophelia of her bindings and leapt down to the ground, holding a hand out to help her down. Ophelia leapt down and stood beside Luquin.

"You may say that but the way that you talked about her before, you sounded so wounded," Astra said.

"Why are you even talking right now, woman? No one cares about your opinion," Luquin snapped.

"Hey, stop it," Sapphira said. She closed the distance between herself and Luquin. Beside him, Ophelia growled beneath her breath. "Think about what she did to you. Think about the fact that she could do it again. Listen to her, she'd rather you burn than let you have a second chance at living."

"Stay with me. Please," Ophelia turned Luquin's face to look at hers. "We can be together again like we were always meant to be. I've always loved you."

Luquin frowned. "But then... why did you leave me?"

"You know that you don't belong up there. You belong here with me."

"Why did you leave me? Why did you not say something when the gendarme came for me?" he backed away, his head shaking.

"Luquin, please..."

"No, answer me, why?"

"Because you were boring me! It wasn't exciting anymore. You weren't exciting anymore."

Luquin gasped. Even Maxwell seemed to be hurt by what she said. They stood silent for a long while before Luquin composed himself and turned. Ophelia grabbed him.

"Everything that you've done, even though I may have had a hand in coaxing you, you did of your own free will. What makes you think that you deserve to live again when there are so many other people who, if what you say is correct, the goddess misplaced?"

Luquin's shoulders slumped.

"Don't listen to her," Sapphira said.

"Come on, werewolf," Maxwell said.

"Let's just keep going," Astra added.

"I..." he said.

"Please, my love," Ophelia begged. "I don't want to be alone anymore. Stay with me."

Luquin looked from her to Sapphira, and at that moment Sapphira knew exactly what he was feeling, could see the anxiety in his eyes. Even before she met Dante, there was always something that kept her awake at night, making her heart pound. As a teen, it was the conditions of the orphanage. As an adult, it was whether she and Persephone would have enough money for rent, food, and sundry. She knew that they were doing fine, but that didn't eliminate the constant anxiety she felt wondering not if but when the other shoe would drop. Then the string of boyfriends and girlfriends, all of whom made her feel anxious for one reason or another, until Dante. He'd been the worst of them all. And when she was in those moments, all she'd wanted was someone to see her, *really* see her, and help her out of the dark places she'd mentally settled into.

Sapphira took Luquin's hand.

"In a way, Ophelia is right. There are probably so many souls here who, just like us, do not deserve their fates. But if we don't get to the goddess and demand her to release us across the veil and show her and the great beast himself what's possible, nothing will ever change. And I know how hurt you are, I can see how much you want her love. But you don't deserve to burn to prove yourself worthy of it. I know that leaving somebody who you love behind will hurt. But what lies ahead of you is so much more. Please, don't stay in this darkness. Come with us and step into the light."

Luquin's eyes were glassy as Maxwell approached them and pressed a hand against Luquin's cheek.

"You and I have not always seen eye to eye. We have fought. We've wished each other ill. And yet, we've made it this far. I've grown to trust you. I've even grown to call you a friend. I don't want to make the rest of this journey without you. You deserve redemption in the same way," Maxwell paused. "In the same way that I deserve redemption."

Tears streamed down the werewolf's fur. And when he looked at Ophelia again, Sapphira could see the woman's face harden.

"I want a second chance. I deserve a second chance. I want to live again, and I wish, for once, what I wanted could be enough for us. But I must leave."

"No, you must stay with me!" Ophelia shouted and clawed at the fur at his neck when he turned away from her.

"You broke my heart when you left me without saying goodbye. And now here we are, and you haven't apologized. You call me boring. And the one thing I asked of you, before I was to be executed, was to name our daughter Désirée and you couldn't even do that. I never got to know our child, but I pray to the gods that she was beautiful and just and loving and all the things that you are not."

"You'll regret this," Ophelia said. "You don't belong up there. You belong here with me."

Luquin didn't reply, only continued holding Sapphira's hand, and walked away.

"Goodbye," he said.

They were quiet as they journeyed through the rest of the island. The sun had set and risen again in the time it took them to get to the beach. The path to the first and final island, reserved for the misdeed of Envy, stretched out before them, unsullied.

"One more island between us and the goddess," Sapphira said. They were the first words any of them had spoken since they left Ophelia. "I cannot believe how far we've come."

"Best to hold the celebration until we reach Purgatore, kitten,"

Maxwell said. "These islands have a habit of surprising us."

Sapphira sighed and began to cross the path, with the vampire on her left and Astra on her right. Behind them, Luquin trailed. She could feel his sadness and looked back at him.

"Leave him to his thoughts, he'll come around when he's ready," Maxwell said.

"When did you get so insightful?" Sapphira asked.

"It's always been a gift of mine. That and my impeccable wit," Maxwell said.

Sapphira scoffed. "Maybe to some."

Maxwell put his arm around Sapphira's waist and leaned into her. "Hopefully to you."

She felt her cheeks redden. "Perhaps."

She could feel his breath on her neck before he planted a kiss there, and the feeling of it sent electric shocks throughout her body. His arm around her waist felt so right, but then so had the kiss she shared with Astra. She looked at the woman now, who walked with perfect posture and confidence beside them. How was it possible for her to go from a broken heart to being infatuated with not one but two people?

As though sensing her tension he removed his arm from her waist but threaded his fingers with hers.

"How bad do you think the torture on this island will be?" she asked. "It's envy..."

"My father used to say that envy is the ultimate thief as it steals your joy and eventually your life. They said that Tartagnon punished the envious by torturing them from the inside out, like how envy does."

Sapphira's brows knitted as the first island came into view. It looked nothing like what she expected, nothing like any of the other islands. It looked like the wildflower meadow in Central Park—yellow daffodils blanketed the brilliant green grass. Th sky was cloudless. It was warm and windy, like the perfect spring day. They moved across the beach and into the interior of the island and when she saw the souls of the damned, she stifled a scream.

All around her, souls roamed the meadow in various states of decay. Their flesh was gone in spots, revealing muscle and sinew and in some cases, bone. Some of the souls lay on the ground, too ravaged to move. One of them, a vampire dressed as a Minuteman, was missing one leg and his arm seemed barely connected by bones ravaged with holes. Another was missing its nose, the skin near its mouth completely gone, revealing bloody, blackened gums. They all reached out toward Sapphira and her companions, as though touching them would make them whole again.

Tortured from the inside out. Sapphira gagged as the realization of this island's torture hit her. Whatever it was that caused it led to these souls rotting until they died.

"We need to hurry up," she said.

"What is causing their degradation?" Luquin marveled.

"I don't know, and I don't think we want to find out." Maxwell gripped Sapphira's hand tighter and began to run. The wind whipped Sapphira's hair, and a sweet smell carried in the air. She inhaled, and instantly her nose began to burn. The air. *It's the flowers and the wind, it's—*

"It's in the air!" Astra shouted, seemingly having come to the same realization as Sapphira "Cover your faces!"

Sapphira let Maxwell's hand go and held her coat before her face. The further inland they got the more it was packed with souls all reaching out to try to grab them, still envious.

She heard a strangled cry beside her and Sapphira stopped, eyes widening as she slowly turned. Maxwell had fallen to his knees and scratched his throat, the skin blistered and bubbling. They ran toward him and pulled him to his feet. He cried in agony as his ankle snapped.

"How is this happening to you so fast?" Sapphira asked. Luquin slid his arm under Maxwell's to stabilize him.

"This was always my most common misdeed. I was envious of my siblings, and now, I envy Astra," he breathed.

"Why?"

"Because she has your affection."

"And so do you," Sapphira said.

"I know, but the heart doesn't always see logic."

"We must leave, the longer we stay the worse he'll get. Look at what happens to those who've rotted fully," Astra said, pointing at a soul that was barely recognizable, little more than a heap of damaged bones, bits of skin, and brain matter. Sapphira screamed.

"We've got to carry him."

"Leave me, I'll only slow you down."

"No, we will not."

"Kitten, you must, you—"

Sapphira pressed her lips against his, wishing and hoping he could feel just how much she cared for him. Electricity shot through her whole body. She was breathless when she pulled away.

"C'mon, I'll take his legs, Luquin his arms. Cover your face with your free hand, and Astra," Sapphira turned toward the woman. "You lead the away."

Astra nodded. Luquin hoisted Maxwell's arms while Sapphira grabbed his legs, holding them delicately, because she could feel the blisters forming on his calves already. They fast walked across the island, the wind kicking up and the sickly-sweet smell of the daffodils and decaying flesh burned her nostrils and stung her eyes.

The afternoon sun cast the island in a blinding, clementine haze. Her legs ached, her head ached, her ears ached. Beneath her armpits blisters formed and when she looked back at Luquin she could see tufts of his fur had sloughed off.

"We're almost there!" Luquin called. In the distance, she could make out the high walls of the canyon that marked the start of Simyasha's territory. Her heart leaped at the sight.

"Please, hold on," she begged. She could feel her own body

succumbing to the blisters and the rot from the first island. Her legs felt like jelly and her teeth were loose, her stomach twisted and when she shifted her grip on Maxwell, she saw that two of her nails had fallen off.

They approached the beach as the sun began to set and started along the pathway, all the while Maxwell groaned in agony.

Almost there.

They were halfway across the path when Florizeel and his retinue appeared before them. Sapphira shrieked. The demon smiled.

"No," Astra said. "No. This won't happen."

"What's the matter, sister? Mad that I'm sticking to the script you should have been following all along?"

Sapphira knitted her brows. "What..."

And then before her eyes, the great beast, the god of Pandemonia, Tartagnon himself, landed before them, his robes setting around him like a cascade of clouds, a wicked smile on his beautiful face.

CHAPTER 21

TARTAGNON

H E WAS PACING again. Back and forth, back and forth, with no regard for time. It'd been weeks since he sent his daughter to capture the errant souls who thought they were brave enough to escape his domain. But he hadn't heard anything from her. At first, he'd been fine without a word. She was his deadliest weapon, after all. A knife sharpened over eons of training and torture, who was desperate to redeem herself after centuries in captivity. Tartagnon had thought this mission good for her. Perhaps it would reinvigorate her lust for Pandemonia and what it stood for — what its purpose was.

But then Simyasha had left her throne and come all the way to his island at the end of the realm. He'd been watching his demons put on a play in his honor, a typical evening for him, when she descended from the skylight, her silver robes shimmering around her. The demons in his retinue balked at the sight of her, and though they tried to scrape and scoff as she was used to, it didn't stop her from sinking her teeth into the neck of his most trusted and annoying advisor, Garwill.

When she was done, she tossed his dead body to the side and planted a bloody kiss on Tartagnon's lips. He licked the blood from her lips and pulled the goddess onto his lap, but not before lifting her dresses to expose the nakedness beneath. He nipped at her neck as she unzipped his trousers and pulled out his dick, stroking it though he was already rock hard. Wordlessly he gripped her ass and thrust himself into her. She grunted and he wound one hand around her neck and squeezed.

Hours later they pulled themselves apart from one another, bruised, clothes bloodied and torn, but their desires sated. Only then did Tartatgnon gesture for his demons to take their leave.

"What an excellent visit, lover," Tartagnon said.

Simyasha bristled. "I did not come here just to bounce on your dick."

"Oh?"

She rolled her eyes and strode to the other side of the throne room. "I've come to tell you that our daughter may be compromised."

He waved a hand at her.

"She killed your demon, Aleteo. Then she came to me and practically begged me to release that fresh young soul back across the veil."

Tartagnon scowled.

"Why would she do that?"

"Because the woman's lover sold her soul. Our daughter is convinced that she has no place in Pandemonia as a result."

Tartagnon chuckled. "She gets her sense of order from you."

"And she gets her disregard of authority from you. I told her to leave the woman be, that my decisions are fated, and final. But I'm not so sure she listened."

"You think she's helping them?"

Simyasha didn't reply. She simply shrugged and ascended into the sky, leaving him to his thoughts.

His pacing began the second she left. He was uncertain of how to handle the possibility of his own daughter aligning herself with the damned. He called another demon to him and bade him to bring him his son.

An hour later Florizeel's large body filled the doorway to his throne room.

"Father?" he said. Tartagnon bristled. He never wanted his progeny to call him that. It was far too caring for the type of relationship they had, yet the demon insisted on using the word anyway. Tartagnon stifled a frustrated sigh and plastered on a smile.

"Florizeel. Have you come across your sister of late?" he asked. He watched Florizeel's nostrils flare, his eyes narrow, and he admired the healthy hatred he had for Astraphelle.

"Yes. She was with those escaped souls. Masquerading as one of them. When me and my men tried to capture them, she tried to kill me."

"That sounds pretty typical of you two," Tartagnon said. "If I recall correctly, you spent the whole of the Middle Ages chasing each other around the world, butchering one another in the most extravagant of ways."

The ghost of a smile passed over Florizeel's face. "Yes, I remember the time when I broke every bone in her body and tossed her off a bridge into the Tigris."

"And I'm sure you remember when she disemboweled you, pulled your intestines out, and stuffed your belly with rats, sewing them inside of you and letting them eat their way out."

Florizeel grit his teeth but nodded. Tartagnon laughed heartily before resuming his serious demeanor.

"Do you think her efforts to kill you were just typical fare or do you think there was something more?"

"I think she's always been your favorite," Florizeel said.

"Yes, she has."

"And I think she is helping them, and I think you won't do a thing to stop her before she gets to Simyasha's domain," Florizeel said. He clenched his fists and leaned back ever so slightly, and Tartagnon was grateful that he had the good sense to be afraid.

He smiled, a plan coalescing in his mind. "Why would I stop her?"

"What—"

"Why would I stop her when I could just carry out our plan? Only, instead of simply capturing the souls, I could force her to reveal herself? Imagine the look on all their faces, when they realize how close they were, only for it all to be ripped from them at the last minute, because of her. How sweet it will be to see the helplessness on her face when she realizes that they will spend the rest of their eternity in the pit all because of her."

A twisted smile spread across Florizeel's face. Tartagnon walked over to his son and wrapped an arm around him. "Spread the word. Tell the demons on the remaining islands that the escaped souls are not to be touched. Tell them their lord means to handle them himself."

On the thirty-first day, just at sunset, Tartagnon received word that the group had passed through the first island. He leapt out of his throne with glee and bade the painter who sat drawing him in cubist fashion, to wait. Then he dressed in his most regal attire — a crown of bones dipped in gold, inlaid with rubies, robes of white opalescence, golden cuffs, collar, and belt. And at his side, a sword forged in the eighth century, by a blacksmith who made a deal with him in exchange for the secret of alchemy.

The god floated out of his palace and flew over his domain, delighting in the breeze that caressed his hair. He saw the damned being tortured, heard their screams, and smiled.

Then he saw them, the escapees and his daughter, moving across the final path between his domain and Simyasha's. The woman and a werewolf carried the rotting body of the vampire between them. His daughter led the way across the causeway, still glamoured, bone knife in hand. They were almost there. Mere steps away. He landed in front of Florizeel and a small group of demons. He was not surprised at the woman's beauty despite the blight that ravaged her. She had to have been to keep not one, but three creatures captivated by her enough that they'd willingly go through all Pandemonia to help her.

"No," Astraphelle growled when she saw him. Her anger sent a delicious thrill through his body. He smiled. And took a step forward.

"What's the matter, young one, did you think your change of plans would go unnoticed?"

"I'm just surprised it took you this long," she spat.

"I'm sure you are," he said. "Now, step aside. I've got to meet these souls brave enough to escape."

"Astra, what's he talking about?" Sapphira asked. Tartagnon quirked a brow.

"Astra? You haven't even given her your full name?"

Astraphelle's eyes widened briefly before narrowing. She always recovered gracefully.

"Time to drop the charade, my dear," he said. He snapped his fingers, removing the blight from the trio of souls. The vampire gasped and stood at attention.

"What did I miss?" he asked. And Tartagnon rolled his eyes. He snapped his fingers again, dropping Astraphelle's glamour. The woman gasped, the werewolf and vampire looking equally as horrified.

Astraphelle turned to her companions and reached out for them, but Sapphira stepped backward.

"What the fuck are you?" Sapphira asked.

"I think you know the answer to that, Sapphira," Astraphelle.

"Why are you here with us? Were you supposed to kill us?"

Astra shrugged. "That was one option."

"Option? You had options?"

"Yes. I could have killed you all when we first met and moved your bodies back to the seventh island. Or I could've captured you alive and bound you for eternity to some rock or at the top of a mountain, maybe even the bottom of that lake you found yourself in. But in the end I went with a more covert approach... at my lord's behest."

"You lied to us! Why? Was it some kind of twisted game for you?"

"Not for her." Tartagnon chuckled and moved to Sapphira's side. The woman squeaked and backed away from him. "For me. I don't often ask my children to get involved in such matters but, this extraordinary case called for extraordinary measures."

"Your father is the god of Pandemonia?" Luquin asked.

Astraphelle nodded once. The woman's knees buckled, and the vampire rushed to her side to steady her. Tartagnon watched curiously as he soothed her then handed her to the werewolf. When he turned toward them all, the ferocity he was used to seeing in a vampire returned. He ran quickly toward Astraphelle and grabbed her by the neck, lifting her off the ground.

"I knew it. I knew you couldn't be trusted."

Astraphelle didn't bother to move the vampire's hand away.

"My father sent me after you, I didn't realize you'd added Luquin to your party until I saw you all, but that didn't matter. I was to stop you from getting to Purgatore. But somewhere along the way, I realized I couldn't do what my father asked of me. I knew I had to help you."

"Why?" Sapphira asked. "Why did you help us?"

"Isn't it obvious? She's infatuated with you," Tartagnon said, mimicking the softness of Sapphira's voice.

Astraphelle pushed the vampire off her, knocking him into the werewolf and rounded on Tartagnon, punching him in the mouth. His head didn't snap back but the punch split his lower lip open. She held her hands up, knuckles tightening over her knives.

The god smiled his blood oozing down his chin. He'd hoped she still had the same violence in her. He'd wanted to use his sword after all. The sun set, plunging them into darkness. He snapped his fingers, brightening the moon.

"I want your new friends to see this," he said.

He brought his sword down in an arc, the metal clashing with her daggers. The sound was beautiful, as was the way his daughter fought. She pivoted correctly when he thrust at her, jumping back when he tried it again. She slashed at him, tearing his robes. He chuckled and thrust again, the blade glancing off her thigh.

She grunted but twirled and slashed again, this time connecting with the side of his neck.

"You're still an amazing fighter," Tartagnon said.

"And you're still a showboating whore," Astraphelle barked.

"Careful, now, your feet are awfully close to the edge," he said, bringing his sword to her feet and making her jump to the side. Her balance was unsteady, and she teetered on the edge.

"Why do you care if these souls go free? They are three of billions," Astraphelle said.

"Yes, but they belong to me now," Tartagnon said. "They are mine to torture, mine to move about at will."

"Are you talking about them, or me too?"

She swiped at him again, catching his side. He stumbled and laughed. He switched hands and turned, catching her off guard. He walked toward her, pushing her back and making her turn so her back was not to her friends but the abyss. Then he issued his parting blow, driving the blade into her chest, just below her rib cage. Astraphelle cried out, spitting blood onto his robes. He lifted her off the ground, the movement driving the blade further into her stomach.

"You've always belonged to me. It's a shame you forgot that," he said. He pushed her off the blade with his free hand and into the abyss.

"No!" Sapphira screamed. "No!"

Despite Astraphelle's betrayal, she still seemed to care for her. She ran to the edge of the path where Astraphelle had disappeared under the water. Tartagnon caught her in his arms.

"Be careful. You don't belong in there, not yet anyway."

"You monster, how could you do that to your own daughter?"

"I am the god of Pandemonia, sweet thing. There is nothing I can't do." He grabbed the woman and tossed her over his shoulder. "Florizeel, grab these two. It's time to show them all how transcendent torture can be."

PART 3: KNOCK ON WOOD

CHAPTER 22

ASTRAPHELLE

THE LAST THING Astraphelle saw before plunging into the heat of the abyss was her father's satisfied grin and beside him, Sapphira, wailing, horror etched across her features. Then she went under, sinking into thick, viscous water. Though her demon eyes could always see in the darkness, she still struggled to make sense of what was around her.

It wasn't nothingness. She could make out the faintest movement, could hear fins as they displaced the water around them. But when she reached out there was nothing there but thick, brackish water that made her skin blister from its heat and smelled like sulphur. Then there was her stomach, slit open and bleeding out, the water stinging the wound. Normally it wouldn't take long for her to heal but this was the abyss. The ancient place from which all things came from, even the gods. The thing which they were all terrified to return to. Would she heal in the same quickness as she always did? Would she even heal at all? And beyond that, would she be able to escape the abyss's clutches?

She pumped her arms, desperate to reach the surface as the water seeped into her lungs and infiltrated her wound. But it was like trying to swim through honey. She closed her eyes and envisioned Sapphira, trying to teleport to the woman. But it seemed her powers didn't work here.

You must get to them, she told herself.

She knew firsthand the kind of cruelty her father could dole out if given the chance. Even before she'd spent time in the pit, she'd run afoul of his temper after he got in the middle of her constant fighting with Florizeel. She'd stabbed him, and he'd returned the gesture in kind. Only it hadn't felt like the kind she'd get from her brother or any other demon. This had burned. It ached down to her very essence. What's worse is that it hadn't been the only one. The god of the damned stabbed and slashed at her face, her stomach, her very eyeballs. He'd rendered her into a pulp, little more than a scrape of cells and a brain stem. She vaguely remembered the pain she'd been in, how he'd taken her mangled bag of bones and placed her in a warded circle which kept her from healing. She stayed in that fractured state, in that excruciating agony, for what felt like a millennium.

Finally, he released her. He tenderly carried her back to her quarters and put her to bed. It took weeks for her body to coalesce.

Longer still for her to regain her strength. After that, she'd tried to lay low, even though every bone in her body tensed at the sound of his voice, and the fact that when she allowed her mind to wander, she often fantasized about butchering him until his flesh was liquid and his bones were dust. This fantasy was one of the only things that kept her going while she was in the pit.

Astraphelle's fingertips grazed the surface of the water as she wondered why she'd become so eager to defy him now. What was so special about the group she'd saved that it made her forget the pain of that incident and the promise she made to herself never to put herself in that position again.

Was it lust? She asked herself. And she knew that was certainly part of it. Their kiss had set her body aflame. Sapphira was gorgeous, the kind of beauty Astraphelle would have been drawn to no matter the lifetime. But it was more than that. It was the woman's heart that she was also drawn to, however wounded it was. Despite all she'd been through she still trusted. Nurtured. Saved. And that saving had included Astraphelle, more than once.

Astraphelle contemplated her infatuation, Sapphira's face in her mind's eye, when she saw a light shining before her. It swung slowly in the brackish water, as though trying to hypnotize her. The closer it got the more she could see what creature it belonged to. It was a long, eel-like creature with a tentacle that arced over its head and ended in a lamp, which it swung to and fro. Its eyes were the same black as the water around it, mouth a cluster of needle-sharp teeth.

She gripped her daggers in one hand and tried to swim away with the other. She shook her head, momentarily dizzy from the blood loss. The setback allowed the creature to move closer to her, and when she swiped at it with her daggers, an electric charge shooting up the length of her spine. Astraphelle's mouth flew open, the sticky, hot liquid flowing down her throat. She'd been so focused on this creature's gimmick and its ugly, goggle eyes that she hadn't realized that it had slithered around her body, waiting for the right time to shock her. Then came another shock, this one harsher, pulsating through her nervous system. Its skin was spongy and where it touched her body it shocked her. Her body floated backward as her limbs grew numb.

No, no, no.

She struggled to push herself out of its grip, to send energy to her arms and hope that at least one could work long enough to bury her daggers into its skin. But her hands couldn't grip. All she could do was lay limply as the creature swam through the abyss, taking her down, down, down to the depths. They passed a castle, a large chunk of it caved in on itself. There was the wreckage of a boat, and Astraphelle thought about those sailors who'd tried to cross the abyss all those millennia ago.

Her head lolled to the side and made eye contact with a creature whose eyes were bigger than her whole body. A mass of tentacles stretched below it, and clutched in one of them was the skeleton of a fairy. Again, she tried to move, and a tingling pain shot through her. The creature tightened its grip on her, sending more shockwaves through her body. Black dots danced in front of her eyes as they plunged deeper into darkness. The water's increasing pressure made it hard to breathe. For only the second time in her long life, Astraphelle prayed to the creator.

Enefri be my strength.

CHAPTER 23

SAPPHIRA

SAPPHIRA HAD BEEN dragged away from Purgatore, away from salvation, by the god of the damned himself. But they hadn't left the way she'd arrived. Instead of trekking through each island they flew, and within minutes they were moving beyond the seven islands themselves. They'd come to one obscured by clouds, with a black sand beach and a palace whose spires stretched above the atmosphere. An arid, dizzying heat settled over this island. The air smelled like burning wood.

They were taken through the palace to a grand ballroom with black marble floors and pillars. Ropes dangled from the crumbling ceiling and each of the pillars. In one corner stood a bronze bull statue, in the other a large wooden wheel with ropes dangling from the sides. There was a large vat filled with silver on the right side of the room and across from it, a spiked metal plate big enough to be a bed, with an identical plate hanging above it. Knives and swords and other weapons Sapphira didn't recognize hung on a wall.

I'm in the torture chamber of the god of the damned.

Tartagnon tossed her to the floor, and Florizeel wasted no time rushing toward her. She backed away, ready to punch him, but then he rounded her and ripped her jacket off.

"Hey!"

Her hands covered her breasts just as the demon cut her panties off with a dagger. He picked up her and tossed her over his shoulder.

"Let go of me, asshole!" She cried. She punched his back and when he dropped her between the two pillars and grabbed one of her hands to tie, she bit him, her teeth sinking into Florizeel's hand. The demon backhanded her and stars danced before her vision. Her head pounded as the demon bound her wrists and ankles between the pillars. Naked and spread eagle, Sapphira shivered despite the heat.

She watched helplessly as her companions struggled against their torture. Florizeel threw Maxwell onto the spiked metal plate as though he were little more than a doll. The spikes pierced his skin upon contact. He cried out as the demon slammed another metal plate onto his body. Sapphira flinched at the sound of the vampire's bones crunching, his blood squelching as it spurted from his wounds.

Luquin was tied to metal beam that jutted from the ceiling. His body dangled over a vat of silver and with the pull of the end of the rope Florizeel lowered him into the vat, just enough to cover his legs and torso. Tears sprang into Sapphira's eyes as she watched the metal bubble. Luquin howled as he was lowered into the vat. His fur was singed off his snout and the front of his body. His clothes glittered.

Standing before Sapphira was the god of the damned, beautiful and terrifying in his bloody white robe. It hung open to expose his chest, black pants, and a crown of bones dipped in gold and studded with rubies. His skin and cinnamon-colored beard gleamed in the light of the sunset. It was his eyes that Sapphira was drawn to the most. They were like ink spills glowing, pulsating, drawing her in to their depths. He strode around her, his fingertips never leaving her body. She hated how her body responded to him; the way her stomach fluttered, chest tightened, clit throbbed. She was altogether turned on and afraid of Tartagnon. But as he stopped before her, his other hand on her body, she realized that these feelings were nothing new. Dante had often inspired that bodily dissonance in her. So had Maxwell. And Astraphelle.

I guess I have a type, she thought bitterly.

The god stepped back and held out a hand. A knife materialized in his hand. Sapphira's heart thumped in her chest.

"I suppose I should've been the one to do this from the beginning," he smirked. She hadn't seen him move but she felt the blade slash across her shoulder. She dug her nails into her palms as he slashed across her areola. Then her inner thigh. Her forearm. Her navel. She fought the urge to scream or to beg. She'd screamed and begged for her life already more times than she cared to count. She wasn't about to do it again.

Soon her body was covered in cuts. Some were deep enough that she could see her skin flapping open. Others barely broke her skin, blood beading up to the surface like fat, red pearls. Tartagnon dropped the knife and a copper bowl appeared in his hand. He dug his fingers into .it then lifted his hands, showing the coarse salt that cascaded back into the bowl.

"You're a lot more resilient than then Florizeel gave you credit for. But I am a selfish god, Sapphira, and I want to hear you scream."

"Fuck you," she spat.

"And I'm sure you'd enjoy that," Tartagnon bit his lip and smirked. "Maybe once you've been properly tortured, I'll have my guards bring you to my bed."

He traced her lips with his finger.

"I won't apologize for trying to escape," She replied.

"You should never apologize for trying to survive. And you'll need that fight once you return to the seventh island."

Her stomach dropped. "You know I don't belong here."

"Oh, sweet thing. You see that's where you're wrong."

He pressed his salt-covered fingers into the cut on her neck, then licked the wound. She bit her tongue as she looked into his eyes, endless and searching.

"How? Simyasha is the goddess of order," she whimpered as he applied salt to a cut on her pubic bone, his fingers tracing the salt down to a deep cut on her inner thigh. "How could she think it's orderly for a soul to be in a place they don't belong?"

"But she is also the goddess of fate and the arbiter of death." More salt, this time across her areolas, the long slash across her stomach, the one severing her Achilles tendon on her left foot. The tears fell freely but still she didn't beg. Still, she didn't scream. "Have you not considered that this your fate?"

"No. It can't be. If Dante hadn't bartered my soul then—"

Tartagnon pressed a kiss against her lips, taking her breath away. He pulled away and ran a hand over her body. "Perhaps your fate may have been different. Maybe in another life you would've gotten married, had kids, grown old. Enefri might have welcomed you to Caelum with open arms. But you chose him, he killed you, and so here you are," he said, leaning down to whisper in her ear. "With me. Forever."

He plunged his hand into the wound in her stomach. The salt on stung and the pressure from his hand made her feel as though she were being ripped apart. He twisted his wrist, and Sapphira finally screamed.

"There it is," he said, tilting his head back and closing his eyes as if in ecstasy. He pulled his hand out as quickly as he thrust it in, her kidney in his palm. Blood splattered out of her wound onto the floor.

"I ... don't ... belong here," she sputtered. Sweat beaded on her forehead, plastering her hair to her head. Her body stung from the inside out and all she wanted to do was crawl into her own skin and rub out the salt. He gave her one last pitying look before walking over to Luquin. Tartagnon grabbed the rope from Florizeel and released it, plunging Luquin completely into the vat of silver. The werewolf thrashed wildly before settling. The silver bubbled then stilled, and Luquin didn't emerge.

"You see the thing about Pandemonia is, there are many souls who may not have belonged here. But Simyasha sends them here all the same. Perhaps it's because, like you, their souls were bartered. Or, perhaps, some of them pissed the goddess off enough she decided to teach them a lesson. Whatever the reason, eventually they all become the things they said they'd never be — killers, defilers, sinful creatures for all eternity."

Tartagnon sat casually on top of the metallic plate that had crushed Maxwell, his weight driving the plates further into the vampire's corpse as he brought her kidney to his lips and began to lick the blood off as thought it were an ice cream cone.

"With the things you've done in your short time here — killing demons, that poor fairy, almost slitting the throat of your own companion in retribution — and with the things you imagine yourself doing to the souls here, to me, Simyasha, Dante... perhaps this *is* the place you belong. Perhaps the only place you've ever belonged."

Tartagnon slid off the metal plate and walked out of the room, tossing her kidney over his shoulder, leaving Luquin and Maxwell dead, and Sapphira in agony.

Sapphira didn't know how much time had passed since she'd been in Tartagnon's palace. All she knew was that since he left the moon had risen then set, replaced by the sun again and again. But no demon had come to torture her or to untie her. She was unaccustomed to silence, to stillness, since she'd been in Pandemonia. Each day had been a new nightmare, but it had also been filled with noise and activity.

Both Luquin and Maxwell were still dead. She was still tied between the pillars. Her wrists and ankles had grown numb, turned red then an angry shade of purple. Her wounds had yet to heal, keeping her in a not quite alive but not quite dead state. As she looked around the room and noticed the symbols carved into the floor in a circle around them, she wondered if that was this room's purpose. Maybe this was where souls truly died in Pandemonia.

The thought sent a spike of fear through her belly. What would it mean to truly be dead here? To never make it across the veil? She thought of her sister and their friends. She wondered how much time had passed. Did they still dance on Saturday nights? Had Persephone graduated, published books, become a professor like she dreamed? Had she married a man who looked like Billy Dee Williams like she wanted? Had Frankie found success as a poet and did Claudia get to open her own club?

Her chest grew tight as she thought of them all living on without her. All the things she'd miss. Then she thought of the night she died and about Dante and her stomach twisted in on itself. She loved him. Truly loved him. She hadn't known whether that love was meant to be for forever or for just a short time. Even now after she knew what he'd done, after she sifted through some of their worst moments in her mind's eye, there was a part of her that still loved him.

She pictured him now, sitting on the windowsill of his apartment, one leg dangling out onto the fire escape. She imagined him taking a long drag from a spliff and staring out at the city. Would she be on his mind like he was on hers? Would he have cried at least after he was chased away by that couple?

Her thoughts twisted and she saw him on stage, his name in neon lights behind him and his band, as he crooned into the mic just like Johnny Mathis. She saw him dressed in a lush velvet suit, new platforms, a brand-new chain at his neck. He would be on all the talk shows, singing and interviewing about his big break. About how his star had risen meteorically overnight, and would he dare say it was because of her? Would the world even notice she was gone?

I guess he wins, she thought. *After everything he put me through, Dante still wins in the end.*

And it was that thought, not the stinging ache of her wounds nor the seemingly endless deaths of her companions that finally broke her. She began to scream, shouting the names of her companions, of the demons who'd captured her. Of Astraphelle, who was no doubt completely lost to the abyss. Thinking of her made her knees buckle. Her mind raced.

I'm a failure.

Dante wins.

Nothing I do matters.

Nothing I did ever mattered.

He never loved me.

I am unlovable.

The others are better off without me.

Maybe I do belong here.

As though listening in to her thoughts, Tartagnon appeared before her, a smile on his beautiful face and a blade in his hands.

"I knew you'd see things my way, eventually," he said. He planted a kiss on her forehead and walked to the far side of the room. He bent down and pressed the blade to the floor, breaking the sigil. He didn't look back as he walked away.

She screamed deep into the night, until her vocal cords were raw. But her cries went unnoticed.

The sun rose and set once again, and all Sapphira could do was cry.

She still felt the echoes of her wounds though they were now healed. But she was still bound. Luquin had reanimated but he was barely able to keep his head above the caustic liquid, and when his eyes met hers, Sapphira saw the fear within his golden eyes before he lost his ability to stay afloat. He sputtered and gagged as the liquid entered his throat.

"Help..." he trailed before sliding back down into the silver. She watched the liquid go still and she cried all over again. She lost count of how many times Luquin fought against the silver but lost every time. And it was the same with Maxwell.

When he'd first reanimated, he'd tried to push at the plate that held him down, but the movement only pressed the spikes beneath him further into his body. She watched as blood spewed from his mouth, winced as his bones eventually shattered and his skin burst open like overripe fruit. His gaze found her, and he looked at her pleadingly.

"Kitten, please..." he breathed.

An hour later he reanimated, and again the metal crushed him. The sun rose and set and all Sapphira could do was watch her companions die.

"Tartagnon, please," she rasped. "I'll bear the punishment of our escape, just spare them."

Her cries went unanswered for another day. By then her voice was gone and she stared, unfocused, at the marble floor.

Over and over again, Luquin and Maxwell reanimated, they spared what little breath they had to plead for help, and again they died. Memories played like a kaleidoscope in her mind's eye, flashes of her granny, of the kids at their orphanage and all their bullying. Of Persephone, Frankie, and Claudia all on the dance floor with her, their bodies warm as they pressed against her. Of her past girlfriends and boyfriends. Of Dante. Her mouth hung open and drool fell from her lips. She was so drawn into her brain that she didn't hear the footsteps approaching her. She didn't feel the gruff demon as it grabbed the back of her head in one hand and lifted her head. Her eyes were unfocused and blurry, but she still knew that it was Florizeel standing before her and pressing a blade to her throat.

"The lord of the damned wanted me to tell you he hears your cries. He's asked me to put you out of your misery, for now."

She didn't respond as the blade slid effortlessly across her throat. Her blood was warm as it cascaded down her chest and as she stopped feeling the pain in her limbs and joints, a sense of peace washed over her.

CHAPTER 24

TARTAGNON

H E SCRAPED ONE of the binding sigils on the ballroom floor, breaking its power. Now it no longer held the souls in a suspended state, preventing them from healing, but he didn't remove their bonds. He wanted them whole, not free, so he ignored the woman's cries and shouts as he walked down the hall to his throne room where Simyasha awaited. She stared at him as she sat with her legs across one arm.

"What a pleasure it is to see you, god of the damned," Simyasha crooned. Tartagnon was altogether irritated and aroused at the sight of her sitting on his throne, silver dress gauzy and see through.

"You can skip the niceties, lover. We've got business to discuss," he said. Her playful expression soured as she stood. Tartagnon replaced her on his throne.

"Yes, I heard your... employees talking. Other souls are following the woman's lead and trying to escape," she said lightly.

He bared his teeth at her, hating the false nonchalance in her voice, as though this wasn't also her problem, too.

"Yes. They're trying to leave my realm and come for yours. So, before you gloat, you may want to decide how you'll handle that, seeing as how you're the goddess of justice, after all."

She clenched her jaw, menace written across her features before she smiled.

"Where is our daughter?" she asked. Her tone was light, but he could tell there was an undercurrent of care within it.

She'd never been particularly nurturing or concerned with Astraphelle's wellbeing. After all, there were several times where she'd tried to kill the demon. And hadn't she been the one to tell him of Astraphelle's deception? He almost wanted to laugh at her sudden hint of maternal concern.

"Probably being fed on by some wretched creature at the bottom of the abyss, I imagine," Tartagnon replied. The goddess's eyes widened momentarily before returning to normal.

"You cast her into the abyss..."

He shrugged. It hadn't been his first choice. He'd hoped that she'd turn on the wannabe escapees the second he and Florizeel appeared, but when she stepped in front of the woman, he knew he had no choice. She'd made up her mind and once she did there was no changing it,

Tartagnon knew.

"Yes. She decided that her loyalty was to these souls, rather than her true purpose."

Simyasha shook her head bitterly. "I wish you would've just taken her captive and tortured her. She deserved punishment but to be permanently lost? Cast back to the place from whence we came? I cannot think of a worse fate."

Tartagnon snorted. "Oh, I highly doubt that, *fate-bringer*."

She swiped at his face with her nails, drawing blood.

"Is that it?"

"Where are the souls?"

"They're in the ballroom. Their torture has only just begun. I can show you if you'd like."

She waved a hand at him. "No. I've not come here to watch. I've come to take them with me."

He quirked a brow. "Why?"

"Because it's my due," she said. "They defied my decision with their escape attempt. It's only right that I should be the one to punish them."

He rolled his eyes and stood, his feet fitting into the grooves of the path he'd paced for millennia.

"They attempted to escape my domain, not yours."

"Actually, they attempted to escape both of our domains. And, as you reminded me when we first spoke about these pitiful creatures,

I'm the goddess of order and it's not very orderly for them to defy me."

Tartagnon grit his teeth, anger blooming in his chest at her throwing his words back in his face. All of this made his ass itch. He wanted nothing more than for things to return to normal. He wanted to pose for his portraits and paintings as the sound of the tortured echoed through the palace, soothing him. But no. These souls, *these souls* were taking up too much time and energy.

He fixed the goddess with a glare. "These souls tried to escape Pandemonia. If they were simply stuck in Purgatore do you really think they'd have tried what they did? Think they would've tired if their only punishment was to scrape and bow to the goddess, and bare the possibility of being eaten by her? No, lover. It is my domain they feared. My torture, my demons, my lands. Not yours."

"Yes, it was also your demons who failed to stop them," Simyasha replied, staring down at her nails. "I sent that girl to the seventh island, the very bowels of this cesspit and she, a mere human, was able to escape. She, along with her vampire and werewolf, escaped a kaimong, bested your general, and somehow, she was able to beguile our daughter, who should have been drooling to comply with your orders after the years she spent in the pit. So, if we're honest with each other here, should you and your retinue really be the ones responsible for carrying out their punishment?"

Tartagnon launched himself at her, pushing her against the stone wall. He heard the cracking sound of her skull connecting with the stone, breaking a little because of it, and he smiled. The goddess growled and pushed him away, leaving a bloody reminder of her injury on the stone. She tackled him and pinned him, her razor-sharp nails digging into his flesh.

He grabbed her arms and twisted, breaking the bones of her forearm. He tossed her to the side as she shrieked, but her eyes were wild with anger. Her bones healed quickly, just as his cuts had, and when she got to her feet, they circled each other.

"Quite bold of you to cast such harsh judgment on me in my own domain," he snarled.

"Don't act like you're wounded by this, you sent our daughter to her death," she spat. She punched him in the stomach, the blow doubling him double over. He returned the gesture in kind, hitting her in her clavicle hard enough to break bone.

"You think you can beat me? The one who invented brutality? The one whose torture casts fear in the heart of every creature in this realm and the next?"

She kicked him square between his legs. The pain made his eyes water and knees buckle but he didn't crumble. He wouldn't give her the satisfaction.

"The only thing you invented was how to be mediocre at your job and still keep it for eons," Simyasha said. She closed the gap between them once again, punching him in the throat, his belly, and his shoulder. He fell to the ground. "Those souls are mine, and I'll be taking them back to Purgatore where they'll receive proper judgement."

He clutched his already-healed throat and waited for her to walk away. When her back was to him, he stood and tackled her, slamming her head into the marble floor with such force the tiles cracked. After a while she went limp, and he sighed. He bent forward and whispered into her ear, knowing she was already healing from his assault on her:

"Your bravado is sexy but falsely applied here, lover. These souls belong to me, and I alone get to decide what happens now. But because I'm feeling magnanimous, I suppose I'll let you watch."

Tartagnon stood. The goddess moaned beneath him.

He looked down at his bloody tunic and rolled his eyes. "Forgive me, but I must change. Your blood is staining my favorite tunic."

He walked out of the throne room, his steps heavy against the marble floor.

CHAPTER 25

ASTRAPHELLE

THE EEL SLITHERED through the water, clutching Astraphelle in its tail. Her limbs dangled limply in the creature's grasp, and her head lolled to the side. All she could do was stare through the darkness of the abyss as it grew more oppressive the further down they went. The heat increased, as did the sulphur smell. She wished she could do something to shield herself from how cloying it was.

The creature plunged down quickly, moving through a hole in the ground. Astraphelle's hands scraped against the tunnel, the pressure so thick that her eyes bulged, and her head felt like it would burst open at any second. There was a light ahead, and as they swam out of the tunnel they surfaced into a small cavern. Astraphelle struggled to breathe through the searing pain in her lungs.

The creature uncoiled its tail and Astraphelle floated down to the sandy beach outside of the water. Her muscles twitched and spasmed as her body slowly started to regain feeling. Above her the creature's lamp bobbed to and fro as it stared down at her. Its jaw hung open, its pupils dilated, readying itself for the kill. Astraphelle knew she didn't have time to let her body regain feeling. She had to act, or she would die her true death. She willed her hands to close around the metal bar in her palms, further securing her knives, and when the creature dove toward her, she brought her left hand across her body and tore into its face.

It shimmed back but lunged for her again, and this time she dug her knives into the length of its tail. The connection sent a shockwave throughout her body and Astraphelle bit down hard on her tongue. The coppery taste of blood filled her mouth, but she ignored it, instead gliding her daggers along the creature's side, opening its body in ragged gashes. With her other hand she slashed at the cartilage that connected the creature's lamp to its head. The lamp came loose, and she was surprised to find that it kept some of its luminescence. The creature made one last attempt to bite her before she buried her knives into its gullet. It twitched then dropped to the ground in an unceremonious heap. Astraphelle groaned.

She lay on the beach staring up at stalactites, willing her breath to steady and the pain in her chest from her father's sword to dissipate. *I've got to get out of here*, she thought. She had to get back to the palace and save Sapphira, Maxwell, and Luquin, even if that meant dying at her father's hands in the process. She rolled to her side and looked down at the tunnel she'd just emerged from. Then she stood, her legs still tingly, and took a deep breath before jumping in, using the creature's lamp to illuminate her path.

Her eyes widened at the pressure of the tunnel, the ragged rocks digging into her skin and drawing blood as she emerged swam through it. The sulphur smell stung her nose as she swam, her barely healed lungs protesting from the lack of oxygen. The water was hot enough to make her skin blister. She swam past the tentacled creature, moving slowly, hoping that it would ignore her. But she could feel its large eyes on her even as she passed it. Her heart leapt when she saw light from above and realized she was nearing the surface. *Almost there*, she soothed. *Almost there.*

A tentacle wrapped around her ankle, jerking her downward. Her mouth flapped open, sucking in the brackish water before she quickly closed it. She whirled around in time to see the open jaws of the tentacled creature, its teeth spiraling down its throat in rows. The lamp dropped from her hands. She could barely see now, but that didn't stop her from reaching out wildly and lashing out at the creature with her blades.

She connected with a tentacle. It let her ankle go and she tried to swim up again, the tips of her knives barely piercing the surface. The creature lashed out at her with another tentacle and Astraphelle swam to the side, narrowly missing its reach. Then another tentacle reached out, grabbing Astraphelle and clutching her other leg. Teeth dug into her leg and she screamed, letting in more water. Another tentacle, this one wrapping around her waist, the end of it digging into her wound. She hacked at it but just as she removed the grip of one tentacle, another jutted out toward her. She looked down, eyes widening at the sight of the dozens more tentacles splayed out around the creature. There was no way she'd be able to kill it before she ran out of air. Already her brain was starting to feel fuzzy, vision curling in at the surface. Her arms and legs were moving slower.

The creature brought her down closer to its giant maw, wide open to receive her. At first, its teeth seemed never-ending, but then she looked closer. There, in the center of the top row of teeth, at the roof of its mouth, was a small area devoid of teeth — its soft palate. Astraphelle smiled wickedly as a plan to defeat this beast formed in her mind. She rallied her strength and flipped upside down so that her arms would be the first part to go into its mouth. Then, just as it tried to clamp its jaws down on her body, she used all her strength and pierced its soft palate with both sets of daggers. It let her go but she kept carving, pushing in through the creature's head as it thrashed.

Her daggers connected with some type of organ which leaked hot, putrid-smelling fluid onto her as she pressed forward, through what must have been its stomach and lungs, until she finally reached the large throbbing vessels of its heart. She cocked her arm back and grunted as she plunged her daggers into the organ. It beat feverishly before slowing. By now she was completely submerged into the head of the tentacled creature and losing oxygen fast. She hacked and slashed at its body, its brain, its flesh until she burst through the top of its head. She pressed herself through the opening and wasted no time swimming out of it and toward the surface, her body and lungs aching.

Astraphelle's daggers breached the water first, then her hands, and finally her torso emerged. She gulped down a breath and blinked rapidly, willing the dots that moved before her eyes to stop.

When she was finally able to focus, Astraphelle noticed that she was only a few yards away from the causeway. She swam toward it, urging her tired limbs to work. When she reached it, Astraphelle groaned pressed her knives into the dirt road and slowly, painfully, slid out of the abyss. She rolled onto her back and stared at the pale pink sunrise and tried to slow her breath. She lifted her hands to examine her skin, wincing at the popped blisters and bite marks.

The sun had risen by the time she stood and examined her surroundings. She was on the causeway between the fourth and fifth islands. She closed her eyes and teleported herself to one of the various streams on the fifth island, ignoring the stunned looks and murmurs of the demons dispensing their torture. No doubt they'd heard about what her father had done to her. She slipped into the water, letting it wash away the gore and soothe her peeling skin. She paid special attention to her braids, and when she emerged minutes later, she felt powerful once again. Then she closed her eyes and pictured Sapphira in her mind's eye and in the next moment she stood before her father's palace. The guards outside were visibly shaken at her presence.

"Thought you'd seen the last of me?" she quipped.

"How is it possible that you escaped? No demon's ever done that before," questioned one of the guards.

"I'm not just any demon. I'm *the* demon," she said stepping forward. The guards stepped in front of the door to block her way. "What is this?"

"We know you conspired with the souls to escape. You're a traitor."

Astraphelle rolled her eyes and sighed. "I really don't think you want to do this."

One of the demons lashed out at her, landing a punch across her jaw and snapping her head to the side. Anger stoked in her belly, and the orange network of her veins pulsed in pleasure. Unlike the creatures she'd fought in the abyss, this was one fight she was absolutely sure she'd win. She returned the gesture, her daggers slicing the demon across his cheek, then ducked to slice his thigh, bringing him to his knees. The other demon ran toward her, spear out and ready to skewer her, but she leapt back and sliced the weapon in half. The edge of the spear dropped to the ground limply. The guard looked down, then back up at her, but his moment of distraction gave her the opening she needed. She raked her daggers across his throat, digging so deep her blades brushed his spine as she pulled out.

The demon fell to the ground and Astraphelle turned back to

the first demon, just as his mace connected with her sternum. She stumbled backward, grunting, but after what she'd been through the wound barely registered. She thrust her palm up against his chin, snapping his spine. His body thudded against the ground. Astraphelle sighed as she stood.

"That felt right," she said. Then she walked toward the doors to the palace and pushed them open.

CHAPTER 26

SAPPHIRA

S HE FELT THE sun's warmth on her eyelids. She opened her eyes, dread filling her as she realized she was still in Pandemonia. But she was no longer bound. She wiggled her fingers and toes, moving them along the floor next to her. They brushed against a hand and Sapphira turned to see Maxwell there beside her, alive, his eyes on her. He smiled.

"Kitten, you're awake," he whispered. Her heart swelled as she entwined her fingers with his. There was a low grunt to her right and Sapphira turned. Luquin was there, his eyes blinking as thought trying to focus.

"Luquin," she whispered.

His head whipped toward her. "Bijou! I thought we'd all gone to our true deaths."

"So did I," she said. She looked down at her body, expecting to see her nakedness but instead she was back in her jumpsuit and fur coat, which had seemingly been stitched back together and cleaned. She marveled at how pristine her clothes were, as though she hadn't spent her time trudging through mud and getting it all slick with blood. She ran a hand through her hair and realized it, too, had been cleaned.

As though reading her mind, a deep voice said: "You've been cleaned to properly stand before the gods. Now rise to your feet."

Sapphira searched for the source of that statement as she and her companions stood. They were in a great throne room. Marble pillars stretched up as far as her eyes could see. There was no ceiling, and the warm breeze of this island carried the scent of burning wood and cardamom. Thousands of demons stood in the room, eyeing her menacingly.

The god of the damned sat before them on his marble throne, one leg casually tossed over the side, his head resting on his palm. Simyasha stood at his side, arms crossed, an irritated look on her face as she locked eyes with Sapphira.

"Welcome back to Pandemonia, sweet thing," Tartagnon drawled. Sapphira fought the urge to grimace. She kept her face blank, but fear unfurled in her chest as she looked at the gods. She was surprised to see the goddess in Tartagnon's domain — she hadn't thought she'd had the time nor the desire to leave Purgatore and come all the way to the ends of the realm. But seeing her straighten, eyes never leaving

Sapphira, made Sapphira's stomach clench. The punishment they'd face was to be even more sever than she expected it seemed. Why else would Simyasha come to watch?

"Whatever you're going to do, just do it already," Sapphira said. She hated the way her voice trembled but the last few days in the ballroom had robbed her of her determination. All she wanted now was for it to be over.

"Kitten, no," Maxwell whispered. He wrapped his arm around her. Then he turned his attention to the rest of the room. "I think what she means is, she doesn't belong here."

The goddess scoffed. "Is that right, leech?"

Maxwell's lips drew into a thin line, but his eyes were bright with fury.

"Wolf, did this woman not try to slit your throat?"

Luquin took a measured breath. He looked at Sapphira and took her hand, squeezing it reassuringly before he turned back to the goddess. "She did, in retribution. It was my actions that lead to her death by a kaimong. It was only right that she repay me, but she did not kill me, as I'm sure you know."

"She may not have murdered you, but nevertheless, she meant you harm. And she may not have killed you, but there were others whose lives she didn't hesitate to end," Simyasha trailed. She clucked her tongue. "There's just no reason to send her back across the veil."

"She murdered those demons, those creatures, in defense! For survival!" Luquin exclaimed.

"You cast her down to the seventh island, the worst place in this realm and the next and what did you expect? That she wouldn't pick up a blade and defend herself?" Maxwell added. "You call yourself the goddess of order and fate yet you act as though an innocent soul has any place in Pandemonia. With creatures like them."

He pointed at Florizeel and the demons that surrounded him. Many of the snarled at him, some gripped their weapons. Florizeel only smiled.

"And creatures like us," he finished, gesturing between himself and Luquin. Simyasha stepped toward Maxwell, a murderous look on her face, but Tartagnon grabbed her hand and brought her back to his side.

"Well, it's obvious what this woman's pets seem to think," he said. The comment drew titters of laughter throughout the crowd. "But you've been quiet, Sapphira Gail. I'm interested to hear what you think. Given everything you've done, gone through, and discovered — the torture, watching your companions die again and again at my hands knowing that they're only here because of you, the revelation that your lover sold your soul for his own gains — do you still think there's a place for you across the veil? Do you still want freedom?"

Sapphira felt the weight of all the eyes in the room upon her and though she held Maxwell and Luquin's hands, she still felt unsteady on her feet as though the ground would rise up to meet her at any moment. Tartagnon's words stung. She'd been so sure that she hadn't belonged in this place for so long. The thought of her virtue and the eventual taste of freedom had propelled her through much of their journey. But when she took stock of all the things she'd done, that she'd thought about doing, she wasn't so sure of her virtue anymore.

And when she thought about how she'd gotten here, the fact that Dante had bartered her soul to ensure his success with no regard for her life or her afterlife, it made her chest tighten. She'd trusted the wrong man. Let him into her bed, her mind, her heart. And he'd betrayed her.

She thought about Astraphelle, how even though the demon had fought her own father for them in the end, she'd still deceived them. She hadn't been able to see through her ruse, hadn't listened to Maxwell and Luquin when they warned her, just as she hadn't listened to Persephone or her friends when they warned her about Dante.

There was a part of her that wondered if she'd known who they were all along and allowed their behavior, their betrayal. And what did that make her, then? An accomplice? Why hadn't she left Dante sooner? Why hadn't she called Astraphelle out before they stood before Tartagnon on the path of the damned? How could she ever trust her own judgement again when she'd allowed herself to be manipulated and abused and lied to?

If she made it back across the veil, would she truly be free? Free from the pain of what her misjudgment had caused her? She knew

Dante bartered her soul for his music career. How could she be free when his songs would be on the radio or in the disco or on Soul Train? His face and voice would be everywhere, a visceral reminder of how he'd succeeded.

And the weight of all of this, of the ways in which she failed herself and those around her collapsed in on her. Dante won. Not because he was smarter or cleverer. But because she wasn't smart or clever enough. Because when it came to loving herself, Sapphira had always been so many steps behind.

She lifted her head, ready to surrender to the gods, when she saw Astraphelle creeping up the side of Tartagnon's throne. The demon nodded at Sapphira, and before Sapphira could do anything else she drove her daggers into Tartagnon's back.

The god growled at this and spun around on her, slapping Astraphelle across the face and sending her flying across the room. She scrambled to her feet and got back into a fighting stance just as Tartagnon rounded on her once again.

"We've got a fight to continue, father," Astraphelle spat.

"That we do. I'm surprised you managed to claw your way out of the abyss," Tartagnon said. He punched her, his blow glancing off her temple. She slashed his arm, blood blooming across his obsidian skin. All the demons and even Simyasha shifted toward the fight between the god of the damned and his daughter.

"Now's our chance," Maxwell whispered. He nodded toward the

door. Sapphira shook her head. The vampire scowled.

"We can leave this place."

"Yes, bijou, we must go," Luquin replied.

"No, I can't... I don't deserve..." she stammered. She was weary. She wanted to fall to her knees from the sheer weight of the sadness that racked her body.

Luquin and Maxwell stepped before her.

Maxwell cupped Sapphira's face in his hands. "Oh, kitten, can't you see? You deserve the world."

"But I failed," she replied, her voice breaking. "I'm the reason we're here, the reason why they'll probably toss us all into the abyss. We'll be forgotten. And he wins."

Luquin pressed a kiss to her temple as Maxwell wiped away the tear that slid down her cheek with his thumb.

"Bijou, they only way he wins, the only way they win, is if we stop trying."

"You've fought so hard, please don't give up on yourself now, because we're not," Maxwell soothed.

"We never will," Luquin said. "Even if it takes us centuries, we will carry you to the other side."

Sapphira looked down, unable to keep Luquin's gaze. How could they be so kind to her when they'd never be in this position if it hadn't been for her.

"But all I've done is endanger you."

Maxwell scoffed. "You've given us more than you could ever imagine. You've given us a reason to hope."

Her heart swelled at Maxwell's words. Hope. It was something she hadn't had in a while, not even when she first hatched her plan to leave. She'd been determined. She'd been ambitious. And when she realized what Dante had done, she'd been spiteful. But in all the time she'd been in Pandemonia, she'd never been hopeful. But now, as she looked up at her companions, her friends, both of them looking at her with such care in their eyes, she wondered how it was possible that they could feel hopeful. And she wondered if she could feel it, too.

"Come, let us try for freedom once more," Luquin said. He gripped her hand. Maxwell gripped the other. And without looking back at the fight, the trio ran.

They made it out of the throne room and into the long foyer. The palace doors hung open and as she stared out at the black sand beach glinting in the sunlight, she picked up the pace. Maybe they'd make it this time. They were out the door and running toward the causeway that stretched between the palace and the seventh island. She let go of their hands and pumped her arms, her will to live returning with every step. *I'm going to make it. I'm going to—*

A whip cracked in the distance, and she fell face first onto the sand. She had no time to reach for purchase, before she was pulled back into the palace. She screamed and watched as her companions were struck down with arrows as they tried to run back toward her. They still looked at her with such tenderness it made her heart ache. Once their bodies hit the ground they were rounded up and brought back into the throne room, where Astraphelle lay at the foot of Tartagnon's throne, wrists and legs bound. He resumed his position on it and rested one foot on her head and the other on her waist. The demon looked at Sapphira sorrowfully. Sapphira nodded at her, hoping she understood that she bore her no ill will. Sapphira was pulled to her feet, and a tall, grey-skinned demon gripped her arm, rooting her in place.

"It seems you haven't been broken of that will to escape after all," Tartagnon said. "I was certain you'd resigned yourself to your fate."

Sapphira held her head high. "My fate belongs to me, no one else."

The statement drew murmurs from the crowd.

"That's a pretty sentiment, Sapphira," Simyasha said. "But it's false. Your fate belongs to me."

"Then how did you not see any of this coming, goddess?"

Her statement drew murmurs from the demons in the room. Even Tartagnon quirked a brow, the hint of a smile playing on his lips.

"You say my fate was yours to decide, so that must mean it was you who knew that I... that we," Sapphira began, gesturing to Maxwell and Luquin's bodies as they bled out on the marble floor. "Would do all of this. We're simply acting out the fate chosen for us by you."

Simyasha opened her mouth then closed it just as fast.

"Well done, Sapphira," Tartagnon said after a long silence. He leaned forward, resting his elbows on his knees. "It's been ages since

I've seen the goddess this flustered. It's got me feeling magnanimous. You want out of Pandemonia and right now I'm inclined to help you. I wish to see the fight in you once more. If you can defeat the demon of my choosing, then you can leave here."

She considered this. There was no way there wasn't a string attached. This was the god of Pandemonia, after all. But what other choice did she have? She couldn't give up now, not when there was a chance she could leave.

"If I say yes, will you allow my friends to come with me?"

He chuckled. "Ever the caring soul."

Sapphira stared at the god, not backing down as his ember eyes bore into hers. He looked down at the vampire and the werewolf, who groaned, barely alive. Tartagnon heaved a deep sigh.

"Fine. If you win, they can leave with you as well."

"And they'll be alive?"

"What kind of monster do you take me for?"

"The kind that would kill his own daughter for sport," Sapphira replied. "When I win, Maxwell, Luquin, and I will leave this palace *and* your realm alive."

He looked at Simyasha, who stood seething. Then he tossed a blade made of bone down to Sapphira and said: "you have my word."

Sapphira nodded and bent down to pick up the sword. It felt light in her hands, familiar, and she laughed momentarily at just how acclimated she'd gotten to the feel of a blade in her hands.

"I choose Florizeel."

Her stomach dropped. She hadn't expected him to choose such a strong opponent, but then of course he had. He wasn't going back on his word, but he knew that Sapphira stood virtually no chance against his general. His son.

Florizeel smirked and strutted toward her, an axe in his large hand. Sapphira looked down at Astraphelle. The demon's eyes were fiery as she watched her brother circle Sapphira.

"It seems we keep coming back to this, Sapphira," Florizeel said.

Sapphira grimaced at the sound of her name in his mouth. She let out a slow breath. *I can do this*, she thought. She didn't make the first move. She wasn't preternaturally strong like her friends, nor was she particularly muscular. She was short, lithe, capable of staying on her feet and dancing for hours but in all her life she'd never really fought until she died and came to Pandemonia. She circled the demon, hoping to catch him off guard when he lashed out at her.

Florizeel seemed to be following the same tactic, though she could see his impatience creeping up.

Finally, he slashed at her, and she brought her blade up just in time to avoid a blow that would have split her head open. He struck again and she dodged, but the third time the axe struck her shoulder, and she almost dropped the blade.

"Shit," she cried. Florizeel laughed.

"Not too late to give up."

"Fuck you," Sapphira spat. She lunged at him, the blade glancing off his chest. He smiled and with his free hand punched her in the throat. She gripped her blade but brought her other hand to her throat, the wind knocked out of her. He seized the opportunity and brought the axe across her forearm. She screeched as the axe split her flesh, rendering her right arm completely useless.

Sapphira backed up, creating some distance between them.

"You know, I've been chasing you this whole time. I can't figure out how a small, insignificant thing like you has caused such ruckus," he snarled. He landed another blow, splitting her thigh down to the bone. She fell, her knees connecting with the floor and sending pain shooting through her thighs. Her body felt like she was on fire and blood flowed out of her wound in crimson rivulets. She dodged a blow from Florizeel, but she could feel her strength waning. She tried to stand but her legs were unsteady.

"I mean look at you, you can't even fight. You can't defend yourself."

The derision in his voice reminded her of Dante. The way his voice dripped with judgement, always so smug. Florizeel wore a pitiable expression on his face that made her think of every time she'd spoken to Dante and he'd thought she was wrong. The more she spoke the more his smugness grew, the antsier he got for her to stop talking so he could tell her all the ways in which she had said or done something incorrect.

"I'm just trying to prevent you from looking stupid," Dante had said once.

Sapphira's vision went red as she thought of all the times he'd made her feel less than. It'd happened so often that she started to believe the things he'd tell her, that she had poor judgement, that she didn't deserve to leave this place. In that moment it became clear to her that it had been Dante's voice in her head all along telling her that she didn't deserve freedom. That she didn't deserve to win. Sapphira grit her teeth against the pain and stood, rounding on the demon.

She spat in his face and he shook his head, bewildered by the action. It was the opening she needed, and she dug the blade into his stomach. He doubled over as she pulled the blade out. He landed a blow on her clavicle, sending pain shooting down her arm and making her drop the blade. She screamed as she rammed into him, tackling him, and when he lifted his arm to hit her with the axe she leaned down and bit his forearm, and pulled, taking some of his skin and veins with her. She spat the mixture into his face and grabbed the axe that lay limp in his arm. He bucked his hips, trying to remove her but she clamped her thighs tight and brought the axe down across his face.

She hit him again, splitting the bridge of his nose. And again, splitting his jaw, the bones cracking open and his tongue splitting in a sickening squelch. Florizeel's warm blood coating her arms, her chest, her face. His body slackened beneath her and all she could hear was the sound of her heartbeat reverberating in her ears and the axe splitting the demon's bones. Her head spun and she screamed as she brought the axe down one last time across Florizeel's chest, breaking his ribs open with a crunch, before falling to her side. She locked eyes with Astraphelle, who lay there smiling. The room was silent, but she felt the weight of thousands of eyes upon her, no doubt wondering how she'd been able to take Florizeel down. She looked up at Tartagnon, who stared down at Florizeel with a cold detachment.

"Such a disappointment my children have become," he said. He stepped over Astraphelle and strode toward Sapphira. He grabbed her hand and pulled her to her feet. "You have earned you and your friends the right to leave Pandemonia."

Relief washed over her like a tide and she bit her lip to stave off the tears. She nodded and let the god's hand go. She searched the room for her companions, who were being released from the grip of two demons the same size as Florizeel. They ran toward her, and she closed the distance between them. Maxwell was the first to wrap her in his arms. He planted a kiss on her cheek and Sapphira smiled. Luquin wrapped his furry arms around them both. When they pulled apart, she turned back to the god.

"Do we have your protection? None shall harm us on our journey?" she asked.

"I promise you no harm shall come to you or your friends as you leave my realm," he replied.

"But you best get going. The causeway will be flooding soon, and I might just change my mind."

He walked back to Astraphelle and yanked her to her feet. Alarm shot through Sapphira.

"But wait — what about Astraphelle? She shouldn't be punished because of us. We—"

The god scoffed. "You ask a lot of a god, Sapphira Gail. If I were you, I'd be happy with the victories I'd already secured. My daughter and I have unfinished business."

"Sapphira, please. Just go. I'll be ok," Astraphelle said. Sapphira's stomach sank at the thought of leaving her there at the mercy of her father. Even though she'd deceived them all, she didn't deserve what Tartagnon no doubt had in store for her.

"C'mon, kitten, we've got to go," Maxwell said.

"Thank you," Sapphira said to Astraphelle. The demon's mouth twitched but she didn't smile, only nodded once. Sapphira turned toward the door and with her hands entwined with Maxwell and Luquin's once again, walked out of the palace of the damned.

CHAPTER 27

ASTRAPHELLE

S HE WATCHED SAPPHIRA, Maxwell, and Luquin run out of the throne room, a single tear falling from her eyes. Part of her wished she was running with them, feeling the wind whip through her amber braids as she sprinted with the trio toward Purgatore. Toward freedom. But as she was carted out of the throne room by her father's retinue, she realized bitterly that their fate was never meant to be shared, not with her. She realized now that she was always meant for this, to succumb to the torturous whims of her father as he punished her for whatever wrong he felt she committed. Whatever would happen to her next, Astraphelle thought, at least she'd been able to help them. At least she'd been able to see Sapphira one last time.

They walked down the long corridor to the ballroom. In the

corner sat a vat of silver tinted crimson, no doubt the blood of the werewolf. On the other side, metal plates coated in blood and in the center four strands of ropes tied between two pillars. Dread spread from her stomach throughout her limbs as she looked at the sigils on the floor. This was the same place she'd been tortured by her father before, when he'd rendered her into almost nothingness. She'd heard his deliberate footsteps trailing her all the way to their destination. He was quiet, and so was she. Astraphelle had no reason to talk to him. She wasn't about to beg him for forgiveness or for her life. That same numbness that she'd had before she met Sapphira returned, and she was grateful for it.

The demons positioned her in the center of the ballroom and retreated, but not before retracing a sigil that had been broken. Her father closed the distance between them and she clenched her fists at her side and tilted her chin up, daring him to strike.

"I wish I could count the ways in which you've disappointed me, Astraphelle," Tartagnon said. "But I'm afraid they're too numerous to list."

She kept her expression blank and remained silent. He glared at her, and the longer she kept quiet the more his anger radiated off him. She smiled inwardly.

"It's a pity we've come to this. You always were my favorite."

She clenched her fists even tighter, her nails burying themselves into her palms.

"If you torture your favorites into bloody pieces, I'd hate to think what you do to your enemies," she replied.

"You won't have to think much longer, young one. Because you're about to find out."

He lifted his hands and a set of chains slithered down from the ceiling. Hooks jutted out from the ends, and Astraphelle ran a hand over one dispassionately.

"I see you mean to gouge my skin and hang me. Such a novice type of torture for one so accomplished in the art," Astraphelle replied.

The god glowered before picking her up and flipping her upside down, her braids dusting the marble floor. He thrust her onto the hooks with such force that they pierced her hip bones and poked through the other side of her body. She grit her teeth and pressed her lips into a thin line but kept her vacant stare locked onto her father's.

He leaned forward, whispering into her ear. "You have no idea the suffering that I've prepared for you."

He spread his arms out and more hooked chains glided toward him.

"Trying to keep up a brave face I see," he said as he dug one of the hooks into her left wrist. "No matter, that'll change soon."

He hooked the next one into the crook of her right elbow. The next, into the space between her second and third rib. She grunted at the pain, and a smirk played at the edge of his lips.

"Such a pity, this route you've taken. Had you done what I asked you could be rewarded by now. I'd have given you anything you wanted — a pack of hounds, allowance to spend some years across the veil tempting souls again, your brother's head on a platter. But somehow you were corrupted."

Astraphelle gagged when he dug the next chain onto the side of her neck. Her blood spilled down her throat and out of her mouth, seeping down her face and into her eyes.

"It seems some of that woman's humanity took root in you. I suppose you get that from your mother, being as she's not of this realm and still has the capacity for compassion." Tartagnon buried two more hooks into her, one in each breast. Astraphelle's body throbbed. "Then again, perhaps it was your years across the veil that made you vulnerable. After all, your mother does intend to kill those souls once they reach her realm."

Panic spread throughout Astraphelle's body. *Simyasha intended to kill them?*

"But you gave your word no harm would come to them," she rasped, struggling to speak with the hook digging into her throat.

"I gave them my word no harm would come to them in Pandemonia. Once they reach Purgatore, they are no longer in my realm or under my protection," he said. He knelt down before her and pulled the hook out of her throat before burying it into her left eye. She gasped at the pain, heard her own eyeball pop open and leak onto her forehead. "I can no more control your mother than Xira can control Umiyo's tides."

Astraphelle seethed at the mention of the other gods and at her father's revelation. She knew her parents were conniving. To a certain extent, so was she. But the thought of the three of them making it through Pandemonia again only to be stopped so close to the veil? She'd resolved herself to accept whatever plans her father had for her but now she knew she couldn't give in so easily. She had to find a way to escape and catch up with them, stop her mother from keeping them in Purgatore.

"So that's it, then? The great beast of Pandemonia is not only bested by a human but the goddess of Purgatore as well?"

Tartagnon narrowed his eyes. "Silence."

"How is it that she's the one who gets to do what you wanted so dearly?" Astraphelle asked. She watched him with her good eye as he took to pacing across the room, something he only did when he needed to think. Good. She was getting to him. "While you're here with me, torturing me in a way that barely even hurts."

Tartagnon roared as he turned back to her. He pulled a knife from his robes and quickly drew it across her lips, splitting her skin in two. The wound stung but Astraphelle had to keep going. She had to get out of there.

"You want pain?" he snarled. He stepped closer to her and she felt the blade at her womb. As swift as her position allowed, she drew the hook out of her eye and thrust it into his thigh. He grunted and stepped backward. As he leaned over to remove it, she pulled the hook from her wrist and buried it in his hand, pinning it in place. He dropped his knife and tried to remove the hook from the limb.

Astraphelle pulled the hooks from her elbow, breast, and ribs and promptly inserted them into her father's body, claiming his forearm and stomach. The chains bound his arms but he struggled against them. She looked at her hips, her vision fuzzy as she pulled herself up to reach for the chains, groaning against the pressure on her wounds as she did so. Her hands were slick with her own blood. She screamed as she pulled herself off the hooks. Pain jolted up her body as she fell to the floor with a thud.

She scrambled to her feet just as her father freed his pinned hand.

"You will not win this," he spat between gritted teeth.

"You know I already have, father," she took the hooks that had been shoved in her hips and punctured both his ears with them. His eyes crossed. His mouth gaped. But still the god of the damned lived.

He reached out at her as she bent to pick up his knife. The blade was slippery in her bloody hand.

"No matter what you do to me I will come back, child. And when I do, I will find you, and I will make you wish you died in that putrid abyss."

"Maybe you will," she said. Her eyes watered, the vision in her left eye a swirling gray mass. "I've seen you drowned, burned, butchered. You've recovered from them all but I suspect not even a god can recover from the loss of their heart."

She dropped the knife and plunged her fist into his chest. His mouth flew open and he screamed. She grabbed hold of his heart and pulled it through the cavity. His veins snapped as she freed the organ, which still beat slowly in her hand.

Tartagnon's eyes focused on hers, his brows drawn up in a look of fear, mouth open and nostrils flared. Then the heartbeat stopped. His eyes glazed over. And the god of the damned was dead.

Astraphelle brought his heart to her mouth and took her first bite.

The first thing she did after consuming the heart was break the sigils on the ground. The second thing she did was dismember her father's body. Her wounds healed as she butchered the corpse, and by the time she was done her eye was renewed and the skin on her face had fused back together. She made a bag out of his robes and slung it over her shoulder, placing his pieces within.

Astraphelle walked out of the ballroom and down the corridor. The demons were still gathered in the throne room as she walked in and stood at the threshold. Before they could rush her, she held up her father's severed head.

"I have killed the god of the damned. I have severed his body and consumed his heart," she said. And, realizing the opportunity she'd created for herself, added: "This kingdom is now mine."

Hushed murmurs rang throughout the crowd.

"Is there anyone who would challenge me?" She made eye contact with Florizeel, whose face was still healing from Sapphira's parting blow. He sneered at her but remained silent. *So, the death of our father has cowed him*, she thought. *How fortuitous for me.*

"Then you will submit to my command, bend to my will, or be executed as my father has been."

One by one the demons bent the knee before her. Astraphelle smiled and dropped her father's head in the bag. Then she removed his crown and placed it atop her head.

CHAPTER 28

SAPPHIRA

THEY RAN THROUGH all the islands of the damned, barely stopping to rest. But like Tartagnon promised, they remained unscathed. Her chest grew tight as they crossed the causeway between Pandemonia and Purgatore, hand in hand. They let go of each other as they balanced across the large boulders that covered the shoreline. Halfway across was a stone staircase that led toward Simyasha's cave, the top obscured by the clouds.

"Here we are, kitten," Maxwell soothed. "The veil awaits us."

Sapphira exhaled, all the tension that had settled in her shoulders releasing. Here they were. After so much torture and terror, they'd finally made it to Simyasha's realm. She took the first step, leading her friends up the stairs. The temperature grew colder as they ascended, the air smelling less like sulphur and more like cinnamon, clove, and decay. Once she stepped into the cave Sapphira was shocked to see the goddess standing there waiting for her, flanked by her retinue, each of them bearing weapons.

"Welcome to Purgatore, Sapphira. I hope you're ready for what fate has in store for you now."

Before she could protest, the goddess's servants grabbed each of them, dragging them across the floor.

"Why are you doing this? Did you not hear Tartagnon's promise?" Sapphira spat.

"Foolish girl, how could you think that the promise made by the god of Pandemonia holds any weight in my realm," Simyasha replied. She sat back on her throne as her servants forced Sapphira, Maxwell, and Luquin down to the ground. The tip of a spear pressed against the center of her back.

"Just let us go, you have no reason to keep us," Sapphira rasped.

"Please, goddess, we beseech you," Luquin said.

"Beseech?" Simyasha said. "Such a pretty word to use now. You should've been this contrite when we saw each other in Pandemonia, but instead you insisted on gloating. Well, now it's my turn. Look to your friends, memorize their faces, because this will be the last time you will ever be together."

Sapphira craned her neck to look up at the goddess. Simyasha met her gaze and said: "Each of you will bear a different fate. One will be sent back to Pandemonia. Another will remain here to serve me for all eternity. And the other will be a sacrifice."

Sapphira's blood grew cold as she stared at Simyasha and shook with fear.

"Werewolf," the goddess shouted. Sapphira shuddered as the goddess spoke. "You shall remain here as my servant."

"Vampire, you will be cast back to Pandemonia. And that leaves you."

Sapphira felt the servant's spear move from her back and then Simyasha stood before her, gripping her chin in her hand.

"Sapphira. You will be sacrificed."

Maxwell and Luquin thrashed beside her.

"No, please, take me instead," Maxwell replied. "Please."

"Or me, leave the girl alone," Luquin pleaded.

Simyasha rolled her eyes. "Such a hold you have on these men and you didn't even have to use your feminine wiles."

"I would sacrifice my life for them just as they would for me," Sapphira replied. The goddess let go of Sapphira's chin and stood.

"And so you shall."

Maxwell was pulled from the ground first. Sapphira scrambled to her feet but was stopped from running when the goddess delivered a blow to her stomach. She heard a bone snap and felt a stabbing pain when she breathed.

Simyasha's servant, a burly vampire with a long beard, pulled Maxwell toward the rear of the cave. Maxwell fought him all the way, but it was to no avail.

The servant tossed Maxwell out of the cave, just as she had been when she first arrived. Sapphira's knees buckled. Luquin caught her in his arms.

"I've got you," he said.

"No," Sapphira whispered. She closed her eyes and pictured Maxwell's smile in her mind's eye, the way he cupped her cheek, the way he called her "kitten." All the warmth and care she had for him surged within her body and when she felt the absence of his presence a tear slid down her cheek. "No."

Luquin's arms were ripped from around Sapphira's waist. She reached out for him, but the werewolf was pulled to the other side of the cave, where a trio of demons began to beat him. The werewolf fought, but Sapphira could hear bones breaking. Simyasha approached Sapphira, her teeth bared, and her fingers pointed like claws.

"I'm going to enjoy tasting such a strong-willed soul."

Sapphira closed her eyes against her fate but when she heard another scuffle, her eyes shot open. Standing before the entrance to the cave was Astraphelle, a crown on her head and Tartagnon's head in her hands. By her side stood Maxwell. Sapphira's eyes widened. The trio of demons who fought with Luquin stilled. She started to run but the goddess grabbed Sapphira by the hair.

"Oh no you don't," she said.

"You will unhand her, mother," Astraphelle said.

"And what authority do you have, child?" the goddess said, but Sapphira could hear the wavering in her voice. It was clear that she saw Tartagnon's head in her hands. They all did. Nevertheless, Astraphelle held it up, eliciting a huff from the goddess. A smirk settled on Maxwell's face.

"The authority of Pandemonia, for I am its new leader. But if you'd like to test me..." Astraphelle tossed Tartagnon's head across the room. It landed at Simyasha's feet with a sharp thud. "I've already eaten the heart of one god today. It was the purest thing I've ever tasted. And I'm eager to know if yours tastes the same."

The goddess shook beside Sapphira, her anger changing the very temperature of the room.

"What do you want?" she gritted.

"Unhand the woman," Astraphelle said. She waited patiently as the goddess untangled her hands from Sapphira's hair. She stepped away from Simyasha, backing into Luquin's arms. "Now you will send them back across the veil. Alive and unharmed."

The goddesses' lip curled. "Fine. I will do as you ask."

She waved her hand and the mark across Sapphira's chest disappeared. Sapphira wondered if she was supposed to feel any different now that there was no mark on her soul. Now that her fate was in her own hands. She looked at the goddess, whose face was a mask of fury as she stared at Sapphira. In an exaggerated moment, Sapphira curtsied before the goddess.

"Thank you, Simyasha, for your magnanimity."

"You listen here, girl," the goddess growled. "You may be alive again, but some day you will die. And after all of this do you really think you'll end up anywhere else?"

Sapphira leaned forward toward the goddess. "Oh no, I know exactly where I'll be going next time. But I'll be ready for you then."

She straightened just as a horse whinnied in the distance. The clip clop of hooves echoed through the cave and Sapphira smiled despite herself. The carriage of the dead was now coming to take them back to the land of the living.

She walked over to Astraphelle and Maxwell. She threw her arms around the vampire, who pressed a hand to the back of her head and placed a kiss on her temple.

"I thought I'd lost you."

"I would've spent the rest of my eternity finding a way to bring us back together," he said, clutching her in his arms. She leaned into his affection, her heart swelling before he pulled away. Then she turned toward Astraphelle, who regarded her with such care despite the tears in her eyes and blood coating her body.

"So, do I call you goddess, now?" she asked. Astraphelle smiled.

"No, just Astra. Always Astra for you."

Sapphira took Astraphelle's hand.

"Will you walk with us to carriage?" Sapphira asked.

"I'd be delighted." She fell into step beside Sapphira, none of them bothering to look back at Simyasha as they walked out of the antechamber to the floor of the canyon. Just as he had when he dropped Sapphira off, Gwydion sat atop the carriage draped in black smoke, his eyes glowing red embers. Maxwell and Luquin walked toward the carriage to grant Sapphira and Astraphelle a moment alone.

"You saved us," Sapphira said, turning toward the demon. "How can I ever thank you?"

"I did it all for you," Astraphelle said as a matter of fact. Her amber eyes held such warmth when she regarded Sapphira that it made butterflies swarm in her stomach. The demon took one of her hands. "I haven't had the courage to defy my father in centuries. You gave me that. You made me feel like I could be something more than a demon spending her days doing her father's bidding and pining for change, even if that change was permanent death."

Sapphira reached up and touched the golden crown atop Astraphelle's head. "And now you can remake Pandemonia as you desire. I'd say that's the biggest change of all."

"Yes. I only wish you could stay to be a part of it." Sapphira stroked the back of Astraphelle's hand with her thumb. Astraphelle sniffed. "What will you do when you cross the veil?"

"Find my family and try to get my life back."

Astraphelle caressed Sapphira's cheek, drawing her closer. "If there's anyone who deserves a second chance, it's you."

She pressed a kiss to Sapphira's forehead, and for a moment

Sapphira closed her eyes. In another life, perhaps they could have known each other and under different circumstances, fallen in love. She pictured what it would be like to hold Astraphelle in her arms, to kiss her lips, to wrap her legs around her and caress her body. Maybe they'd grow old and die together, climb into the carriage of the dead beside each other, their hands never parting. But for now, Sapphira was content to have known Astraphelle, this demon whose eyes reminded Sapphira of a dancing flame and who smelled like burning wood. Without her, Sapphira would be stuck in the realm of the damned, lamenting her fate forever.

Astraphelle pulled away.

"Please just do me one favor?" Astraphelle said.

"Anything."

"Don't forget me."

"I never could. I will live the life you helped me reclaim to the fullest and when the carriage comes for me again, I won't be sad. I'll delight that I may be able to see your face again," Sapphira replied.

Astraphelle smiled. Sapphira stared at her, committing her face and body to memory. The demon dropped her hands and, after nodding at Maxwell and Luquin and casting one last look at Sapphira, disappeared.

CHAPTER 29

SAPPHIRA

T HEY HELD EACH other's hands as they pierced the veil. Again, Sapphira marveled at the canyon, at the wispy blue fog that marked the delineation between Purgatore and the land of the living.

The journey back across the veil seemed to go faster this time around, and when the carriage came to a stop in Central Park, Sapphira's heart leaped. She couldn't help but scoff when she realized the carriage had come to a stop beside the same bench that she'd been stabbed on.

Gwydion was silent the whole journey, but when they got out of the carriage, Sapphira turned back toward him, the coachman nodded. He snapped the whip in his boney hands and his horses galloped, moving at lightning speed. Then they were gone, taking the sound of whinnying with them.

Maxwell patted his body, his eyes wide as he looked around the park.

"I can't believe we did it," Maxwell marveled. "We're really alive again!"

He scooped Sapphira in to his arms and lifted her, twirling her around and for the first time since she met him, he smiled a smile that bore no malice or wickedness, but pure joy. She brought a hand down to caress the apples of his cheeks. He set her down and pressed his forehead against hers.

"You did this. You saved us," he said.

"We did it together. You, me, and—"

Her eyes widened. Standing in Luquin's place was not a werewolf, but a man. He was shorter than Maxwell but more muscular, with dark brown skin and long, jet black coils tied back with a blue ribbon. He had full lips and a wide nose, and though his almond shaped eyes were no longer yellow, they still held the same warmth.

"Luquin!" Sapphira cried. Beside her, Maxwell gasped.

"I can control the change again, thank the gods! Luquin breathed. "Never have I been so delighted to be in my human form again."

"You look great," Maxwell said and clapped him on the back. Luquin smirked and quirked a brow.

"Oh? Is that a compliment, Maxwell? Be careful now, if I didn't know better, I'd think you were flirting with me."

Maxwell groaned and rolled his eyes. "See? This is what I get for being nice to him."

Luquin giggled. "Don't worry, I've got eyes. I can see that you're already spoken for."

Sapphira and Maxwell looked at each other and she couldn't help the warmth that crept up to her cheeks. She bit her lip and looked away.

"You may as well make it official. It's obvious you care for each other. You two have kissed, and you've been seconds away from hate fucking from the moment I met you."

Luquin turned on his heel and slid his hands into his coat pockets, walking ahead of them. "Come, love birds, let's explore this city together."

Maxwell draped an arm over her shoulder as they began to follow the werewolf. It was winter still. Snow fell in quiet flurries, and the streetlamps illuminated the night in a cool blue glow. All around them people roamed the park, some focused on their own lives, others looking at them strangely — wondering why a man dressed in Renaissance clothing and another in Victorian garb were walking around with a woman dressed so modernly. Sapphira ignored them and leaned into Maxwell as she pointed out some of the notable areas of the park. Snow crunched beneath her shoes as she led them through the park and out to 110th Street. They turned left on 5th Avenue, coming to a stop before a news stand. Sapphira stopped and grabbed the newspaper, searching for the date.

December 10, 1979.

Almost exactly a year to the date that she'd been killed. She bit her lip, trying to quell the thoughts of all the things she'd lost in that last year. But when she saw the wonder on Maxwell and Luquin's eyes as they took in the city around them, she realized how much she'd gained. Two friends willing to fight and go through hell to help her secure her freedom. Two friends who she could show all the wonders of the world to, and in that moment, she realized how much she cared for them. And with Maxwell, she realized she'd found somebody who she could possibly spend the rest of her days with. She realized that, even if she never found her sister and friends, she wouldn't be alone. As her gratitude and care for her new friends swelled within her, her eyes filled with tears. Maxwell looked at her and lifted her chin to look him in the eyes.

"What's wrong, kitten?"

"Nothing I'm just... happy."

He planted a kiss on her temple, and Sapphira turned her face up and kissed him on the lips. She heard him gasp but he leaned into the kiss. His lips were cool against hers and he wrapped his arms around her, tenderly placing one hand on the back of her head and the other on the small of her back. Despite the tenderness with which he held her, his lips pressed against hers passionately, making her whole body feel aflame. He pulled away and playfully bit her lower lip before letting her go. She smiled, her cheeks warm, and entwined her hand with his.

"So, what the hell am I looking at?" Luquin asked. Sapphira laughed as she saw him staring at a car.

"Don't worry, I'll explain it all to you."

She led them up 5th Ave, telling them about things like electricity, plumbing, cars, and phones. She felt lighter, buoyed by her relief to be alive again, but when they turned on her street, she couldn't help the sense of dread that overcame her. She squeezed Maxwell's hand and tried to steady her breath and her anxious heart. When they stood in front of Sapphira's old building, she paused.

"Is this it?" Maxwell asked.

Sapphira nodded.

"Then, what are you waiting for?"

"I — what if she's gone?"

"But if she's still there? Waiting for you?" Luquin asked. He gave Sapphira a reassuring smile and gestured toward the stairs. She walked ahead of them, just as she had when they approached the stairs to Purgatore. She thanked the gods as someone exited the building as she approached the door, preventing her from having to ring their apartment. She held the door open as she looked beside it to see the names by the buzzer. Her heart leapt when she saw "P. Gail" and "F. Henry" by apartment 518.

She stepped inside the foyer. Her hand shook as she touched the wooden banister. She leaned on it for support as she walked up the five flights of stairs until she stood before her apartment. Sapphira fought to steady her breath.

"You can do it, we're right here, kitten," Maxwell said.

"Yes, you're not alone, bijou," Luquin added.

She sucked in a breath and let it out slowly. Then she turned back to the door and knocked three times.

"One sec," someone said and Sapphira pressed a hand to her heart when she recognized the voice as her sister's. She heard the chain come undone, then the lock snapped. The door opened and Sapphira was looking into the eyes of her twin. Persephone drew in a sharp breath, eyes widening behind a pair of glasses.

"Sapphira?" she questioned. "What the fuck?"

Persephone backed into their apartment. Sapphira grimaced as she walked toward her.

"It's me, Per, really," she said.

Her sister backed up into the dining room table, the table leg screeching on the linolium floor. She kept her eyes Sapphira as she pawed the table behind her, grabbing a fork and holding it up like it was a knife.

"I don't believe you! You... you died. The hospital told me... I examined your body!"

"I did die," Sapphira said. "But now I'm alive again."

"How?"

"I—"

Persephone held the fork up higher. "I said how!"

"I can see Sapphira's fire is a family trait," Luquin said.

Persephone's eyes darted toward him, then Maxwell.

"And who the fuck are they?"

"Per, please. Put the fork down and I'll explain everything. It's me, it's me."

She closed the distance between them and pulled Persephone into her arms. After a moment Sapphira heard the fork clatter on the ground and felt her sister's arms wrap around her tightly. She buried her face into the crook of Persephone's neck, the familiar floral scent of her Diorella perfume making Sapphira break down. Her knees buckled, and Persephone sank to the ground with her, joining in her sobs. They held each other for a long while, rocking back and forth. When their sobs dissipated they held on to each other as though afraid to lose each other again.

"I thought for sure you'd be in Caelum with Granny."

"I didn't go to Caelum. I was sent to Pandemonia."

Persephone looked at Sapphira in disbelief, her dark eyes welling with tears.

"Why?"

"Dante. He bartered my soul to become famous."

A murderous look passed over Persephone's face. "I knew that motherfucker had something to do with it. I couldn't prove it, and then he got fucking discovered at The Mean Bean. Just last week he was on Soul Train."

Persephone's comment stung, but she didn't respond.

"I'm so sorry, Sapph," Persephone said. "I should've fought harder to keep you from leaving. I should've..."

Sapphira pressed a hand against her sister's cheek. "No, it's not your fault. Please don't blame yourself. I'm here now."

She stood and helped Persephone to her feet. Once again her eyes darted toward Sapphira's friends.

"Are they with you?"

Sapphira nodded.

"Persephone, I'd like you to meet Maxwell and Luquin. We escaped Pandemonia together."

Her sister gasped, looking between the men.

"It's a pleasure to finally meet you, Persephone. Your sister spoke of you so often I feel like I know you," Maxwell said. He held his hand out and Persephone shook it.

"It's nice to meet you," Persephone said.

"Persephone. What a lovely name for a lovely woman," Luquin said. He bowed deeply before Persephone. Then he took her hand and planted a kiss on her knuckles, smirking at her all the while. When Sapphira looked at her sister she could see her expression turn bashful.

"Alright, lycan, how about you dial down the charm right now and let Sapphira reunite with her sister," Maxwell groaned.

"Oh Maxwell, still a wet blanket after all this time," Luquin said.

"Come on, take a seat you must be... cold? Hungry?"

She ushered them into the living room and Sapphira felt such relief to see that it looked so much the same. Their velvet orange couch, the Mahogany poster behind it. Their rattan coffee table, the cream-colored shag carpet that Sapphira always hated because Dorothy's nails always got tangled in it.

"Dorothy..." Sapphira's voice trailed.

As if on cue the black cat sauntered out of the bathroom. Sapphira bent to her knees and the cat ran toward her. She scooped it in her arms and pressed the cat to her chest, delighting in its purring.

"Can I get you anything?" Persephone asked.

"I could use a drink," Sapphira chuckled. She took a seat on the couch and suddenly it felt as though all the tension she'd been keeping in her body for the last year released. Suddenly her calves ached. Her feet were numb. Her shoulders throbbed and she hoped her sister had enough aspirin to cure the pulsating headache at the back of her head. Luquin and Maxwell sat beside her. She heard them both sigh and she realized they were probably having similar feelings. Maxwell put his arm around her and Sapphira leaned up against him and sighed.

"All this must look so strange to you," she said.

"I must confess, I don't think I could even guess what that is," Luquin said, pointing toward the television.

"Don't worry. I'll help you through it."

Persephone came back into the living room with a bottle of wine and four glasses. Sapphira set Dorothy on the ground and reached for the bottle. She poured them all a glass then paused as she went to hand one to Maxwell.

"Wait, can werewolves and vampires even drink wine?"

"What?" Persephone asked.

Maxwell chuckled and in response grabbed the glass.

"I recall wine being quiet exquisite in my day. Let's see if your modern versions hold up."

Sapphira lifted her glass, ready to toast.

"I'm sorry, did you just say werewolf and vampire?" Persephone asked. And Sapphira laughed. For the first time in ages she laughed, not from pain or disbelief, but from pure joy.

Persephone lit a fire and put Four Seasons of Love by Donna Summer on the record player. Frankie arrived home minutes later, and when he saw Sapphira he nearly collapsed. She'd held onto him for a while, breathing in his cologne and relaxing in his strong embrace. Then she'd introduced him to Maxwell and Luquin, and he marveled at their clothes.

"Don't worry, I'll be taking them shopping first thing," she said. Maxwell and Luquin looked down at their clothes and shrugged.

Persephone called Claudia, telling her it was an emergency and twenty minutes later she'd arrived, a gun in hand.

"What the fuck happened? Someone break in because I—"

Her eyes roamed the room and when she saw Sapphira she backed up into the door.

"Holy fuck," she said. Sapphira drew her friend into a hug and then poured her a glass of wine.

They sat in the living room for hours as Sapphira told them everything, from when Dante stabbed her to when she said her goodbyes to Astraphelle. Maxwell and Luquin added to her tale, speaking about what happened when Sapphira had been pulled under by the kaimong and how fierce Sapphira had been when she defeated Florizeel. All the while, Persephone and their friends looked at Sapphira in disbelief, taking sips of their wine and hanging on every word. When she was done, she sat back against the couch cushions. Her head swam from the wine. Her cheeks were warm and coated in tears.

"I don't even know what to say. I can't believe you went through all of that," Persephone said tearfully. Sapphira reached across the table and took her sister's hand to soothe her.

"That asshole," Claudia said. She downed her wine and walked over to the kitchen. She grabbed the newspaper and sat back down, spreading the paper across the coffee table. There in a large centerfold was a picture of Dante. He was dressed in a crushed velvet suit, his hair pressed and his beard lined up. He wore his signature chain around his neck, gold, with the symbol for Xira on the end. He smiled at the camera as he held the mic in one hand and lifted the other above his head. Behind him were his bandmates. The headline read: "From Humble Beginnings to The Apollo: How This Coffee Shop Crooner

Went Platinum."

"Just look at him. He's proud of what he did," Claudia said.

Sapphira's mouth went dry at the sight of him. It felt like her heart stopped and the room went silent around her. He was still so beautiful, that smile still enough to light her aflame. But there were new emotions now as she looked at the photo. Rage sparked her belly, moving from a dull simmer to a full-blown flame as Claudia read the article. It spoke about his upbringing, his time as a busboy at different restaurants in the city. It mentioned the tragic unsolved murder of his beloved girlfriend, the year before. Claudia read his statement about her death aloud:

"Losing her really fucked me, mentally. That girl was the love of my life and it took me a long time to crawl out of the dark place her death put me in. I wrote this album for her, in memory and celebration of her. And I hope that wherever she is, she can hear me serenade her every time I perform."

Sapphira sat still, gripping her wine glass. She heard Persephone quietly weeping, saw her sister leaning against Frankie's strong shoulders. She watched as her friends cleared tears out of their eyes. Even Luquin seemed taken by the swell of emotion in the room. He dabbed at his eyes with the edge of his shirt.

She set her glass down, stood, and walked toward the window. Her arms were crossed as she looked out into the night turning his words over in her head. He killed her. Sold her soul and became an overnight success who got to guest star on Soul Train and play at the Apollo. Sapphira didn't know much about the music business, but she knew that was the big leagues. And now he had a sold-out show there playing songs that he said he'd written in her honor. He was proud of what he'd done, Claudia said. Sapphira could see it now. The easy way he smiled, the way he made jokes throughout the interview, only getting serious enough to say what her death had done to him and how it had inspired him to write another album. Even in her death he still found a way to center himself. The thought set her teeth on edge, and it wasn't until she felt a hand on her shoulder that her eyes refocused. She saw Maxwell's reflection in the glass and turned back to him. He wrapped her in his arms, and she leaned into the gesture.

"Are you alright?" Maxwell asked. She pulled back and looked into his eyes.

"Do you think we will return to Pandemonia when we die again?" she asked softly.

"Yes. Though it seems we may have a friend in a very high place. That may make all the difference when our bills come due."

"If I'm to return there, will more blood on my hands make a difference?" she asked. He smoothed a hand over her hair, a smile crawling across his face. His fangs gleamed in the light of the fire.

"What did you have in mind, kitten?"

Four weeks later on a Saturday night, Sapphira stood outside of Dante's dressing room wearing a new pair of gold dancing shoes, only this time she was dressed in black. Her hair was curled and teased like Donna Summer, her lips red and her eyelids painted gold.

She'd worn her signature perfume, carried a sequin purse she borrowed from Claudia, and carried a new knife discreetly in a pocket she added into the interior of her jacket. Beside her stood Maxwell and Luquin their hair down and natural, both dressed in modern clothes. Oddly it had taken Maxwell more time to acclimate to the clothes than Luquin, who loved the silken ruffled shirts and brightly colored suits. Though he wore all black, like Maxwell, his shirt was ruffled.

Sapphira looked at them, each wearing a look that said they were game for whatever violence would occur. Down the hall, Persephone stood with Frankie as lookouts, and further still was Claudia, who flirted with the security guards.

Maxwell nodded to her in reassurance, and then Sapphira knocked on the door.

"Who is it?" grumbled Dante. Sapphira squared her shoulders at the sound of his voice. She didn't answer, only knocked again. "What the fuck you want?"

Dante whipped the door open. He wore a baby blue suit with a silver shirt. His hair was still in rollers, a blunt sticking out from between his lips. His eyes widened then narrowed.

"What do you want, Persephone?"

Sapphira didn't hide the menacing smile that crept across her face.

"I said the fuck do you want? Who are these jokers with you?"

"Joker?" Luquin wondered. "Is that supposed to be an insult?"

Maxwell chuckled. "Strange times, indeed."

Dante reached out and grabbed Sapphira by the arm and jerked her toward him. Both Maxwell and Luquin darted to her side.

"Didn't you hear me? I said what the fuck do you want, Persephone?"

"I'm not Persephone," Sapphira said.

Dante's mouth slackened. He let her arm go so fast it was as though touching her had burned him. She pushed her way past him and into the room, where a vanity sat on the right side. A second pre-rolled blunt sat on it, along with a bottle of Moët & Chandon.

She sat in the chair at the vanity as Luquin closed and locked the door behind him.

"That's not funny," Dante said. But she heard his voice waver. She crossed one leg over the other and grabbed the champagne, taking a drink straight from the bottle. Then she lit a match and took a long puff of his blunt.

"And I'm not joking," she breathed as she exhaled the smoke.

"Sapphira?" Dante questioned. He looked from her to Maxwell

and Luquin, both men standing on either side of the door with their hands crossed in front of them, wicked expressions on their faces.

She took another puff as if in response.

"No fuckin' way. You died. You're dead."

"Yes, you would know, wouldn't you? After all, three stabs should be enough to murder anyone, let alone the slit throat. Oh, let's not forget the deal you made with that demon."

"Yes, though I'm happy to report that he's the dead one now," Maxwell said. Dante scoffed.

"Then you should be..."

"Getting tortured for all eternity?" Sapphira said. She took another swig of champagne, then tossed the bottle to Luquin. He caught it and followed suit, then handed it to Maxwell who drained the bottle and tossed it to the ground. It shattered in a satisfying splat, and Dante jumped. Maxwell chuckled.

Sapphira stood and walked toward him, closing the distance between them. "Your plan worked. I did die. I was sent to Pandemonia, to the seventh island, in fact, for the misdeed of maleficence. But I escaped and I fought my way back with a blade made of bone and the help of that werewolf, and that vampire."

"Don't forget our demon queen," Luquin added.

Sapphira smiled. "Ah yes, there was also a demon involved. She's the goddess of Pandemonia now."

Sapphira gestured to her companions. Dante's eyes widened as he looked at them. The men bared their teeth at him. Maxwell growled and Luquin held his hands out, his nails growing and sharpening to claws. Sapphira put Dante's blunt out on the collar of his suit then reached up and grabbed Dante's face, holding it in her hands, bringing his gaze back to her.

"I made it out of Pandemonia, through Purgatore and across the veil for this." She pressed her lips to his. Snaking her tongue into his mouth. His fear turned to desire, as he wrapped an arm around her. Seconds later she felt his dick harden in his pants as it pressed against her waist. She pulled away from him, her lips hovering against his.

"And for this."

Sapphira pulled her knife out of her pocket and held it to his throat. Dante looked down, eyes widening, and backed away with his hands up.

"Wait a minute, we can talk about this."

"Nothing to talk about. There's nothing you could say to me that would make anything you've done better."

"If you kill me, you'll just go back."

She shrugged. "I'm already going. And remember, I know the goddess of the damned."

"They are rather intimate," Maxwell added.

"Oh? I didn't take you as one to be ok with your girlfriend having a girlfriend," Luquin asked.

"Sapphira's a grown woman. She can do whatever she wants. I'm just happy to share her heart... and her bed," Maxwell said. Luquin dapped him.

Dante looked from the vampire to Sapphira. But the longer she pressed the knife against his throat, the less afraid Dante looked. Even as a smug expression crossed his face Sapphira couldn't bring herself to kill him. *What's wrong with me?* She thought. He deserved this. She'd thought about this moment for over a year, fantasized about feeling his blood coat her hands and being there when he took his final breaths. So why was she so unable to end him?

"Can't do it, can you?" he taunted.

"Shut up," she said. But her hand had started to shake.

Maxwell moved to her side. "Do you need my help?"

Her shoulders shook and her vision went blurry as her eyes filled with tears, which betrayed her. She didn't want to cry in front of him, didn't think he deserved the satisfaction, but she couldn't stop the deluge that ran down her cheeks.

"I don't know why I can't... I killed so many demons. I literally split Florizeel's face in two," she said. "So why can't I do the same with this piece of shit."

Maxwell wrapped one arm around her waist and pressed the other over her hand.

"If you need me to guide your hand, I will. And if you need me to pull you way, I will. Tell me what you need, kitten."

"I..."

There was a knock at the door, and Sapphira's stomach dropped.

"Yo, Dante? You good?"

"H—"

Maxwell pressed Sapphira's hand, letting the knife draw blood. Dante went silent.

"Get them to go away," Maxwell whispered. "She may have difficulty hurting you, but I can assure you, I would revel in it."

"As would I," Luquin added.

"Yeah, I'm good. Just smokin.'"

"Aight. Sound check in ten."

"Aight, then," Dante replied.

Footsteps echoed down the hall and then disappeared.

"I will support you whatever you decide, kitten, but you best decide soon. Don't want to risk being seen."

Sapphira took a deep breath to try to steady herself. All this time she thought about ending him and the satisfaction she'd get from his death. But as she stood before Dante, knife pressed against his throat, she realized that killing him would only bring temporary relief. She'd spend the rest of her life either in jail or on the run. While Dante had been supernaturally protected from the clink by his deal with the demon, she had no such protection. Though she knew Astraphelle would do anything for her, she had no idea how to even contact the new goddess of the damned. No, she would not spend her life with his life or his death at the center. She dropped her hand and took a step

AMANDA B. WEAVER • • •

back. All the while, Maxwell held on to her to steady her.

"You're not worth it. Killing you would only be my ruin. I fought too hard to get my life back to ruin it by going to jail or spending my life on the run."

Dante scoffed. Now that he was no longer in immediate danger, his bravado returned. He straightened his suit jacket.

"I knew you didn't have it in you. Always were a coward."

Maxwell's hand snaked out and gripped Dante's throat, lifting him off the ground. He bared his fangs. Dante's legs and arms shook. Luquin laughed.

"You will not speak to her that way, insignificant little fool. It would only take seconds for me to drain every last drop of blood from your body. I'd tear your throat, ripping vein and tendon, until my teeth grazed your spine. Sapphira need only give me the word."

The front of Dante's suit darkened as he peed his pants. Sapphira looked at him dispassionately.

"Let him down, my love. He's not worth spoiling your appetite."

Maxwell growled before he dropped Dante and removed his hand from his throat. Dante gagged and doubled over.

"You might want to change your pants," Maxwell spat. He walked back toward the door to stand beside Luquin.

"You missed doing that, didn't you?" Luquin asked.

"There's some things that never get old," Maxwell replied.

Sapphira turned her attention back to Dante. "If you tell anyone

394 • • •

what happened or try to come after us, or my sister, or Frankie and Claudia, I might just change my mind."

Dante sniffed.

She turned away from him.

"Have a nice life," he said. "Good luck, I see you still need other people to fight your battles for you."

Without warning, Sapphira cocked her arm back and punched Dante in the throat. Then she hit him again in the eye, and finally kneed him in the groin.

"You evil bitch."

"Evil? Well, that's just a matter of perspective," Sapphira replied, looking at Maxwell as she did so. The vampire smiled at her, his face a mixture of pride and desire.

EPILOGUE

SAPPHIRA

THEY SLIPPED OUT of the theater and into the night. Dante played to a sold-out show, and to sold-out shows all over the country. But he never could replicate the success of that first album. And with the steady decline in disco's popularity, his audience dwindled, and so did the wealth he accumulated. Soon, he was barely able to play local venues, and the last thing Sapphira heard about him was that he was living in Hoboken with his sister and working at their father's car dealership. That is, until this evening.

It'd been five years since the night she confronted him at the concert, and her life had changed astronomically. She reapplied for her summer internship at Yves Saint Laurent and was accepted. With Luquin's help, she learned French and spent the summer in Paris with Maxwell, Luquin, and Persephone at her side. Both Luquin and

Maxwell had taken to the modern world exceptionally well. By the time they left for Paris, they barely balked at the sight of a taxi, though they were both anxious when they got on the plane.

They all rented an apartment together in Saint Germain. Sapphira got to study under one of the world's best designers, made connections she'd only dreamed of. The others spent their days touring the city, where Luquin got to revisit his old home and marvel at how much it had changed. One evening Sapphira walked in on him and Persephone kissing, and gasped.

"Er... don't think this is me secretly wanting to kiss you, bijou," Luquin said. "It's just... your sister is exquisite."

Sapphira sighed and Persephone giggled. Sapphira knew that sound, and so she simply nodded and closed the door, happy that her sister was happy. And so was she. Maxwell was everything she needed in a partner — attentive, kind yet firm, romantic, and a passionate lover in and out of bed. He made her feel alive, like she was capable of anything. When she told him this, he'd scoff.

"Kitten, you did what no other human has done before you in recorded history — you took on Pandemonia itself and won. You don't need me to be your guiding light. You are a beacon onto yourself."

She was offered a job at Yves Saint Laurent when her internship finished, to the delight of them all. Paris had become their home, and the American distaste of disco had not quite reached the French shores, so she resumed her Saturday night ritual.

Persephone published her first novel in the spring of 1981. That same year, Luquin was accepted into the Paris Ballet. Maxwell graduated from Parsons Paris, and soon began a career as a photographer. In 1982, Luquin and Persephone married and moved out on their own. In 1983, Sapphira designed and curated her first fashion show under her own label, Kitten, where she showed a collection of evening wear in green, red, and gold. The reception was overwhelmingly positive, with critics noting the prominent themes of bones and blood in her designs.

They traveled back to the States to visit Frankie and Claudia often, both of whom were equally successful — Frankie now taught at Pratt, and Claudia owned Kaleidoscope. They were in New York, celebrating Frankie's thirtieth birthday, and staying at Claudia's apartment when the phone rang.

"Hello?" She said.

"Hi, may I speak to Sapphira Gail?"

"This is her."

The person on the other end of the line sucked in a breath. "Sapphira, it's Kira."

Sapphira gripped the phone at the mention of Dante's sister's name. She exhaled unsteadily, before responding. "Hi Kira. How may I help you?"

"Listen, Dante... he's not doing well. Doctors say he's only got a little more time left, but I don't know. He asked for you and I thought...

well, I don't know what I thought. Maybe you could come to see him?"

"What's wrong—"

"Car accident. He crashed and the car caught fire. Most of his body burned."

Sapphira was quiet for a long while. It'd been years since he crossed mind, longer still, since she felt the sting of his betrayal. Now all those emotions came flooding back to her.

"Um... maybe. Can you give me the details?"

She shakily wrote down the name of the hospital and his room number before wishing Kira well. She hung up and sat on the edge of the bed, staring at the black and gold curtains.

"Will you go?"

She sighed at Maxwell's question. Of course he'd heard, that damned vampire hearing.

"I don't know."

"I think you should."

"Why?" she turned to him. "Why after all these years? I'd forgotten him. Moved on. My life is... I've got everything I..."

He moved to sit beside her and stroked her cheek. "I know, kitten. But it's ok if you still want to see him. Or feel like you need to."

"I wouldn't even know what to say."

"You'll figure it out when you get there."

Sapphira sighed. "Do you want me to come with you?"

After a long while, Sapphira responded: "No, I've got to do this alone."

Three hours later Sapphira stood at the foot of Dante's bed, her mouth agape as she stared at the man she once loved. He looked so frail, covered in gauze. When Dante opened his eyes to look at her, she winced.

"Hi."

"Hey," he rasped.

"Your sister said you wanted to see me."

"I want to apologize. For everything."

Sapphira's mouth dried up.

"You *what?*"

"Yes, I... I'm sorry," Dante said. The beeping of the vitals sign monitor brought back the memory of when she was in the ambulance just after he stabbed her. She remembered how afraid she'd been, both of him and of Gwydion.

"I forgave you a long time ago. Though I will say it's convenient that you apologize on, from what I understand, your deathbed."

"I 'm sorry. I was so blinded by my desire to be something, that I would've done anything."

"How did that work out for you?" she asked, though she knew the answer. Dante laughed bitterly."I ..." he took a breath. His heartbeat quickened momentarily, and Sapphira could see his oxygen levels dropping. "I wanted to ask..."

She scoffed and crossed her arms. "What's it like in Pandemonia?"

Dante nodded. She should have known he'd ask her that.

"I know after what I did to you, I've got no shot at Caelum. So, I thought I'd... get prepared. Maybe get a leg up."

"I can assure you there's no way to truly be prepared for that place. But," she started. She grabbed a chair and sat at his bedside. He was even more tragic looking up close. What little of his skin wasn't covered in gauze was crusted and scabbed over. His right iris was completely gray. His hair that he'd always fussed over was ruined, only a handful of strands on his head. "First, you hear the horses. Then you see the carriage. It doesn't matter if you run, Gwydion will find you. You'll cross the veil, and the first thing you see on the other side is a canyon and Simyasha's palace. It's warm, smells like cinnamon, but the goddess is more terrifying than you can imagine. She will taunt you. Maybe even try to bite you."

"Bite?"

Sapphira nodded. "Bite. Then, she'll toss you out of the cave and you'll fall thousands of feet, so far and so fast that your body should liquify on impact. But it won't. You'll land, probably on the seventh island, and the beach will be full of bloody teeth."

Dante squirmed. His heart rate stayed raised. "And you'll spend the rest of your eternity fighting for your life. You'll be tortured, ripped apart, killed in ways you can't imagine. And then you'll come back to life and do it all over again. If you're lucky, you'll find friends. But, knowing your personality, you'll probably spend your eternity alone."

Dante shuddered. He reached out for Sapphira's hand and she sat back, crossing her arms.

"That's a nice ring," he said. She looked down at the sapphire and gold ring on her left hand. Maxwell had proposed in the only place that was ever truly sacred to her — Kaleidoscope, on the dance floor.

"The vampire?"

She nodded.

"Least he takes care of you... I never..." Dante began to cough. His vitals spiked, and Sapphira leaped out of her chair.

"Do you want me to call—"

"Too late, the carriage..."

And Sapphira was shocked to find she could hear the sound of hooves, the neighing, the wheels spinning against the concrete.

"Not again! I'm not fucking dying!"

The edge of the room grew dark, stretching and stretching until she couldn't see the end. Through it emerged Gwydion, still draped in black smoke. When the carriage ground to a stop he tipped his hat at her.

"You're not here for me, are you?"

"You still have decades, Miss Sapphira," Gwydion's voice echoed in her mind.

She sighed and looked down at Dante. His body lay limp in the bed, mouth open, eyes unblinking. Beside the carriage his soul stood, body absent of scares and damage. He patted himself down, surprised.

"How am I breathing?" he asked.

Sapphira shook her head and looked at Gwydion. "Are you going to tell him, or should I?"

"Don't worry," came another voice. Sapphira's heart quickened as the door to the carriage opened and Astraphelle stepped out. "Dante and I will have plenty of time to discuss the function of his organs."

The goddess of the damned looked more beautiful and terrifying than Sapphira had thought possible. Her blood-red gown pooled on the floor at her feet. The neckline plunged down to her navel, the sleeves resting off her shoulder. Her braids were gathered up into two horns that circled her head like ram horns, the ends dipped in black. On her wrists were twin gold bracelets and atop her head, a crown of bones dipped in gold and studded with rubies.

She smiled sweetly at Sapphira and she ran toward the goddess, throwing her arms around her. She smelled sweet, like cardamom, but there was also the coppery tang of blood just beneath the surface.

"I've missed you," Sapphira whispered into her neck.

"You have no idea," Astraphelle replied. They pulled away from each other and Sapphira could feel Astraphelle's eyes assessing her. "You look..."

"Older?" Sapphira quipped.

"Lighter. Happier."

"You were a big part of that."

"I'm very glad," Astraphelle said. She kissed Sapphira, and Sapphira sighed at the warmth of her lips. She opened her mouth to Astraphelle's tongue, and for a moment their tongues danced with each other before Astraphelle pulled away. "I hope that vampire is treating you right."

"Better than I could've hoped. Certainly better than him," Sapphira gestured toward Dante.

Astraphelle stepped away from her and back toward the carriage. "That's not a tall order."

"I didn't think I'd see you until..."

"Well, when I heard he was not long for this world, I knew I had to come to collect this soul myself. But we best be going. I cannot leave Pandemonia without a god for too long. The demons will start to riot."

"Florizeel?"

Astraphelle shook her head and smiled deviously. "No. I strangled him, stuffed him in a coffin, and tossed him into the abyss. Though I must admit I do miss the excitement of having someone try to kill me all the time."

Sapphira laughed. "Gods, I'm gonna miss you all over again."

"You'll be alright. You've got love, inside and out. We will meet again one day, and then you can decide whose bed you wanna share —

mine, or the vampire's."

"Must you make me choose?" Sapphira asked.

Astraphelle chuckled. "Greedy girl."

The goddess turned serious. "Goodbye, Sapphira."

Sapphira nodded, not bothering to wipe the tear that slid down her cheek.

"Goodbye, goddess."

Astraphelle smiled before she turned to Dante. She grabbed him by the collar and tossed him into the carriage.

"Ok, Dante. I hope you're ready to see what I have in store for you."

"No! Please, I... I'll repent, I'll..."

"I don't think you'll find a single god who'll be receptive to your pleas," Astraphelle said. "But by all means you're welcome to try. I love it when you souls scream."

The door to the carriage shut, Dante's cries echoing as the carriage turned back through the darkness and disappeared. Soon, the only sound was that of a consistent beep from the vital signs machine, announcing that Dante had flatlined. And as Sapphira gathered her purse and walked out of the room, a smile slowly spread across her face.

ACKNOWLEDGMENTS

2023 was an exceptionally difficult year for me, one in which I thought about giving up multiple times. There were times when I was so depressed or angry or afraid of the future that I could barely do anything but get out of bed. But through it all this book was my constant companion, my saving grace. I'm not lying when I say this book saved my life. And I am forever grateful for it.

But this book wouldn't be possible without the help of several people, including my editor, La Purvis, who gave me the honest truth when I needed it; my cover designer, RaeKwon Groover, who captured the essence of Sapphira and the horrors she faces in such brilliant detail; and my interior designer, C. M. Lockhart, who—beyond making this book look amazing— is also someone I am lucky enough to call a friend, one I am very thankful for.

I'd also like to thank my beta readers, Samara, KJ, Evangeline, Sharae, Cyrin, Ashley, Tia, Bre, and Michael. Special thanks to Michael LaBorn, who was a beta reader and who promoted my books on TikTok and who tirelessly supports Black and brown authors.

I want to thank my family, especially my mom, for putting up with my hectic schedule, my anxiety, and my late night, music-blasting caffeine addled self. I love you all.

To my readers, you truly make all of this worthwhile. Thanks for sticking with me, and I've got so much more dark fantasy and horror in store for you.

Finally, I want to thank me. I saved myself, finished this book, and made myself proud. And I hope that anyone who reads this and is searching for someone to save them from whatever storm they find themselves in can realize that sometimes, the hero you're searching for is the one in the mirror.

ABOUT THE AUTHOR

AMANDA B. WEAVER (formerly Ross) is an indie fantasy and horror author. Her books include _In The House of Transcendence_, _To Astera, With Love_ and its sequel, _To Ilaris, In Desperation_, the YA fantasy anthologies _Girls of Might and Magic_ and _Kindred Kingdoms_. When she's not writing, Amanda is spending too much time on TikTok, X, and Instagram, (@amandabweaver) or recording her horror podcast, Horror Heaux Support Group.

Printed in Great Britain
by Amazon

44187271R00239